MORE RAVES FOR CRYSTAL!

"Crystal is a glamourous career woman with spunk. I would love to play her in the movie."
—Angie Dickinson

"People are fascinated by the book. They all want to know who this woman [Crystal] is."
—Diana Vreeland

"I'm proud to be one of the characters in *Crystal Clear*."
—Halston

"It's a fun book. Crystal is someone I'd really like to meet. I liked her ingenuity."
—C. Z. Guest

CRYSTAL CLEAR
a novel that takes you
inside the glamourous world of beauty
By Eugenia Sheppard and Earl Blackwell

"It's amusing from start to finish. Nedda and I hope there will be a sequel."
—Josh Logan

D0907998

CRYSTAL CLEAR

Eugenia Sheppard
and
Earl Blackwell

CRYSTAL CLEAR

*A Bantam Book / published by arrangement with
Doubleday & Company, Inc.*

*PRINTING HISTORY
Doubleday edition published February 1978*

Bantam Books are published by Bantam Books, Inc. Its trade-
mark, consisting of the words "Bantam Books" and the por-
trayal of a bantam, is registered in the United States Patent
Office and in other countries. Marca Registrada. Bantam
Books, Inc., 666 Fifth Avenue, New York, New York 10019.

PRINTED IN THE UNITED STATES OF AMERICA

To *Carriearl* on the enchanted island of Great
Harbour Cay in the Bahamas, where this book
was born.

PART ONE

1

"Bitch!"

"What a bitch," she said a moment later.

The uniformed chauffeur driving her elegant little town car down Fifth Avenue didn't turn his head, but he smiled. She spoke like the girls announcing the flights in the London airport. Every word was shaped like a little silver bead. No matter what she said, it always sounded wonderful.

He heard the crunching of paper. At a red light, he looked into his rearview mirror, saw her throw the crumpled tabloid across the car floor and reach for her handbag. Crystal Young took out her lipstick and fortified herself with a fresh coat of bright pink, which she usually did when things weren't going her way.

"Vincent, will you get the apartment on the car phone, I want to speak to my husband." Crystal was now sitting back on the leather cushions and was completely under control. "Tell Celeste if he isn't up yet to keep knocking gently at his door until he's awake and answers."

It took Vincent several minutes to make the connection and a few more for Eliot Tyler Young's voice to come over the phone. Vincent held on to his receiver long enough to hear him ask, "What the hell's the emergency?"

"It's not really an emergency, darling. I just wanted to remind you that the architect is coming to see you

3

about the glass wall we want in the living room. He'll be there around eleven, you know."

"I remember. But I'm not sure it's a good idea. You know it means our place will be torn up for at least six months."

"Talk to him anyway, darling. If it works, it will give us the most dramatic room in New York."

"Shall do. What else?"

"Just remember that we're giving a small dinner tomorrow night. Jackie and the Paleys are coming. John Fairchild and Jill are coming, too, but I wish I hadn't asked him now."

"Why? I always find him an interesting guy."

"It's just that he gave me a nasty little dig in *Women's Wear* this morning. He didn't like the dress I was wearing at the Museum party the other night."

"Neither did I, but what did he say?"

"He was raking a lot of people over the coals. It was one of those pieces he writes under the name of Louise Esterhazy when he wants to be especially mean. I had thrown the paper away, but wait a minute and I'll read you the part about me." She bent down, picked up the crumpled paper, smoothed it out and read, " 'Crystal, the wonder woman who is making a fortune in cosmetics by not looking her age, doesn't have to prove her point by dressing like a baby doll. That cutie-boo dress of hers certainly missed.' There are a few more jabs but that was the worst."

"He was quite right, my love. Ribbons and laces are not for you, as I've often told you. Better let me pick your dresses. I know how you should look and I've never chosen a loser yet."

"I promise to listen next time. We're at the office, so goodbye, darling." As she hung up the receiver, he was saying, "You've never—" and she knew the rest of the sentence would have been "listened to anybody yet."

The car slid to a stop in front of the GM Building. Vincent jumped out, opened the door and stood at attention. He admired the way she always got herself out of the car, all in one piece, without any visible effort and showing just enough of what he considered a good pair of legs. As he handed her the briefcase and stack of magazines with turned-down pages that she had tossed into the front seat, he noticed approvingly, as he always did, the way her blond hair was pulled back, clubbed at her neck and tied with a navy blue ribbon to match her suit. A good-looking woman, he thought to himself, and unbelievable for her age.

"Thank you, Vincent, I'll call you if I want you to pick me up this evening," she said. "It's such a lovely, warm day that I may want to walk up Madison Avenue for a while when I finish work, and then grab a cab." Walking up Madison Avenue was a hangover from the days when she had no money and desperately wanted almost everything. Now it was equally delicious to feel selective and critical.

As she often did, Crystal stopped for a minute to look up at the General Motors Building. The sun would just be reaching her windows, which were near the top.

As she passed the sunken plaza with its shops and umbrella-shaded tables, she turned back once more. She loved the whole scene, the old Plaza, which seemed to be squatting reverently across from the tall new skyscraper; the splashing fountain and the patient horses with their still empty victorias. It was just ten o'clock, early for New Yorkers, and everything had a damp freshness about it like a newly painted picture.

She took a deep breath, lifted her head and went into the building like a racehorse on its way to the track.

Inside it was like a chorus. "Good morning, Mrs. Young. How well you're looking today," said the porter, who was echoed by the elevator starter and the operator who took her to her own floor.

She realized it was a backhanded compliment and that she had to accept it, much as she often longed to come back with "Look at me. I'm a successful young woman. Why shouldn't I look well today?"

On her own floor she passed through swinging doors with *Adam and Eve* in block letters and *Cosmetics* in smaller script. She waved at the receptionist and then passed through three offices, all furnished with blond desks, cane chairs and brass and Lucite tables. At each desk a secretary, with her hair pulled back and tied at the nape of her neck to show off a flawless skin and unbelievable eyelashes, was talking intensely into her white telephone, probably to her best friend about what happened last night, Crystal was reasonably sure.

The fourth door she came to was lettered *President* in one corner. The big office inside was her own.

Her executive secretary, Herbert Pomeroy, was still arranging the papers on her desk and putting the mail into action and we'll-take-it-up-later piles.

"Don't tell me a thing, Pomeroy, good or bad until you call Fred or one of our other hair stylists and get him to come over here immediately. Every girl in this office has her hair done exactly like mine and I prefer to be different."

"A good idea," said Pomeroy, taking off his dark glasses and putting on his perpetual smile. She knew the answer would have been the same if she had said, "Get me a barber. I want to be as bald as Yul Brynner."

Crystal's office was like the living room in a country house. It was almost blindingly white and bright. At the far end, tall windows that reached almost from floor to ceiling looked out above the top of the Plaza. They were flanked on each side by big, healthy trees in tubs concealed by straw baskets. More trees scattered throughout the room were nourished by lamps in the ceiling.

Other windows faced south and offered a glimpse of the traffic as it inched its way downtown. When she stood there looking down she never failed to think: This is almost exactly the spot where I spent my first night in New York. The difference is that the old Savoy Plaza is gone and there were fewer cars then.

She had ordered her floors painted white and covered them only with white handwoven scatter rugs. The walls were covered with a blue-and-white fabric in a small provincial pattern, and tall étagères held some of her collection of blue-and-white porcelains, bowls and plates. She liked only white flowers, either growing azalea plants or her favorite white daisies in the room, and when more colorful offerings arrived, the cards were filed for thank-you notes, but the flowers were sent off to decorate other offices. Since there was no fireplace, white couches and chairs stacked with blue-and-white cushions in half a dozen different prints were arranged around a white bookcase wall with a big round coffee table that had a revolving top in the center. On the table Margot Fonteyn's biography was open to the title page, on which the ballerina had written, "Darling Crystal, you are an inspiration to us all."

On a table behind one couch, magazines from all over the world were neatly arranged. Every inch of another table was covered with silver-framed photographs of all sizes. One of them showed Crystal and Eliot Tyler Young at their wedding. The rest, all lovingly inscribed, came from John and Jacqueline Kennedy, Diana Vreeland, the Duke and Duchess of Windsor, Gloria Guinness, Shelley, Yves Saint Laurent, Halston and Jamie Wyeth.

Crystal had given in recently to what she considered her first extravagance. In one of her previous offices she had tried abstract paintings. They bothered her, because she couldn't accept them as design and kept trying to understand them. Wyeth was clear to her, she hung his painting on a plain white wall in her working quarters, a small bare room with nothing but a big desk, a typewriter and files. She had hung it opposite the desk. It was beautiful and peaceful to look at as she worked.

Pomeroy sat down in a chair, put the stack of papers on a small table and began to nervously adjust his bow tie as he always did when he wanted Crystal's complete attention. "Mary Lasker would like you on the dais for some sort of award luncheon. I couldn't quite make out what it's all about but I was sure you would want to go . . . But did you want to use your married or professional name?"

"Miss Crystal, of course. I've worked hard enough to establish it. You ought to know by now, Pomeroy, that I use Mrs. Eliot Tyler Young only for my private life."

"Mrs. Isabelle Leeds also wants you next Tuesday for a luncheon in honor of the wives of the Democratic governors," Pomeroy continued.

"It's yes to both. Find out how many ladies at each and we will try to arrange gifts. For Mary Lasker's group, the new packages that hold my Young Forever eye cream and eye shadow, and for the governors' wives, sample-size jars of my own special Young Forever night cream, along with the latest pink lipstick, I think."

At this moment, there was a commotion at the door as Fred, consultant on all hair problems for Adam and Eve, arrived with two helpers. "Now, Mrs. Young, if we are going to change your hairdo, it must be thoroughly shampooed."

Crystal's own private bathroom adjoining her office was equipped completely to cope with all kinds of emergencies and changes of mind. The cabinet above the sink was full of Young Forever shampoo and hair creams, scissors, razors, brushes and rinses, to say nothing of both standing and hand dryers.

It wasn't long before she returned to Fred, looking freshly clean and blond. "What magnificent hair you still have, Mrs. Young," he said, running his comb through the heavy strands. "There's hardly a silver thread among the gold, to quote an old song my grandmother used to sing."

"Just look at the three pretty girls in the offices you came through, and you'll see why I want a new hairdo," Crystal said. "I'm thinking in terms of a part right down the center and the hair hanging almost to my collarbone, like the old-time page but limper and absolutely no teasing."

"Any curl, Mrs. Young?"

"Curls are tacky as far as I'm concerned. Just turn the ends under slightly," Crystal ordered.

When she was dry and brushed, Fred brought her the big magnifying mirror from her desk. She studied herself for a minute and then turned to hug Fred. "Just what I wanted," she exclaimed. "You caught it exactly!" She pranced around the room, turning her head from side to side and letting her hair swing across her cheeks. "I feel like a girl in one of our own Adam and Eve commercials."

"Mrs. Young," said Pomeroy as she finished gyrating, "I forgot to tell you that Mr. Adam Adler's secretary called you while you were being shampooed. Mr. Adler would like to see you at either noon or four o'clock. He is in his office now. I was told to remind you that there is a press conference tomorrow morning and he has many things he wants to discuss with you."

"No chance before luncheon, which I really shouldn't keep because you and I are so far behind. Look at that stack of unanswered mail. I'd like to put off Adam but maybe I'm not being respectful enough to the almighty boss. Tell Mr. Adler I'll be in his office at four o'clock," she said as she picked up her handbag and went out the door.

2

Adam Adler had awakened about nine-thirty and turned over, only to find that the place beside him in the huge king-size bed was empty. He rang for the butler.

"What time did Mrs. Adler leave the house, and was she alone?"

"It was about a half hour ago, sir. She was driving her own car and she took Rose. She left you this note."

Adam took the folded paper on which Lynda Adler had scrawled, "Darling, you can reach me at Southampton by noon." She had a childish trick of drawing a little smiling face at the end instead of signing her name.

He telephoned his office, and while he waited for his secretary to come on the wire, he had looked around him. The room was warm and pretty with its peach-colored slipcovers, but he couldn't understand why Lynda liked it so much better than the rest of the house.

When finally his secretary, Pat Haley, picked up the receiver, he said, "You must be having a lot of calls this morning."

"It's been unbelievable, but actually, Mr. Adler, the operator didn't cut in and tell me it was you."

"Get the operator's name and see that she's dismissed this evening. In the meantime, please call Miss Crystal's secretary and tell her I want to see her in my office. Check her calendar and ask her to make it either at twelve or four."

Adam was in a bad mood even before he came downstairs and found out that his new car had developed an ailment and the chauffeur had to substitute another.

"What the hell has gone wrong with the damn thing this time?" he asked as the chauffeur opened the door and he got in.

"A Rolls is a very delicate car, Mr. Adler. I don't know exactly what happened but I believe Mr. Alan took a young lady to a party in it last night."

"My son has rich ideas. Uh, well, I suppose I would have done the same thing if my dad had a town car when I was twenty-five." Adam sat back in his seat, unfolded the *Wall Street Journal* and looked with disfavor at the heavy traffic moving down Park Avenue.

He made a point of never arriving at his office before noon. Since he had bought the town house that had once belonged to multimillionaire Lawrence Mackay, he liked to have an hour or so to enjoy it, and to keep on personally supervising the improvements that would surely make it the most spectacular and talked-about place in town.

From the minute he saw it, Adam had fallen in love with the old Mackay house and making it a showplace had become a fetish with him. In the beginning, Lynda had wanted to have Billy Baldwin do the whole planning and decorating job, and to humor her he called Baldwin.

The three of them had met at the new house, and Adam was prepared to be even more generous than he had originally planned.

"This is the greatest house in New York and my wife tells me that you're the greatest decorator, so that's why I had my secretary call you," Adam had said as he shook hands with Billy Baldwin.

"Thank you Mr. Adler," and as Baldwin's eyes wandered about he commented, "The proportions of this entrance hall are perfect."

Everything had seemed to be going well. Lynda was

pleased and smiling and Baldwin was more than enthusiastic about other rooms in the old mansion.

When they reached the second level, Adam had said, "Now I'll tell you some of the things I propose to do here. I want to tear down the partitions and throw these two rooms together for a larger drawing room. I haven't decided about the staircase yet. The railing doesn't seem to be impressive enough for the rest of the place."

Baldwin had interrupted by saying he thought the staircase a perfect example of the architecture of the period. Baldwin had also ventured a mild protest against destroying the built-in shelves around three sides of the library, but Adam knew he hadn't the books to fill them or the desire to buy them.

Adam decided he would settle the fate of the staircase later, but in the meantime he would hire the decorator. "I want you to do the whole job, Mr. Baldwin, and I want you to start from today. As soon as I get back to the offices I'll arrange to put you on a retainer, just as I do with my lawyers. All I want is for you to be available twenty-four hours a day, so that if I get an idea even late at night I can always reach you. I do a lot of my thinking late at night, and if I happen to read about something that's coming up for sale in Paris or London, I'd like you to be able to hop right on a plane and go over and get it for me."

He had brushed aside Baldwin's protest that he had other clients with "Forget them. You won't need any other clients for two or three years, and this house is going to put you into every magazine and newspaper in the country."

When Billy Baldwin left them, Adam had felt confident that everything was settled and he turned to Lynda. "Now, honey, I hope I've made you happy."

Two days later he was astonished when a polite note from Baldwin appeared on his desk. It stated how beautiful he thought the house was and how much he regretted that he had committed himself to too many clients to take on another assignment at this time.

"The damn fool. He doesn't know a good job when

he sees one," Adam had shouted on the telephone to Lynda.

Though he didn't say so to Lynda, he longed to see his own conception of wealth and elegance come to life in the house. In the beginning, it had to be completely gutted to accommodate the air-conditioning system that Adam felt was essential for comfort. After that a new water tank had to be installed to bring up the pressure.

When Adam's car reached the Madison Avenue entrance of the GM Building, which he preferred to the Fifth Avenue entrance which Crystal used, he was greeted as if he were royalty. The elevator starters were aware that the Adam and Eve offices occupied three floors.

As the elevator doors swung open on the executive floor he walked past the receptionist to his own office, and he wondered if Crystal would be waiting there, and was rather annoyed to find that she wasn't. "You gave my message to Miss Crystal?"

"She was booked up this noon for one of those big charity luncheons she's always going to, but she'll be with you at four," said Pat Haley, who never failed to press home the number of Crystal's social engagements.

While Pat Haley went back to her desk to pick up the sheaf of letters to be answered and her own notebook, Adam asked the operator to call Southampton for him.

In a minute, Lynda was on the wire. "Hello, darling, I just got in the door. This place is a real mess with ladders and painters. I'm glad you aren't here. You wouldn't be able to take it."

"How will you be able to have luncheon and dinner if things are as bad as all that?"

"The painters aren't in the kitchen, so I'm sure we can manage, or if we can't, Rose and I will go out and find some little restaurant that will keep us from starving. You know how hungry I always am."

He had just finished talking with Lynda when his son, Alan, came in and dropped into the chair in front of his desk. Alan was six feet one and as Adam looked at the long, lanky figure, the wavy auburn hair and the freckled face, he couldn't help smiling. Alan returned the smile with the grin that was a duplicate of his own.

"Hi, Dad, I'm afraid I've done it again."

"How badly was the car damaged?"

"The news isn't very good. The operation will be expensive, but the Rolls will live and look as well as ever."

"I ought to make you pay for it, damn it, but this time I'll just say don't take it out again. Your goddamn girl friends will have to settle for your Buick."

"Thank you, Dad."

"Besides, you've got to start putting more effort into your work. Your figures aren't very good. I was going over them, and I also noted you've been reporting for work at nine-thirty and ten."

"Selling cosmetics to drugstores in New Jersey can be pretty damn boring, Dad."

"I didn't find it so."

"Maybe it makes a difference that it was your own business. I think I'll improve when I get more responsibility, and don't have to answer to a woman president."

After Alan left, Adam had lunch in his private dining room with some of his executives and the Viennese doctor he was thinking of hiring for a new project.

3

As chairman of the board, Adam had his office at the other end of the Adam and Eve executive floor. When Crystal tapped at the door promptly at four o'clock, and went in, he was sitting at his desk, looking bored and depressed, she thought.

Adam's office was completely different from hers. Instead of being bright and provocative, it was done in shades of brown. It looked deliberately shabby.

Crystal once told him that it reeked of old money, but what she really thought was quite different. She felt it was exactly the setting a man would choose if he hadn't finished NYU but wanted to look like a Harvard graduate and a member of one of New York's founding families like the Van Rensselaers.

When Adam saw her he got up and came around his desk. She stood on tiptoes to kiss his cheek but he didn't return the caress. Instead he picked up her hand with the long nails covered with their latest color. He looked at it for a second and then bent down and kissed it.

"What on earth, and why so formal?" she asked.

"I've hardly seen you in weeks, but Lynda and I are always reading about you in the columns."

"I managed to get myself publicly spanked this morning by John Fairchild in *WWD*. Did you happen to see it?"

"Yes, I did, and I didn't like it. What could he possibly have against you?"

"It didn't hurt me all that much." But tears came to her eyes.

"Now, don't cry, Crystal, I always hate it, if you remember," said Adam, handing her a piece of Kleenex from a tortoise-shell box on his desk. "I'm about to ask you a favor. It's not for me but for Lynda."

"Just ask me anything, and I'll do it, Adam."

"It's this way, Crystal. You know I have been very happy in Westhampton since we bought the beach house there, but for a long time Lynda has thought that Southampton is much nicer. She tries to be a good wife and a good stepmother to my Alan. I want to make her happy. So this past week I have just closed a deal for a house near the beach in Southampton. It was built by an architect called Stanford White and it has a two-story living room and a swimming pool, and fourteen bedrooms."

"How pleased Lynda must be."

"Yes, she's happy and she loves the house. Actually she bought it with her own money. It has great character and she'll have fun decorating it, but we don't know anybody there. It doesn't matter to me except as far as Alan is concerned. He'll expect that we'll belong to the Meadow Club. The way most of his friends' parents do. I've read the list and I see that your husband is a member."

"Of course, Adam, I'll do anything to help."

"I know you will." He smiled at her across the desk. "Now let's get down to business. I've got lots of plans to tell you about." He pressed the buzzer and when Pat Haley came in he said, "Please bring in all the material about the new promotion and the layouts. Miss Crystal and I will be in conference for at least an hour, so don't put any phone calls through."

"What on earth is this all about and why hadn't somebody bothered to tell me?" Crystal wanted to know as Miss Haley put down a stack of papers on the desk and went out again.

"I wanted to talk to you about it, but I've been in

conferences all week and I knew how wrapped up you were in your own Young Forever division. This will be another entirely separate division, Crystal."

"Tell me quickly, Adam."

"Well, to make a long story short, I believe that cosmetics are going medical. Both men and women are going crazy today on the subject of rejuvenation. Not necessarily by using cosmetics but by shots or pills that contain the same formula. "We've all heard about Niehans and I checked him out. Even sent Gotwin and his wife to have the treatment. They came back like converts to a new religion. Niehans, as we know, is dead, but plenty of people are around today peddling the secret of his shots. I've found a doctor who knows what it's all about and I'm planning to build a rejuvenation center in Westchester around him."

"Darling, it's the most marvelous idea, but you're doing it all wrong," snapped Crystal. "The AMA will never permit it in this country. Why don't you buy one of these ocean liners that are now going for a dime a dozen? Look at the poor *Queen Mary*. You could make one of them into the greatest rejuvenation center and beauty spa in the world—with only Adam and Eve products on board. Once you are out past the three-mile zone you can do whatever you like."

"Bring your chair over here, Crystal. I've always said you were a genius," Adam said, with his broadest smile.

They spent the next two hours discussing the idea and going through the press release on the already finished product to be launched the next day, crossing out words and rewriting the copy. It was Crystal who finally looked up and saw that it was dark outside the window. The whole building was eerily still. The staff had slipped away and left them working.

"I must go," she said and, picking up her handbag, she started for the door. He followed her and as she reached for the doorknob his hand closed over hers.

"Lynda is in Southampton. Come home with me tonight," he said.

Crystal had looked forward to seeing Adam's new

house, but the evening began badly. Adam seemed withdrawn and almost antagonistic, but she tried to make herself believe that it was she who was feeling the antagonism, not towards him but towards the freshly decorated room they were sitting in.

While Adam went to fix the drinks she looked around at the heavy suede-covered chairs and couches and the paintings that she supposed were part of a collection he had bought hurriedly at auction. He had come back from the auction full of enthusiasm and even called her on the office telephone to tell her how lucky he had been because the paintings were just the right size. The room was Adam personified and she thought what a pity that he hadn't allowed some of Lynda's taste to come through.

Adam came back with a bottle of Dom Pérignon. He poured it over a glassful of ice cubes, just the way she liked. After the second glass they were laughing and talking just as they used to when they started working together twenty years before.

They had dinner on a card table in what Adam called his den. It was just big enough for a token desk and a couple of chairs, and the butler had trouble getting around the card table to serve the meal.

"Lynda and I usually eat in the little sitting room that's next to our bedroom. It's fitted with a small refrigerator and a stove."

"It's a beautiful old house, Adam. You must love it."

"It's just what I've always wanted. The house in Southampton is all Lynda's from the deed to the decoration. There are things she doesn't seem to like about this place, but out there she'll have her own way."

After coffee he asked, "Like to see the rest of the house?"

"Of course. There's nothing in the world I'd like better. I've been longing to see it ever since you first bought it."

They walked up the spiral staircase that Adam had decided to leave intact and went into the master bedroom. Adam liked the idea of platforms, and he had had one built in the center of the floor. The bed he had placed on it was lighted by spots and there seemed to be almost nothing else in the room. It looks like a shrine, Crystal thought.

"I don't think there's another bed in the world like it," said Adam. He showed her the headboard that was as full of push buttons as the panel that confronts the driver of a car. Both the head and foot of the bed could be raised or lowered. Each side had its own reading light and telephone and there were buttons to ring bells in most of the rooms of the house.

"I designed a makeup table for Lynda that I'm pretty proud of."

He led her into the bathroom and showed her the mirrored table that had a section for her perfumes, a built-in rack for her lipsticks and a button she could press to bring her makeup mirror closer or push it away.

When they reached the main floor, Adam turned her towards the dining room. "Lynda says it looks like a goddamn boardroom," he said as he turned on the light.

"Well, you can hardly blame her," said Crystal when she realized there were twenty-four chairs around the table and that they were swivel types and firmly screwed into the floor. "Do you always have twenty-four for dinner, and what on earth are you going to do, Adam, if somebody drops out at the last minute?"

"I know you're laughing at me a little as you sometimes do, Crystal, but you still turn me on." He put his arms around her, pulled her close and kissed her.

Crystal felt herself responding for a minute, but when his fingers began fumbling with the zipper of her dress she reached up and pushed him away.

"I'll never get over wanting you, Crystal."

"Darling, I was crazy about you for a while years ago, and it was wonderful. I still care for you, but in a different way."

"You're playing the faithful wife, I see."

"I'm not playing. I really am. Besides, Lynda is one of my best friends, and I adore Eliot."

"But, baby, we're together, and Lynda and Eliot needn't know."

"Oh, Adam, don't be foolish. We're grown up now. I want to be fresh and bright for that press conference tomorrow. It's terribly important for both of us to launch those Before and After face-lift products just right."

"Maybe so, Crystal," but Adam was no longer smiling.

"Meeting the press is not easy, you know. It takes so long to produce a product after you first think of it that by the time it's finished you lose your enthusiasm. I want to lie quietly in bed tonight and remember our original excitement."

"You've never failed us yet." He picked up her handbag from a chair in the foyer, gave it to her and kissed her cheek.

His car was waiting outside the door to take her home and, as the chauffeur got out to help her in, she turned back to wave to Adam, but he had already closed the door and turned out the light.

4

The next morning when Crystal finished her coffee, she showered and dressed hurriedly. When she arrived at the office, television cameras were still being set up. The room was already full of reporters, most of whom she knew well. Coffee was being served from an urn in one of the outer offices and she helped herself to a cup as she began to make the rounds. Angela Taylor was there from the *Times*. Ruth Preston had come from the *Post*, and Kathy Larkin was representing the *Daily News*. As always, the beauty editors of the magazines were huddling together in a corner, leaving the newspaper girls to form their own group. Most of the journalists had brought their own photographers, who were in a huddle discussing the prospect of a proposed strike. The TV and service crews were setting up lights and working out camera positions.

The only person she did not recognize in the crowd was a young man she had never seen before. He seemed to have no contact with anyone in the room, so she went to him and held out her hand. "I'm so glad you could come. Have we ever met before?"

"I'm a bit of a strange bird here, I guess. I'm from the London *Daily Globe* and you're Crystal of course."

"And what's the strange bird's name?"

"It's Roderick Ramsey, and I write a gossip column several times a week, in the London *Daily Globe*, which has one of the largest circulations in England."

"It's very flattering to find a gossip columnist who is interested in a business presentation of new cosmetics," she said.

"I don't know how interested I'm going to be in your new creams and lotions, but I'm deeply interested in you and everything about you, Miss Crystal."

"Well, thank you."

As they talked, she examined him closely. He was not unattractive but he needed some grooming and pressing. He had pale blond hair, a narrow face and a sharp nose and chin that looked as though they had been cut out with a razor blade. His pale blue eyes did not warm up when he smiled.

"A few weeks ago, I wrote a bit about your success in my column," he said. "To my surprise the international edition of World noticed it. They've commissioned me to do a cover story on you that will run in the American edition, too."

"How exciting."

"I wonder if I could see you for a few minutes after the regular press conference is over."

"Of course. I can't give you much time because I have a number of other appointments. But if you wish, we can set up another date."

As she began her presentation, Crystal noticed Adam standing quietly near the door. Speaking in her most precise English voice, as she always did at conferences, she began:

"It was so good of all of you to make this your first stop today. I never send for you unless I feel that we have a real story and I am sure that we have this time." She took the brown paper from a big package beside her and said, "Today's surprise is the first book I've ever written and it will probably be the last. It's a complete survey of all the possible face lifts and body lifts that are available for both men and women."

As she talked on about breast lifts, fanny lifts and thigh lifts, Crystal became steadily more articulate.

"It's a strange thing, but with all the prevalence of facial surgery, and we give you the statistics, it is still surrounded by a certain amount of mystery. Many women are still averse to acknowledging that they've had it. That's why, at the end of the book, we publish a complete list of surgeons involved in the subject along with the special techniques for which they are famous."

"Give us some names, please," called a voice from the back of the room.

"Dr. John Converse, of course, was a pioneer way back in the days when he was ashamed to admit it. Dr. Tom Rees is famous for doing a fabulous job on the eyes. Dr. Michael Hogan, a young surgeon, has done spectacular face transformations for girls in the TV world. Dr. Pitanguy in Brazil does a miraculous job of lifting breasts, but those are just a few of the dozens who are mentioned in the book."

"Have you had a face lift yourself?" asked Angela Taylor.

"Not yet. People have suggested that I have, but if you look behind my ears, you won't find any scars. I plan to do it, though, the minute I feel my face is drooping. My book is simply a helpful guide to go along with our new Before and After products . . . It's a paperback that will be sold in bookstores and will also be available in department stores where the creams and lotions are sold. It will cost much less, of course, when it is bought that way.

"There are several products in the line, and their type and purpose are thoroughly described in the releases I've given you. The skin should be in especially good condition before the operation. I'm not speaking from personal experience, Angela, but I learned from many of the women I interviewed for the book that their skin felt tight and irritated for several weeks afterwards. One lotion is designed to help this condition. Another cream and lotion is designed to stimulate the skin and to keep it from relaxing into its old look for as long as possible. In spite of its popularity, the prices of reliable surgery have not decreased, and every woman is anxious to protect her investment that is anywhere from three to five thousand dollars."

"Do you recommend an anesthetic or a local?"

"A local anesthetic costs less, but I cannot personally recommend anything. The choice depends on the temperament of the man or woman." She looked over at Adam and he nodded and smiled.

She noticed that Roderick Ramsey was taking notes throughout the conference. When most of the reporters had gone, she sat down on one of the couches, and he joined her.

"Well, Miss Crystal, when I first got this assignment I thought it was going to be a bore, but now I'm beginning to think I'll like it."

"I'm glad. I hate to bore anyone."

"Just for starters, Miss Crystal, do you remember a boy named Richard?"

"I expect I've met dozens of Richards in my life. Richard who?"

"Well, he's rather a pal of mine. When I come to New York I stay in his flat, and when he goes to London he visits me. He's a hair stylist."

"I don't believe I know him."

"He's top dog at Arden nowadays. I just happened to mention the other day that I was researching a piece about you, and he said he did your hair the first day you came to New York."

"That's more than twenty years ago."

"He told me he wouldn't have remembered you had not your hair been so beautiful. It was down to your waist and you told him to cut it off."

"Of course, now I remember. He did it very well."

"He told me that you showed him a woman's picture and said you wanted your hair to look like hers. He didn't pay much attention but he thinks you said it was your twin sister. Do you have a twin sister, Miss Crystal? I'm curious about your family background."

"I have no sister at all, let alone a twin. I'm afraid I'm a spoiled only child."

"How many languages do you speak?"

"I speak three languages well, and another two not so well. Why don't we continue this later, Mr. Ramsey? We are having a small dinner tonight. You might

want to meet my husband and a few of our friends."
She took a pen out of her handbag and wrote the
name, address and the time on a little card.

"Just one more question. What is your connection
with Frieda Franken?"

"Frieda Franken? I don't believe I know anyone by
that name. Who is she?"

"I had a letter from her after I wrote that short
piece about you in the London *Daily Globe*. It came
from a nursing home in Holland and she was anxious
to locate you."

"My God, you must mean fat old Frieda." Suddenly
Crystal's eyes softened and she smiled. "How can I
find her?"

"I tried to get in touch with her last week before I
left England, and found she had just died. She was
eighty-six."

"Dear, dear Frieda. She spent most of her early life
with my family."

5

Berlin, 1936

It was Crystal's grandmother who first told her that the earth was round. This information came as a great surprise to her, and the scene was still vivid in her mind.

She could see the freshly scrubbed white tile floor of their Berlin kitchen, her grandmother very erect in her black dress, and the cook, Frieda, fat and smiling, stirring a pot of soup on the old-fashioned stove.

Crystal remembered dropping her grandmother's hand, walking to the window and squinting her eyes to look as far as she could. She went back to her grandmother and tugged at her dress, to interrupt her conversation with Frieda. "I don't think so," she said.

"*Liebchen,* we'll discuss the universe another time," her grandmother said, resuming her conversation with Frieda.

Even at the age of four Crystal did not completely believe elders. She was determined to prove everything they said for herself. She had conceived of the earth as a platform with a fearful dropping-off place somewhere. It disturbed her even more to think of them all clinging to something as round as an apple. After a few minutes of speculation, she began to listen to what her grandmother and Frieda were saying.

"But how can I leave you, Countess Casalet?"

Frieda asked. "It's now 1936 and I started with you in 1912—almost twenty-five years ago, the day before her mother was born—to say nothing of her"—pointing to Crystal with her soup spoon.

"I know, Frieda. We've been together for a long, long time. You are very much a part of my life. It will hurt me deeply to lose you, but it's no longer a question of affection or loyalty. You are not safe in Germany."

"But don't you think this will all pass, Countess?"

"I do not. And I can't afford to take the chance. You must face the fact, Frieda, that you are half Jewish and can't get the necessary papers to live safely in Berlin. Almost every week now we see one of our neighbors leaving for another country."

"But where shall I go, Countess?" Frieda started to cry.

"To your sister in Holland, of course. I will give you the ticket and I promise that the minute this is over we will all be together again."

Crystal felt tears coming to her eyes at the thought of such a fundamental change. Whenever anything went wrong in her life Frieda was the one who said, "Never mind, little Crystal. You are a good girl and the sun will shine on you." She turned to her grandmother. "What will we ever do without Frieda?"

"We'll have to manage," she said.

Though Crystal lived with both her grandmother and her mother, for whom she was named, she felt much closer to her grandmother. Even when she was very small, her grandmother had never talked down to her. She still remembered her last ride along a path by the Wannsee in a little open pushcart. When they came home her grandmother said, "This is your last ride, Crystal. You might as well start walking, for you will walk the rest of your life."

She understood. That winter her grandmother rewarded her with a sled. She took her to the park, showed her how to steer and to coast down the hill on her stomach.

Crystal's mother was young and pretty, but she

often seemed more like an older sister. Every morning she got up from the breakfast table, leaving a faint trail of fragrance behind her, and went off to a dramatic school that she was sure would turn her into a famous actress.

Crystal's grandmother often reminded Crystal that she looked exactly the way her mother did when she had been four years old, and that when she grew up she would surely be just as pretty, if not prettier. "You have stronger bones than she has, more like mine," she said.

After her mother had left for her acting lessons Crystal sometimes went to her room. She liked to look at all the dresses in her mother's closet, some of which her mother had bought in Paris long before she was born. The dressing table was crowded with dozens of fascinating little bottles, brushes and jars. She liked to dip her fingers into the special jar of cream and rub it over her face and then look at herself in the hand mirror. Even when she dabbed on a lipstick, she couldn't see any resemblance to her mother, whose flawless pale face and very red mouth was framed with bangs and shoulder-length hair.

Years later, when she analyzed it, Crystal realized she had had a lonely childhood. They lived in a homely but comfortable house in an upper-middle-class Berlin neighborhood near the Wannsee, where her grandmother and grandfather had once owned an estate with a stable, a conservatory and all kinds of gardens. Their living room was furnished with pieces from that house—a pair of bulbous-front marquetry commodes with marble tops and damask-covered sofas and chairs that were beginning to fray a little.

Next to it was a library where they spent most of the time and where the radio played constantly. The dining room had cabinets full of her grandmother's porcelains and the drawers of the buffet were equally filled with her silver, engraved with her crest and carefully preserved in felt covers.

Crystal's grandmother had often told her how much she loved giving parties and arranging her table, but there had never been one since she was old enough to remember. Her mother and grandmother exchanged friendly greetings with their neighbors when they met on the street but nothing more, and the disinclination for anything further seemed to be mutual.

As a replacement for Frieda, Countess Casalet had hired a daily maid who came at noon and stayed through dinner. At Crystal's former nap time she was storming through the house with vacuum cleaner and dustcloth.

It was the beginning of a new regime. She and her grandmother went somewhere every afternoon. Usually it was just a walk, but once it had been a movie, Crystal's first. It was a German film with a Russian star, Olga Zarov. Crystal sat frozen with excitement as she watched Zarov sweep through the picture in chiffon and feather boas.

Once a week her grandmother hired a car and they drove to the cemetery where her grandfather was buried. She was aware that there were fathers and sometimes grandfathers in many of the houses on their block. She knew her grandfather had been killed in the Great War, so when Gerda, the little girl who lived next door, had once asked her, "Where's your father?" she had answered, "Oh, he was killed. I guess it was a long time ago before I was born."

"My mother sometimes sees your mother on the streetcar and says she doesn't wear a wedding ring. Why is that?" Gerda had said.

"Oh, my mother has lots of rings but she is an actress and doesn't like jewelry. My grandmother has a big box of jewelry, and she says when I grow up she's going to give me some. She's a real countess."

6

New York, 1976

Crystal was confident that her press conference had been a complete success but her contact with Roderick Ramsey had left her chilled. It was as though she had come close to an iceberg. When she returned to her office she instantly rang for Pomeroy, told him to cancel her luncheon date and to go out and find as many back copies of the *Daily Globe* as possible.

She ordered a salad and a glass of milk to be brought to her desk and while she was eating she thought to herself: I'm being very silly. I must be overtired. Perhaps Eliot and I should go away for a few days. I think I'll speak to Adam.

She was just finishing her luncheon when Pomeroy came back with the London papers. He had managed to find three and they all happened to carry the Ramsey column that was called "I Spy."

"He's an unpleasant kind of fellow . . . hasn't a decent word to say about anybody as far as I've read," he said.

"I'm sure you're right, Pomeroy, but I've already asked him to dinner. Do you think you can find me an extra girl to make an even number?"

While she skimmed through the beauty pages in the latest *Vogue* she could hear Pomeroy telephoning.

It was a quarter of an hour before he came back to her room.

"Lee Radziwill is available but only if she can bring Peter Tufo."

"That's all right. I can expand my table but I still need another girl."

"Fortunately I have already located Carroll de Portago, who just returned from Nassau last night. Now, why don't you go home and get a little rest before your party, Mrs. Young?"

"I might do that."

"Something I forgot, Mrs. Young, but perhaps it doesn't call for an immediate answer. Mr. Adler has sent you a memo asking for all possible details on the beauty cruise that you mentioned to him yesterday."

Crystal had already started to get together the papers and magazines that she always referred to as her homework, but she sat down again and reached out her hand for the memo. "Anything he wants is always immediate. I'd better sit right down and try to dictate an answer. If I don't I wouldn't put it past him to call me away from the table at my own dinner party tonight to answer some questions."

As Crystal began to dictate, Pomeroy was ready with his pad and pencil poised. "First of all, say that I plan to contact some of the cruise lines, and find what we can do on special rates for a large group, or whether it would make more sense to charter an entire ship. Say that I think we should accept no more than two hundred applications, so that we can give everyone personal attention."

"If I may interrupt for a minute, Mrs. Young, I don't quite understand the advantage of taking these ladies off on a boat."

"It's simple, Pomeroy. The ship will cruise outside of this country's boundaries so that the passengers can take the Niehans-type shots that are forbidden here by the Food and Drug Administration."

"I've never quite understood the Niehans treatment."

"Remind me to call Montreux, Switzerland, tomorrow, Pomeroy. That's where the clinic is located. Celebrities like Charlie Chaplin, Merle Oberon, and dozens of others have taken their shots there."

"Do they really look younger afterwards, Mrs. Young?"

"Not necessarily. It's not a face lift, Pomeroy. The shots are said to replace nonworking cells in your body, though I must say that lots of people who have had the shots manage to look terrific, too."

"Perhaps there might be a chance for me to go on the cruise with you. I assume you'll have to be there, won't you, Mrs. Young?"

"Since I've suggested the whole thing, I suppose I will, but, at any rate, I'm sure I can arrange for you to have some of the shots. But if you like we can also consider whether you might not prefer the shots that were developed by Aslan, a Rumanian doctor."

"Thank you, Mrs. Young. Even though I'm still in my thirties, I can't seem to keep up with you, and this may help."

She dictated a few more paragraphs suggesting Gayelord Hauser might be contacted to give his talks on vitamins and diet suggestions. "If we can get him, it will make the trip. He not only makes sense but he's very amusing, and the ladies will love him."

Pomeroy picked up the telephone and announced that Roderick Ramsey was calling.

Crystal stood up. "I think he's going to pester the life out of me. Tell him I've already gone home." When she reached the door she turned back. "Better give me his three columns."

On the way home in the car, she read the three "I Spy" columns from beginning to end. When she arrived at the apartment she went to her room, stretched out on her chaise longue and slept for an hour.

She woke feeling refreshed and able to cope with the whole human race, including Roderick Ramsey. She put on a robe, went into the kitchen to give instructions to the two extra maids who were there for the evening, and was circling one of two round tables in the dining room with her place cards in her hand when Eliot came in.

"Hello, my love. Who's coming to dinner?"

"Don't try to pretend you don't remember we're having a party for the Patinos. You'll be sitting between Jackie and Beatriz Patino. I really started out to have just one big table but today I enlarged it because I invited a London gossip columnist named Roderick Ramsey. He came to my press conference and afterwards he told me that World had commissioned him to do a cover story on me."

"That's very good, isn't it? Even better than a Time cover."

"It would be if I trusted him, but I know from reading his columns that he's one of those writers who're out for the kill. I'm putting him beside Jill Fairchild at dinner. She is English and she leads such a nice, straightforward life that he won't be able to take any digs at her."

"He'd better not try any funny business with you if he knows what's good for him," Eliot said. "But you've left yourself wide open, I'm afraid. The magazine won't leave a stone unturned, for a cover story."

"Oh, Eliot, what should I do? Do you think I can get out of it?"

"My advice is to play along with it for a while and not let him see that you are worried."

As she went upstairs, she thought: Easier said than done.

She remembered Roderick Ramsey's steely blue eyes, and was terrified that their probing would prove disastrous to her career.

She chose the dress she was going to wear that night and then opened the little wall safe that held her jewelry. Though she picked up the necklace that Eliot had given her and watched the light sparkle through the pale yellow diamonds, she put it back and took out the little circle of tiny diamonds that had belonged to Countess Casalet. It was the only tangible thing she possessed to remind her of her grandmother.

She could imagine her wearing it at her debut ball in Vienna that she had often described to Crystal in detail. Looking at herself in her makeup mirror, she thought: I wonder if I really am like Grandmother?

7

Vienna, 1887

Crystal's grandmother, Vilia, Countess Casalet, grew
up on her family's estate in the countryside near Vienna. Since the house was only fifty years old, it was
larger and more luxurious than some of the castles of
the nobility.

When she woke up in the morning, Vilia pulled a silk
tassel that hung among the draperies of her four-poster
bed. Her little maid, Tina, brought her breakfast while
she was still lying in bed, and pushed back both the
curtains that enclosed the canopy and the window
draperies. All the hills and woods which she could see
in the distance belonged to her family. When she got
up, stretched and actually went to the windows, she
looked out on the wide, shallow stone steps that led
up to the front door, the graveled drive that was as
smooth as sugar, her mother's rose gardens and, a little farther off, the stables where the horses were kept
and the lake her father had built purely for his aes-
thetic pleasure. He had decorated it with a family of
swans.

Early in life, Vilia realized she was something of a
beauty. Her father told her so frequently, and wherever she went women looked at her appraisingly and
the men always smiled.

It made her happy to know that she had the famous

Viennese skin that looks like pink marble and that she had the reddish-gold hair to go with it. Vienna was full of pretty girls, but she envied none of them. She made up her mind early that she liked pretty women and wanted them as friends.

She also made up her mind she would never interfere with another girl's romance, a promise she kept for the rest of her life. "I think the pretty ones are the happiest and the easiest to get along with if you play fair. The plain ones are the most troublesome," she once told a friend.

In the private school in Vienna to which her parents sent her she was a good student and immensely popular among her classmates. She wanted to be part of everything, whether it was a class party that she had actually organized or, in the country, a sleigh ride, a hay ride or a dance. She had her own little horse that she rode every weekend. She rode side saddle with her hair clubbed and tied in a black ribbon at the back of her neck, a black jacket, a white shirt and a long skirt over boots; she was an exhilarated and fearless rider.

From the time she reached her teens, Vilia's name was never missing from the guest list of a Vienna party. The success of their only child delighted Baron and Baroness von Krantz, who were well connected and well respected among their friends.

At least once a year, a big party was given for Vilia in the big red-and-gold ballroom that occupied a wing of the house. The parties ranged from those for fifty little friends with a magician to the later well-chaperoned dances for boys and girls.

Among Vilia's friends was one girl who was not exactly beautiful, or even pretty, but had a strange mystic charm. She was Marie Vetsera, daughter of Baroness Vetsera, whose name was greeted with raised eyebrows by her mother and complete silence by her father when she mentioned it one night at dinner.

"Quite a dreadful woman," commented her mother. "She is said to have a great deal of money, though nobody knows quite where it comes from, and she is determined to push her daughter into the best possible marriage."

At school Marie clung desperately to Vilia, whose positiveness, she sensed, could carry her through any situation. "Aren't you afraid of anything?" she once asked Vilia, who laughed and answered, "Not yet."

When Vilia's parents finally consented to let her invite her friend for a weekend, even they had to admit that Marie had charm.

"A nice child. She listens," remarked her mother.

"She's a little mouse, with that soft brown hair and those bright eyes," said her father.

At luncheon in school, Vilia and Marie sometimes managed to get a table by themselves so they could exchange secrets. One day Marie's secret was: "Guess what, Vilia. In a few months Queen Victoria will be celebrating her Golden Jubilee and my mother is going to ask your mother and father if you can come with us to London. What's more, we are going to stop in Paris on the way, and my mother is going to give each of us a ball gown and perhaps more. Oh, I do hope you will be allowed to come, for I shall be so lonely if you can't."

When the invitation was delivered, though, it seemed at first that the answer would be no. "You are just about to be sixteen and you won't be coming out for another year, at least," her mother protested.

"Besides, though Marie is a dear little girl, I'm not sure that I like your name to be linked so closely with Baroness Vetsera," her father said.

"But, Mother, I do so long to see Paris and London. Queen Victoria will never have another Golden Jubilee, and everybody from Vienna is going, even Crown Prince Rudolf will be there and so will the Empress's cousin, Countess Larish."

After several notes were exchanged and Baroness Vetsera came in her carriage to call on them, permission was finally granted. Baron von Krantz drove with Vilia to meet the Baroness and her entourage that in-

cluded her own maid, a footman, as well as her own
sheets and blankets.

The two girls shared a compartment on the train and
they talked all night. "I'd like to meet lots of men, not
just Viennese but English and French," Vilia said.

Marie, though, was only hoping to get a glimpse of
Crown Prince Rudolf. "I love his face," she said.

They were hardly settled into their rooms at the
Hotel Crillon in Paris before a carriage was waiting to
take them to Worth's fashion salon.

"It's very late to be ordering clothes for the Jubilee," said Baroness Vetsera. "Mine have been finished
long ago, but I'm a good customer and I feel sure he'll
be able to finish two gowns for each of you."

At Worth's with its satin brocade walls and draperies and a dramatic mixture of flowers in a Ming vase,
fashion models began showing them dresses from the
latest collection. When Worth himself came in Vilia
was surprised. She had expected to meet a man who
looked like an artist, but instead he was bald and
looked like a tired businessman.

The Baroness chose pink and blue for her daughter,
who whispered, "I don't like either." She told Vilia to
pick her own fabrics from the samples and Vilia
picked white moire with a bustle draped back and ruffled shawl of the fabric draped around her shoulders.
The second was apple green taffeta. It was arranged
for all the dresses to be brought over by a special messenger and delivered to them at Claridge's in London
within a week.

Vilia's mother and father had written ahead with
advance notices of their daughter's arrival. There was
a pile of notes and invitations waiting, but Vilia was
too polite to accept unless Marie could be included.
She was soon aware that they weren't going to some of
the most exciting parties, but since they went out
every evening to the theater, to dinner or to dances
where they met young guardsmen and diplomats, it
didn't seem to matter. Marie was still shy and one
night Vilia's heart bled for her when nobody rescued

her from dancing for hours with the same man who had, obviously, been told to take care of her—Count Krinsky, the Englishman in charge of Prince Rudolf. He spent his time constantly teasing the habitually nervous Prince and even mimicking him to his English friends. When the Baroness finally maneuvered to meet Count Krinsky he found her an equally sharp wit and she and the two girls soon received invitations to what promised to be the most spectacular of the Jubilee balls.

The night arrived. Vilia was hooked into the tight top of her white moire dress from Paris by the Baroness's maid. A hairdresser arrived who brushed back her hair into a pompadour, fastened it with a barrette concealed by two camellias and twisted the ends into two long curls that fell over one shoulder. Marie chose her pink silk as the lesser of two evils, but her hair was brushed up to curls on top of her head to show her long, slender neck.

Vilia could never forget the ballroom with the men in full-dress uniforms, and the ladies with bare shoulders and bustles, dancing the minuet, the mazurka and the waltz. She was presented to the Prince of Wales and, about the middle of the evening, to Prince Rudolf. He asked her to dance but she found him an uncertain dancer, who sometimes missed the beat, and he didn't hold her tightly enough.

Later, she saw him bending over Marie's hand and, at the end of their dance, she watched them talking together and walking towards open doors that led to a balcony. It was a warm June night, and she remembered there was a full moon.

At their hotel later, she asked Marie, "Well, how was it?" and Marie told her, "He was wonderful. He says he is very shy, too. He said he hoped to find me again in Vienna but probably he was just talking. I don't suppose I'll ever see him again."

The next morning she and Marie went shopping for souvenirs of the trip and Vilia bought two white cotton handkerchiefs embroidered in red and blue thread with a crown and, under it, the words "Victoria 1827 to 1887." She gave one to Marie and kept one for herself.

The following morning they were up early to see the actual Jubilee parade from a friend's window as it moved from Paddington Station to Buckingham Palace. The Queen was not riding in her glass carriage but in an open landau driven by six cream-colored horses. She was wearing a lace cap embroidered in diamonds. Many of the court ladies had copied it. She and Marie decided it would be fun to design their own versions as soon as they were back home.

When they returned to Vienna, Vilia and Marie continued to be close friends. Now they were old enough to go to shop or have hot chocolate and a pastry together at Sacher's. One afternoon after they had sat down in their favorite red velvet corner with the potted palm and the waitress had brought their hot chocolate topped with a tower of whipped cream, Marie leaned across the little marble table and said, "Vilia, I would rather not mention names again. First came a note, and then another. He arranged to send a carriage for me and I met him in quite a remote place that I'd rather not mention. If it happens again, I may tell my mother I'm with you."

It did happen again and again. Marie began to look very pretty in a soft romantic way and to Vilia she seemed to be walking in a dream. One day she told Vilia, "We love each other completely. I would rather be dead than try to live without him."

Vilia said nothing at home but at the dinner table one night her father surprised her with "So, Vee, it seems that the little brown mouse has managed to catch the lion, Prince Rudolf. Servants talk, you know, and all Vienna knows about it.

"The Emperor will never let them marry. What a pity. It will break her heart and no man in Vienna will want her after all the scandal."

Since she had got no further than a boy-and-girl kiss, Vilia sincerely envied and admired Marie for her grand passion. Now that they had both finished school they saw less of each other. When they did meet,

Marie talked only of Rudolf's and her happiness together, and seemed not to mind that by this time all Vienna was talking.

Early in May a note came from Marie asking her to be one of a house party she and Prince Rudolf were planning at Mayerling, which she described as "a hunting lodge far up in the hills in wild country. We have been happy here and would like to have you like it, too."

Vilia couldn't go. Afterwards she never knew whether she was glad or sorry, and she often wondered why Marie wanted her and whether the double suicide was decided far ahead or really came as a last-minute decision. The news reached her at Baden-Baden, where she had promised to go with her father for a week, and she was stunned and unbelieving. When she and her father arrived home she found a package had been delivered to her by Baroness Vetsera's coachman on the day Marie died. In a pretty little jewel box was a small amethyst heart on a gold chain. On the card Marie seemed to have scribbled hastily, "With love to my dearest friend."

Though Vilia grieved for Marie and realized that probably she would never form such an intimate friendship again, she soon became engrossed in details for her coming-out party. The party was given at their home. There was a formal reception first, followed by dinner and after that a ball, for which two orchestras played, one inside in the ballroom and the other outside under a tent on the lawn. While her mother's maid was putting the last touches to her hair and giving a last press to her petticoats, Vilia looked out of her window and saw the first carriages beginning to arrive. Guests came from London, Venice, Paris and Berlin. The magnificent panorama of carriages, horses and coachmen was one she never forgot.

Vilia never cared whether it was a mazurka, a polka or a waltz as long as she was dancing. She wore yards of white hand-embroidered cotton, a blue sash and a small diamond necklace that had belonged to her grandmother. She danced with wings. .

As the evening wore on, she became aware of a sandy-haired young man, somewhat older than most of her friends, who kept watching her with amused interest. Around three o'clock in the morning, after he had spent a long time leaning against the piano, he said something to the pianist, who got up and let him take his place. When he finished playing, Vilia went over to the piano.

"It's the most enticing music I ever heard," she said. "Nobody could possibly resist dancing to it."

"Thank you, then let's try it," he answered, beckoning to the pianist. "I wrote it and brought the score with me. Perhaps you will play it for us."

When he put his arm around her for the waltz, it was unlike anything that had ever happened to her before. As they whirled around the floor she felt as if the music were beating through both their bodies, and she felt almost faint when it stopped and they separated.

"Come, let's have a breath of air. You've been dancing all night, but I can see that you love it."

They could smell the roses in her mother's garden and they walked towards the perfume.

"Do you know that dancing is an expression of sex?" he asked. "The savages use it to rid themselves of their sex repressions and, without realizing it, so do many civilized people."

Vilia had scarcely heard sex mentioned and certainly never at home. She felt it was the most sophisticated conversation she had ever had in her life.

"Do you think I'm a savage?" she asked.

"No, I think you are young and want to discover everything in life," he said. He put his finger under her turned-up face and kissed her full on the mouth.

As they strolled back to the tent, Vilia began to think quickly how she could arrange to see him again. "I do so wish I could learn to play the piano. Could you possibly suggest someone?"

"I'm sure I could find a teacher for you. I'll write you a note and thank you for the party. If you are really interested in learning to play, I will tell you how to reach me. My name is Franz Lehár. This is my address."

The note came in a few days, but she put it in the drawer of her desk and didn't answer it right away. She felt so violently attracted to young Lehár that it frightened her.

"My father wouldn't approve and I would rather live for love than die for it as Marie did," she told herself.

Three months later she hadn't forgotten him, so she wrote a note saying that she still longed for piano lessons. Perhaps he has forgotten me and perhaps it's a good thing, she thought when a week passed with no answer.

At the end of the second week it arrived with the explanation that he had been visiting his home in Hungary. He gave her the address and said he would have a possible teacher ready and waiting for her at the studio.

For the appointment, Vilia put on a new brown velvet suit with a tight, little Basque jacket and a little brown ribbon hat that ducked over one eye.

He opened the door of his studio and she could see at one quick glance that there was no teacher there. "Did you really think there would be?" he asked. "I only said so to soothe your conscience for coming here."

He followed her around the room and when she stopped to look at a painting he gently took out her hatpins and then took off her hat. "It's adorable," he said, "but you should never wear a hat. Your hair is too glorious."

When they came to the piano he said, "Sit down and put your fingers on the keys. Let's see if your fingers are made for playing."

She spread her hands over the keys and he put one of his hands over hers. "You don't really care about playing the piano. You came here because you wanted to see me, didn't you?" he asked.

"Yes," she said.

He kissed her again and again and she felt as though she were on fire.

"You're very desirable," he said. "But you are also very young and vulnerable."

Vilia longed to have him go on kissing her but instead he said, "Next time."

After that, they saw each other at least once a week, though Vilia never mentioned him at home. She met him at the studio and sometimes they stayed there while he played or they made their own luncheon in his kitchenette. Other times they went to an art gallery or a concert, and at one of the concerts Vilia caught a glimpse of one of her mother's friends in a box.

The next time she came to the studio he told her he had written a special waltz for her. "The music sounds the way I see you," he said. "It's your own music. I'll give you the score. It will be published, and whenever you hear it, you'll think of me."

When he kissed her goodbye he said he was off to Hungary for three weeks. "It's an opportunity for me, but we will see each other the minute I return."

Actually she never saw him alone again. At dinner that night her father said, "Vilia, your mother and I have something serious to talk to you about." Vilia felt sure that her mother's friend had tattled and she braced herself.

"At your party last year you met young Count Curt Casalet," her father went on, and Vilia had a quick recollection of a tall, handsome, rather serious gentleman very elegantly dressed and with a neat mustache.

"His family and our families have been good friends for a long time. He has a high and very responsible position in our government. We had luncheon together today at our mutual club, and it makes me very happy to tell you that he asked my permission to speak to you. He wants you to become his wife."

Vilia sat quietly for a moment, and then her father said, "Liebchen, you are not made for the role of a strolling musician's wife."

When she reached her bedroom Vilia faced the fact

that she had known all along this was the way her pretty little love affair with Franz would end, and she was certain that Franz knew it, too.

She and Curt Casalet were married six months later after a flurry of shopping that Vilia couldn't help enjoying even though she missed the gaiety, the music and the lovemaking with Franz. She had written him a sad little note and he had mailed her the score of her own Vilia waltz.

Vilia's trousseau was incredible. Her underthings had all been embroidered in a convent with doves, roses and four-leaf clovers. She had tablecloths of all sizes, some with cutout embroidery and others with deep lace hems. She had enough sheets for a mansion.

Though Vilia often wondered how she was going to get through the first night of her married life, she was not one to worry and Curt made it easy for her. By the time they reached London, which was part of their wedding trip, she was feeling happy and adjusted.

Though they stayed at Claridge's, which made her think of Marie, they were invited to Warwick Castle for the Countess of Warwick's famous masked ball, to which four hundred had been asked to come in medieval Italian costume. The banquet was set out in the great splendor of the period and the guests ate and danced in the flickering light of hundreds of torches.

The hostess, an old friend of Curt's, was delighted with his young wife, so they went the following weekend to her favorite Eastonby Hall. Curt explained to her that Daisy Warwick was famous for her charm, and that she and England's Crown Prince Edward had been carrying on a long-playing romance. At the station he showed Vilia the siding that had been installed for the Prince's private car.

Vilia had a natural liking for England, and she enjoyed the whole routine at Eastonby Hall. She was thankful that, passing through Paris, she had bought one of the new tea gowns that were replacing some of the more upholstered fashions. The tea gowns fell from the shoulders with no waistlines and long, sheer sleeves, and the ladies looked more Oriental than English as they fluttered downstairs in them.

At dinner Vilia expected Lady Warwick to arrive with the famous bullfinch on her shoulder but instead she arrived late from London looking rather distraught. The English newspapers had criticized her masquerade party and when she called on one of the editors to complain he had given her a lesson in world economy that she would never forget.

"My dears, I plan to give up all frivolity. There won't be any more masked balls," she announced to her dinner guests. "Already I have plans for establishing a cottage industry on my estate that will turn out trousseaus like Countess Casalet's. I intend to upgrade the status of women, too."

"Don't you find her a little extreme?" Vilia asked Curt as they left Eastonby.

"Not really. She has become aware overnight. Women have previously been happy to remain loved and pampered, but Daisy will start a trend. She is the prototype of the new century's woman."

She learned quickly to love Curt and to depend on him for understanding her thoughts, which, for a while, seemed juvenile beside his. It had been difficult when he first told her that he had been given an important post in the Kaiser's regime as a representative of their country. This meant that they must give up Vienna and move to Berlin. She was happy to go wherever he went, but it took a long time to learn to enjoy the grand house on the Wannsee in Berlin. She would have preferred the easy-going life of Vienna to stiff-necked Prussian Society, but she never complained.

Soon after their arrival in Berlin, Vilia realized that she was pregnant at last, and she and Curt were as eager as children for the arrival of the baby. She lost the baby at three months. Many years later, when she had almost given up hope, she became pregnant again.

This time she gave up the balls and the dancing and spent most of the nine months reading and dreaming in her own big bedroom that overlooked the Wannsee. Since she was no longer a young girl the birth was difficult. When she began to feel herself swimming out of the darkness from the anesthetic, the first thing she saw was the crystal chandelier in her bedroom that sparkled in the morning sunlight with hundreds of colored lights.

Curt's voice, which seemed to come from far away, was saying, "Liebchen, we have a beautiful daughter."

"Curt, how wonderful! Then let's call her Crystal," she said.

Curt had only two years to enjoy the baby before he was summoned by the Kaiser for staff work in the war that was still going Germany's way. He came back frequently, and at first Vilia didn't worry too much. She felt they led a charmed life.

When he was killed three years later at the Battle of Verdun it took her months to realize she would never hear his voice again. She often felt in her heart that when they sent her his Iron Cross her real life ended and the rest became an epilogue.

8

New York, 1976

For the Patino dinner party, as with all her large dinners, Crystal arranged for an expert from one of the Adam and Eve cosmetic counters in a Fifth Avenue department store to come to make up her eyes, a job she had never been patient enough to do as well as she should. She put on Shelley's latest hand-painted chiffon tunic over chiffon pants. Shelley was one of her oldest friends in New York and would be one of the dinner guests that night. Actually, he was the first to arrive and was standing by the window watching the lighted boats on the river as she came in.

"We're thinking of an all-glass wall there. Would you like it?"

Shelley came over to her and kissed her on both cheeks. "Divine," he said.

Shelley had been bought recently by one of the big conglomerates and had become a millionaire overnight and he and Crystal often laughed about the years they had felt extravagant if they went to luncheon at one of the French restaurants. Now Shelley's romantic label that was one of his assets was already appearing on gloves, scarfs, shoes and raincoats. He was thinking of china and tablecloths, but had just turned down a manufacturer who wanted it for bathroom fixtures.

"I've just found the most incredible town house," he told Crystal. "It has a three-story living room and an indoor swimming pool. I'm planning a big party soon to open it, and you simply have to be there."

She was just promising that she would when the rest of the guests began arriving. Jackie, in black crepe, was the last. She had known Jackie ever since she was First Lady and had given an all-girl luncheon at the White House.

Soon after Jackie's appearance they went into the dining room that was lighted by votive candles in little white frosted-glass cups. They flickered on the window ledge, the mantelpiece, the buffet and around the low bowls of white flowers on each table. It was all very pretty and peaceful, thought Crystal as she talked to Antenor Patino about the new home he was building in Mexico on the hills near Las Hadas. And then to Winston Guest about the just published book on gardens written by his wife, C-Z, who was sitting on Antenor Patino's other side.

Before dinner she had taken Roderick Ramsey around the room to meet everybody and had found that he not only knew them by name but knew all about their reputations, homes and hobbies down to the last detail. She looked across at the other table several times and each time she could see he was talking avidly to Jill Fairchild.

The lemon soufflé was delicious but while she was eating it she heard Jill's voice raised several times in protest. When dinner was over Jill came to her in the drawing room.

"Your journalist friend from London spent the whole time quizzing me about you. I didn't know the answers but I wouldn't have told him if I had."

"What on earth did he ask?"

"He wanted to know how long I'd known you, did I think you're as old as you say you are, what was your mother's name, and I forget the rest of the things."

"He's thinking of doing a *World* story about me, but I hope he didn't bother you too much," Crystal said.

Roderick Ramsey lingered after the other guests. "It was good of you to have me tonight, Miss Crystal, or do I call you Mrs. Young at home?"

"Whichever you like."

He reached into a pocket and brought out a small black notebook. "There's just one more name I wanted to mention. Does the name Marlene Duna mean anything to you?"

She frowned. "No, I don't think so, but I'll try to remember."

"Then I will call you in a few days to see if you've remembered," he said. "I'll be around New York for a while talking to your boss, Adam Adler, about you and to some of your many friends. I may have to go back to Berlin for a little more research but I promise I'll see you before I take off."

"A real s.o.b.," said Eliot after the elevator door had closed.

"I suppose he has his job to do and the competition between the gossip columnists is pretty tough these days," Crystal said.

"I find your charity very sweet and not entirely like you. You can be pretty tough in business, yourself, my dear."

"I suppose that's why I understand him. But he frightens me to death."

He put his arm around her as they walked down the hall. "Keep smiling, darling, and let me do the worrying. I'll start a little personal investigation on this bastard tomorrow. Everyone has something in their lives that they'd rather not reveal. I'll try to find out what he has to hide. Maybe my pal Clive in London can help."

"Oh, darling, thank you." She threw her arms around him.

"I look forward to the job. I'll be doing something really useful."

In spite of Eliot's promise, Crystal lay awake for a long time. As she repeated the name Marlene Duna, it began to have a more and more familiar sound. She was half asleep when the phone rang. It was Ramsey again.

"Another thing that bothers me, Mrs. Young, is your voice. You speak English perfectly, without a trace of a German accent."

PART TWO

9

London, 1938

It was just before her sixth birthday that Crystal was told she was going to school in England instead of Berlin. She had come into the library and announced, "I got married this afternoon." Her mother cried, "What do you mean?" but her grandmother simply smiled and said, "Oh, really, and to whom?"

"To Friedrich Schultz," answered Crystal.

"What is Friedrich like?" asked her mother.

"He has yellow hair and blue eyes but he says all the Master Race is blond. He wears a swastika band around his arm just as some of the men do."

"And the wedding?"

"Oh, it was exciting. We were married under the Schultz wisteria tree that has long, drippy branches down to the ground. Afterwards I came home."

"Do you like Friedrich?" asked her mother.

"He's nice, but I was just being polite about getting married. His father owns the market, but I plan to marry somebody who is very rich and important. Like Grandmother did."

"I told you so," said her grandmother, turning to her mother. "She's a true Casalet. It is born in her. Her grandfather would have adored her."

It was that night that Crystal heard the two women talking about her.

"She must go to England immediately. This maniac will ruin what is left of the country," she heard her grandmother say. "She must learn the English ways of thinking and living. I'm afraid she will never be happy here. It was so different when I was growing up."

Crystal couldn't hear her mother's reply, but her grandmother went on. "You don't have to write Keith. I will communicate with him and see that the papers are signed, and I will take her to London myself."

"But how can we afford it?" she heard her mother ask.

"I've already had my amethyst-and-diamond brooch appraised. Herr Kruger says it is worth at least fifty thousand marks and I may be able to get more in England," said her grandmother. "I'll sell it there since Hitler has forbidden anyone to take more than two hundred marks out of Germany."

As she drifted off to sleep, Crystal wondered who Keith was.

A week or two later her grandmother suggested going to the big KDV department store instead of taking a walk. It was a glorious afternoon. The store was full of women who looked like the photographs in the magazines that her mother often brought home. Even more fascinating than the ladies was the paying routine. She could hardly wait for her grandmother to buy something so the salesgirl could enclose the marks in a brass tube that went spinning off on ceiling cables and came back with the change.

For the trip to London she would wear her new navy blue jumper with a white blouse. When she added the navy coat and sailor hat, she felt a great surge of happiness. England would be something new, and she felt ready for it. Even though she cried a little when she kissed her mother goodbye, because she was afraid her mother would be hurt if she didn't, Crystal was eager for her first visit to another country. She loved the boat trains, but the most amusing sight in London was the long, thin doorman with the tall black hat who opened the taxi door for them at Claridges. As they walked into the hotel she remembered her grandmother saying, "It's expensive, but there is an old Austrian saying: 'Believe you deserve the best each day, and the best is sure to come your way.' "

The next morning her grandmother took a taxi to a jewelry shop for which she had a card. Crystal stood with her while she pulled a jewel box out of her handbag and took out her amethyst-and-diamond brooch and showed it to a man who put a small spyglass to his eye to observe it.

"You don't see these any more," he said. While they talked business, Crystal walked along the store's glass cases, looking at the antique shoe buckles, the necklaces of colored stone and even the little crowns for ladies to wear in their hair.

The business must have gone well, for Crystal's grandmother looked flushed and happy as they left the shop. Afterwards they went to Fortnum and Mason and, with her sandwich, Crystal had the largest double chocolate ice cream soda she had ever seen.

The next morning they set off for the school Countess Casalet had selected. It was an hour's train ride from London and a short drive from the station. The school, once a country house, was surrounded by a park full of enormous trees and the whole thing was enclosed in a high iron fence with iron gates. The headmistress, Miss Clairborne, greeted Crystal's grandmother as an old acquaintance.

"We are delighted to have your granddaughter, Countess Casalet. She will be one of our youngest pupils, but there are several others her age, and we shall hope to continue with her until she finishes school."

"That may not be possible," her grandmother said. "Germany is in the hands of a maniac. I don't need to tell you that the situation is growing every minute more desperate. I'm very much afraid, for your sake, that England will become involved with him before long."

Before they finished talking Crystal heard her give Miss Clairborne a list of friends she had asked to visit

Crystal or to take her out, if possible, and among the names she heard was Keith Dunston, whom she described as a young professor of languages in London.

When Countess Casalet rose to go, Crystal clung to her for a moment but her grandmother said firmly, "Enjoy your English year, *Liebchen*. Learn to write English well, and we will write to each other. I will come for you in June." She bent down and kissed her.

When the door closed behind her grandmother, Crystal felt a moment of complete panic before she remembered that she had heard her grandmother call her a true Casalet.

When Countess Casalet returned to the hotel the man behind the desk told her, "Professor Keith Dunston is in the tea lounge waiting for you, Countess. He said you were expecting him."

She went toward the tea lounge and he got up from his chair when he saw her. He hasn't changed at all—almost too good-looking for anyone except an actor, she thought as he came towards her with his most ingratiating smile.

"I received your letter, Countess Casalet," he said. "You asked me to mail the necessary papers to prove that I'm Crystal's father and you can be assured, as far as my family is concerned, she is certainly one hundred percent Aryan. I wanted to bring them to you instead of posting them."

"Thank you," she said.

They sat down. He beckoned to the waiter and ordered tea.

"I have recently read *Mein Kampf* and I feel uneasy at the idea of the three of you living there alone. Wouldn't it be possible for you to go somewhere else?"

"We are in no danger of being taken off to a concentration camp. I wrote to you because little Crystal's birth certificate was questioned without your signature."

As he handed it to the Countess he said, "I had it notarized this time, and here it is."

She put it into her handbag. "Obviously, this man Hitler is crazy," she went on. "It's hard for me to believe that he plans to go on with the wholesale destruction of so many worthwhile citizens of his country."

They talked politics for a few moments until finally he asked, "And how is Chrissy?"

"My daughter has finally found something that really interests her," said Vilia Casalet. "She wants to be an actress. I don't know how much talent she has, but she has been going to dramatic school and has just got her first part in a play that will open in about a month. It's a minor part but Curt Jurgens is the star."

"I'm glad to hear that. She deserves to be happy. I have thought of her often and that happy carefree summer at the university."

"And your wife?" the Countess interrupted.

"Oh, she's fine, thank you. She and the children are at Brighton until the end of the month.

"There is a note to Chrissy enclosed with the certificate, and please assure her, too, that I will look after little Crystal like a fond father."

"Thank you, she has been told to call you Uncle Keith," said the Countess.

As she watched him pay the check, she thought: How typically English, so tall and thin and with all that wavy blond hair and skin like a scrubbed baby's—it's hard to dislike him. When he was studying for his Ph.D. in Berlin and he and her daughter first started going out together, heads turned to look at them wherever they went. Their coloring was so similar they could be an angelic brother and sister. If they only had been, thought the Countess grimly.

Keith Dunston's first visit caused a near panic in Miss Clairborne's school, and while Crystal and Keith sat stiffly in the visitors' room getting acquainted, dozens of teen-age students passed and repassed the door, craning their necks.

After he had left, Crystal was the center of attention, surrounded by girls who had never noticed her before.

"Who is he? He must be a movie star. What a lucky girl you are. He's absolutely divine. When is he coming again?"

"He's just my Uncle Keith. I never met him before, but I do think he's very good-looking," said Crystal, who had a crush on him already.

The next time Keith Dunston came to see Crystal, he asked permission to take her to London for luncheon and to have a look at the city. "All the girls think you're a movie actor," she said after she settled beside him in his car.

"I guess I've heard that before, but I'm not that kind of fellow."

"Then what kind are you? I can't think of anything more fun than being a movie star," she said.

"Not for me. I like living in the country. I read a lot and do a little writing. But I enjoy teaching."

"You are not really my uncle, I know, but just a close friend of my mother. Where did you first know her? She's an actress, you know."

"I was teaching a summer course at Berlin University and she was one of my students. We saw a great deal of each other that summer, and then I had to come back to my family and work in London."

After luncheon he took her to the Tower of London and the Crystal Palace, which looked to her like a giant conservatory.

"Your mother may have been named for this, I don't know," he said.

"Oh, no, she was named for a chandelier in my grandmother's bedroom. My grandmother has often said so," Crystal told him. "Most German girls with the same name spell it C-h-r-i-s-t-e-l. Mother and I spell it differently."

On the drive home, he told her he was learning to fly and would have less time, between his school and his planes, to see anyone. Late in the spring he took Crystal to his flying field, showed her his plane and let her watch him take off and return from a short flight.

As he drove her back to the school he said, "We all still hope there won't be another big war, but if there is, I want to be ready to join the Royal Air Force instead of fighting on the ground."

"England will be fighting Germany, won't it?"

"If the war really comes, yes, I suppose it will."

"Then does that mean you will be bombing Berlin?" she asked.

"Not if I can help it, Crystal."

It was the last time she saw him, but she was so busy with studies, dancing classes, swimming lessons and school parties that she hardly realized that the weeks and months were passing.

The day before the school year ended, Miss Clairborne sent for Crystal. "We hope to have you with us again next year, Crystal," she said. "We have arranged with one of the older students to take you as far as Paris tomorrow. She will put you on a train to Berlin and your grandmother will meet you at the other end. And I almost forgot that your uncle, Professor Keith Dunston, has sent you what looks like a five-pound box of candy to make the trip seem faster. The card reads, 'Until next year, dear Crystal.' "

10

Berlin, 1951

Crystal was sitting on a high stool beside a cash register at the check-out counter of the Schultzes' market. It was Saturday morning, weekly marketing day for many Berlin women. Crystal not only knew by heart the price of everything in the store but could call two-thirds of the customers by name. As her fingers nimbly touched the correct figures, she managed to carry on friendly little conversations at the same time.

Now that she had turned nineteen and was taking only a few courses at the university, she spent most of her time at the market, and was virtually managing the operation on the floor. Wearing her hair pulled back into a big, soft snood, she felt every inch a successful businesswoman.

When she started five years ago the market had still been a sad kind of mockery with almost nothing for the women to buy. For the first two years after the war ended, she had still felt half starved and their only luxury had been the American CARE packages that held fluffy white bread, dried milk and delicious bits of chocolate. Recently, though, the food products, both fresh and packaged, had begun to come in. Men were finding work and women were able to buy. Today as she ticked off the figures, exactly six years after the cease-fire, Crystal could feel Germany panting like a racehorse at the starting gate, eager to get into the race again.

Customers called her Fräulein Schultz, and she had slowly grown accustomed to the new name. After the first few weeks of desolation that followed the bombing, when she lost her mother and grandmother, Emma and Hans Schultz had told her that they had grown fond of her and wanted her to stay with them instead of going to a strange foster home. It was Hans Schultz who said that it would be simpler if she used their name, Schultz. It would help with the food rationing. Crystal said yes to everything. She wanted desperately to stay with the Schultzes, since they seemed like a last link with her family.

If Uncle Hans wasn't at the market that day, which Crystal felt would be the biggest since she had been working there, it was because he had already made bigger and better plans. A few years after the war ended he had read that Coca-Cola was going all-out for increased European distribution, and he acted instantly. Two days later, he was on a train to Coca-Cola's German distribution center in Essen, and asked to be a distributor for Berlin.

I'm sure he'll get it, Crystal had thought when she heard the project discussed. Uncle Hans, she felt, had an almost overwhelmingly positive personality which was good for business, and he never backed down on anything he started but drove through all obstacles like a high-powered truck.

She wasn't at all surprised one evening when he announced that a letter had just arrived from Essen, and part of Berlin's consumption of Coca-Cola was in his hands.

The next morning he was out looking for a warehouse. The property next to his market was available. It had an old building on it that he knew he could remodel. He bought it, and the renovation was completed by the time the first Coca-Cola shipments arrived.

"Wait and see—we'll be driving a Mercedes one day," he had announced only last night at dinner.

After the doors of the market had closed and she was locking up, he came in through the back entrance from the warehouse next door.

"Since we're finishing at the same time, I thought we might as well go home together, Chrissy," he said.

"Oh, thank you, Uncle Hans," but she was aware of a slight feeling of uneasiness that she couldn't quite analyze.

On the way home she chattered on about the run on the new detergents that had to be restocked in large quantities as soon as possible.

"You have a real feeling for business, Chrissy," he said. "I've decided to let you in on the buying end of the market. You'll like it, and if you use your head, you'll be in line for general manager soon. Of course, your salary will be increased a little now and more as time goes on."

He's very kind, after all, thought Crystal when she reached her own bedroom that night. She felt ashamed of herself for thinking that Uncle Hans had occasionally seemed to be peering into the neckline of her white shirt with unnecessary interest. She remembered he had made her so self-conscious one time that the next day she had buttoned her shirt up almost to her neck.

I must have imagined it, she thought as she switched on her radio to the American station and turned it on low so that the Schultzes wouldn't be disturbed downstairs. She sat down in a comfortable chair, put her feet up and waited hopefully for some Glenn Miller dance music.

Crystal knew better than to probe into whether she was happy or unhappy. She simply accepted each day as it came along, and she found that she liked work.

After the bombing, the first weeks had been the worst. When she finally returned to school she wore her one and only dress for two weeks. At the end of that time, Aunt Emma had said to her one morning, "I think I must face opening Friedrich's closet. It's almost impossible to buy new clothes now, but we will go to

KDV's tomorrow and see if we can find you a skirt or two."

They went to Friedrich's room and Aunt Emma cried all morning, as she took out his shirts and sweaters and gave them to Crystal.

"They will be too big for you, of course, but the fabrics are good, and you can roll up the sleeves. I will give you a needle and thread and you must alter them yourself if you can. I'm not able to touch them yet."

When Crystal picked up the clothes and carried them to her room, it seemed to her that they still smelled of pine needles.

The whole nightmare had happened on her eleventh birthday.

"We'll have a celebration tonight," her grandmother had said as she wheeled her bicycle out of the cellar and had come running back to kiss her goodbye. "I'm afraid I can't promise a cake but at least there will be eleven candles."

As always, when she started to school, she half turned around and guided her bicycle with one hand and waved to her grandmother, still standing in the doorway.

As they were almost through the pine woods that morning, the sirens started screaming. Friedrich, who, as usual, was pedaling along beside her, said, "Go on ahead, Crystal. I forgot my damn math homework and I'm going back to get it. Tell the teacher I'll be late and if I think there's any danger I'll stay until those cursed Britishers decide to go back home."

When they reached school, the children and their bicycles were all hurried into the basement, along with the teachers. The bombing was louder than it had ever been, so loud that there was no possibility of lessons, or even much talk.

They all sat huddled in little groups. Finally, one bomb exploded with such a crash that the whole room seemed to rock, and Crystal felt a cold shiver run down her back.

"That was a close one," yelled one boy.

After that, the bombs became less deafening but the

noise seemed to go on for hours. Finally there was quiet. The teachers went upstairs but the children were still kept in the bomb shelter.

It must be getting dark, and I ought to be getting home for my birthday party, thought Crystal.

At that moment she heard her name called, along with some two dozen of her schoolmates, and they all went upstairs together.

Miss Rowland, her music teacher, came forward and took Crystal into her office. "Sit down, my dear," she said. "I hardly know how to tell you what I have to tell you."

Crystal simply sat staring at her.

"It's your mother and grandmother," began Miss Rowland.

"You mean they've been hurt?" Crystal cried.

"I'm afraid it's worse than that, dear, you heard the bombing that went on all day."

"No, no, no," cried Crystal. "We are having my birthday candles tonight." She began to feel faint.

Miss Rowland took a bottle of smelling salts from her desk drawer, uncorked it and held it under Crystal's nose.

"Crystal, you must listen to me. We are in the midst of a war and there are at least twenty-five of your friends in this school who are facing the same kind of crisis that you are."

Crystal choked a little from the smelling salts and then took a few deep breaths.

"A whole neighborhood has been wiped out of existence. I think it is only fair, though it's hard for me, to tell you exactly what happened. A bomb hit your home directly and, along with some of the nearby houses, it has burned to the ground."

"But the bomb shelter. It was such a good one."

"When a house collapses, no shelter is good enough," Miss Rowland said. "Your mother and grandmother were killed instantly by a falling beam and, you must realize that, fortunately for them they never knew what was happening. Many others were much less fortunate."

Crystal tried to speak but not a sound came out of her mouth, and when Miss Rowland rose and she tried to stand, she had to hold on to the back of a chair. Miss Rowland took another bottle from her desk, went to the water cooler and handed her a small white pill along with the water.

"Take this, Crystal," she said. "It's a light sedative and it will help you through the next few hours. Herr Schultz, your neighbor, has kindly invited you to stay with them. I will walk back with you to the Schultz home, where you will stay for the next few days at least. Your bicycle will be brought there tomorrow."

It was twilight as they went through the pine forest. Crystal stumbled along but, though her eyes were clouded with tears, she neither spoke nor cried. The street she knew so well had become a shambles. There was a dreadful odor of charred wood and what she realized later was burned flesh, and a few houses were still flaming. The street was so full of fire fighters, ambulances, stretchers and curiosity seekers that it was impossible to get near her home, but she could see that it was nothing but a gaping hole in the ground. Tears began flowing down her face. As they came near the Schultz home, which was miraculously undamaged, she could hear Mrs. Schultz screaming at the top of her voice inside. She was repeating over and over. "Why should it have to be my son?"

Crystal didn't have to be told that Friedrich hadn't been able to make it back to school but had been hit by the same bomb that destroyed her home. The handlebars and one pedal of his bicycle were lying on the front lawn. As they went into the house and she heard Mrs. Schultz screaming louder than the radio, she felt her tears drying on her face.

I must keep my grief to myself as much as I can. It is all mine and no one else really cares, she thought. I must be a true Casalet, as Grandmother said so often.

It was not so easy the next morning. Mrs. Schultz had stopped screaming but the doctor had come and she was lying limply in bed when Crystal was taken in to see her.

"My Friedrich did nothing but talk about you," she said. "He has loved you since he was a little boy, and I'm sure you felt the same way about him."

"Yes," said Crystal in a small voice. Her throat still felt so full that she was unable to speak, and she had to pinch her arms constantly to keep from crying.

Later that day, one of the firemen came to the house. From the top of the stairs, Crystal heard him say, "I brought this for the little girl down the street whose house was hit yesterday. I heard she was staying here."

Crystal ran down the stairs, and Mr. Schultz handed her the metal box that her grandmother always carried with her to the bomb shelter. Crystal took it and, in spite of herself, broke into a terrible flood of tears. She rushed upstairs, closed the door and lay down on the bed with the box in her arms. She cried for hours until she fell asleep. When she came downstairs the next morning Mr. Schultz told her that many more had died the preceding day from injuries. "Separate services for each one would be impossible, so we have decided on a single service, both in the church and at the cemetery." It would take at least two days to make all the necessary arrangements, and he asked her if she had a black dress.

"I have nothing but what I have on, but I'm sure God will understand," Crystal said.

Later that afternoon Miss Rowland came to call on both Mrs. Schultz and Crystal.

"Will I see my mother and my grandmother?" asked Crystal, and her teacher answered, "I think not, Crystal." She accepted the decision without arguing. She felt she would rather think of her mother as she looked on the stage in The Gypsy Princess and her grandmother as she waved goodbye on her birthday.

The services were held at the same church to which Crystal's grandmother had taken her every Sunday to pray for peace. This time, as she kneeled down and buried her face in her hands to try to keep her tears controlled, she found herself suddenly thinking of

Uncle Keith. She prayed that he wasn't the Englishman who had dropped the bomb.

That night Mr. and Mrs. Schultz asked her to call them Aunt Emma and Uncle Hans. As they sat around the table making a pretense of eating dinner, Aunt Emma asked her, "And what was in the metal box that they brought you, dear?"

"I haven't opened it yet," she said. She knew perfectly well that she hadn't opened it because she would break down completely, and she had already started hardening herself for a new and, she was sure, a difficult life.

"It's locked and I don't have a key, but I'm not going to open it for a long time—not until the war is over," she added quickly.

For weeks Crystal clung desperately to her grandmother's metal box. It was the first thing she looked for when she came home at night. She caressed and sometimes kissed it, and every night she put it at the top of her bed beside her pillow. Waking each morning was a nightmare, since for the first few minutes she expected to be in her own little bedroom with the white painted furniture.

Years later when Germany had surrendered and they were finally at peace, she picked up her grandmother's heavy metal box one morning and managed to get it to a locksmith's shop. She waited while he made the key. Late that night, when the rest of the house was asleep, she opened the box. Now she could do it with a lump in her throat but no tears.

The metal container had been ordered by Countess Casalet to protect another, more precious box made of ivory stripes set in rosewood squares. It was the jewel box she had often seen on her grandmother's dressing table. When she raised the lid even the scent of the wood was familiar. The top layer was a series of shallow compartments, each with its own inlaid lid, but most of the compartments were empty. As Crystal remembered, her grandmother had sold almost everything to keep them alive.

Only three of the compartments were still occupied. From one of them she took a gold ring set with a large golden-brown topaz framed in small diamonds. In another compartment was a small amethyst heart on a tiny gold chain. In the third there was a necklace of small, rose cut diamonds that her grandmother had worn as a young girl in Vienna.

Under the compartments was another layer where she found her grandfather's Iron Cross laid on top of all kinds of private papers. Crystal went through them very carefully. A few were personal notes, like the one from Marie Vetsera that had come with the amethyst heart. A faded piece of paper was covered with musical notes and inscribed in one corner: "To Vilia from Franz Lehár." Her grandmother had kept dozens of receipts for the sale of her jewelry along with an estimate for the topaz ring. The little diamond necklace, Crystal realized, must have been the last thing she had wanted to part with.

Underneath everything else were the passports for her grandmother, her mother and herself. The certificates that proved their Aryan ancestry were neatly folded. Crystal looked at hers and saw that Keith Dunston had signed it as her father. She was surprised, but not really shocked. "I had a good-looking father, at least," she said, and went to sleep with the feeling that she had known it all the time.

11

Berlin, 1952

Encouraged by Uncle Hans's hint that she might become the manager of the whole market, Crystal threw herself more eagerly than ever into her work. The next semester she signed for a course in economics and business administration. Though she went out sometimes at night, it was usually in groups. She had no desire to attract the kind of steady date most of her friends had. Word had come back to her through the girls that the boys thought she was good-looking but frigid.

"I must make a secure life for myself because I have no one else who will do it for me," she told herself every morning as she dressed for work. She contributed a part of her salary to the Schultzes for support, but since their food all came at cost price from the market, she was allowed to keep most of it for herself.

Crystal started a bank account, but she felt it was smart, too, to look fresh and attractive at the market every day. The only problem was to have enough time to shop. But by looking at the magazines that were already starting to encourage the Berlin fashion designers to compete with Paris, and by following the store advertisements, she managed to put together what, at the time, seemed quite a fashionable ward-robe.

She decided to stop classes forever at the end of the next term since she felt she was only marking time. Just before the end of the semester, she said to Uncle Hans, "You know, you have that other little building that's between the market and the warehouse. Wouldn't it be a good idea to put in a dozen or so washing machines and dryers? Women could bring along a load of dirty clothes when they come to market. They could put their clothes in the machine and do their shopping, collect the clothes and go home with a whole day's work done."

Uncle Hans looked at her. His eyes narrowed but he said nothing.

"I've been thinking about it for several days," Crystal went on. "Of course, they'd have to wait if they wanted to go and dry them, but you could even put in a Coca-Cola machine to keep the children quiet if they brought them. I think women would love it, part-ly because of the companionship. The things most of them dread isn't housework itself but the fact that they have to do it alone."

"You're so right, Crystal," put in Aunt Emma, who had been nodding to her husband all the time Crystal was talking.

"If you're still in doubt, Uncle Hans, you could have some questionnaires made to pass out at the check-out counter. You could find out what percentage of the customers are interested so you could gauge the num-ber of machines to buy and you could even find out if most of them would prefer to take it home wet or wait for the dryer."

"Crystal, you seem to know a great deal about peo-ple for your age," Uncle Hans said.

The questionnaires were ready early the next week for the cashiers to pass out, and when the first three days' responses were counted, the yeses were so over-whelming that Uncle Hans hurriedly ordered the ma-chines and started repainting the little building inside and out.

It was opened the first of September and on the same day Crystal became general manager of the market.

"You deserve it, Crystal," said Uncle Hans, who added that from now on her salary would be nine hundred marks a month.

Uncle Hans had now become a minor tycoon who involved himself only in the major decisions of a little empire that seemed to be running smoothly of its own volition. Crystal had her own little office with an important-looking desk and two chairs. To celebrate, she bought a couple of inexpensive prints for the walls and a little crystal vase for a single flower from the florist's shop that she passed every day.

The Schultzes not only had a car but Uncle Hans had ordered Aunt Emma to hire a cook. Aunt Emma had fought violently for some time. She came from a long line of dedicated German housekeepers and to ask her to relinquish the broom or the frying pan, or even to watch someone else putting her favorite knife in the wrong drawer, was like robbing her of her importance in life.

Uncle Hans always had his own way. For the first two weeks, Aunt Emma followed the new cook forlornly around the house but the time came when she and Crystal arrived home at the same time.

"This afternoon I went to the American movie *High Noon* that's playing at the Adelphi," Aunt Emma said, and for the first time she seemed happy that dinner had been prepared.

Later that evening, Uncle Hans announced that he wanted to give a small dinner party.

"When I talked to Essen on the telephone today they told me that the nephew of one of the top Coca-Cola executives from America is here. He is a test pilot with the occupational forces that are stationed in Berlin. I don't know his age but I would think he's in his early twenties. He doesn't know anyone in Berlin except his own group and I feel we should entertain him at least once."

Crystal couldn't help remembering some of the language Uncle Hans had used to describe the Americans during the last year of the war, but she also knew that, when it came to business, he could put on blinders instantly.

"We'll do our best, won't we, Aunt Emma?" she said.

Uncle Hans set the date for the following week. He reported that the young man's name was Mathew Lanier, and that he came from Atlanta, Georgia, the headquarters of Coca-Cola. During the next few days he talked so often about Mathew Lanier and underscored the importance of the dinner so heavily that she realized he must have in mind a further rise to power, possibly as one of the executives in Essen.

She took an advance dislike to the American pilot but dutifully helped plan the menu, and shopped with Aunt Emma for attractive dessert plates and small after-dinner coffee cups, which the Schultzes had never needed before. She also rehearsed the cook several times in the routine of serving plates on the left side and taking them off at the right side of each person.

The night of the dinner she came home later than usual after an irritating day of settling an argument on where to place a new product. She decided to wear a new cornflower blue blouse with an almost off-shoulder, gathered neckline, and a wide skirt in the same color. He'll expect me to look like a milk-fed, German peasant girl, so why not please him? she thought. At the last minute she brushed up her hair, coiled it on top and fastened it with two amber-colored pins.

When she came downstairs, Uncle Hans was walking around the dining-room table, on which she had arranged a low white bowl of white flowers and ivy leaves. Two low white china candlesticks that she had found in the department store were ready to light.

"It looks very nice," he said. "And so do you. You're growing into quite a beauty, Chrissy. I realize it especially when I see you in party clothes."

He came around the table to kiss her, and Crystal

let her lips lightly touch his cheek. She felt his arms tighten around her just as the doorbell rang. Aunt Emma scurried out of the kitchen, where she had been lecturing the cook about not cooking the asparagus too long, and the two of them hurried into the living room, where Uncle Hans was greeting Mathew Lanier.

"Captain Lanier, my wife and our adopted daughter, Chrissy," said Uncle Hans with an inclusive wave of his hand.

It would be impossible to dislike Mathew Lanier, Crystal had decided even before they went in to dinner. His eyes were soft and so was his voice, and there were no hard edges to his personality.

He listened to Uncle Hans's monologue on Coca-Cola's success in Europe, delivered in halting English with frequent stops to ask Chrissy for the right word. At the end he smiled and said, "You know, for me the best thing about Coke has just been drinking it, especially the way we do in Atlanta, poured over a big glass of crushed ice." He went on. "My uncle wanted me to come into the business but when I finish this stint I'm enough of a rebel to want to start something on my own."

If I'm ever alone with him I'm going to ask him what he plans to start, thought Crystal. She liked both his independence and the way he spoke, not actually leaving off all the r's, but suggesting them faintly. At the dinner table she spoke to him directly for the first time.

"Is there really a Tara," she asked, "or is it just a place that Miss Mitchell, who wrote it, invented?"

"No, it's really not there, though I often expect to see it when I drive out to Jonesboro, where it was supposed to be located."

"It's a wonderful book. I've read part of it several times. It's not just an American book at all. The deaths, the sufferings and the deprivations touch the people who have lived through a war in any country. Did you know the author?"

"No, but my mother went to school with her at Washington Seminary and called her Peggy. I believe she was a newspaper reporter. She spent three years writing the book, and didn't have the courage to show it to a publisher until nine years later."

"She must have made a fortune," said Uncle Hans.

"I don't think that's what really interested her," Mathew Lanier answered. "It's funny, but I just read a little story in the *Stars and Stripes* this morning that might interest you. Margaret Mitchell's husband died this week, just three years after her fatal accident. He left an annuity to pay for a box in a bank vault that holds the original notes and manuscripts of *Gone With the Wind*, just in case anyone ever tries to contest her authorship. The article said that the box also holds two unpublished manuscripts that no one, except possibly her husband, has ever seen."

"What a gold mine," exclaimed Uncle Hans.

The film version had played in Berlin several years ago and at the time was paying a second visit to a Berlin theater with long queues waiting to get in. Aunt Emma, who now considered herself something of a movie critic, launched into extravagant praise of Clark Gable's performance. When she had finished, Mathew Lanier looked across the table and smiled at Crystal.

"Have you ever seen the movie, Fräulein Schultz?"

"Actually I haven't."

"Then perhaps you would go with me some evening. I'm homesick for the sight of Atlanta, even if it's burning, and I can tell you quite a lot about the South."

"That would be nice. I'd like to," she said.

The cook was serving their after-dinner coffee at the table and, as she turned to leave the room, Crystal said, almost to her own surprise, "Gretel, won't you turn out the chandelier, please?"

As they left the table, Mathew Lanier said to her, "Do you believe in mental telepathy? How else could you know that I always like my coffee by candlelight?"

Crystal thought several times of his nice voice and engaging smile. Only a few days later, when she was making her daily inspection tour of the market, she found him in the home-baking section, studying the labels on the prepared cake and cookie mixes.

"What on earth are you doing here?" she asked.

"I had no idea there were so many things you could make by throwing an egg and a cup of milk into a package of mysterious flour, then end with something as glorious as this," he said, pointing to the color reproduction of a chocolate cake.

"Are you interested in cooking?" she asked.

"Only somebody else's," he answered. "I suppose I could tell you that I came here to do some shopping, but the plain truth is that I came to find Miss Chrissy Schultz. When they told me that she is the general manager, I was a little intimidated. I was undecided whether to slip away quietly or to persevere."

"And which did you decide?"

"To persevere, and to ask her to have dinner with me and, afterwards, take in *Gone With the Wind*. Perhaps through headquarters I can wangle some way to let us in without standing in line."

"Come into my office, and let's talk," she said.

In her office he sat down in a chair in front of her desk.

"I feel a little as if I were being interviewed for a job," he said. "I can see that you're a very successful businesswoman, Chrissy, if I may call you that," he said.

"Of course you may, and what do I call you?"

"Everyone but my mother calls me Mat for Mathew."

"Mathew Lanier is a very nice name."

"I've always rather liked it," he said.

"Well, then, Mat, I'd like to go to the movie with you, but first I have to tell you that Chrissy Schultz is not my real name. My real name is Crystal Casalet."

"It's much prettier, but spell it for me."

"I know you're laughing at me for being so serious," she said after she spelled it out. "Eight years ago both my mother and my grandmother were killed when a bomb destroyed almost our whole neighborhood. I escaped by being at school. Aunt Emma and Uncle Hans had an only son about my age, who was killed by the same bomb. They took me into their home and have been very kind to me. So it has seemed the right thing for me to take their name."

"At home we read about the bombings, but I expect we didn't want to really think about them too much or visualize the horror of them in our minds. I was shocked when I first saw Berlin. Mr. and Mrs. Schultz are good people," he added, "but I could see very plainly that there was no blood relationship between you."

Both Aunt Emma and Uncle Hans seemed delighted that Mathew Lanier had asked Crystal to go to dinner and a movie, but Crystal herself was startled that she had talked about herself so quickly and so frankly to a comparative stranger.

When they came out of the movie they strolled along the avenue looking in the windows and discussing the film.

"Much as I wave the flag for Atlanta, not all my friends are Southerners," Mat said. "My buddy at the air base, Jack Larsen, comes from Minnesota and I often kid him about being a damn Yankee. He and his wife, Laurie, have a little apartment here. I've told them about you and they'd like to meet you. How about a double date with them next Saturday night? The movie will be *Sunset Boulevard* with Gloria Swanson."

"Oh, I'd like to very much."

"Otherwise, I don't plan to share you with my squadron," Mat went on. "The boys are all eager for a girl who can speak English, and you'd soon be so popular that I wouldn't have a chance."

"So it's because I speak English that you're taking me to the movies. Well, if it interests you, I speak French, too."

"I think you have already guessed that I would take you out if you could only say *ja* or *nein*," he said, "but I do wonder where that perfect little English voice of yours came from. My mother would love it. When I was a young kid my mother sent me to a teacher to get rid of my southern drawl but it hasn't helped much.

So far my sister Susan has refused to do anything about hers."

"I spent a year at school in England," Crystal said. "Besides, my father was English and my grandmother, with whom I lived, thought it was important. The three of us often spoke English at home."

"Was your grandmother German?"

"I'm not really German at all," she said. "My grandmother was Viennese, and it just happened that both my mother and I were born in Berlin."

"I can't help wondering why you didn't go back to some safe place in the English countryside and wait out the war," he said.

"No more confessions from me tonight. Now I want to ask you why you don't want to become a big Atlanta banker like your father."

"I suppose because I don't want to lead a banker's indoor, orderly kind of life," he said. "A banker always has to present the image of the man that everybody trusts. He has to be careful of what he wears, does and even thinks. I have in mind something a little more invigorating."

"Like what?"

"Like flying, right now," he said. "I've been flying since I was five years old. There was a bankers' convention in the city where my grandmother lived, so my father took me with him. The planes were smaller and it was more of an adventure in 1934. They let me sit in the seat beside the pilot and I'll never forget the thrill of watching him land the plane. I knew right then that flying was for me."

"But you won't always want to do it, will you, Mat? It's terribly dangerous, isn't it?"

"I like to hear you say that, because you sound as if you care about me. After I get out of the service, I don't plan to fly professionally, but I'd like to have my own private plane that I could fly myself. My father has a beautiful plantation in Thomasville, in southern Georgia, near the Florida border. I don't know what will actually turn up for me to contribute to the world but that's where I'd like to end up. I'll show you some

snapshots of the plantation one of these nights," he
said.

Next weekend she met Jack and Laurie Larsen, both
of whom were in their mid-twenties. The Saturday
nights became a fixed date in her life whether she
spent them alone with Mat or whether the four of them
did something together. In between, she and Mat saw
each other once or twice during the week on some
pretext or other. Once he brought some color snap-
shots of the plantation to the Schultzes' home and
they all looked at the rambling house, the pool, the
stables with the riding ring for training horses, the
greenhouses and the special poultry yards where
the Rock Cornish hens were raised.

The next day Uncle Hans said to her he had already
heard that Mathew Lanier's parents were very
wealthy. "You must watch yourself, Chrissy, and make
sure he intends to marry you before you become any
more intimate," he said.

"We have no intention of becoming any more intimate than we are right now," Crystal replied.

Actually, Crystal sometimes wondered why Mat had
never tried to make love to her more seriously than a
very warm, very affectionate good-night kiss. Since he
obviously found her attractive, she supposed that he
didn't want to become involved.

They had been seeing each other constantly for
several months before he kissed her at all.

"Why didn't you do this before, Mat?" she whispered, clinging to him.

"Sometime I'll tell you, Chrissy, but in the meantime
kiss me again."

"Most boys try to make love on the first or second
date. I suppose it's more or less a gesture to show
their virility but I've never liked it. I'm glad you are
different, Mat. Maybe you belong to a girl in Atlanta?"

He laughed. "I'm glad you seem interested. It makes
me happy. To tell the truth, I did have a girl at home,
someone I grew up with and always thought I would
marry. My mother has sometimes told me that I'm not
aggressive enough with girls and I was too deliberate

for Adele. She has been married for a year now and she's a satisfied young matron with a baby on the way, my family writes. She is not the least bit like you, physically, mentally or emotionally. She's a pretty little brunette who hands out the sweet southern kind of talk that makes you feel you're something special. She is spoiled rotten, and though I'll always be fond of her, I've long since stopped hurting."

"How old are you, Mat?" asked Crystal, trying to hide her relief and happiness.

"I guess I'm about three years older than you are, which makes things about right. I sent a write-in vote for Eisenhower last year. It's the first time I've been eligible to vote. I like politics, and remember a funny mess we got into in Georgia a few years back. They elected a character called Ole Gene Talmadge as governor and he died before he could be sworn in. His son, Herman, claimed the office, because of a huge write-in vote and the lieutenant governor said it was legally his. For a while, every day was moving day at the Governor's Mansion in Ansley Park while the three families tried to move in and out."

Crystal laughed at the story, but she had picked up the words "just about right" that Mat had used when he told her he was three years older than she was. "I hope he means what I think," she said to herself.

When Christmas came she gave him a heavy, hand-knit Bavarian sweater, since he had once told her he liked to ski. He brought her a bottle of Joy perfume and she thought this would be her perfume forever.

She was surprised a few months later when he tossed a package into her lap. "Here's an Easter present from my sister Susan that was tucked into a box I received from home. I can't deny I know what's in the box," he said with a big smile.

It was a half dozen pair of the sheerest nylon stockings, the first she had ever owned.

"Does your family really know about me?" Crystal asked.

"Of course they do. I talk about you all the time when I write home. They know what you look like and what we do. They're begging me to send some snap-shots but I don't have a camera. I'm afraid I'm no good at mechanical gadgets. I started out left-handed. I learned to write with my right hand because my teacher used to hit my knuckles with a ruler when I didn't, but I still throw a ball with my left."

Through the summer they spent Sundays rowing in the Wannsee, feeding animals at the zoo or eating a picnic lunch which she had prepared. The months passed quickly and it was early December when Mat said to her, "Start making plans right now. We're going to spend the whole Christmas holidays in Garmisch. Jack and Laurie are going with us, so your Aunt Emma and Uncle Hans won't object. The snow reports are good, and we'll have a marvelous time."

"I've never learned how to ski," Crystal said.

"Never mind, I'll teach you a little and you'll be an adorable snow bunny. Besides, you'll love the after-ski evenings in front of the roaring open fireplaces."

Uncle Hans, who had grown less and less enthusiastic about Mat as the months passed, took a firm stand against the project, but Crystal was equally determined. Aunt Emma was on her side, and when Crystal promised to work until noon at the market on the day before Christmas, he stopped arguing.

Early that afternoon they flew to Munich, and then took a train to Garmisch, and a few hours later were driving through the village in a sleigh.

"It looks like a stage setting for *Hansel and Gretel*," cried Laurie as she looked at the row of tiny houses with snow up to their front doors and icicles dripping from their peaked roofs. Through the casement windows they could catch glimpses of lighted trees and tables set for supper. Many of the houses had a lighted candle in every window.

"The Germans love all the details of Christmas. They spend weeks planning and baking. I've brought along a box of Aunt Emma's cookies."

Crystal was always pleased to be able to say something kind about Germany since she had to spend so many years hating its wartime world in silence.

They arrived at the inn with sleigh bells jingling. As they started for their rooms, Laurie said, "Let's change fast and have presents in our room. We'll order some wine sent up and at the same time reserve a table so we can eat afterwards."

Mat's gift was another bottle of Joy.

"Because I know you love it," he said, "and this is from my mother."

She opened the box and, as she reached into the folds of tissue paper, Laurie, who was peering over her shoulder, shouted, "It's nylon. I know it's nylon. I'm mad for it and nobody over here can get it."

Crystal pulled out a nightgown, low-necked and sleeveless and outlined in white lace. Something else in the box turned out to be a lace-trimmed jacket to wear over it.

"For breakfast," said Mat as Crystal threw her arms around him.

"I'm giving you kisses for your mother," she said.

They were the most luxurious things she had ever owned.

As they left the room Mat held her back and let the Larsens go on ahead.

"The perfume was just for fun, Chrissy, and because I know you like it. I'll give you my real present later when we come upstairs after supper."

They ordered red wine with their dinner and sat around the fire afterwards with hot toddies. When Mat took Crystal to her room he said, "I'll come in for a few minutes."

As soon as the door closed, he took a small box carefully wrapped in gold paper from his pocket and handed it to her.

"It's past midnight, so merry Christmas, darling, and many more of them—to be spent with me."

She tore off the paper with hands that were trembling. Inside was a small velvet jewel case. She looked up at him for a minute and then opened it. Inside was a wide gold band, and when she picked it up she recognized it as a Victorian wedding ring that had been hammered into three-dimensional flowers and scrolls.

Before she could speak, Mat said, "It's an old one but it looks romantic to me. You'll only wear it for a while, anyway, until I give you the real thing. I guess this is my usual left-handed way of making a point. I want you to marry me. Will you?"

She felt Mat's arms close around her, and she could never remember afterwards whether she had ever said yes.

Mat told her that he was planning to go back to Atlanta the first of May when his duty was up, and that she would go with him. "You'll have plenty of time for Uncle Hans to find a replacement and I have a feeling he'll be relieved to see the last of me. He's been scrutinizing me for a long time to determine whether I was a seducer of lovely young girls."

Mat had planned everything. "Since you have no close family, we'll be married in Atlanta," he said. "My family will like that. I would like to marry you at the Sacred Heart Church, where I was baptized, but I'm sure Mother will prefer Christ the King, where we all go now."

"Will they really like me?" Crystal asked.

"My mother will love you, and so will my sister Sue. Strangely enough, that's the name of a song from a Broadway musical. I really mean it. They'll adore you," he replied. "We're not going to live with anyone else, though. My grandfather was thoughtful enough to leave me quite a chunk when he died. We may have a lean year or so, but I get the first part when I'm twenty-six. I think we'll buy some land somewhere near the Thomasville plantation and then look around to see what kind of business we want to start. If we fail, we can make a fresh start when I'm thirty-six and get the second half of Granddad's estate."

"We won't fail," Crystal said.

The next morning Crystal showed Jack and Laurie her ring. She had already told Mat she never wanted him to replace it.

"Wait and see," he said with a smile.

After breakfast the four of them set forth, each of them, except Crystal, loaded with skis, boots and poles. They boarded the little trolley that crawled laboriously to the top of the mountain. There Crystal watched them take off. She re-entered the trolley with her book and amused herself until they were re-united for luncheon at the little restaurant that was halfway down. After they finished in the afternoon, Mat always gave her a lesson.

"You'll be ready for an easy downhill run when we come back in March," he promised.

On the fourth day, though, Laurie appeared for breakfast in city clothes.

"We're going home," she said. "We've just had a call from Berlin. Jack's parents are there. They came to surprise us."

"It's too bad," Jack interrupted. "But Mom and Dad have been saving up for this trip for a long time. They wanted to see Europe while we are still here. We only have about three months more."

"You're lucky," Mat replied, "but I only have four months to go. Hell, Chrissy and I are going to miss you two."

"Thanks, buddy," Jack said. "But in your state of mind, I don't think that you are going to miss us."

Crystal and Mat met every noon at the midway restaurant, which became more and more social as the New Year's weekend approached. All week Jack and Laurie, who had come to Garmisch several times before, had been introducing her right and left as "our friend Chrissy Schultz," but she noticed that Mat had now amended it to "my fiancée," and when he ran into an Air Force chum at the bar one evening, he said, "This is Chrissy Schultz, who is about to become Mrs. Mathew Lanier."

On New Year's Eve they decided they would dress for dinner, so Crystal put on a new black taffeta dress that the store said had been adapted from a Paris design by Christian Dior. As she looked in the mirror, she thought to herself: Grandmother's little diamond necklace would be so perfect with this. I'm not going to tell him about it but I'll take it with me to Atlanta, of course, and I'll surprise him one night.

They ordered a bottle of champagne, danced and blew whistles with the rest of the crowd when midnight came.

"Darling, I think we have really got it made," Mat said as he kissed Crystal for the first time in 1955.

As they got off the elevator and walked towards her door, she said, "Once you promised to tell me sometime why it took you so long to kiss me for the first time. Why was it?"

"Girls, like elephants, never forget, do they? That factual little mind of yours wants to know all the whys and becauses," he said as they opened the door and went in.

"All right, Chrissy, I'll tell you." He put his arms around her but it was unlike any other time he had touched her. She felt a wild tremor run through her body.

"I knew if I ever really kissed you I'd never be able to stop," said Mat, and even his voice sounded quite different.

"Don't stop, Mat. I don't want you to," she said, pressing even closer to him.

He started kissing her neck and shoulders and then began fumbling with her dress. "Where does the damn thing unfasten, darling?"

"It zips down the back and I can't reach it when you're holding me."

He gave the zipper a tug and the dress slipped down to the floor.

"Good God, you're still fully dressed," he said of the crinoline petticoat that, earlier in the evening, she had thought was so fashionable.

Mat's fingers soon found her breasts, and she tried to unhook the waist cincher.

"Lie down on the bed, Crystal, and let me take off your shoes and stockings. I want to see every inch of you and learn it by heart."

He sat down on the side of the bed, took off his own

shoes and socks and dropped the rest of his clothes on the floor.

"I often thought of this happening and I pictured you just like this. You're lovely, Chris." He bent over her and smoothed back her hair. "You look happy, darling, but your eyes are tightly closed. Are you afraid to look at me?"

She opened her eyes as he lay beside her.

"I'll try not to hurt you, Chrissy, but tell me if I do, and I'll stop."

"Don't stop, don't ever stop, Mat," she said, returning his caresses.

They slept after a while, but when she awoke in the middle of the night and felt the warmth of Mat beside her, she knew that she was happy for the first time in her life.

The next morning she ordered breakfast for two in her bedroom, and Mathew hid in the bathroom while the table was being wheeled in.

"Chrissy, darling, I hope you don't feel sorry that I didn't wait for the ceremony," he said as he returned smelling fresh from a shower and draped in a terry-cloth towel. "After our wedding in Atlanta, we'll be dead tired from the round of parties, but as things are now, we can just go quietly to bed after the reception, like an old married couple."

"I love you, Mat. And I'm completely happy," Crystal said.

As he pushed the breakfast table away and came toward her, Mat said, "You know, Chrissy, I have never gone to bed with a girl before and I know that you were a virgin, too. I'm glad it was that way but from now on we're going to make up for lost time. We're going to sleep together every possible chance we get. I'll keep my clothes in my room but I'm sleeping in here with you."

That night they undressed properly, laughing and talking. Crystal put on the nightgown Mat's mother had sent her, but he said, "Take it off and save it until after we're married."

When Crystal came back from Garmisch even Aunt

Emma noticed how happy she looked. She went around the house bemused, humming a tune. When Aunt Emma asked her what it was, she said, "Just an old Viennese waltz that was written for my grandmother. I haven't thought of it in years."

At the office she had started thinking of trying to find a successor at the market. It would not be easy. She also wondered how she was going to break the news to Aunt Emma and Uncle Hans.

Mat called her excitedly to tell her that Buddy Morton, a friend of his, was vacating his apartment and that he had rented it. "We'll spend our weekends there and have a wonderful time together, and we'll go back to Garmisch in March."

The apartment furniture was meager but it had everything they really needed. Crystal brightened it with fresh flowers and a few pillows from the department store.

"What a relief not to have to eat in a restaurant," said Mat as they checked through the kitchen drawers to see what equipment they needed.

"I don't see how he got on without a tea kettle; an egg beater or a pastry brush," she said.

"Guess he didn't do much cooking," Mat said, "but I'm looking forward to some good southern food. I like to eat."

"I don't know if I can cook southern dishes."

"I've noticed you can do anything you really want to."

Crystal, who had always thought of the market as business, began to study the shelves like a housewife. She found that almost everything in the new after-war world came half prepared and that she could produce in a few minutes the cookies, cakes and biscuits that Aunt Emma still worked over for hours.

Mat taught her to love hamburgers and he liked to cook them himself, while she set the table, watched over the baked potatoes and mixed the green salad. They pampered their kitchen by adding extras like a maple chopping block and bright-colored casseroles.

"We'll take them with us when we leave, to remind

us of this place, though I guess we'll never forget it," Mat said.

One evening he came home with a calendar and they started marking off the days until the first of May.

Moreover, Crystal finally found a replacement who, she thought, understood the nature of the business and could get on well with Uncle Hans.

When she came home that night she told Aunt Emma that she and Mat were going to be married and that they were leaving for his home in Atlanta in about two months. Aunt Emma cried a little and Crystal knew she was thinking of Friedrich. She left it to Aunt Emma to tell Uncle Hans, who greeted the news as a personal disaster to all of them.

"You will be a great loss to him in his business and he realizes it," Aunt Emma reported later, "but he also feels that to move to another country with a man whose family you have never met is wrong for you. You should stay here and marry a substantial Berlin businessman."

Crystal had started shopping cautiously for clothes to wear when she reached Atlanta. She bought a dirndl skirt and a sweater and, as with all her new clothes, had them sent to their apartment.

She had just opened the box and was trying on the skirt when Mat came in.

"Sorry, honey, but no Garmisch this time. A lot of the top brass is flying over from Washington that weekend, so I'll have to put it off until we get rich and can afford to fly over."

"As long as we're together, who cares?" said Crystal.

The flight parade was scheduled for Sunday afternoon. Laurie telephoned on Saturday afternoon and said, "Jack's parents have just come back from a month in Rome and they're dying to see the show.

"We have box seats. Jack and Mat can join us when the parade is over, and we can all go somewhere for dinner."

Sunday was clear and cold. Laurie telephoned early in the morning. "I've already been out and I can tell you you'd better wear the warmest coat you've got, if you don't want to freeze this afternoon."

It was peaceful in the apartment. Mat read the newspaper and, as usual, strewed the sections all over the floor. Crystal ran the dishwasher and made the beds.

They dashed off to church, and as they walked back Mat said, "That's a beautiful coat you're wearing, Chrissy. I hope it's part of your trousseau."

"I wondered when you'd notice. You told me Atlanta can get very cold in the winter. I thought I'd have this ready but I've decided to wear it this afternoon."

The navy blue fitted reefer was the most elegant thing she had ever bought, but she hadn't felt extravagant. I want only the best, she had thought.

They had a leisurely luncheon and then Mat got up to go. As he buttoned his leather jacket, he said, "Honey, I'm going to give you my binoculars so you can watch all the maneuvers." He went to a drawer, took them out and hung them around her neck. He bent down and kissed her and patted her cheek. "See you," he said. "And watch for me. I'll be in 602."

Jack was waiting for him in his car, and Crystal watched Mat as he ran down the walk and got in.

Though the sun was shining, it was cold in the stadium. Crystal felt uncomfortable and wished it was all over.

"I don't understand the maneuvers," she said to Laurie. "Do you?"

"Not really, but I know they're dangerous because so many planes are taking part. Mat didn't discuss them with you because he senses that you're a little nervous about his flying. He told Jack so."

"Aren't you ever nervous, Laurie?"

"Not really, or else I've just got used to it. Jack has been in it longer than Mat, and since he wants to be a professional pilot, I guess I've taught myself to take it in my stride."

When the parade of planes came in sight, Laurie began to share her binoculars with Jack's mother and father. "Jack's plane is 805," she told them, "and Mat's is 602."

Though it was a beautiful sight, Crystal felt herself trembling with both cold and fear. She kept her binoculars trained on Mat's plane. "Oh, Lord, let it be over soon," she kept saying to herself.

After what felt like hours, everything seemed to be going well. Suddenly she heard someone shout, "Look! My God, there's a plane on fire!" She saw Mat's plane seem to halt in mid-air and then a bright spurt of flame shot from it into the clear blue sky. The plane following directly behind tried to change its course but couldn't and there was an instant crash, with both planes bursting into flames.

Crystal would never forget the terrible cries of horror and fright that rose from the stadium as flaming parts of both planes began falling into the field and the stadium.

"Is Jack safe?" cried Jack's mother.

"Yes," said Laurie as she put her arms around Crystal.

Crystal tried to speak but couldn't and then everything went blank. After that she was vaguely aware that someone was picking her up and carrying her. She could hear the screams, the sirens and the noise of the stampeding crowd, and then came total blackout.

12

It was late the next morning when Crystal opened her eyes. She was in a strange bed in a strange room with whitewashed walls. As she moved slightly and tried to lift her head, a white-uniformed nurse got up from a chair by the window and came to the side of the bed.

"I hope you're feeling better this morning, Miss Schultz," she said, picking up Crystal's hand and looking at her watch as she took her pulse.

"I don't know how I feel yet," said Crystal. The whole scene at the stadium flashed before her eyes again. She closed them and turned away.

"A breakfast has been ordered for you, Miss Schultz, and you must make an effort to eat it. You need building up," went on the nurse.

I wish she'd keep still, thought Crystal, who neither answered her nor moved.

The door opened. The orderly who brought in the tray was followed by a doctor.

"We are all deeply sorry for yesterday's tragic happening, and we feel we should keep you here for a few days," said the doctor as he stood by the bed looking down at her.

"I should like to go home as soon as possible," Crystal said.

"When you were brought in here late yesterday afternoon you seemed to be bleeding a little internally," the doctor went on. "When we examined you, we realized, of course, that you are at least two months pregnant and were starting to miscarry. You are still bleeding slightly and we can only wait to see what will happen."

"I want the baby," said Crystal. "I want it more than anything in the world. What can I do to keep it?"

"Just relax and try to rest," said the doctor. "We will give you a mild sedative to help and, for the next twenty-four hours, only liquid food."

The room was half darkened and Crystal lay quietly, feeling that a part of Mat was still with her. Late that afternoon she was aware that Laurie was standing beside her.

"What can I say, Chrissy?" said Laurie. "We all loved him, you know," she said.

"Don't say anything now. Just tell Aunt Emma and Uncle Hans that I'm all right and am staying here for a few days."

"I've already done that."

"I had missed one period," Crystal went on, "and if I missed this one, I was planning to go to a doctor, but I hadn't had any of those symptoms women are supposed to have. Because of yesterday, they're afraid I'll have a miscarriage, but I want so much to keep the baby. Oh, Laurie, I want Mat's baby."

"Isn't that a little foolish, Chrissy?" Laurie asked. "I know how you feel now, but how can you raise a child without a father? Is it fair to the child?"

"I can do it and I will," Crystal said. My mother brought me up without a father, she thought to herself, and I'm better equipped as a businesswoman to carry it off.

"Then I hope you keep the baby, Chrissy."

"One thing you can do for me, Laurie," Crystal said. "Please go to the apartment and take all my clothes back to Aunt Emma's. Leave the little things we bought or take them if you want. I will never go there again."

"I'll do that this very minute," Laurie said, "and I'll be back tomorrow at the same time."

The next afternoon Crystal was lying in almost the same position in which she had left her the day before, and Laurie could tell that by sheer force of will she was trying to stop the miscarriage. She kissed Crystal and left.

Crystal had another sedative but sometime in the middle of the night she woke. She felt the bleeding had increased, and she began feeling pains at regular intervals. Through the night Crystal dragged herself back and forth between her bed and bathroom. She saw the first ray of morning light through her window and heard the early milk trucks rattling down the street. She didn't need the doctor to tell her that she had lost her and Mat's baby.

Three days later, when she was discharged from the hospital, the doctor said, "You're a strong, healthy girl, Miss Schultz, and you have no real injury. You will be able to bear as many children as you like."

"Thank you very much," said Crystal.

When she reached her room at Aunt Emma's and looked into her dressing-table mirror, she hardly recognized herself.

I mustn't die of this. I want to live, she thought.

Aunt Emma kept Uncle Hans away from her, and for a few days Crystal stayed in her room trying to eat everything that was brought to her and resting as much as she could. She picked up the European editions of *Time* and *Newsweek* that Mat had brought into her life but put them down almost as quickly. Each day when Laurie came to see her she told her how much better she looked. The Larsens were due to return to Minnesota and when, at the end of the week, she came to say goodbye, she was able to say truthfully, "Chrissy, you look like your old self again." Jack had wanted to come with her but Laurie thought better not.

"We do hope we will see each other again, Chrissy. You know we both love you," Laurie went on.

"It would be nice and I hope so, too, but I have no idea where I'll be. I've been thinking things out this week and I see very clearly that I have to get out of here. I want to start a completely new life somewhere. I don't know quite where. I'm never going back to the market. I still have a little money left in my bank account. I plan to leave this house next week, though I haven't told Aunt Emma yet. I'm sure I can find some interesting work. I know that I must be on my own."

Early the next week, Crystal told Aunt Emma what she had decided. Aunt Emma cried and Uncle Hans offered her more money to remain as manager of the market, but Crystal was adamant. The one burning wish that kept her going was to get out of Germany and to the United States. At one point she even thought of asking Mat's mother's help, but in the sad little note she finally sent to Mrs. Lanier she didn't mention that she intended leaving Berlin, but simply said how much she had cared for Mat.

Crystal started packing. She had bought quite a few clothes for Atlanta, so she went out and bought a second suitcase. In a few days, almost everything was ready except for her grandmother's box. She picked it up and carried it to Aunt Emma's room.

"Aunt Emma, I'm sure you remember this box and the things that were in it," she said to Mrs. Schultz, who was making a needlepoint chair seat.

"Of course, dear."

Crystal laid it on Aunt Emma's needlepoint and opened the lid. "I want you to have one of the three pieces of jewelry, whichever you like, so that you'll often think of me."

"Oh, no, dear, I couldn't think of it," began Aunt Emma, but Crystal could see that her eyes were riveted on the topaz ring.

"I think the diamond necklace is too small for you and so is the little heart. It must be this."

She took out the ring and put it on Aunt Emma's finger.

"It looks wonderful on your hand and you must wear it often."

"But, Crystal, it's so beautiful. You really shouldn't."

"I want to," said Crystal.

She went to her room and packed the ivory-and-rosewood box in the middle of her soft woolen clothes so that it wouldn't be damaged. She carefully put on a pair of the Atlanta nylons she had been hoarding, laid out her coat to carry over her arm and ran downstairs to call a radio cab.

When it pulled up in front of the house she called to the driver to come in and pick up her two suitcases.

"But where are you going, Chrissy, and when will we see you again?" Aunt Emma called from her open doorway. "You will come to see us soon, won't you?"

"I don't know where I'm going, Aunt Emma, and I haven't any idea what I'm going to do," Crystal said. "I'd like to go to the United States, but I promise you that as soon as I'm settled, you and Uncle Hans will hear from me." She ran upstairs again, kissed and hugged Aunt Emma. As she went out the door, she was happy that Aunt Emma was still wearing the ring.

Actually, Crystal knew exactly where she was going. When she got into the cab, she said, "Take me to the Kempinski, please." She had read about the old hotel being completely remodeled and refurbished and that it was going to cater to Americans. Later, it might even lead to getting out of Berlin.

She went to the reservations desk and asked for a room and bath. "Something very light and cheerful," she said.

"And how long do you expect to be with us?" the clerk asked.

"I don't know. I'm more or less in transit, but I'm sure it will be a week or longer," using her most British voice and manner.

"And the name, please." The clerk pushed the register towards her.

"Crystal Schultz," she said. She picked up the pen and wrote it, and opened her handbag and gave her identity paper to the clerk.

13

En route to New York
August, 1955

Crystal was early for the plane that would at long last get her out of Berlin and take her to New York. In the waiting area she found herself unable to sit quietly. She paced around the enclosure, changed her seat several times and, with all her strength, willed the plane not to be late taking off. When it was finally announced, she was one of the first to board and she sank into her seat with a sigh of relief. Though she knew it was ridiculous, for the past few days she had been haunted by the fear that something or somebody would stop her from leaving Berlin.

She sat quietly at her window seat and closed her eyes while the plane filled. She opened them only when it started to move towards the runway for its takeoff. She felt it going faster, gathering power. As it left the ground, she looked out the window and wanted to shout, "Goodbye! Goodbye forever, Chrissy Schultz! I never want to hear your name again. I'm Crystal Casalet. I'm my own self again."

Being up so high above everything seems to make everything much clearer—I like flying, she thought, and now she could think of Mat tenderly, and without the terrific pain.

She closed her eyes and thought of the last six

months at the Kempinski Hotel. It had been a valuable experience, and the key to her escape.

The first day at the hotel she had gone to the passport office. She took all her documents with her—the passport that had been issued when she went to school in England as well as the certificates that the wartime government had demanded.

"You must have yourself photographed. There is a machine you can use downstairs."

The machine provided four photographs for the same price. She had been told she must look straight ahead, but she tried both smiling and looking serious as she pulled down the handle.

The woman at the passport counter chose one of the serious photographs and clipped it to the application forms. "In two or three weeks, Fräulein, your passport will be mailed to the hotel."

Her next stop had been to the American Embassy, where she applied for a visa, and signed the necessary papers, but was given little hope.

Back in her room she placed her documents in the rosewood-and-ivory box. Her mother's passport was there on top and she picked it up to look at it.

I do look like her. I never paid any attention when people said so but now I see it's true, she thought. She looked back and forth from her mother's to her own passport picture. Her mother, she felt, must have been about twenty-three when her passport was issued, probably to go somewhere with a theatrical company, Crystal guessed.

She looks softer and sweeter than I do, but it's as if someone had painted the same picture twice but used a stiff brush with a finer point for me, Crystal thought.

As she brushed her hair before going to bed that night, she thought again of her mother's face, framed in bangs and the long bob that young women wore in the early thirties. Someday I must try that look, she thought.

As always, she had her radio turned to American

music. As she came out of the bathroom that evening, she heard the announcer saying something about an Ethel Merman festival of songs. A man's voice said, "Here she is in *Annie Get Your Gun*." Later, he announced songs from another Merman hit, *Panama Hattie*. A voice began singing, "My mother would love you, and so would my sister Sue. My dozens of cousins . . ." but by that time she had reached the radio and turned it off. She was shaking, and the tears she hadn't shed when Mat died now flowed freely. She lost complete control and cried herself to sleep.

The next day she had put on her navy blue coat, her American nylons and her high-heeled pumps. She had already noticed that the manager looked young and aggressive, so she went directly to his office and asked for a job.

She remembered describing what she wanted as a kind of hostess job. "Whenever I go through the lobby, I always hear people asking where to go for luncheon or dinner, or what's playing at the theaters. I've lived in Berlin all my life. I speak English fluently and French quite well."

Mario Buschel, the manager, studied her for a minute, adding up the blond hair, the Viennese skin, the expensive looking clothes. "Class," he thought. Aloud he said, "I find this interesting but let me think it over. I will call you tomorrow morning."

At ten o'clock the next morning she was called to his office. "I've decided to give it a try, Miss Schultz. I've discussed it with my colleagues and they are in agreement. We are a new management team and trying to attract new guests, you know. This may be a great help."

She settled for a room in the hotel and a small salary that was increased when she suggested getting out a weekly mimeographed bulletin about what to do and where for circulation in all the rooms.

Her job was never dull. She arrived at her desk every morning at ten and stayed until one. Her afternoon hours were from half past three to seven-thirty.

Each day was a panorama of personalities. Many of them were men who invited her to share with them the entertainment she suggested, but she accepted only one luncheon with an American businessman, who offered no solution to the quick trip to the United States that she wanted so much.

One morning just before luncheon break she looked up to see what she considered a fabulous-looking woman coming across the foyer toward her. She was tall and broad-shouldered and she was wearing an open white jacket, a white shirt unbuttoned halfway down her chest and immaculate white pants. Her dark hair was carelessly curled and flowing over her shoulders, but Crystal realized instantly that such effective tumbling could have come only from Berlin's most expensive salon. As she came closer leading a snow-white poodle by a gold leather strap, Crystal could hear the jangling of gold bangle bracelets. It came to her in a flash that the woman must be Olga Zarov, the movie star she had worshipped ever since her very first movie.

"I hear you understand Russian, my dear, and I do hope so because I don't seem to be making myself clear to the man at the desk," said the husky voice that had sent thrills and chills up and down Crystal's spine when she first heard it at the age of six.

"No, I don't speak Russian, Fräulein Zarov, but I'll be glad to help you, especially since I'm a great admirer of yours."

"Oh, then you know me," said Olga, leaning on the desk and giving Crystal one of her famous glamour movie smiles. "The situation is this, Liebchen. I have my jewels with me since I am here to make a personal appearance with my new film. I want to place them in a vault or a safe-deposit box but I cannot make that foolish man at the desk understand."

"That will be very simple, Fräulein Zarov. The hotel is very proud of having the very last word in a vault for the storage of jewelry or important papers. If you have your precious things in your handbag now, we can go together and I can show you how to reach the vault. They will be listed. You will have a duplicate of the list and be able to take out what you like whenever needed."

"Not all my things are in my handbag but I'd like to get those that are to a safe place, if you would be kind enough to help me."

Crystal signaled to her replacement to take over, and they started for the elevator.

"How wonderful to be both businesslike and beautiful," said Olga Zarov as they walked down the long basement corridor to the vault. "I have always enjoyed the creative part of my work but I have made an abominable mess of managing my life."

"Have you really?"

"Perhaps I will tell you all about it some night at dinner, or are you a married woman?"

"No, I'm not, Fräulein Zarov."

They deposited the jewels, Olga Zarov put the receipt in her handbag. As they walked back along the corridor, she slipped her arm through Crystal's.

"I am here only for a few days, but as I look at you, I can see that great things are in store for you. If you are free, let us dine together and I will tell you all about my world."

"That will be lovely. I'd like to very much."

She showed Olga Zarov an outside door to the street and watched her until she reached it, with the poodle paddling along behind her. When she went upstairs to her room, the elevator was still fragrant with the film star's perfume.

When Crystal came on duty later, her assistant said, "That movie star you took down to the vault was one of Hitler's girl friends, you know."

"I remember but it may just have been gossip," Crystal said.

The next morning, two dozen half-opened, long-stemmed pink roses were delivered to her room with a note thanking Crystal for her kindness and ending with a postscript: "Tonight at 8:30 in my suite."

As she filled two green glass vases with the flowers, Crystal thought: The Russians must be very effusive people.

Zarov had rented the hotel's penthouse, and when Crystal arrived the dinner table was already set on the terrace and she could see a silver cooler with the neck of a champagne bottle sticking out of the ice.

Zarov's arrival was preceded by a whiff of her perfume. She came in wearing a white Moroccan robe that clung to her like wet tissue paper. There was nothing underneath and her feet were bare. She cried, "Good God, how beautiful you are," as she saw Crystal. "You should become a movie star. You would go straight to the top. Your face is far more moving than that Grace Kelly's whom everybody is raving about."

"It's so nice of you to say . . ." Crystal was beginning when Zarov interrupted her.

"But why do you come here tonight in that prim little black dress? There is a full moon that will light our dinner table. We will drink champagne and talk about life together but you must look like the beautiful, seductive creature you are instead of like a schoolteacher."

She took Crystal's hand and led her to her dressing room. "We'll see what we can do for you," she said, opening the louvered closet.

Though Olga Zarov was in Berlin for only three days, she had brought more clothes than Crystal had ever seen in one place before.

"Try these," went on the movie star. She handed Crystal a pair of sky-blue satin breeches that fastened just below the knees and a sleeveless, lace-edged organdy vest with tiny crystal buttons. "All my clothes come from Molyneux in Paris. People say he's conservative. I often take the rejects that the fuddy-duddy ladies pass up, but often I buy the same things. I just wear nothing underneath and it makes all the difference."

Olga Zarov's fingers lingered lovingly on Crystal as she buttoned the little vest for her.

"Now you are perfect for the evening," she cried.

"Especially with your pageboy hairdo, you look like a wonderful, unawakened little boy in a Mozart opera."

They went to the living room and Zarov ordered the waiter to uncork the champagne.

"Dom Pérignon is the only kind," she told Crystal. "I started drinking it when I was making silent movies with Emil Jannings. In those days it was Garbo in Hollywood and Zarov in Germany."

"You were wonderful," Crystal said.

"Hollywood wanted me but I preferred to stay in Germany," Zarov went on. "Then the war came. I was a friend of the Führer's but never his girl friend as they say. Gossip, gossip, gossip. Some women make their whole lives out of what happens to other people."

They moved to the dinner table and she went on with her story.

"Of course, I'm half Russian, but when the Russians occupied Berlin they were beastly to me because of my connection with Hitler. After the war, Hollywood wouldn't touch me for the same reason. I've been living quietly, but now I'm back again with my first film in seventeen years and ready for another chance."

"Tell me about your new movie," Crystal asked.

"Oh, my dear, it's the story of a silent-movie star living in retirement. Something like Gloria Swanson in *Sunset Boulevard* except in this one I don't kill my young lover."

They went back to the penthouse living room for the coffee and sat on the sofa.

"I sincerely want to help you, Chrissy," she said. "Of course, you must take a more romantic name, but I honestly believe you could be a star."

"I've never even tried acting in school plays," said Crystal, who was beginning to feel slightly uneasy.

"It's the face and the voice that count," Zarov said. "You must come to visit me in my country house. We will see what we can do about your career. You won't find it boring. Two women can have a very good time together, you know." Her arm slid down and her fingers brushed lightly across Crystal's breast.

Crystal found the dark Gypsy face with the big

mouth attractive and she found herself not even dis-
liking the touch of her hand.

"I must go," she said, standing up. "It has all been
like seeing a film with you starring in it. I will send
the little suit back tomorrow."

"No, *Liebchen*," said Zarov. She rang a bell and
asked the maid to bring Crystal's black dress. "Keep
the suit and wear it to a masquerade some night." She
kissed her goodbye.

The next day there was a note for Crystal telling her
exactly how to reach Zarov by letter or telephone. A
ticket to her opening that night of her new film was also
enclosed. Crystal went to the opening and stopped for
coffee and pastry afterwards. She was relieved that
Zarov had already left for the airport by the time she
returned to the hotel.

The next day, Mario, the manager, came to Crystal's
desk and said, "You did a very nice job with our famous star and I want to thank you, Miss Schultz." He
smiled, "I must say you have quite a way with the
guests. They all sing your praises."

After that she noticed him frequently in the lobby,
either standing at the newspaper counter, leaning
against the reception desk or even sitting briefly in one
of the easy chairs. She felt he was watching her co-
vertly and longing to be close enough to hear what she
and the guests were talking about.

Finally Mario Buschel invited her to luncheon in the
Bavarian Room, but they talked strictly business most
of the time. Over coffee he told her a little about himself. His German father had married an Italian girl
from Genoa and they had settled in California after the
First World War. He had been brought up speaking
German, Italian and naturally English. He had attended
Cornell University, majoring in hotel management, and
this was his first important assignment. He was married
with two children but had left his family behind in
California until he was certain that he was a permanent
fixture in Berlin and not subject to transfer to another hotel. Crystal already knew about "the wife and
children," often followed by "It's a lonely life for me

here," and an invitation for her company in bed, but Mario Buschel seemed genuinely to enjoy her company and, after the first luncheon, they met several times.

By mid-July they had reached a Mario and Chrissy relationship. She wasn't surprised when he stopped at her desk one morning and said, "Chrissy, I don't usually ask personal favors of you like this because I figure you should do what you like about your free time. But an old friend of mine arrived this morning, and I wish you would have dinner with him. He's a retired congressman, pushing seventy, I guess, but he has had a fascinating life and is here on a special ambassadorial mission, straight from the White House."

I feel totally overdressed, thought Crystal as she looked at her bare neck and arms in the mirror, but if he asks me where I want to go for dinner it's going to be the most expensive nightclub in Berlin.

The minute she entered Mario Buschel's living room she knew Zarov had been right.

"Well, Chrissy, I had no idea you could turn into such an exotic butterfly at night or I would have asked you to go out dancing myself," he said, rising. As he introduced her, he slurred over the names of the Japanese diplomats, so she knew he wasn't quite sure of them. Then, "Chrissy, this is an old friend of mine, the Honorable Alban W. Breck from California."

"I'm Alban Breck," said the man, who had been patiently waiting his turn to be introduced. He was almost half a head shorter than she was and he had the small, bright eyes of a little animal sunk in a deeply lined and suntanned face.

He turned to her as they sat down. "I had no idea that I was going to have the pleasure of escorting a Berlin beauty, and I'd like to know two things before we start out on our date. Do you like to dance, and do you like Cuban cigars?"

"I adore dancing and I like cigars when someone else is smoking them," she said with a smile. She was already suffocating from the smoke of the cigar he had laid down when he got up to meet her.

She was pleased when they got into a taxi to hear him give the address of the most fashionable spot in Berlin to dine and dance.

"Good evening, Mr. Breck," said the maître d' as they came into the room. They were shown to what she knew was the best table, and it was ready for them with champagne in a silver bucket.

"I collect maître d's, among other things," Mr. Breck said as they sat down. "I never forget a good one. The maître d' here is an old friend of mine. The last place I ran into him was a very dull nightclub in London. I'm sure he likes it much better here."

When the glasses were filled he lifted his and said, "To you, Chrissy. Nothing as young and lovely as you has come into my life for many a year."

"Thank you, Alban."

"Al is easier."

"Then where do you live, Al?"

"California is the state that sent me to Congress for many years. My home base is a wild and wonderful ranch in the northern part of the state. I'm the lord of some eight thousand nine hundred and ninety-nine acres adjacent to the very best California wine country."

"And where did you spend your holidays when Congress wasn't in session?"

"In my spare time I've always been something of an adventurer and explorer," he said. "I don't just visit, I like to probe into all kinds of situations, and the result is a number of unusual friends, many of them unknown but very powerful. I often know where the bodies are buried, and that's why I'm here on this special mission for President Eisenhower though I'm no longer a member of Congress. Shall we dance now? This is one of my favorite Cole Porter tunes."

He was a good dancer but Crystal would have enjoyed it more if she hadn't felt herself towering above him.

When they returned to the table the Scotch salmon had already been served. "I didn't ask for the menu. Roger, the headwaiter, understands my likes and dislikes. You'll see, after this he will bring us a lightly poached chicken, surrounded by fresh, boiled vegetables, a green salad and, finally, a very delicate pomegranate sherbet with our coffee."

A few minutes later he put his hand over Crystal's. It was the size of a small boy's and just as eager.

"You know, my dear," he said, "you remind me of my first wife."

"It's a great compliment, I'm sure."

"She was born in Sweden," he went on. "She won all the beauty contests and finally became Miss Universe. I met her soon after that and we were married within a month. She was much taller than you, almost six feet, and she had beautiful skin. Hers was snow white and yours, I would guess, has some warm, Viennese blood flowing underneath."

"How could you possibly guess?" cried Crystal. "I'm half Viennese and half English."

"Experience, my dear," he answered. "My granddaughter Kitty is actually more like you and is about the same age, I should think."

"If I could only get to the United States, I'd love to meet her," said Crystal.

He paid no attention and went on with his story.

"My wife was born with a faulty heart valve. The birth of our son was hard on her and she was a partial invalid for a while. I had made arrangements for a boat trip up the Amazon and she wanted so much to come along that I foolishly gave in. When we were at the farthest possible point from civilization she had a heart attack and died in my arms."

He signaled to a waiter. "Bring us liqueurs with our coffee, please. Brandy for me and Grand Marnier for the young lady." He turned to Crystal and went on. "It was impossible to bury her in the jungle and it would have taken too long to bring the body back. We had to cremate her on the spot."

"Oh, no," cried Crystal as a horrifying picture of the scene flashed before her eyes. She gulped down the Grand Marnier so fast that she choked.

After he finished his Cuban cigar, Alban Breck called for the check. All the way to the hotel, he was telling her about his second wife, a Texas oil heiress, who had died just recently and left him her fortune. Crystal kept wondering how she could get him to listen to her. She felt sure that perhaps he could at least hasten her visa to the United States.

At the hotel, he said, "It has been such a beautiful evening for me. I wonder if we couldn't continue it for just a little while. I have a little bar in my room and I should like to smoke a goodnight cigar."

It's my last chance, Crystal thought desperately, so she smiled and answered, "Of course."

They went to his suite and when he brought her the drink she saw that his hand was shaking. She put down the glass and said, "I don't really want a drink. I've had enough and I think you have, too. Let's just sit and talk a moment."

"If I were a young man, Chrissy, I would ask you to jump in bed with me but I'm afraid I'm a little over the hill. All evening I have been admiring your body. I wonder if you will be kind to a lecherous old man? Will you take off your clothes and let me look for a few minutes at your beautiful young body?"

She went to the window, looked out for a moment. It was still twilight, although close to midnight, but summers in Berlin were like that. She turned and then walked back toward him. She started taking off her dress very slowly. Then she crossed to the sofa as she unfastened her bra and took off her pumps, nylons and panties. She could see that his bright little eyes were watching her avidly and she thought: Who'd ever think I'd be doing a strip-tease act? He came and stood over her, caressing her chin and throat and then moving his hand down between her breasts, but when he tried to go further she winced and turned away from him.

"There is only one tragedy in the world—old age. Time cures everything else," he said as he went to the bedroom. He came back with a light blanket that he threw over her. Then he pulled over a chair and sat down beside her. "I told you I was collector of maître d's," he said. "But I'm a collector of many other things, like emeralds." He took a brown envelope, opened it and shook a few green stones into the palm of his hand as casually as if they were pills.

"The clear ones that are neither too dark nor too light are the most valuable. I started investigating emeralds on the same trip I told you about earlier this evening. For some reason their color gives me a great sensuous pleasure. In a bank vault in Washington, I have thirty-three of the most perfect emeralds in the world that I am willing to Kitty and to my grandson Bob, who is only nineteen now. These are less valuable but you have made me feel so young and happy tonight that I want to give you one."

"Oh, no, Al," said Crystal, sitting up but keeping the blanket around her. "It's been a pleasant evening but you must give them all to your grandchildren."

"I see that you're not a gold digger. I've noticed all evening that your eyes never lighted up, as many women's do, when I mentioned my material possessions. What, dear, can I give you as a remembrance then?"

"I'd like to meet Kitty," she said. "I lost all my family when Berlin was bombed during the war. I want desperately to get away from Germany, even for a little while. I would love to see the United States."

"And you can't get a visa, I suppose?"

"Not for two years at least," she answered with tears welling into her eyes.

"Put on your clothes and go home to bed like a good little girl," he said. "I will arrange everything. Bring the papers to me by nine o'clock tomorrow morning. I am quite sure that the necessary permit will be sent to you within a short time. And my gift to you, Chrissy, will be a round-trip ticket to San Francisco. I'm on my way to Russia for six weeks or more and won't be in California when you arrive, but I will write Kitty and you will enjoy each other. She lives in San Mateo. She is married with an eighteen-month-old baby."

It was four o'clock when Crystal finally reached her room and her one thought was: Will he remember all this tomorrow?

She set her alarm and was at the door of his suite five minutes before nine.

To her surprise, Alban was bright-eyed and in a brisk, businesslike mood. His official portfolio was already under his arm.

As she handed him the duplicate form which she had filed at the American Embassy along with her passport, she said, "My real name is Crystal Casalet. Schultz is the name of my foster parents."

"What's in a name?" he said, opening the portfolio and putting in the papers and returning the passport to her.

The next morning a long envelope was delivered to Crystal at her hostess's desk. It held a note and a travel agency folder with a ticket inside. She opened the note first. "Enjoy yourself and try to think kindly of a blundering old man." The ticket was a forty-five-day excursion trip to San Francisco and back to Berlin. I can't believe he really did it, she thought.

Five days later a messenger arrived from the American Embassy with an official-looking envelope that he asked her to sign for.

When she reached her room she tore open the envelope. The visa was there along with other documents. She picked up the visa and kissed it, and as she put it down, she noticed that it was stamped Top Priority. Al must be as important as he kept intimating he was, she thought.

The stewardess tapped her on the shoulder and Crystal opened her eyes with a start.

"We'll soon be stopping in Paris," she said. "If you are one of the passengers going on to New York, you'll change to one of our Boeing Stratocruisers there, but don't worry—your baggage will be transferred for you. The other plane will be waiting and all you have to do is follow the In Transit signs."

It was a clear day and the plane began its descent to Orly Air Field. Crystal could see the Seine winding its way along under many bridges, and got a glimpse of the Eiffel Tower. She even enjoyed the walk through the In Transit part of the airport, stopping for a moment to send a postcard to Aunt Emma.

As she climbed the steps to the Stratocruiser she thought: Sometime I'll be back and really see Paris. When she found her new seat she felt a sudden wave of confidence and for a moment she could clearly see a new life for herself.

When the passengers from Paris got on the plane Crystal acquired a seatmate. She was about her own age, Crystal decided, and when she spoke to the stewardess, she knew that she must be American. Her dark hair was completely hidden by a black silk babushka printed in an occasional pale lavender-violet and tied at the nape of her neck, a technique that Crystal instantly planned to duplicate. Her features were nice but unremarkable. So her eyes passed on to the blouse and skirt made of the same silk print as the babushka. The skirt was much shorter than Crystal's and showed the most extraordinary legs she had ever seen. They seemed to start right under the belt, which even at a distance she could spot as genuine leather, and they ended in long, narrow feet.

She decided that when the stewardess brought her ginger ale, she would ask her seatmate a simple question like "Do you live in New York?" But it happened the other way around. When the girl beside her realized that passengers just a few rows in front of them were being served, she let down the tray that was attached to the seat in front of her and Crystal quickly followed suit.

The stewardess set down a plastic glass of ginger ale in front of each of them, and the girl smiled at Crystal and said, "I see you're on a diet, too."

"Oh, yes," said Crystal, who would have agreed to anything to keep the conversation going. After a few sips of her drink, she ventured, "Do you live in New York?"

"Where else? It's the only place for a girl who really wants to make her own way. Every other place in the country is a small town, and I got out of my town early."

She reached down into the leather bag, pulled out a red pencil, outlined her lips with it and filled in with pale pink lipstick. Crystal's eyes avidly followed every move.

"You're English, aren't you?" said the girl as she put away her tools.

"My father was English but I grew up in Germany. However, I went to an English school for a while."

"Well, you've got a beautiful voice. I love a British accent."

Crystal began to feel that she was genuinely friendly.

"Look here," said the girl, "we might as well get acquainted. My name is Lynda Lancaster. I'm a fashion model. If the name sounds phony, it really isn't. My family just happened to like the alliteration of the two L's as much as the model agencies do. The only change I made was to spell the Linda with a y, because there are so damn many Lindas around New York these days."

Lynda had gone to Paris a couple of weeks ago to model for Christian Dior. "It was terribly exciting," she told Crystal. "I've got a pal there who designs the windows. His name is Yves Saint Laurent. He and Dior are like that, if you know what I mean," she said, holding up two fingers close together.

Crystal wasn't at all sure what she meant but she nodded.

"My pal Yves will get there someday, so remember his name," went on Lynda. "Doing fashion shows in Paris doesn't pay much but it gives the model great prestige."

"Do you suppose I could possibly become a model?" Crystal asked.

"I've been sizing you up. You've got a great face with wonderful skin and hair, but you seem about an inch and a half too short for a runway model. On the other hand, I'm no good for anything but a movement shot in photography. My features don't come through definite enough in a close-up and yours might. Actually, you never know what the camera will do to you until you try."

"How would I go about trying?"

"I can send you any number of places, like the Ford Agency that has always handled me. The only thing I don't know is how you're fixed financially. Most of the best agencies want you to spend four or five hundred dollars having test shots made by a good photographer before they take you on."

Crystal had been soaring high, picturing herself as a much-in-demand model, but the financial sum plunged her into darkness again. She remembered that all she had in her purse was a round-trip ticket and $900. She nodded gamely, though. "Maybe I could manage it," she said, thinking to herself: It's more than half of everything I have.

"A successful model can make quite a lot of money," Lynda went on. "Last year I cleared fifty thousand dollars. I try to save some of it because a model's career doesn't last forever and I've developed some pretty luxurious tastes by now."

By this time Crystal felt there was nothing she wanted so much as to become an American fashion model, and she could hardly believe her good fortune at having met Lynda Lancaster, who seemed friendly and willing to help.

"My name is Crystal Casalet," Crystal said. She almost said Chrissy Schultz but stopped herself just in time. "I'm on my way to San Francisco but I intend to spend a few days in New York."

"By the way," said Lynda. "Don't let anyone talk you into ever becoming a showroom model on Seventh Avenue where all the top designers work. Lots of them would snap you up in a minute, but it doesn't pay. It's not only that the salaries are less but it's a blind alley as far as men are concerned. You're young and you don't look to me as if you're headed for any convent.

"Believe me, Crystal," Lynda went on, "there are only two choices in the fashion industry as far as men are concerned. Most of the designers are homosexuals or iffy in-betweens, and anything that goes on with them always blows up in the end. The other group is the rich manufacturers, who are older and always out for fun and games. They are sweet and generous but locked into wives, children and country clubs in the suburbs. Hell will freeze over before they get a divorce."

When their dinner arrived Crystal ate every bite of hers but Lynda toyed with her plate. "I suppose I should ask for a doggie bag, but I don't think even my dog would like it. You must be hungry," she said.

"I was," Crystal replied. She closed her eyes and when she opened them again they were landing in Greenland. She and Lynda got out just to stretch their legs and went into the airport, where Lynda bought two postcards and gave her one. "Just to remember the place by," she said.

After they had returned to the plane and strapped themselves into their seats, Lynda said, "I guess I should have told you, Crystal, why I blew my top about the men in the fashion industry. I'm in the same position as some of my friends I told you about, waiting for a man to get a divorce. He's a builder and I met him at the advertising agency. We've been together two years. His wife has been in a mental institution for five and a half years and next winter he can get an annulment without any fuss. Then we can be married and live happily forever."

"It sounds as if you can't lose," Crystal said, and though she felt she should say something about her own life in return, she didn't.

The plane was flying much lower and when she leaned forward she could see that the ground was getting greener as they flew south towards New York. When the stewardess announced that in twenty minutes they would be landing at Idlewild Airport, Crystal felt a moment of panic. She tried to calm herself by watching Lynda gather together all her luxurious possessions, like her gold clock, her cashmere sweater and her oversize dark prescription glasses with the lavender frames. Lynda must have sensed it, for she said, "I don't know how you're fixed, Crystal, but if I were you I wouldn't fool around with the model agencies. I'd go straight to some of the cosmetics companies. With that skin of yours, you'd be a natural for an ad."

"Where would I go to find something like that?"

"Well, there's Arden, Rubinstein, Revlon. Dozens of them. Try the yellow pages of the telephone book. They are all listed."

As they gathered up their belongings to leave the plane Lynda said, "Nice meeting you, Crystal. If you decide to stay a bit longer in New York, let me know. You can always get me through the Ford Agency."

Crystal followed the crowd along the corridors until they came to the booths that admitted or rejected returning travelers. Crystal joined the line of non-American citizens. She felt a little nervous as she presented her visa, but there was no trouble at all.

"Welcome to the United States and enjoy your visit, miss," said the man who stamped it.

"How long will I be allowed to stay, sir?" she asked.

"You have top priority, as you see on your papers," he said. "You can stay a long time without being questioned, and even have it extended after that."

Crystal found her two suitcases quickly. Customs inspected one of them in detail and she realized afterwards it was lucky it wasn't the one with her grandmother's box in it. The heart and the necklace might have called for an explanation.

As she followed the porter who was trundling her bags out of the terminal along with half a dozen others, she caught a last glimpse of Lynda as a uniformed chauffeur helped her into a limousine.

She went to the bus that would take her into the city and found a window seat. It was four-thirty on a warm Friday afternoon, and the bus moved slowly in the traffic that was headed into town. The outgoing lane, she noticed, was bumper to bumper with long, expensive-looking cars full of children, dogs, golf clubs and all kinds of other paraphernalia. Of course, this must be the beginning of the great American weekend that she had read and heard about, she thought.

When they reached the East Side Airlines Terminal, she checked her bags and asked the way to Fifth Avenue.

"Just keep going west," the porter said, pointing. "It's about five blocks, and you can't miss it."

Everything was taller, bigger, brighter and more electrifying than she had imagined. When she reached Fifth Avenue she discovered Lord & Taylor on the corner and she absorbed every detail of the new fall college fashions that were in the windows. She walked up the street in a trance, past the library lions and on to Rockefeller Center, where the flowers were blooming and the sun was still shining on the gilded statue in the sunken plaza.

She crossed the street to Saks Fifth Avenue, went up the steps of St. Patrick's Cathedral and went in to light a candle. Then she continued on up the avenue, past the great stores like Best and Company, Cartier and Tiffany's, where the tiny windows were like looking suddenly through the wrong end of binoculars. In one of them was a crystal vase, holding a single daisy with a huge topaz for a center. It was about the same size stone she had given Aunt Emma.

This has to be the most exciting city in the world, she thought, as she crossed Fifty-seventh Street. She could see that she was almost at the end of the shops, and for the moment she was too tired to investigate Central Park and the elegant-looking apartments that seemed to be coming next.

She stopped in front of the Savoy Plaza and thought: This is it, I think I'll stay here. She went to the desk and, without asking the price, she said she would like a room and bath overlooking the park.

"I'm afraid most of those are large suites," said the reception clerk, "but we can give you a pleasant one facing Fifty-eighth Street with a nice view down Fifth Avenue."

She signed the register and said she would return in half an hour with her luggage. She liked the room and for a while that night sat beside the window watching the endless stream of lights moving down Fifth Avenue.

14

When Crystal woke the next morning she ordered coffee and was happy when the waiter brought a roll with it. Last night when she undressed she had found the price of her room posted on the back of her door, and forty dollars a day came as something of a shock. Grandmother used to say, "Believe you deserve the best each day, and the best is sure to come your way." But this may not have been the time to test her wisdom, Crystal thought.

As she finished her breakfast, she decided to follow Lynda's advice and try to become a model. No more markets or hotel jobs. I hope you're right, Grandmother. I believe I deserve the best.

As she dressed, she calculated that she could afford to spend five days in New York. If nothing turned up by that time, she would have to fly on to San Francisco and see if she could do better out there. She knew in her heart that she was desperately anxious not to go back to Berlin.

Before she left the hotel, she opened the telephone book with the yellow pages and turned to "Cosmetics." The first name, Adam and Eve, amused her, so she took down the address and telephone number. Also listed under the A's were Arden, Angel Skin and Avon. There were a lot under the B's, too. She made a list and made up her mind to try all of them.

When she came out of the hotel, she found Fifth

Avenue much quieter than it had been the day before. It felt like early morning, even though she knew it was nearly ten o'clock. A few women were giving their dogs a morning walk. Across the street the fountain area that had been crowded yesterday was almost deserted. The horses and the hansoms were ready but the drivers were dozing in their seats.

She strolled down the avenue and saw that Tiffany's was just opening its doors. I guess New York makes a late start, she thought.

At Elizabeth Arden, there was a doorman to open the red door.

"I'd like to see Miss Arden," she said to a girl at the cosmetics counter that was just inside the door.

"I'm afraid this is the wrong place," the girl answered. "The executive offices are all around the corner at 3 East Fifty-fourth Street, but they won't be open today. It's Saturday, you know, and even we just stay open until noon."

"I only arrived yesterday from Europe and I didn't stop to think what day it is," Crystal confessed.

"I'm sorry to tell you that you'll be living in a ghost town until Monday. Everybody who can, gets away on weekends."

"I wonder if you would make me an appointment Monday for a haircut and a shampoo?" asked Crystal.

Why didn't I realize I was arriving on a hot summer weekend and that everything would be tightly closed? she was asking herself. Two of the five days she had decided to allow herself would be completely wasted. It was even more vital than ever to look her best and, she realized, the hairdo she had liked so much in Berlin, didn't seem quite right here.

The girl behind the counter was telephoning upstairs and in a minute she said, "Everything's okay for ten Monday morning on the eleventh floor. You'll have Richard, and he's one of the best."

Crystal left Arden feeling completely deflated. She debated whether she should go back to the hotel and sleep or try the others on the slim chance of finding someone there.

Adam and Eve at 5 West Forty-sixth Street didn't seem too far away, so she started walking again.

"I must not take taxis except when I have to, and I must eat lightly to make up for a wasted weekend," she told herself.

Adam and Eve was a far cry from Elizabeth Arden's pink elegance. The foyer of the building hadn't been swept. The sand-filled containers by the elevators were still full of cigarette stubs.

"Where will I find Adam and Eve, please?" She asked the man who was sitting on a stool in the elevator and sweating profusely in his shirt sleeves.

"Fourth floor and turn to the right. I don't know if Mr. Adler's still there, but you can try."

Well, I know his name anyway, and that's a help, she thought as the elevator crawled upward to the fourth floor.

Adam and Eve Cosmetics seemed to be nothing but a group of office rooms. Crystal felt she was wasting her time but she decided to knock on the door anyway.

"Come in," said a man's voice, and when she opened the door she found he was quite young. He was sitting behind a big desk beyond the small reception area and seemed to be alone in the office. He broke into a broad grin when he saw her.

"Surprise, surprise," he said. "What on earth brings you here on a day like this, sweetheart? You ought to be sunning yourself on a beach somewhere."

Crystal laughed. "I wish I were, I just came from Europe yesterday and I'm finding out that I picked the wrong day to arrive."

"I don't know why you picked me to call on, but since you're here, you might as well sit down and tell me. I'm more or less killing time until I take a train."

"I thought you might be needing a model for your advertisements, somebody to personify your products," Crystal said. "Perhaps I could come back next week and meet your advertising director or whoever hires your models."

"You flatter me," he said. "I'm Adam Adler, and I'm

the owner, the president, the board of directors and the advertising manager of this company."

"That must keep you busy," she said, smiling at him, "but what a marvelous challenge to be starting your own company this way, being able to do whatever you want with it. I'd like very much to work for a company like that."

"Sometimes it seems too much of a challenge. My wife, Eva—she's the Eve of the label—and I started our firm nine years ago on almost nothing. We make enough to keep going but so far we haven't managed to make the league of the big advertisers."

Crystal found herself rather liking him. She wished she could think of some angle that would persuade him to hire her, for the struggle of a small firm against giants, and the ingenuity it would take, was the kind of business that intrigued her most.

"I'm sure you'll succeed" was all she could say, and she started to get up to go.

"Here, hold on a minute," Adam Adler said. "I'm not through with you yet. Who are you, anyway?"

"My name is Crystal Casalet."

"All right, Miss Crystal Clear. I'm about to ask a very personal question."

"But why Miss Crystal Clear?"

"Probably because of those cloudless sky-blue eyes of yours, but don't worry, I'm not going to make a pass at you. I'm just going to ask what any man who makes cosmetics would ask. What the hell do you use on that complexion of yours?"

She burst out laughing.

"I guess good, healthy skin runs in my family. I wash my face night and morning, and I use the same old cream that my mother and grandmother used. It's nothing special or expensive."

"For God's sake, have you got any with you?"

"Not on me personally. I brought along two jars but they're back at my hotel."

"Be kind to me, lady, and let me have one of them. The one that's partly used will be okay. We'll run it through our lab and see if it holds some unexpected little ingredient that will make us all millionaires."

"I'll bring it to you on Monday, if you like."

"No, sweetheart, a messenger from my laboratory will pick it up early Monday morning. I'll have it analyzed right away and you'll come back here Tuesday morning. Anytime after ten. We'll know if we have struck gold." He added, "By the way, where are you staying?"

"At the Savoy Plaza."

She watched Adam give her another appraising look.

"An upper Fifth Avenue girl, just as I thought," he said with his wide grin. "Say, what's that lipstick you're wearing?"

"Something I got in Berlin. I don't remember."

"Here, try one of ours." He reached into his desk and brought out a few samples. "This should be right for you. These are our blond colors number seven and nine. I think the nine will be the best."

"Thank you."

As she left the building and started to walk up Fifth Avenue again, she was reasonably sure that Adam would discover no secret ingredient in her cream. She decided that after her hair was done on Monday she would make the rounds of every name on her list. In the meantime, there was no use worrying.

She wandered into Central Park and followed one of the winding paths for a while. What a strange mixture of people, all ages and all types, she thought. There were children eating ice-cream cones, young couples making love on the grass and old people reading their newspapers on park benches. Before she reached the zoo she had heard at least half a dozen different languages spoken.

She bought a sandwich in the zoo cafeteria and sat down at a table to eat it. Everybody in the strange parade of people but herself, she thought, had seemed to be deeply involved in something or somebody. She longed desperately to be a part of the New York scene.

Crystal braced herself for a solitary Sunday but it was more bearable than she expected. After church she hunted out a newsstand. She had decided that, instead of a movie, she would buy the Sunday papers and three or four of the current magazines. If I'm lucky enough to get something to do here, I've got to know what people are thinking and doing and how they look, especially the women, she thought.

"Which is the best Sunday paper?" she asked the man at the newsstand.

"That depends on your taste, miss. You have your choice of the *Times*, the *Journal-American* and the *Herald Tribune*, also the *Daily News* and the *Daily Mirror*, which are tabloid size."

She remembered that Mat was always reading the Paris *Herald Tribune*, so she said, "I'll take the *Tribune*." She also bought *Vogue* and *Mademoiselle*. Back in her room she went systematically through the paper, page by page. The front page had a story on President Eisenhower's operation. The women's section had a full page on the Paris fashion collections. It predicted loud and clear that skirts were going up and up and urged women to shorten their clothes at least two inches if they wanted to have today's look. I'm afraid I won't have today's look until I get myself a job, Crystal thought.

She went through the "For Rent" pages avidly, finding many small, unfurnished apartments available for one hundred and twenty-five to two hundred and fifty dollars. There were also any number of fascinating sublets like "actress going on tour wishes to sublet sunny room and bath quickly," "leaving city, willing to sacrifice duplex apartment with terrace." She dreamed of herself in all these places. She picked up a pencil to circle several of them, but put it down. How silly of me, she thought. I don't even have the vaguest prospect of a job yet.

She lingered the longest time on the theatrical section. It was the slow season for Broadway, but there were many Off-Broadway productions she would love to see and dozens of both old and new films. As she turned a page, suddenly she saw a familiar name. There was a revival of The Gypsy Princess at the Cherry Lane Theatre.

For a minute she was back in Berlin, sitting in a dark theater with her grandmother, watching her mother perform on the stage.

My mother seemed old to me at the time but she was really so young. She was just the age I am now. As she looked back from a distance at her child life in Berlin, she could see that her mother had a certain style and a kind of creative elegance she had been unable to understand. Probably because she belonged heart and soul to her grandmother. Perhaps her mother had deliberately handed over the upbringing of her daughter to Countess Casalet to make up for the suffering she must have caused her by producing an illegitimate child. She could only guess at what had gone on between her mother and her grandmother at the time she was born. Crystal got up, opened the ivory box and took out her mother's passport. If she was still alive, she would be only forty-three now and still young and beautiful, she thought as she looked at the face that was framed in a long, soft bob.

Crystal had always analyzed her own face as being a little too strong for real feminine beauty, and she had never been able to think of any way to hide the determination she saw in it. As she looked at her mother's photograph, she wondered if a hairdo like her mother's would soften her own.

I'll take it to the hairdresser's tomorrow, she decided as she closed the passport and dropped it into her handbag so she wouldn't forget. I'll have him cut off my hair and do it just like that.

When she arrived at Elizabeth Arden on Monday morning at ten, she took the elevator to the eleventh floor and asked for Richard.

"I know exactly what I want," Crystal said as she took out her mother's passport picture from her purse. "I want it to look like this, and a blunt cut, no tapering, in case I want to let it grow again. The part should be on one side so that a lock will fall over my forehead and the length must be shoulder length with the ends curled under."

Richard studied the passport photograph. "You know exactly what you want, don't you, Miss Casalet? Is this your twin?"

"No, it's my mother at twenty-three, which is my age now."

The hairdresser picked up his scissors and paused a minute with the blades open and ready.

"You have magnificent hair, Miss Casalet. It is real honey color. Are you positive you want to do this?"

"I couldn't be more positive. Please put a ribbon or a rubber band around the part you cut off and put it in a manila envelope. I may want to have it made into a hairpiece later on."

Losing the weight of her hair made Crystal feel light-headed for a few minutes. She thanked Richard and walked away feeling rather pleased with her new look. She left the salon, went around the corner to 3 East Fifty-fourth Street and up in the elevator to the executive offices.

"I'd like to see Miss Arden, please. I have no appointment but I'm here from Europe for only a few days."

"I'm sorry but Miss Arden is spending the month in Kentucky, where her racehorses are bred," the receptionist said.

"Then perhaps I might see the advertising director?"

"I'm afraid he's vacationing in Southampton and even Miss Arden's publicity director, Count Lanfranco Rasponi, is off in Italy. Why don't you give us a ring next month?"

Crystal went next to the Avon office, where she was met with the flat response: "Sorry, but we don't do any advertising. We're door-to-door sales, but if you're interested in becoming a saleswoman you might fill out an application. It pays very well."

She wasn't a bit interested but filled out the paper and left.

Her next stop was at Breck, whose advertisements,

always girls with blond hair, had intrigued her in the magazines she had bought yesterday.

"You seem to me exactly the type our advertising director is looking for," said the man who was interviewing her. "It's very hard to find a natural blonde whose hair retains enough color in a photograph. Most natural blondes fade to platinum in front of a camera, and we don't like to use the bleached ones. Your hair, I assume, is natural, isn't it?"

"Completely," she said. "It has never had anything but a soap-and-water shampoo, and I have usually done it myself."

He rang a bell on his desk and said to the girl who came in, "Please put a bottle of our special hair care shampoo, number seven, in a shopping bag and bring it to this young lady." Turning to Crystal, "I want you to try out one of our most famous products. I will take your name and address and when the head of our department comes back we will get in touch with you."

"When will that be?" Crystal asked.

"Directly after Labor Day, though he might not have time to call you until a week later."

"And when is Labor Day?"

"Oh, of course, you're English—I can tell by your voice. It's not very far away. Labor Day is always the first Monday in September."

September might as well be sometime in the next century as far as she was concerned, but Crystal left her name and gave her address as the Savoy Plaza. She would leave a forwarding address with the hotel.

She stopped for a salad at Schrafft's and went on to Coty. How I'd love to work here, she thought as she came into the salon that was right in the heart of Fifth Avenue and had just been decorated by Dorothy Draper, she had read in the Tribune yesterday. The walls were painted blue with white moldings and the cushions and slipcovers were a shiny, pale blue fabric.

At the desk the response was the same.

"There might be a job for you somewhere but all the department heads are away."

As an interlude from the cosmetics companies, she decided to try the Ford Model Agency.

"I don't know if you're quite our type," said the girl who seemed to be in charge both for interviewing would-be models and for booking those who had already made the grade. "Only Mrs. Ford can tell you what your possibilities are and she's taking her vacation in Venice."

"She won't be back until after Labor Day, I suppose."

"Right," said the girl. "Drop in again when she's back."

She picked up the telephone, and as Crystal left the room she heard her say, "Gee, you're in luck. Yes, you can have Lynda Lancaster tomorrow. She's just had a cancellation."

By the end of the day, Crystal was totally frustrated and depressed. She knew she must leave the hotel no later than Wednesday morning. She would go to San Francisco, but it, too, would be a ghost town until Labor Day, she supposed. It occurred to her that Kitty, also, might be off on a holiday. She got out the number, but decided not to call.

I'll go to bed and forget everything, she thought.

She undressed and lay down and when she opened her eyes it was eight o'clock the next morning by the traveling clock beside her bed. She showered and dressed as fast as she could, ordered her coffee and was thinking of her interview with Adam Adler. She was dreading it.

As she was about to leave, the telephone startled her by ringing. It was the first time it had shown any sign of life since she arrived.

When she picked up the receiver a man's voice said, "Miss Casalet, this is Bob Allen, with whom you talked at Breck yesterday morning. It just happened that our advertising director telephoned the office later in the day. I told him about you and he asked me to set up a date to have some photographic tests made on September seventh."

"Thank you so much, Mr. Allen," she said. "Please

make the appointment. I may possibly be going out of the city but I'll either confirm or cancel it in plenty of time."

Crystal's spirits rose. Though she didn't believe the Breck job would work out, the call was giving her the courage to spar with Adam Adler.

When she arrived at the Adam and Eve offices there was an older woman sitting at the reception desk. Behind her she could see Adam sitting at the same desk as before. He motioned for her to come in.

"Hello, sweetheart, I've been expecting you," he said. "Sit down for a minute."

As she sat down across from him, she saw that her jar of cream was in front of him on his desk. She had a sinking feeling that he was about to hand it to her and wave her out the door with a casual "goodbye and good luck."

"Well," Adler began, "we're not going to become millionaires after all."

"What do you mean?" Crystal managed to say.

"We sent your miracle cream through the lab yesterday and the report is nothing new. We have practically all the same ingredients in our cream. I'm sorry, sweetheart, because I was looking forward to working with you."

"Thank you, Mr. Adler."

Adler leaned back in his chair and grinned at her again. "I see we've treated ourselves to a new hairdo. I like it. It makes you look more like a good-time girl," he said.

Crystal started to explain, "I copied it from my mother's," but instead she heard herself saying, "You don't think it's too juvenile for a forty-three-year-old woman, do you?"

He stopped smiling and stared at her.

"I guess I heard you wrong. You're not trying to tell me that you're forty-three years old, are you kid? Because it just ain't possible."

"I did say it, and I am."

"Come on, Miss Crystal Clear. You're having a good time pulling my leg. You couldn't be a day over twenty, or I'll start eating your damn cream," he said.

"You'd better start eating it then."

She reached into her handbag, opened her mother's passport and held it in front of her eyes.

He looked at the photograph, read the name, then the date of birth, December 4, 1912, and the place of birth—Berlin.

"My God," he said, "you were born before the First World War?"

She nodded.

"Sweetheart, here I was thinking of making a pass at you eventually, and you turn out to be eight years older than I am."

"Serves you right," she said.

"When you came in here this afternoon, I was about to say politely that it had been nice meeting you, and so long, baby. Now I've got to rethink the situation a little."

She sat quietly, still smiling.

"Talk, girl, talk and don't spare the details," he said. "Tell me how any woman can go through forty-three years and still have a body like yours, to say nothing of skin like a baby's. You haven't a gray hair in your head, and I'm going to be snow white by the time I'm forty."

"I honestly don't know," Crystal said, "but I don't see that my age really changes the job situation as far as you're concerned."

She picked up her handbag and started to reach for the jar of cream on his desk.

"Not so fast," he said. "I know there's something we can make out of this. Why don't you stick around town for a while and we'll play with some ideas."

"I'd like to but I'm planning to leave for San Francisco Wednesday to visit friends, and I may fly straight to Europe from there."

This time she picked up the cream and put it in her bag.

"What are you planning to do with that cream?"

"Well, use it, I guess. I've often thought of trying to promote it personally. If women see what it seems to have done for me, they might want to buy it, too," she said. "The trouble is that I have no capital." She spoke very gently and looked straight into Adam Adler's eyes.

"You might put it over but there's nothing special about your cream. It's all right, just run-of-the-mill but no pizzazz. It's very like one of Arden's and not quite as good."

"Well, if mine is nothing special, it still seems to work. Perhaps I should try to find some other manufacturer who would want to produce it and let me promote it," said Crystal, who still looked ready to leave at any moment.

Adam hit his forehead with the palm of his hand.

"Good God, sweetheart, am I ever dumb? You must have stunned me with that 1912 passport of yours. Eva and I have been holding back for a year now because we couldn't find a gimmick for some new product. Now the gimmick drops right into my lap."

He leaned across the desk and held out his hand.

"I'm going to hire you, Miss Crystal Clear," he said. "I don't usually make decisions like this without my wife but I guess I have to do it to keep you from taking that plane to San Francisco tomorrow."

"It sounds very nice, Mr. Adler, but in what capacity are you hiring me?" Crystal asked.

"To promote this cream of yours. You will do press interviews, radio and TV interviews, personal appearances in stores and any other thing we can dream up. We'll do the producing while you do the promoting. Christ! We haven't even got a name for it yet but you and Eva and I will get going right away on the whole campaign."

"I like the sound of the job and I feel it's something I'll enjoy doing," Crystal said. "I've had quite a bit of business experience. I really created and managed a market for my uncle in Berlin and more recently had an executive position in a Berlin hotel."

"That's a bonus I didn't dare to hope for," Adam

Adler said, "but since you mentioned business, do you have your working papers?"

"No, I don't. I'm here on a top priority visa that a close friend of President Eisenhower's was able to get for me and I've been told that it can be extended easily."

"I can manage the working papers but in the meantime I'll pay your salary out of the expense account of the company. I'll give you one hundred and twenty-five dollars a week to start, but since you have no permit, you'll have no withholdings and the whole thing to spend. I suppose it will be just about enough to keep you in cigarettes."

"Luckily, I don't smoke," she said. The money wasn't as much as she was making in Berlin but it would do for a start, she was thinking.

"I think we've got something, sweetheart, and I've got a hunch it's going to be very good. A lot better than the queen bee's wax or the urine of a pregnant mare that has sold creams by the million." He paused. "If you're free, why don't we go around the corner and talk some more over luncheon?"

"I'm sorry but I've made a date to meet someone at the hotel for luncheon but I promise he's not in the cosmetics business."

"Well, let's start work tomorrow. Timing is everything."

"I've got a few loose ends to tie up in the morning but I'll be at the office before ten-thirty," Crystal promised.

15

In her excitement, when she reached the street, Crystal hailed the first cab that came in view. "The Savoy Plaza Hotel, please."

At the hotel she went straight to the desk.

"I'm leaving today. I see your check-out time is two o'clock, so please send for my bags in an hour and leave them with the bell captain. I'll be back later this evening to pick them up and to pay my bill."

In her room she picked up the *Tribune* "For Rent" pages that she had folded and left on top—just in case. She ran down the columns and took down the addresses and telephone numbers of four. When she called the first number a man's voice answered and said, "Sorry, but the room has already been rented." There was no response at the second. The third call was to the actress going on tour. The bell rang several times and she was about to give up when a woman's voice said, "Hello."

"I'm calling about the room you advertised in the *Tribune*, Sunday. Is it still available?" Crystal asked.

"Yes, it is, I'm sorry to say, and if you're interested, you'll have to get over here pronto, because I'm leaving for the airport at five. I'm in the throes of packing but you can see what it's like, I guess. I'm Chita Rogers and the apartment is 2B at 50 West Fifty-fourth Street."

Crystal told her she would be there around two o'clock. She pulled out her two suitcases, and it didn't take her long to replace the few things she had taken out to wear in New York. Before the porter came, she was able to write down two more possible addresses and phone numbers in case this one didn't work.

It would be a perfect location for her, she realized, as she turned west on Fifty-fourth Street and walked along the south side looking for the number. I could walk back and forth to the Adam and Eve offices and get to most places easily, she thought.

Number 50 was an old-fashioned brownstone with a flight of stone steps leading up to the front door. The apartment mailboxes and bells were in a little foyer and when she pressed 2B the locked door beyond the foyer clicked open and she was in a long, dark hall with a stairway at one side.

Suddenly the door at the end of the hall was flung open and a voice called, "Come on in if you're the English woman who called about the room. Otherwise I'm too busy."

"I'm the one," said Crystal.

The door was open, so she came into the room.

"I'm just out of the shower," said Chita Rogers, who had a towel draped around her and a shower cap still on her head. "It'll take me just a few minutes to get my clothes on, and in the meantime you can have a look at the place."

It was a good-size room with a high ceiling and it had a big window at the end with the sun pouring through. There were two studio couches that could be turned into beds, an upholstered chair with a lamp and little table beside it. In front of the window a drop-leaf table still held Chita's breakfast dishes, and her robe was thrown over a straight-back chair. The walls were painted a dusty yellow and the whole place seemed to be clean.

When Chita came out of the bathroom she was still barefoot but wearing pants and a shirt. She ran her hands through the short black curls that were still damp from the shower. "Look over the facilities," she said, waving her hand towards the bathroom.

It was incredibly small, with a toilet, a washbasin and a stall shower, but it would do, Crystal thought.

"Can you do any cooking?" she asked.

Chita waved her hand towards a bedraggled screen across one corner that Crystal thought was an effort at decor. Behind it she found a small chest of drawers on top of which were an aluminum pad and a hot plate.

"It's not much but you can make coffee and at least keep from starving," she said. "I keep three or four pieces of china in the top drawer along with some assorted knives and forks and paper napkins. It's not the Waldorf but you can make do."

"What are you asking for the room, Miss Rogers?"

"Oh, well, I guess I could let you have it for two hundred a month. Damn it all, if this were September instead of August, I could have got two hundred and fifty in a breeze, but when you go on tour you gotta go, as the saying goes."

"I like the room but I really can't afford that much at the moment. I'm a stranger here. I'm starting a new job tomorrow morning and the salary is rather small."

"I sure know how that is. I was a slow starter and this part in *West Side Story* that I'm going to play is the best I've had so far. I've got a feeling I'm on the up-and-up now."

"You're a dancer, aren't you?" asked Crystal, who had noticed her well-kept feet and her springy step when she came out of the bathroom.

"Yes, and the woods are full of them, I'm sorry to say. But back to brass tacks, baby, I guess you've got me in a bind. Could you manage a hundred and fifty? You'll be getting the all-time bargain and, for me, it's better than getting nothing."

"All right, I'll take it. I guess I can manage," Crystal said.

"Good enough. Time marches on, so let me give you a few quick facts of life. The electricity is on the house but the telephone is on you. It's unlisted and you get sixty free calls for your basic twelve dollars a month. They'll send a bill and you can watch for it."

"How about the laundry?"

"There's a laundromat around the corner, unless you do it in the washbasin like I sometimes do. My sheets are drip-dry and that sun is a good dryer. I keep the sheets and towels in a box under one of the beds, and they're all fairly new. Another thing, I'll introduce you to Mrs. McCafferty, our landlady. She's a nice old lady but sublets are no-nos, so I'm going to introduce you as my cousin from London. And, by the way, what's your name?"

"Crystal Casalet," she said, laughing.

They agreed that Crystal would go back to the hotel and return with her bags and the first month's rent in cash. After that, the check would be mailed to Chita's agent since her itinerary was uncertain.

"I'm sure to be away five or six months and maybe longer, and I'll give you at least two weeks' notice when I know I'm coming back," Chita promised.

Chita followed Crystal down the hall and they stopped at Mrs. McCafferty's door to make the necessary introduction. Behind her new landlady, Crystal caught a glimpse of a Victorian room.

Chita followed her to the mailbox.

"Don't forget your own name here along with mine in case some good news is coming to you," Chita said. "This sure has been a hit-and-run business transaction between us but I think it's going to work out."

Crystal went back to the Savoy Plaza, paid her bill, cashed a couple of traveler's checks and claimed her bags. When she arrived at 50 West Fifty-fourth Street the taxi driver carried in her bags, and since Chita was ready to go, he agreed to take her bags back and deposit them along with Chita at Idlewild Airport.

"You seem like a nice person. Unglamorous as it is, I kind of like the old place and I don't like just anybody to live in it," she said, patting Crystal's shoulder as she left. She turned back to call, "I hope you don't mind if I left a few of my clothes in the one and only closet and, if you're feeling charitable, maybe you'll water my poor old ivy plant."

Chita had left more than just a few clothes in the

closet, Crystal discovered, but she pushed them to the back of the rack and wrapped a towel around them to separate them from hers. She unpacked the clothes she would need during the next few weeks, just as she had at the hotel, and since the closet was deep, managed to put away the two suitcases in the back. All except the top drawer of the chest that held the china were empty, so she filled them with her underthings and toilet articles.

Later she went out to investigate the neighborhood. Around the corner on Sixth Avenue, she discovered a delicatessen, bought a take-home sandwich, a couple of pieces of fruit and a jar of instant coffee and returned.

As she passed her landlady's door, Mrs. McCafferty stuck her head out.

"If you're looking for a nice place to have dinner, Miss Crystal, the Woman's Exchange is just two blocks east on Madison Avenue. It's good for a woman who's alone."

"Thank you, Mrs. McCafferty. I'll try it tomorrow, but I'm very tired and tonight I'm staying right here."

It was a very warm evening. She took off her dress, shoes and stockings and sat down in her one easy chair, and began adding up her assets. What with my hotel bill and the first month's rent for this room, I've spent about half the money I brought with me, she thought. I've got about four hundred and fifty dollars left and if Adam and Eve doesn't work out, then I can still get to San Francisco.

16

As soon as Crystal had left, Adam decided to call Eva at the house he had rented at Far Rockaway. She would just be giving the two kids their luncheon before they went back to the beach, he figured.

"It sure is hot here in town, honey," he said. "I thought I might knock off early this afternoon and come out for a swim before dinner."

"That makes sense," said Eva. "I told you, you ought to be spending the whole month of August here so we could get our money's worth out of the place, but you never listen to me."

"You're probably right, baby, but we're not that prosperous yet," Adam said.

He was devoted to Eva and proud of his two small sons, but to be cooped up in a domestic scene for more than a short weekend was more than he could take. Besides, he had a steady Wednesday-night date in Newark with a girl friend he hated to miss. She was in Bamberger's cosmetics department.

Eva began talking about Jeff's swimming lesson and then on to what would he like for dinner but Adam cut her short.

"I've got some work to finish, and I want to get there in time for that swim. I'll like anything you cook, babe." He was being especially patient because he wanted Eva to be in the right mood when she heard about the new project. "Besides, after dinner I've got some new business to talk about," he said.

"What business?" He heard a sudden, sharp note of suspicion in her voice.

"Something that could make lots of money for us but I don't want to spoil it by telling you now," he said as he hung up the receiver.

Adam was the youngest in a family of three sons, and his mother adored him from the moment he was laid sprawling in her arms. Her two older boys were good, serious children who presented no problems, but from the start Adam was a tease and a charmer.

Since his two brothers had just started school when he was born, he was left with his mother all day, first watching her from a playpen and then following her around the house as she cleaned and cooked with tremendous zest, talking to him at the top of her voice and laughing at his childish pranks.

As he grew older, he often heard her talking to a neighbor about her three sons, and she always said, "My Adam is the handsome one, and he has the brains, too." It never occurred to him not to believe everything she said.

When he went to school he quickly became the most popular boy in his class. Tall and skinny, with lots of wavy dark hair and a big grin, he was completely sure of himself from the start.

When a few years later the girls began calling Adam his mother was beside herself, half out of pride and half out of jealousy.

"That little girl will never be good enough for our Adam," she would say when the telephone called him from the dinner table.

Neither of the two brothers resented their mother's partiality for Adam. Like their father, they took her violent enthusiasm in stride. They were well adjusted enough in their own worlds to like Adam, too, and to consider him something of an asset to the family.

Adam accepted the adulation of the girls with his usual smile and said yes to some of the invitations but girls weren't necessary in his life at the time. He much preferred to be part of the boys who played on the street in front of his house.

His father, Joseph Adler, was a furrier on Fourteenth Street. He dealt in silver foxes, a business that had its ups and downs during the Depression years. They were neither rich nor poor, and had always lived in one of a long row of identical brick houses on a shady Brooklyn street.

Like everyone else on the block, the Adlers had dinner at six o'clock and for years Adam gulped his down in a hurry so he could join the gang on the corner. Since there was no daylight saving time in those days, the games of baseball or gutter hockey had to stop around eight.

Afterwards, they sat on a bench or squatted on the sidewalk in front of a confectioner's shop. Sometimes a boy told a dirty story, and even those who didn't get the point pretended to. They all smoked cigarettes. It was a clique, and Adam soon became an arbiter of which boys were qualified to join it.

When Adam got into high school he began to take girls more seriously. Whenever there was a school party or prom, he made a point of asking the prettiest, most popular girl in his class to go with him and she invariably said yes. He felt sorry for some of his old gang who by this time were stuck with steady dates.

"Adam," his mother would say, "my friend Rose Hart was talking to me the other day. She has a daughter about the same age as you that she wants you should meet. Her name is Eva. Her mother says she is getting very pretty and the boys like her. Rosie was a pretty red-haired girl, I remember, when we went to school together."

"Oh, come now, Mama, you aren't matchmaking, are you?" laughed Adam. "You know I've got more girls right now than I can manage."

The summer that he finished high school his father suggested that he come to work for him in the new showroom he had just rented on lower Seventh Avenue. He had already put his two older sons to work, one of them as a salesman in the showroom and the other overseeing the workroom that adjoined it on the same floor.

Adam's first job was stacking skins, but he found it so boring and did it so carelessly that his father decided to try him as an assistant salesman. The new job was more to his liking as he soon discovered the two models, who sat around in their dressing room wearing nothing but their lace-trimmed slips and smoking and drinking coffee between showing the furs to customers.

They were ten years older than he was, but one day he asked Francine, the blond model with a mole on her cheek, to have lunch with him. He took her ten blocks uptown to the Arts & Writers Restaurant, where the food was good and all kind of celebrities stood around the bar. He was able to point out F.P.A., whom he liked on the radio show "Information Please." They both had two Bourbon old-fashioneds, the specialty of the place, before luncheon and another afterwards.

They were laughing as they came out of the restaurant and Francine said, "I'm sleepy and I'm damn sure there won't be any customers this afternoon. Let's go to my apartment."

They took a cab to her apartment on West End Avenue and went in.

"Make yourself a drink. There's a bar on the back of that door," she said.

Her bedroom door was open, so after he fixed a drink, he went to the door. She had taken off her clothes, pulled off the bedcovers and was lying on a pale pink sheet. She looked much more appetizing than she had back in the Adler showroom.

"What's the matter? I thought you were never coming," she said.

He took off his clothes and got into bed. Francine wasted no time. Her lovemaking was eager and violent and he quickly forgot that her body was without the curves he expected in a woman's body and that her elbows and knees were sharp.

"You're wonderful, kid," she kept saying over and over.

They were finally exhausted and dozed off for what seemed a few minutes.

"It's damn near half past four, kid," she said. "We've got to make sense and get back to silver-fox heaven before I get sacked."

It was quarter to five when they reached the Adler showroom, and the racks of furs were being stowed away for the night. Since one hour for lunch was the rule, Francine would have been fired if her companion hadn't been the boss's son.

"He's been fooling around with the models again," Adam's father told his wife.

"It's because they've been enticing him, and you can't blame them," she answered.

"He's no worker, either," Adam's father continued.

"Not everybody has to like furs. Just wait until he finds some work that appeals to him; then you'll see," she said.

It was a relief to the whole family when the summer was over and Adam began classes at NYU. If there was anything he enjoyed, it was a new scene and new people to charm. In each class there was always a girl or two who looked as if she would be interesting to date. He took out one after another as long as she was fun but forgot it the moment she got that serious look on her face.

It was well into his second year at NYU that he became aware of a girl in his English literature class who kept staring at him. Once, while the professor was lecturing to them, he turned around and found that the tortoise-rimmed dark glasses she wore were still trained on the back of his head. He put his hand on his hair to feel whether there was anything peculiar about the way it felt but everything was in order. Five minutes later he turned around again and she was still staring.

Adam decided to ignore the whole thing but next day he caught her at it again. This time he took a good look at the auburn-haired girl and what seemed to be a pretty nifty build under her tight sweater.

As the class was breaking up, he stopped her and

said, "I guess we know each other but I can't remember your name."

"You've never met me. I know I was staring at you but I was just trying out ESP."

"What on earth is that?"

"It's extrasensory perception. I was willing you to speak to me."

"You were willing me to *what*? We're in the same class and all you had to do was tap me on the shoulder," he said with a big smile.

Not bad, he thought, looking her over. She was a small girl, but with rounded hips and more bosom than usual for her size.

"That would have been too easy and I didn't want it that way. I wanted it to be more romantic," said the girl.

"Well, Miss ESP, how about a romantic Coke in the cafeteria?" asked Adam.

She amused him and he again gave her his best big smile.

"My name is Eva Hart," she said as they walked along. He felt it was supposed to mean something to him but it sounded totally unfamiliar.

"I'm Adam Adler," he ventured.

"Of course you are. I've been hearing about you for years. I made up my mind I would hate you passionately but instead I think you're the most attractive man I've ever met," she said.

Well, the little one certainly comes on strong, he thought, but Eva was explaining. "Don't you remember? Your mother and my mother went to school together and for years they've been trying to throw us at each other's heads."

"Good God, you're Rose Hart's daughter, the girl I've been ducking ever since I can remember," he said, and they both burst out laughing.

After that they began having Cokes together after English lit. every day. Adam took her to a few Saturday-night movies but he still kept up his friendship with Francine because she attracted attention wherever they went and afterwards was exciting as hell in bed.

"Rosie told me over the telephone today that her Eva likes you very much," Adam's mother said to him one night. "She says Eva keeps a snapshot of you in a silver frame beside her bed."

"I know she likes me. She tells me so every time I see her," Adam said.

"Eva is a nice girl, and her mother says she's a good girl, too, and has never played around with the boys," went on his mother. "You both come from good, hard-working Jewish families and you might make something out of it together."

"Stop it, Mother. I'm not in the mood to settle down yet and become a husband and father," Adam said.

Though he laughed off Eva's adoration, he found it soothing. Other girls demanded flattery and special attention but Eva seemed happy to be with him. It was good to feel that no matter what dumb thing he knew he had done, someone besides his mother would still believe he was the all-perfect man.

Adam was just twenty-one and had six months to go before finishing NYU when he awakened one Sunday morning to hear that Pearl Harbor had been bombed. He knew he was ripe for the draft, so he decided to enlist in the Marines with the hope of getting a commission.

He expected Eva to burst into tears when he told her, but she said, "Oh, Adam, how lucky the Marines are to have you." Then she began to cry.

They were sitting on the couch in the Harts' living room. Eva's parents had gone off to the movies to leave them alone, as they always did when Adam arrived. He put his arms around her warm little body that he had already explored as thoroughly as he could without going the whole way. As she pressed closer to him and he felt her whole body shaking with tears, for the first time in his life he was aware of a craving for a deeper relationship than he had ever had with a girl.

He kissed her eyes with the tears welling out of them.

"Eva," he said, "maybe we ought to do something about this, like getting engaged."

She stopped crying and began to respond even more warmly than she had before. "Oh, Adam," she whispered.

They had told the Harts when they came back from the movies, then Adam walked home to tell his own family. As he walked the few blocks that separated their homes, Adam was thinking: I don't know if I'm in love or what love is, but if I'm going to start growing roots and making a home, I can't think of any woman I could get along with as well as I can with Eva.

For Christmas, Adam gave Eva a gold ring with a one-carat diamond.

"I wish it could have been bigger but that'll come later, honey."

If it had been a twenty-carat marquise cut stone, Eva couldn't have been happier.

Adam was due to leave the next morning for a six-month basic training course at Parris Island, South Carolina. After some unsatisfactory attempts at love-making on the Harts' living-room couch, Adam got up to go but Eva pulled him back.

"Listen, Adam. I've decided to quit school. It won't be the same there without you and I wouldn't learn anything. I'd just be mooning about you all the time and it would be better for me to be working. Uncle Jake thinks he has a job lined up for me, and if it comes through, I'll be starting the first of the year. Since I live at home, I can put most of what they pay me into the bank, and we'll have a little capital to do whatever we want to do when you come back."

"Great idea, my girl," Adam said, kissing her.

Basic training was not too much of a grind, Adam wrote, and he liked strenuous physical exercise. Eva's weekly letters kept telling him that her job was interesting and that she missed him more and more each day.

When he wrote to her that he would be home on a six-day leave the first week in July before probably being shipped to a base in California, Eva asked for time off from her job.

She was at Pennsylvania Station to meet Adam when

he arrived and she flew into his arms. He was deeply tanned and looked handsomer than ever, but before she could tell him so, he said, "Glad you came, honey, because I've been doing some thinking. What do you say we forget about that big wedding when the war is over and get married right now?"

"Oh, Adam, how wonderful! Where, when and what shall I wear?"

"Right away, and just wear that cotton dress you have on. It looks great to me, especially after six months of not seeing my girl."

After he picked up his bag and they started toward the exit to get a taxi, he outlined his plan.

"I'll go home and talk to Mama for a while. You get yourself packed and don't bother about a lot of clothes because I'm looking forward to seeing you without any."

"It will be heaven," she said.

"I'll pick you up in a couple of hours. I have to find out how to get around the rules and regulations but I'll work it out somehow. I won't get home again soon and I'm darn tired of trying to make love to you on the family couch. We'll get married somehow and afterwards we'll go to Atlantic City. I figure we can have at least five days to ourselves. When we get there we can call back our folks and tell them what we've done."

"It'll have to be Connecticut," he said when he came for her. "It's not too easy but it's a matter of three or four days in New York with blood tests and all. Luckily, I called a Marine buddy who has a friend who's a friend of a judge and he'll do the job. We'll check our bags at Grand Central, take a train to Danbury. That's where the judge lives. And after the ceremony we'll come back to town, pick up our bags and take another train to Atlantic City. Can you take it, honey?"

"What do you think, Adam?" she said, taking his arm and squeezing her body close to his.

It was past dinnertime when they finally reached Atlantic City. Eva stood close to Adam as he signed the hotel register. She could hardly hide her happiness as she watched him write: Mr. and Mrs. Adam Adler.

They spent most of the five days in their room and Eva never put on anything but a sheer white net robe. It was part of a set with a matching nightgown that she had bought for her trousseau. Adam quickly discarded the nightgown but he loved the robe. It was a fine veil through which he could see all the details, curves and crevices of her full-blown little body as she moved.

Eva took easily to sex, as Adam felt sure she would. He found her far more satisfying than his previous casual contacts like Francine had been.

"Oh, Adam, this has been so much more peaceful and beautiful than a big wedding would have been," said Eva on the last night at the hotel. "I've never been happier."

"Me, too, sweetheart," he answered as he took her into his arms.

He returned the next day to the Marine base in South Carolina and it was six months before he had his next leave. This time he was wearing lieutenant's bars. He had not seen action and seemed to be enjoying the companionship of his fellow Marines, just as he had enjoyed the old Brooklyn gang and games of gutter hockey. They spent half of his leave at the Harts' and for the rest Adam took a room at the Astor Hotel so they could be alone, go to a couple of Broadway shows and do whatever they felt like together.

One night before dinner Adam ordered two martinis sent up. He was already drinking his when she sat down beside him, put her head in his lap and stretched out full length on the couch.

"I've been meaning to tell you about my job," she said.

"I'll try to concentrate but it's going to be hard," Adam said, looking down at the auburn hair spilling all over his lap and her breasts bursting out of her slip.

"It's a fascinating job, and I really like it. You know how I was always crazy about chemistry in school, and now I'm working in the Elizabeth Arden factory in Long Island City. Uncle Jack is responsible for me getting there. You know he sells all kinds of cosmetics at his drugstore, and he became friendly with one of the Arden salesmen."

"What kind of things do you do there, honey?" Adam asked.

"Well, so far I've been just a helper, bringing the ingredients they need to the chemists," Eva went on, "and, oh, Adam, you should see this Miss Arden. She comes out to the factory occasionally and she hates smoking. So the lab has had an alarm bell put in. Somebody sets it off when they see her getting into the elevator. The other day Miss Arden came in and caught June just putting out her cigarette. She shook her until her teeth chattered. Afterwards June had to lie down and take a sedative and everybody said she should sue, but, of course, she didn't. I would have, I can tell you."

"She must be quite a gal, to have built such an empire," Adam said as he leaned down to kiss her.

This was their last night together before he left for Camp Pendleton, near Oxnard, California, and then on to the Pacific.

It was eighteen months before Adam had his next leave. This time he was a full-fledged captain in the Marines. Eva thought he looked well but older, and though he still had his winning smile, it was not so quick and ready. Adam had always refused to face horror and death, and in the past eighteen months he had seen plenty. Eva let him rest a week before she began to talk about herself.

"You haven't asked to see our bankbook and I haven't wanted to bother you but I've saved nearly ten thousand dollars. I've been banking every cent of your government checks along with mine. Mother and Dad refuse to take a cent from me for my board, so everything is going into the bank. When you get out we'll have a nice little nest egg to start a small business."

"What do you have in mind, honey?" Adam asked.

"Oh, I don't know, but there's an awful lot of money

in the beauty market. Some of these beauty products cost about three cents as far as ingredients go. Even with the cost of the labor and the special labeling that the Food and Drug Administration insists on now, the profits are quicker and bigger than anything else I can think of. Besides, I've got the ingredients of a cream that can be our own."

Eva told him about seeing one of the formulas for an Arden cream.

"It was lying right on the edge of one of the chemists' basins all day. I looked at it every time I went past, and I went back and wrote down all the quantities and ingredients on a pad that I've got right here at the house. Naturally, we may have to change a little but at least I feel we've got something to start on when you get back for good, Adam."

"It sounds interesting, honey, but now we've got a war to win and it's hard for me to think about the future until that's been done."

"I understand, darling. You're still back in the Pacific in your head."

Ten months later, when peace was in the air and Adam's letters told them that he would surely be coming home soon, the Harts decided to convert the ground floor of their home into an apartment and give it to Eva and Adam as a long-overdue wedding present. The area made a large living room with a fireplace, a small adjoining den and a large bedroom with a corridor between horizontally. A passage was left to pass from one room to another but the rest of the corridor was filled with a small kitchen and dining alcove on one side and a bathroom and dressing room on the other. A door from the bedroom led into the Harts' backyard, where there was a large tree. Eva realized she could put an outdoor table under the tree and they could eat there in the summer. With a couple of folding chairs they could get a tan without going to the beach.

She began watching the sales and started cautiously to furnish the apartment. First came the big bed, followed by a mirror and dressing table for herself and a chest of drawers for Adam. Then when Adam's mother heard about the apartment, she sent over enough furniture to complete the whole place.

One end of the bedroom was enclosed behind louvered doors to make a double space for hanging clothes. She put some of her things in one half to make believe they were already established there.

When Adam came home this time he was a major in the Marines. Eva admired his blue-gray uniform and thought to herself that the few gray hairs at his temples were becoming, too. They spent at least a week getting reacquainted. She didn't push him about any future plans and then one day he said to her, "Are you still thinking we should start this cosmetics business, Eva?"

They were sitting under the big tree in their garden. Eva got up from her chair, came over and sat down on the grass in front of him and reached for his hand.

"Yes, I think so. I've been able to save another four thousand dollars since you were last home. That means we have over fourteen thousand in our bank account now. If I hadn't taken this job at Arden I'd never have realized how much the people who make these beauty products are raking in. It's the markup, Adam. You wouldn't believe it. What your father has made out of silver foxes is nothing in comparison. You can take it from me."

"You're thinking maybe we could make a go of it? I've got to get on to something—and soon," Adam said.

"I'm sure of it, Adam," Eva said.

"Okay, honey, it's the cosmetics business for us," Adam said. "At least we've got a ready-made name in Adam and Eve. I have always admired you, baby, for not linking our names with the first man and his mate but it will make a hell of a trade name for us."

When she got home from work the next afternoon. Eva dashed out to their garden, where Adam was reading the sports pages of the Post.

"The luckiest thing you can imagine has happened, Adam," she cried. "I gave them two weeks' notice at the lab today, and as we were all getting ready to go home, one of the chemists came up to me and asked what I was going to do. He's a nice fellow, very quiet, and in his mid-thirties, I guess. I knew he wouldn't blab to the manager, so I told him we were thinking of setting up our own small business. He said he was fed up with Arden and would like to join a couple of young starters if we had room for him."

"Sounds good," said Adam.

"Well, it is, because he knows a lot and is easy to get along with. I asked him to stop in here after dinner, and we could all talk it over."

Adam and Roy Archer were such opposite types that they instantly liked each other, and together they started to plan the organization of the new firm. Roy would be in charge of the laboratory in the space behind the drugstore that Uncle Jake had already promised to lend them. Eva would assist Roy and look after the packaging and Adam would be the salesman.

"I can get a GI loan for starting a new business," said Adam, "and with our savings we should be able to hold our own." Then he turned to Roy Archer. "What were you making at Arden, Roy? Whatever it was, we'll meet it, and give you a percentage of the profits, when there are any."

Adam secured a license for Adam and Eve Cosmetics that week and they were shortly in business. The cream, when it was finished, had a slight yellow tinge. They called it Amber, not only because of its color but because of *Forever Amber*—the wartime best seller. Uncle Jake shook his head at both the name and the color.

"Women like the idea of pure white stuff on their faces," he said, but when Eva managed to obtain some pale yellow jars he had to admit the overall effect was attractive.

"Besides, we mean to undersell all the other good creams on the market," said Eva, "and what we lose in individual profit, we should make up in volume."

It was almost a year after Adam came home that they were able to put their first consignment of Amber into Uncle Jake's drugstore. Eva went in every day to see what had happened to it. Sales were slow but Uncle Jake said it was doing all right for a starter.

In the meantime, Adam had sold a sizable amount of the cream to other Brooklyn stores. They were considering how to distribute further but for the moment were content with the thought of a small but apparently steady income.

Eva became so preoccupied with her work that, three years later, it took her a while to realize that she was finally pregnant. Jeffrey was a beautiful boy who looked like Adam but without his smile. Eva worked up to the last week before her son was born and was back at her desk three weeks later while her mother happily took over Jeffrey.

Two years later she had Alan, who had her auburn hair but Adam's grin.

One Sunday afternoon when Adam found his mother watching Alan, who was jumping up and down in his crib, laughing and trying to talk, he said, "Don't, for God's sake, Mama, start telling him how wonderful he is. He already knows it and Jeffrey is just as cute, if not cuter."

17

Before he took the subway for Far Rockaway that afternoon, Adam bought a copy of *Life*. As the car rattled along, he flipped through the pages but didn't read the headlines or even bother to look carefully at the pictures. He could think of nothing but what had happened in his office that morning.

It's like some kind of a miracle, he thought. He had not been worried but was slightly discouraged about the business recently. After ten years, it seemed to be standing still. He was intensely competitive and it irked him to see other companies like Estée Lauder, who had started only a few years earlier than Adam and Eve, becoming so successful.

"We need a spark. We need a gimmick. We need something," he had said over and over to Eva during the past year, but nothing had been forthcoming. He was ashamed of himself when he realized how close he had come to waving Crystal out of the door.

When he reached the house in Far Rockaway, Eva was in the kitchen giving the boys their supper so that she and Adam could have dinner alone. He kissed her and hugged the boys as they fell all over him.

"Give me a breather, kids," he said. "I'll put on my bathing trunks and then we'll go out in the rowboat."

Behind the house a narrow little canal led down towards the sea. They had a small pier and a rowboat

149

was fastened to it. He rowed them to the end of the canal and all three of them helped pull the boat up on a wide strip of sand that separated the canal from the ocean. As they ran across the sand, Adam grabbed each of the boys by the hand, and they ran into the surf. Though Jeffrey went along, Adam could feel him draw back cautiously, but Alan was mad for the breakers. Already he was like a fish in the water. Adam rowed them back, and Eva sent the boys off to bed.

When he came downstairs in dry clothes he found that Eva had already made the martinis and set the dinner table on a little back porch that overlooked the canal. It was cool and pleasant there. Eva brought out some crackers and cheese to go with the martinis, and sat down near him.

"All I can say is that this is some vacation," Eva said. "I've had it up to here," and she touched her chin. "What with sweeping the sand out of the house ten times a day, cooking three enormous meals and finding pet toads and lizards in places like our bed."

"Thanks for warning me, honey."

"I can hardly wait to get back to the lab right after Labor Day but I'm worried. I know Mother loves keeping an eye on the boys but all she does is make Alice nervous, and a good housekeeper is hard to get these days."

"I'm glad to hear you say that, honey, because I feel just the same way. Come sit here and tell me some of the luxuries you would like in life."

"Are you kidding? But if you want me to daydream, let's see. I would love to live in Brooklyn Heights. The view of Manhattan is magnificent from there. It would also be fun to have a car, too."

"Anything else, honey?"

"I wish we could afford to send the boys to some kind of private school. The school Jeffrey is going to now is pretty tough. He's not too impressionable but Alan will be."

"Don't think I haven't been thinking the same things, honey. We've worked hard. We deserve to get a break and I think it's about to come to us."

"What do you mean?"

Adam got up, refilled his martini glass and sat down again.

"Well, to make a long story short, a woman came into our office last Saturday morning. She was looking for a job as a model for some cosmetics company's advertisements. I guess I must have told her she had good skin and asked whose cream she used. It was something she had brought from Europe and she said her mother and her grandmother both had used it, too."

"How old was this woman?" Eva asked.

"That's the whole story, honey. You know, lots of those European dames are supposed to have beauty secrets, so just on the chance it was something new, I asked her for a jar and Roy ran it through the lab yesterday. Too bad you weren't around."

"Was it anything special?"

"Not bad, but more or less the same old thing. She came in this morning for the answer, and when I said no dice, she said she didn't think it was so special herself but it had done pretty well by her for forty-three years. God, honey, I almost dropped dead. She looks like a kid of twenty, but she brought out her passport and, believe it or not, it's her age."

"What does she look like?" Eva asked.

"She's a natural blonde, you can tell, because her hair doesn't have that painted-on look. She's got this marvelous skin I've been telling you about and a pretty good figure. Oh, yes, honey, and she has one of those English voices that gives her a lot of class. She's a looker, all right, though not especially my type."

"Well, it's a relief to hear that after such a rave notice."

"Call up your mother, honey, get her to take care of the boys and come in with me tomorrow and meet her. You ought to get away from the sand and the kids for a day," Adam said. "Anyway, I want her to know the other half of the firm before she starts."

"Starts? You mean you've actually employed her?

Adam, how could you hire this foreign girl without at least calling and consulting me?"

"Honey, she was going out the door with the cream, and it came to me in a flash that she's the gimmick we've been waiting for so long. She will go around the country promoting the cream, making personal appearances and telling thousands of women what the cream has done for her whole damn family. She was on her way to some other manufacturer when I stopped her."

Eva went into the kitchen, brought their dinner and sat down.

"What's her name, and what kind of deal did you make?"

"I don't even remember her name. It's Crystal something and the definite deal is still to be made. You'll be in on it."

"Do you think she's a phony?"

"Not at all. Women try to lie about being younger than they are but not older. I almost shit when I saw the date of birth on her passport."

Eva was quiet for a minute. Then she said, "I may not like her, Adam."

"Don't like her if you want to, honey, but let me put it this way. We're not getting anywhere. Do you want to live in a nice large home in Brooklyn Heights? Do you want to give the kids a break and send them to good schools? Do you want a trip to Europe, maybe, instead of Far Rockaway, or do you want to worry about whether or not you like some European dame who can maybe get us all those things. We can't lose by taking a chance."

"Well, if you put it like that, Adam, of course you win," Eva said.

As they were getting ready for bed, she said, "I love you, Adam."

"What a surprise! I'm glad you told me."

"Do you think I'm getting fat?" she asked.

"You've gained like fifteen pounds maybe in the fourteen years we've been married but you still have a pretty little figure."

"I'm going to start dieting tomorrow and I think I'll

have my hair touched up, too. Do you love me, Adam?"

"Why don't you quit talking about l-o-v-e and get into bed with me. I'll show you."

18

Crystal slept until the sun that was streaming through her bay window touched her face. It's going to be better than an alarm clock, she thought.

It was only half past eight and she had plenty of time before she was due at the Adam and Eve offices. She got up, showered and dumped some coffee into Chita's little pot. While she was waiting for it to perk, she set the table in the window and even watered the ivy. I haven't been here even twenty-four hours but it feels like home, she thought.

She walked down Fifth Avenue to what she hoped would be her new office. The elevator man recognized her and smiled, which seemed to her a good omen. She opened the door of the office that was becoming familiar to her and greeted the secretary-receptionist.

"Good morning, Miss Ida."

Adam Adler was in the office beyond and she guessed that the woman with him was his wife, the Eve of the firm.

"Come in," he said, rising from his chair, "and, Ida, have some coffee sent up for all of us will you?"

Adam closed his door as Crystal went in. "This is my wife, Eva, the other half of the firm and one of the main brains of our laboratory. She was anxious to meet you. I have to confess I can't get your last name straight."

"I don't blame you. We only talked for a short time,"
Crystal said. "My name is Crystal Casalet."

"What kind of a name is Casalet?" Eva asked. "It
sounds French but you look more like Swedish."

"As a matter of fact, it's neither. It's Viennese."
Crystal had to think quickly as she began describing
her grandparents instead of her own mother and father. "My mother and father were both born in Vienna. However, I was born in Berlin."

"Oh, really," Eva said.

"My father," Crystal continued, "was Count Curt
Casalet. He was killed at Verdun and I still have his
Iron Cross First Class, which was one of the highest
German decorations in the First World War."

"Your father was a count. Adam, why didn't you
tell me?" Eva looked at her husband reproachfully.

"Mr. Adler didn't tell you, Mrs. Adler, because he
didn't know. Our conversation has been only of business."

"I see," Eva said. She was now smiling.

"I called you this morning at the Savoy Plaza,"
Adam said, "but they told me you had checked out and
left no forwarding address. I thought Eva would be as
fascinated as I was when she saw your passport."

"A friend of mine asked me to take care of her
apartment while she's in California," Crystal said. "But
I think I still have my passport in my handbag,
though."

She reached into her bag and held it out for Eva to
see.

As she looked from the face in the passport to Crystal's, Eva's eyes widened. "It's unbelievable, just like
Adam said," she cried. "You look about twenty, Miss
or do I call you Countess since your father was a
count?"

Crystal could see quite clearly that Eva had a pen-
chant for titles.

"Why don't you just call me Crystal?" she said, smiling. "The title passes only to the eldest male child and
I had no brothers. My mother was a baroness in her

own right, but I'm afraid I didn't inherit that title either."

By this time they had finished their coffee. Adam looked at his watch and said, "Let's get down to business."

"A good idea," said Crystal, but she waited for him to make the first move.

"It's my understanding," Adam began, "that you are looking for a manufacturer to produce your miracle cream. In turn, you will be entirely responsible for promotions and selling it."

"Of course, but don't you think you would prefer to have your salesman do the actual selling. I will, of course, sell indirectly by making personal appearances in stores and by interviews on radio and TV and in magazines, and newspapers."

"With your voice and your beauty, you'll be great on TV," Eva injected.

"I also want to be responsible for the packaging. The total look would be my responsibility, including the labels and the appearance of the cream."

"Have you given any thought to a name?" Adam asked.

"Yes, I have," replied Crystal. "How do you like Young Forever?"

"My God, it's a natural." Adam was so enthusiastic that he almost spilled the remains of his coffee on Eva.

"That's okay, honey . . . I agree with you. It's sensational," Eva said.

"I assume, Mr. Adler, that you're going to make this a separate division in your company?" Crystal asked.

"Well, I hadn't thought about that but perhaps that's the way to handle it. Don't you agree, Eva?"

"Why not?" Eva said. "Provided the financial arrangements are satisfactory."

"Since I'm willing to take the responsibility for Young Forever, I thought a fifty-fifty arrangement would be reasonable. Of course, it would have nothing to do with your other products," Crystal said.

"Hell, that's pretty stiff," Adam said.

"You know your costs better than I do. Would you think sixty-forty would be fair?" Crystal asked.

There was silence for a moment, then Eva said, "I think that's reasonable, Adam. It sounds fair to me."

"Okay, girls, we've got a deal." The familiar grin came back to Adam's face. "It's going to take at least ten months to get this thing rolling. What with producing the cream, getting the packaging and starting the promotion. Now, Crystal—do you mind if I call you that? As we agreed, we'll keep you on the small expense account for six months. When you actually start the publicity and promotion, the one hundred and twenty-five dollars a week will have to be considerably increased."

"Thank you," Crystal said.

"Okay. Now we've got to get our lawyer, Eva, and get the papers for the special division drawn up."

Adam rose and opened the office door.

"Our salesmen use the big space in the back but there's an office, exactly this size, over here," he said, pointing to another door. "Why don't you move right in and get to work?"

19

Adam always made quick decisions, dictated almost entirely by instinct. Enough of them had been right to give him tremendous confidence in his own judgment, especially as far as women were concerned.

Even with the proof of the passport she had held out for him to see, he didn't quite believe Crystal's story that she was forty-three years old. But, as he looked at her and listened to her, he sensed that she had something to offer. What she had was something he had always wanted and never known how even to approach. It was what he and his pals often referred to as class.

He was thirty-five and had been only moderately successful, because what he had been selling was only moderately good. It was totally without any special personality to make it appealing to women. He realized that most successes in cosmetics had been due to women's thinking, like Helena Rubinstein's, Elizabeth Arden's and, more recently, Estée Lauder's.

Adam wanted money, and lots of it. He was thoroughly tired of the domestic life in Brooklyn, and his discontent was increasing rapidly as he saw a few friends from Seventh Avenue days living in Park Avenue apartments, buying country homes and traveling to Europe twice a year.

The Saturday morning Crystal had walked into his office he had begged off Far Rockaway to make a thorough survey of the past six months' figures and was not too happy over the results. Something had to happen.

Crystal's arrival had seemed almost like the answer to a prayer. She and her cream might be just what they needed, and he was confident that if it worked he had the drive to keep it going. If it didn't work out, their loss wouldn't be overwhelming, he figured, and besides, he was a born gambler, whether he was playing poker, going to the races or doing serious business.

When she came to the office the next morning he told her that he had already been on the telephone to their chief chemist, Roy Archer, who would start at once to experiment with the ingredients in her cream. Also, he was seeing his attorney at eleven to get the legalities worked out for the new division.

The rest of the week he was occupied with his out-of-town salesmen, but he was aware that she arrived promptly at nine every morning and seemed to be busy at her desk, typing, telephoning and making notes. She wore the same simple dress in which he had first seen her and, unlike the Seventh Avenue girls, never any jewelry.

It was the following week before he finally called her into his office. "Let's see some of those notes you've been making all this time, Miss Crystal Clear."

"Certainly. What comes first? The packaging?"

"It's as good a start as any."

Crystal began. "I know it's obvious but I was thinking in terms of a pink label."

"Sorry, sweetheart, but pink to millions of women means Elizabeth Arden, and just recently that new dame Estée Lauder has grabbed a nice sky blue for her color."

"Then what about mauve?"

"Mauve?" Adam wrinkled his forehead.

"You know, pink trying to be lavender."

"Lavender, sweetheart, is one of those tricky colors that women either love or detest. I have a friend on Seventh Avenue whose wife recently sold him on doing a lavender-and-white cotton dress collection for spring, and did he ever go broke. He even divorced the bag as a result."

"Then what's left, mint green?"

"Lots of women think green is unlucky and sales-girls say it is a jinx in the stores."

"Then what?" Crystal asked.

"What would you think of that mauve pink you spoke about as a background, with deep purple lettering?"

"That would be beautiful. I wish I had thought of it."

Adam continued. "And now about the jars."

"Oh, would it be possible to have them square instead of round? I think they would look so much more elegant."

"No, sweetheart, it wouldn't be. I'll tell you an inside secret. Round jars hold less cream than square ones. You have no idea how the profits mount up from not having to fill those corners, and we're both out for the big profit, aren't we?"

"Yes, indeed."

He reached for her sheet of notes. "Well, I see you're getting around. You've already gotten in to see Diana Vreeland. How in the hell did you manage that?"

"Going through *Harper's Bazaar*, I discovered that Diana Vreeland's fashion photographs are so far out and so fascinating that I called her, and she was nice enough to see me."

"What did she say?"

"What I hoped she would. She believes that the craze for youth is just starting, and that it will become a real mania in this country. I liked her so much and everything about her is fascinating—her looks, her voice and the way she uses her hands. She seemed to like me. I think I've made a friend."

"Good, and what is this note about *Fortune* magazine?"

"I've been to the library going through the past two

years of Fortune checking on articles about who's making money in the beauty world."

"You don't have to go to the library to find that out, sweetheart. Just ask me. At the moment it's certainly Revlon. That damn TV show of theirs, 'The Sixty-Four Thousand Dollar Question,' is certainly putting them on top. Didn't you watch it on Tuesday night?"

"No, I just have a radio."

"Then I'll have to send you one so you can join the rest of the country. Don't plan to go to the library that night but just sit back and watch Revlon rake in the dough. Some of the products the show advertises have had anywhere from 300 percent to 500 percent increase in sales. One lipstick in a new color sold out of stores all over the country before noon the next day."

"Is TV really as potent as all that?"

"Well, this show is. Hazel Bishop did well a few years ago sponsoring 'This Is Your Life,' but they're virtually down the drain now while Revlon is making billions."

"Are you thinking of going into TV?"

"No, sweetheart, not now but maybe later. I'm counting on your Young Forever to put us in the chips and I think you can do it by looking like a kid instead of the middle-aged hag you really are."

"I'll try to ward off the wrinkles until we get the cream going."

"You've got no reason to worry, sweetheart. You can turn on almost any man. You've certainly turned me on. Didn't you know?"

The turned-on approach was part of Adam's standard routine with the lonely middle-aged women who were cosmetics buyers in New Jersey and Connecticut stores, and it had brought in some orders from even a few chic Manhattan stores. Usually it brought a come-on response from the buyer like "How would I know?" or "You're not so bad yourself," which he was an expert at following up, but Crystal showed no special interest.

"I've been too busy to think," she said.

During the next few months Adam found himself thinking of her constantly, not as the gimmick he told Eva he had hired her to be, but as an immensely desirable woman. He began to call her into his office on the slightest provocation. As she stood in front of his desk or sat relaxed in a chair across from him, he kept undressing her in his mind, thinking of the curves, the softness, the pink-and-white texture of the skin and even the golden hairs on her body.

Just to keep her there one afternoon, he said, "You may think I'm hipped on the value of putting cosmetics on the map, but what do you think of all this hoopla in the papers about Mamie Eisenhower and her visit to Elizabeth Arden's Maine Chance?"

"I'm afraid I'm not up on it."

"Then I guess you need me to supervise your reading. It's been making headlines for days."

"Tell me about it, Adam."

"It's a hell of a lot better stunt than Arden ever realized when she got into it. You know that she has this super rest and reducing home that has never, so far as I know, been able to break even. Suddenly she gets the great idea of asking Mamie Eisenhower to spend two weeks there. The public takes all this in their stride, but later when they hear that the taxpayers' money was used for Mamie and her entourage's plane fares, all hell breaks loose."

"How amusing! But won't it hurt Miss Arden?"

"You really flunked that one, baby. Here I've been working overtime trying to make you understand the benefits of free publicity."

"I'm sorry, Adam."

"You ought to be. The answer is that lots of women will want to go there to see for themselves what it's really like."

"I'll do better next time."

"In the meantime, how about you and me having dinner together tonight?"

"Oh, Adam, I'm so sorry, this is my school night."

"School?"

"Yes, I'm taking a couple of night courses in skin care so I'll know what I'm talking about."

"What time is it over? What about meeting me later?"

"I wish I could, but I promised to meet a young milliner for a late snack. I went into Bergdorf Goodman and I met this charming young man. His name is Shelley. We talked a while and he asked me to have dinner, and I wouldn't know where to find him right now to break the date."

"He's taking you to Schrafft's, I suppose."

"No, as a matter of fact, he says it's a rather new French place where everybody seems to be going. He thinks the flower arrangements are special."

"I was thinking of '21.' A former Marine buddy of mine, Bob Kriendler, runs the place."

"I'd love to go there sometime, Adam. In the meantime, though, I've been wondering if I oughtn't to go out to the laboratory someday and see what it's like out there. They might even show me how they're putting together my cream."

He called Long Island City the next day to make sure that Eva and Roy Archer would both be there to receive Crystal and gave her detailed directions on how to find the place. After she left the office, he sat thinking about her for a few minutes. It was impossible to believe that Crystal was an unawakened virgin or disinterested in sex, but it seemed equally improbable to him that she didn't feel as violently attracted to him as he had to her. He decided time would take care of the whole situation. Picking up the telephone receiver, he called New Jersey to confirm the standing Wednesday-night date he had planned to cancel. When he reached her in Bamberger's cosmetics department, he said he would meet her as usual at her apartment.

At the laboratory next morning, Crystal was greeted at the door by Roy Archer, with Eva, covered from head to foot by one of the lab aprons, standing right behind him.

"So glad you decided to come and see us. We want

you to find the whole operation as fascinating as we do," Roy Archer said.

"Yes, we're both positively silly about liking our work," chimed in Eva. "I thought that vacation I took this summer was never going to end."

Crystal expected the laboratory to be small, but just one glance at Roy's meticulously kept hands with the long fingers and manicured nails told her that it would be well organized and scientifically clean as a hospital.

He looks like one of those studious young middle-aged college professors almost every girl falls hopelessly in love with for a couple of months, she thought, as she and Eva followed his slim, erect figure across the hall and into the first room.

"This is the emulsion area, Miss Casalet. It's where all our liquids, like our cleanser, our astringent and even a makeup base are put together."

"It looks a bit like a very scientific kitchen, doesn't it? But since we're to work together, I hope, do please call me Crystal—just as Eva does."

"Thank you, I will. It *is* like a kitchen, Crystal, and the homogenizers and the blenders are just a larger version of what a chef uses. It was right here in this area that we tried to analyze your cream the day Adam first sent it over."

"I haven't the slightest idea of what's in it. I just know that Grandmother, Mother and I all used it."

"Your own skin is its best recommendation. It's absolutely flawless." He bent over slightly to study it through his glasses, but his voice was as impersonal as if he were talking about a china doll, she thought.

"Could I see what state my cream is in now?" she asked.

"I'm afraid that you'll find it still in a rather messy, half-prepared stage. We decided to add some of the more recent elements biochemists are talking about."

"Roy has lots of friends in the scientific side of the business, and we read everything we can," put in Eva.

"I've been reading a lot about hormones," Crystal said. "I hope you've added some of those."

"That's exactly what we did."

"Wonderful. I hope both of you will tell me all you can. I want so much to learn."

"I'm glad to hear that. Sometimes we have a hard time persuading Adam that our business isn't just hope in a jar or pie in the sky, as the cynics say," said Roy Archer, smiling at her for the first time.

"I hope my cream and I aren't just that."

"A little illusion makes anything more exciting, but to keep up with science, we are also adding a moisturizer element to your formula. What women used to do to their skins is unthinkable. It was unladylike to have a shiny skin, and they did everything to subdue the natural oils. The necessity for the moisturizer was discovered in 1931 by Dr. Blank of the University of Massachusetts and has become the big cry in the whole industry."

After she had inspected her Young Forever cream that was still in an almost liquid state, they went on to the area where the Adam and Eve lipsticks were made.

"The big complaint we get is that if lipsticks are soft enough, they break too easily," Roy explained.

"They have to be structured in both horizontal and vertical layers. We have a pretty good record so far."

In one corner of the area was what looked like an incubator, and was. Inside, instead of a baby were lipsticks, not yet in their cases, and apparently a cream rouge.

"We call this our chamber of horrors," Eva said.

"All of our products have to go through it and your cream will, too," Roy added. "In the incubator they are exposed to all the extremes they will run into in real life, like severe cold and heat, and of moisture and dryness. We even try them under extremes of light. All light is aging, you know."

"But we can't live like moles, can we?" laughed Crystal.

"No, but we don't have to bake in the sun until we look like pieces of gingerbread, either. I can't understand the fascination a suntan has for women with all the adverse publicity it has always had. I've had a hard time persuading even Eva that her freckles look just as pretty on an untanned skin."

"Let's show her our lab within a lab," Eva suggested.

"I must admit this is my hobby, and Adam, who is quite medically oriented, has backed me up every bit of the way," said Roy Archer as they went through some swinging doors into a room that was small but even more like a hospital than the others. "This is where we are beginning to put all our new products through bacterial tests. We have been working on a mascara, but we want to make sure that it's completely pure and can't cause an eye infection as one mascara did. Actually we shouldn't be in here dressed like this," Roy added. He nodded towards the man in a surgeon's apron, a covered head and a gauze mask who was working with a test tube.

They left the room and returned to Roy's office, which adjoined a smaller one for Eva. Another door concealed a burner on which Eva soon made tea.

"We're employing about twenty here now, including the delivery boys," Roy said, "but I'm hoping we'll expand soon. I have a hunch that a big boom in cosmetics is on the way and we don't want to be eaten up by the giants."

When Adam asked her next day how she liked the laboratory, she said, "I learned a great deal and I need to learn a lot more. I'd like to spend some time out there, following Roy Archer and Eva around."

"Do as you like. Archer is a nice guy and Eva is always quoting him, but you'd soon get tired of lunch in Long Island City. I can't take it," Adam said.

20

All through February and March, Crystal spent two evenings a week going to night school taking classes on beauty care, and she spent at least two mornings a week at the lab. A special room was set up for the packaging of Young Forever. She asked to have a table equipped with a makeup mirror that switched from daylight to night light, so that she could study the size of the jars as well as the colors.

There were only three weeks left before launching time when the cardboard boxes, sized to hold the jars, arrived at the factory. They were far from being the shade she had anticipated.

After one look at them, she picked up the telephone and called Adam at his New York office. "They're all wrong. They're so pale they fade into gray under strong lights, and they kill the whole thing."

"Can you describe exactly what you want, or get me a sample?"

"I've got a satin ribbon in my apartment that's exactly right."

"Then get the hell out of Long Island City. Take a taxi, hold it at your apartment and bring me that ribbon in a hurry. In the meantime I'll call the box factory and tell them where they can go if they don't fill a new order in time."

As she dashed into her apartment, she stopped long enough to fish a letter out of her mailbox. She saw it was from Chita but stuffed it into her handbag and decided to open it later.

At the office, Adam was as cool as he usually was in times of crisis. "Sweetheart, you caught it just in time. We can't change the launching date, because I've already booked the Rose Room at the Astor and the hotel is dated solid. But the new boxes will be ready in time, they promise. Hell, if they aren't, we'll hand-paint enough of them to have the right look at the press conference."

"Oh, Adam, you're truly wonderful."

"Of course I am, but up to now Miss Crystal Clear hasn't seemed to get the idea."

"Of course I do."

He followed her into her own office and closed the door. "Then prove it." He caught her wrist and pulled her close to him, and, in spite of herself, she felt a tremor run through her whole body as he kissed her.

"That's more like it." Adam smiled and kissed her again. Then he went out. Crystal could hear him telling his secretary, who sat outside his office, that he was going out to luncheon with the buyer at Bloomingdale's and would be back later.

As she sat down at her typewriter she thought of Chita's letter and pulled it out of her handbag. "Dear Crystal," she read. "I don't know whether you will be glad or sorry, but my tour is ending here in California in a couple of weeks. Los Angeles has been glorious fun and I plan to hang on here for a couple more weeks with the possibility of a bit part in a movie. But as of now you can count on my turning up around the first of April. This ought to give you time to find something as nice if not nicer to hang your hat, and thanks again for being so prompt with the rent."

What a day, thought Crystal. If she could only have stayed away another month, Easter would be over and the cream would have been launched. I would have been much more secure. She picked up the letter and reread it slowly to make sure it meant what it said. When she reached the word "hat," she folded the paper and put it away in a drawer. They say that when a woman feels low, the first thing she does is to go out and get herself a new hat. Maybe that's what I ought to do.

Crystal picked up her coat, went out and walked up Fifth Avenue to Bergdorf Goodman. When Shelley came out of the millinery workroom, he found her sitting in a chair in front of one of the mirrored tables.

"Why, Crystal. What a nice surprise. They told me Countess somebody was outside, and I didn't connect the name."

"I was just being funny. I need a lift."

He pulled up a chair and sat down beside her. "You're not feeling nervous about Young Forever's debut, are you?"

"No, not really. I haven't the slightest intention of not being successful."

"I rather thought you felt that way, because it's the way I feel about myself. Let's shake hands on our future." He reached out, clasped her hand briefly and then let it go. "In the meantime I'm going to make you an Easter hat."

"I'd love it. I hear every woman in America buys one at this time of year."

"The Easter parade has been a grand institution for the milliners and the florists, but it's already starting to pall. You'll notice the top celebrities and socialites don't participate any more. They take off for their country homes. But the Easter parade on Fifth Avenue is as much fun as a circus to watch. This year I've been asked to fill one of those horse-drawn hansoms with friends and maybe you'd like to be one of them."

"Oh, Shelley, I'd love to be part of it all."

"Then let's decide what you'll wear."

He got up and stood behind her, studying her reflection in the glass, and she smiled back at him, thinking how well the chestnut hair and the long, oval face with the big blue eyes suited his romantic name, Shelley.

"No flowers for you, Crystal. Girls with strong features like yours are always trying to disguise their vitality with dripping horticulture, but it's all wrong. You should wear something simple and direct. I see you in a navy blue Gibson-type straw sailor. You have exactly that Gibson Girl outdoorsy kind of skin. The only alternative would be a big, plain navy straw with a wavy brim and long satin streamers, but I like my first thought best."

"What should I wear with it?"

"The simplest navy blue coat or suit you own, and be sure to have a long, white crepe scarf to fold into a muffler around your throat. If you're not busy, let's go around the corner and talk about it over a hamburger."

As they were drinking their coffee, Crystal said, "I don't expect you to solve all my problems, Shelley, but the girl whose room I'm subletting is coming back to New York in a few weeks. So do I just read the classified ads or find a real estate agent or what?"

"Usually the best way is by word of mouth." He paused for a moment. "Listen, I've got an idea. Bonnie Cashin, a fashion designer friend of mine, called me yesterday about an apartment in the building she lives in. It's almost across the street from where you live now. It may still be available, and if you have the time, let's go and take a look."

The building was Regent House at 25 West Fifty-fourth Street, a modern one with a doorman, a nice foyer and uniformed elevator men. The apartment itself suited Crystal instantly, as if it had been designed for her. The living room was dropped a step that made the ceiling seem tall and off the little entrance gallery were a kitchenette, a bedroom and a bathroom.

"What is the rent?" she asked the superintendent, who was showing it to them, but even before he answered she had decided to invest in her future and close her savings account if she had to.

"I believe it's one hundred and fifty-nine dollars, miss, and if you care for it, you'd best say so as soon as possible, because it won't be vacant long. The former tenant moved out only yesterday."

"I want it, Shelley, even if I have to sleep on the floor," she said. "Can we telephone to someone and say so?"

They went downstairs and Shelley used the superintendent's telephone to call Bonnie Cashin. After he hung up he turned to Crystal. "Bonnie suggests you see Jerome Riker, the head of the real estate firm that handles this building, this afternoon. In the meantime she will call him with a personal recommendation for you. Now that's what I call being a friend."

Crystal grabbed his arm. "You're a wonderful friend, too, Shelley."

He smiled and then asked the superintendent for a key and they went back to the apartment to look over the rooms again. "Let me help you," Shelley said. "I see it as a blue-and-white apartment. The blue is the kind of blue you find in antique porcelains."

"I can't spend much money at first."

"All you need to move in is a bed with a box spring and mattress. You can buy those in any department store. We'll pick up the rest at Coleman's."

"What's Coleman's?"

"It's the auction place where we all go on Saturday afternoons. Most of my friends have bought their furniture there and so have I. I think I have a bolt of fabric that I bought for my own place and never used. We'll paper your bedroom with it, and the whole thing will be terribly chic. I can see it now."

"Oh, Shelley, that will be wonderful. If you have time, let's hurry and go to the real estate firm. I mustn't lose this."

That afternoon she paid a deposit, and made an appointment to sign the lease later in the week, after the references had been checked.

When Crystal looked at her calendar in the office the next day, she realized that she had to budget her time and move fast. I've been jogging along too peacefully, she thought, but now I know where I'm going and what I have to do. She decided she would go on spending her mornings in the library reading and researching for her speech at the press conference, which she would write at the last minute. Her shopping for the new apartment would fill the noon hour and luncheon would be a quick sandwich at her desk. She would be in the office every afternoon, ready to consult with Adam, unless she was at the laboratory taking a last-minute look at the packaging.

The bed wasn't easy to find, but in the corner of an antique shop she found one she was sure Shelley would consider a conversation piece, and the dealer promised to hold it until the next day when she could bring a friend. She called Shelley.

"It sounds right. I'll meet you there, but I may be a few minutes late. I've just started three hats for Grace Kelly. She's finishing a picture for MGM on the West Coast and telephoned that she'll be in New York Monday and wants to try them on," Shelley said.

"Oh, the actress who's going to marry the Prince next month?"

"Yes, and one of the hats I'm making for her is quite like the one I'm doing for you, but I'll tell you all about it when I see you tomorrow."

Shelley was half an hour late, and the dealer was beginning to fume when he arrived at last, looking his usual composed and unbothered self.

"Perfect. I see you've got the idea," he said to Crystal when he saw the headboard. She paid for it and the dealer promised to deliver it the next day.

"Did you finish the hats for Grace Kelly?" she asked as they started walking towards Coleman's.

"Yes, I made a big, natural Milan straw with ribbon streamers, just like the navy one I'm doing for you."

"I once went to see her in a movie that was playing in Berlin. I think it was *Rear Window*. Somebody had told me I looked like her and I only wish I did."

"There's a certain resemblance. The coloring and the height are about the same, but her face is much calmer and more serene than yours. She's a nice kind of girl, like you, and I'd like you two to meet, but I suppose next week she'll be knee deep in reporters and photographers eager for news about the wedding, and won't have a minute's peace."

Before they left, they wrote sealed bids for two tall standing bookcases and a pair of huge blue-and-white jars.

Outside, Shelley said, "The quality isn't too good

but they'll make a show. You can get by with murder when you start decorating in blue and white. We'll buy lots of inexpensive things and you can replace them little by little when you begin collecting your real porcelains."

"Should I really start collecting porcelain?"

"It's a must. They suit you and, as an investment, they can only increase in value."

During the next week Shelley telephoned to say that he would bring Joe Tula and two boys from his own workroom to the apartment, to assist with putting the material on the bedroom wall.

I can hardly wait to move in, thought Crystal as she lighted the ceiling lights of her new apartment for the first time. The headboard had already been attached to the wall, the mattress and chests were in place and she was planning to buy her sheets and towels from this week's salary.

It enchanted her to hear her own doorbell ring. Shelley kissed her on both cheeks, European fashion. Joe Tula, who was head and shoulders shorter than Shelley, followed him in. The two boys worked in the apartment until midnight.

In what seemed to her only a few minutes, Crystal began to see the apartment come to life. The white cotton fabric with a scattered pattern of tiny blue flowers made her bedroom look as cozy as the inside of a box.

At the office the next morning, when she arrived just ten minutes late by her watch, Adam said, "What the hell have you been doing with yourself lately? And why do you seem to be crying."

"I'm not really crying. I just said a sentimental good-bye to my first New York landlady." She had packed her suitcases the night before and tipped two boys from Regent House to carry them, along with her TV and other belongings, across the street.

"And who's this fellow Shelley who's calling you every other minute?" Adam wanted to know.

"Oh, I thought I told you about him. He's first assistant to Jessica Daube, Bergdorf Goodman's famous milliner, and he's been helping me with my new apartment."

"As long as he's just a milliner or a decorator," said Adam, in a tone that indicated his feeling for both categories.

Easter morning was sunny and chilly, but Shelley told Crystal to wear her big Grace Kelly straw hat and her navy blue coat. "And don't forget to fold your white scarf like an ascot and tuck it into your coat. Joe Tula's date for the day is a world-famous fashion model," he added.

When Crystal arrived at their rendezvous, the Fifth Avenue entrance of the Plaza, she quickly spotted the two men in the crowd, but the girl's back was turned.

When she swung around, Crystal cried, "Lynda!"

"Crystal!" They rushed to hug each other.

"Where could you two manage to meet?" Shelley asked.

"On the plane eight months ago when I was coming here from Berlin."

"I had gone to Paris for the collections," Lynda said. "We talked, or I guess I talked, most of the way home."

As they climbed into the open carriage with a top-hatted driver on the front seat, Shelley and Crystal took the seats that faced the front and Lynda and Joe flopped down across from them. No matter where or how she sat, Lynda was like a cat. She could never look anything but graceful.

"Lynda Lancaster's wonderful," Shelley said. "She can wear anything. Anybody else would look like a tramp in that hat, but she makes it look elegant."

"The girl has almost no bones and you feel you could double her up and put her in a suitcase," put in Joe Tula.

"I wish you guys would stop all this bullshit and look at the crowds," said Lynda in her soft little voice.

From Fifty-ninth to Fiftieth Street, Fifth Avenue was closed to everything but the horse-drawn carriages and the people who filled the street as they paraded up and down. The horse moved slowly, and as the crowd parted to let them pass, Crystal saw a woman with a poodle trotting beside her in an identical rose-trimmed hat, pink jacket and a pink bow tied at the neck.

"Pink seems to be the color this Easter. I've counted ten pink suits," said Lynda.

"It's unbelievable," said Crystal. "It's like Fasching in Munich, though Fasching is at the beginning of Lent instead of the end."

"You're German, Crystal?" Joe Tula asked.

She was on the brink of claiming an English father but stopped just in time. "Viennese, but I was born in Berlin."

As the carriage reached St. Patrick's, the crowd became so dense that they stopped altogether. Men and women pressed against the carriage, commenting on their clothes and calling good-naturedly, "Who are you? Tell us who you are."

How rich, how incredibly rich everyone is here, thought Crystal as she looked across a sea of obviously new hats, coats, corsages and handbags. Even the children seemed to her to be lavishly dressed.

A television unit had been set up just across from the cathedral. A reporter with a microphone, followed by a cameraman, pushed his way to the side of the carriage. "For Christ's sake, Shelley, give us a hand. The boss is yelling for celebrities on tonight's news, and there just ain't that many around. Just get up and say something about the fashions and I'll do you a favor sometime."

Turning to the crowd, the reporter announced, "This is Shelley, one of Fifth Avenue's best-known milliners. He's so well known that Grace Kelly goes to him for her hats."

Shelley stood up and took the microphone. He said that fashion was really in the pink this spring, and he was happy to see so many women so well hatted. He pulled Lynda up beside him and introduced her as today's most famous fashion model. Lynda smiled and waved her hand and the crowd cheered.

When the carriage finally reached the Plaza again,

they left it and went into the hotel's main floor bar, where Lynda ordered a beer and the rest of them drank wine over ice with soda.

Afterwards they made a taxi tour of Harlem. It looked just as rich as Fifth Avenue, Crystal decided. The only difference was the color; here there was lavender and purple instead of pink.

Joe Tula offered to cook spaghetti for them in his apartment, but Crystal begged him to bring it to her new apartment and make it on her own stove. "I desperately need a housewarming."

When they reached Crystal's apartment, Lynda pulled off her hat, kicked away her shoes and flopped down on the couch, looking more like a rag doll than ever, Crystal thought.

After Shelley and Joe had gone out for the food, Lynda turned to Crystal. "Don't worry about being a hostess," she said. "Shelley and Joe will bring back the best food you ever tasted, and in the meantime I need another beer. Monty wants me to gain some weight."

Crystal brought the beer and sat down on a cushion beside the couch. "Who's Monty?"

"Remember I told you about my friend on the plane coming over? He's the man I've been in love with for over two years. Well, believe it or not, he finally got his divorce last week. We thought the wedding bells were going to ring this week, but New York State insists we wait, think it over for sixty days."

"That's not long, and it will seem like nothing after waiting such a long time."

"You are so right. In two months I'll be living day and night with the man I love, and I'll be rich, rich, rich." She closed her eyes and smiled.

"How wonderful, Lynda."

"We plan to live in Monty's house in Rye. It's on the Sound and you can see water from every window. His wife hardly ever lived there. She's lived in this sanitarium in New Jersey for years, so there are no painful memories."

"You'll go on working, of course?"

"Not on your life. I'm planning to retire at the height of my career, shall we say?"

"Are you planning a big wedding?"

"Not really. It will probably be in some judge's chambers in City Hall. I don't have any family and, as far as I'm concerned, New York is not exactly packed with friendly faces."

Just then Shelley and Joe arrived with a market basket that held not only the spaghetti and a bowl of sauce but a loaf of French bread and green salad.

While Lynda remained stretched out on the couch, the three of them cooked the spaghetti, heated the sauce, tossed the salad and set the table. Then they poured the wine and opened another can of beer.

It was after midnight when Joe and Lynda finally left, but Shelley lingered. "I've been dying to ask you all evening about that unbelievably beautiful box on your coffee table. Where on earth did you ever find it?"

"I didn't find it. It's mine. It belonged to my grandmother." She hesitated a moment. "I mean, it was originally my grandmother's and then my mother's. She kept it in a heavy metal box she had someone make to protect it, and when our home was burned, it was the only thing left. I usually keep it in my bedroom, but I decided to try it out here."

Shelley ran his finger lightly over the polished rosewood and the ivory inlay. "Who was your mother, Crystal?"

"She was Countess Curt Casalet."

"May I open it?"

"Yes, of course."

He looked at the velvet-covered trays and pockets. "It must have been full of lovely things once. Do you still have them?"

"I'm afraid that most of them went to feed us during the war. I still have an old-fashioned little diamond necklace that my mother wore when she came out. I put it in the bank and I never wear it."

He closed the lid. "You never know when there

might be the right occasion for you to wear it, but in the meantime your box makes the room look very elegant," he said as he put on his coat.

As she undressed, Crystal thought: I must be more careful. I almost slipped twice today. I must keep reminding myself that I'm forty-four years old, that my grandmother is my mother and my father was a Viennese count and not an English college professor.

21

Adam decided to visit the laboratory before the office Monday morning, so he and Eva left the house together.

"You're worried, aren't you, Adam? You've been tossing and turning and muttering in your sleep for the last week. It's not like you."

"I sure want everything to be just right."

"For Crystal, do you mean?"

"That's just like a woman. Hell, no. For us. There are a lot of fortunes going to be made in cosmetics in the next ten years, and I want a big slice of the dough."

In the laboratory he picked up one of the finished and already filled jars of Young Forever and, while turning it in his hand, he studied it closely.

"Would you buy it if you were a customer, Eva?"

"I might and I might not. It's different and that's in its favor. It would all depend on what I'd heard about it. I can tell you one thing sure. Anyone who looks at Crystal's skin and thinks this cream can make hers look like it when she's forty-four or more will be a pushover for the salesgirl!"

"That's what I'm hoping, but do you think she'll come back for a second jar?"

"Why not? It's a good, rich cream, and it even smells good and wholesome. It could work more miracles than we think."

179

When Adam reached the office, Crystal was already there busy at her telephone. When he saw her put down the receiver, he beckoned her into his room.

"Well, Miss Crystal Clear, you're certainly getting around pretty well for a beginner."

"What do you mean?"

"Come on, now. Eva and I just happened to switch on our TV last night, and there you were, riding in one of those open horse-and-buggies with that fancy fellow Shelley. To say nothing of one of the greatest-looking dames I've seen in a long time."

"Oh, yes. That's Lynda Lancaster. She's a model."

"When we're in the chips, I'd like to hire her."

"It would be great, but it may not be possible. She's getting married to a man everybody describes as a multimillionaire, and then she'll retire."

"Retire? Why, she's just a kid."

"I know, but he wants her to be free to travel with him. But she might be able to pose for us between trips."

"That announcer said she was tops. By the way, I want you to make sure that you get yourself announced, too."

"Nobody would have known my name."

"Never mind. Any time it's mentioned it ups your rating with the public. I'm already starting to boost you." He handed her the *Journal-American* that was folded to show Dorothy Kilgallen's column.

She read the paragraph that was outlined in red: "Adam and Eve, who are Eva and Adam Adler to each other at home, think they've discovered an Austrian beauty who discovered the Fountain of Youth. Won't it be fun to meet the girl (who proves their story) at the Astor next week?"

"How did this happen?"

"It didn't just happen, honey. I'm so hell-bent on getting this cream of yours started right that I called up Bob Kriendler at '21' and asked him to recommend somebody to get the right people to the press conference and to help with the party. He suggested an Italian count named Rasponi or an American named

Taplinger. I discovered the Italian count does public relations for Elizabeth Arden, so I called Taplinger, who, by the way, is a great guy. You'll like him."

"I'm glad."

Adam continued. "I know some of the buyers and I know you'll be working on some of the editors, but we need more. It's got to be a smash."

"You're planning to give them samples to take home, of course."

"Sure, that's standard, but I'm planning on full jars, not sample size."

"That's perfect. Wouldn't it be wonderful if you could half wrap each jar in a piece of pale lavender tissue paper and put the whole thing in a tiny shopping bag the same color as the box?"

"You're right, Miss Crystal Clear. A box that size is too big for a girl's handbag and it's not easy to carry. I hope I've got time to arrange the whole thing."

"I think it would be smart if you slipped in a couple of your own Adam and Eve products, a lipstick and a little jar of that cream rouge of yours that I like so much. You know I plan to talk about other things besides my cream as a kind of alibi."

Adam was shouting on the telephone. "I'm not taking any ifs or probablys." When he got his positive answer, he turned back to Crystal. "What do you mean, an alibi?"

"I plan to outline a whole routine for keeping a young look. You know, there are chronic complainers who'll say the cream doesn't work for them and, in letters, we can fall back on their not eating right or exercising enough."

"Do you know what you're going to say?"

"I think so, but I don't believe in writing speeches. I've jotted down my ideas on cards, and I carry them around with me. Sometimes I go over them when I'm riding in a cab."

"Think you can write a press release or would you rather Taplinger's office did it?"

"Why don't I write a rough draft, and they can work with it."

The next morning three typewritten pages from Crystal were on his desk. When he finished them he burst out laughing for the first time in two months. In the beginning, Young Forever had seemed so simple, so amusing and so sure. It had been more expensive to prepare than he had expected, and as his supply of ready cash had diminished, he felt himself becoming more and more tense.

On the morning of the press conference, Adam was the first to arrive at the Rose Room of the Astor. Taplinger had suggested he order lilacs flown in to go with the packaging, and the room already smelled sweet. A bartender was polishing the glasses on a long table.

"I know you're planning on serving bloody marys, Mr. Adler, but I think you should have more vodka and at least two bottles of scotch in reserve," he said.

"Then order some for me at the bar, please, and right away."

Eva and Roy arrived early with as many of the laboratory staff as could be spared from their work. Adam had wanted to make sure there would be no empty seats in the back of the room, but he soon saw that he needn't have been afraid. The room was soon crowded with all the women editors whom he had longed for years to know but had never known how to go about meeting. When he introduced himself to a tall, rangy girl with at least two dozen gold bracelets jangling on one arm, he discovered she was Sally Kirkland of *Life*. They became instant pals, but as he talked to her he was still able to watch Crystal moving from Bettina Ballard and Carol Phillips of *Vogue* to Kathleen Corey, *Harper's Bazaar*'s blond beauty editor, who spoke with the same English accent she did. Some of the others he vaguely recognized were Pat Peterson of the New York *Times*; Priscilla Chapman, who came from the *Herald Tribune*; *Mademoiselle*'s editor, Betsy Blackwell; and both Constance Woodworth and Peggy Shannon from the *Journal-American*.

When the time came, Adam introduced Crystal briefly. He said her creams were based on an old family recipe, which was the reason behind the party. He handed the microphone to Crystal and was relieved that she seemed not at all nervous and began to talk as concisely and as simply as if she were discussing something with him.

She told of coming to Adam Adler's office on a Saturday morning in early August when she was fresh off a plane from Berlin. "When I told him about my cream, he said that the beauty world was already glutted with products made from old family recipes. I was leaving the office feeling very apologetic for bothering him, when I happened to mention my age. He seemed startled, called me back, and when I said I had never used anything else, he changed his mind about producing the cream."

She paused for just a moment and Adam could see that she had the audience in her hands. "Twenty years from now I may be regretting bitterly that I've told you this today. The truth is that I am forty-three and will be turning forty-four in the fall. I'm happy to say I had to show Mr. Adler my passport to prove it."

She was interrupted by a murmuring of "Can you believe it?" and "It doesn't seem possible!" from the audience.

"I want my sample quick," called out Sally Kirkland.

"Me too," said Constance Woodworth.

"You are all going to try my cream," Crystal went on. "And I truly hope it will do for each of you what it has done for me, and what it did for my mother, too. I plan to travel around the country with my cream and to appear in all the stores that buy it in quantity. I will tell my story, just as I've told it to you, and give them my own personal beauty philosophy that's just as important as the product itself. I firmly believe that the woman who complains that a good cream isn't doing anything for her should know that her own private life is probably to blame."

In the rear of the room, Adam could see Bob Taplinger, who was smiling, and when he caught Adam's eyes he raised his hand and spread his fingers up in the victory sign, and nodded.

By this time Crystal was deep in the beauty routine,

and she was warming even more to her subject. "The first part of my program is nutrition," she was saying. "Most of us have read by this time what we ought to eat. Recent scientific experiments have proved that old saying: Eat your breakfast like a king, your luncheon like a lord and dine like a pauper. Anything eaten after four o'clock tends to add weight, to dry and to age the skin. Also a late-night snack is especially aging to the skin."

How the hell did she get all this stuff together, Adam wondered as Crystal went on to explain how to exercise while riding in a taxi or sitting at an office desk.

"The women of this country are known for many things, but not for their beautiful skins, and the woman who has a lovely skin should be especially congratulated, because she has succeeded against great odds . . . even the elements are against her. Moving from one climate to another is detrimental to the skin until it readjusts, and the weather here provides such violent changes that dermatologists call it the most punishing climate in the world."

Adam watched the pencils keep writing, and Crystal herself seemed to pause to let them catch up.

"Now I'm coming to another point," she went on. "I believe that a regular, happy sex life is an important, if not the most important factor in keeping a woman's skin young and beautiful. It's not just a matter of glands, circulation or whatever. It gives her an emotional balance that reflects itself immediately in her skin."

Adam couldn't suppress his wide grin. He saw Sally Kirkland laughing and nudging her neighbor, and most of the rest of the audience was smiling.

"I've just about wound up my story," Crystal said, "but just let me finish with this. I believe that under my beautiful skin is a woman who eats well, sleeps well and likes to make love."

"Wow! You certainly sprung one on me," said Adam under cover of the applause. The room had gone wild. "Give me the details later."

There was no time to talk later that afternoon. He was surrounded by the store buyers who were there and he could see that the press was clustering around Crystal, asking more questions. On the way out, Bettina Ballard of *Vogue* stopped to say goodbye to Adam. "Crystal is a real addition. We're planning an interview in depth with her next week."

He heard Sally Kirkland say, "Welcome to our age group, but you could have knocked me over with your little finger when you told us how old you were."

Early that afternoon the telephone at the office began ringing so persistently that Adam had to go out to a pay station to call the factory to send any two girls to help with the calls. He made an emergency call to the telephone company for three additional lines in the office.

Later that afternoon he became involved in a tug-of-war between Saks Fifth Avenue and Bloomingdale's for Crystal's first personal appearance. Since both buyers had always been friendly but slow on the orders, he enjoyed playing one against the other. Finally, it was decided that Crystal would belong exclusively to Saks Fifth Avenue. After that she would go to Bloomingdale's. Then she would belong to the rest of the world.

"Saks means bigger orders because of all those out-of-town stores," Adam explained.

The next morning when Adam arrived at the office, it was even more of a madhouse than the day before. Both AP and UPI had sent out stories, and buyers from all over the country, most of whom he knew but had been obliged to court hard for orders, were calling.

"Baby, you're going on a tour like you were running for President," he called when he saw Crystal come in. He picked up all the newspapers on his desk and dumped them down on hers. "Good God, you have made every daily. Miss America never had it so good." He stood looking over her shoulder as she read the headlines. "Happy Sex, Healthy Skin," said the *Daily News*. "Sex Called Cosmetic," reported the *Herald*

Tribune. "Sex May Turn Back the Time Clock," was the more cautious statement in the *New York Times.* All the stories carried a smiling photograph of Crystal, and the *Daily Mirror* added a caption, "Guess what? She's forty-four."

"Perhaps I shouldn't have brought in sex. Has it distracted people from buying the cream?"

"Hell no, not a chance. We've got so many orders now that I don't know how I am going to fill them. We're already increasing the factory staff by a third. I used to worry about orders, and now I'm worrying about deliveries." Her telephone rang and he waited while she answered.

"It was Lynda Lancaster. She just can't believe I'm her mother's age, and she jokingly said she's going to treat me with more respect from now on."

"Don't count on that kind of respect from me, babe. And don't forget we're celebrating with dinner at '21' tonight."

"Won't you be tired?"

"If I am, all you have to do is to give me another lecture on the Fountain of Youth."

22

Adam asked Crystal to meet him at '21,' but he intended to arrive at least a half hour early. He felt if he was alone at the bar for a while he could sense more easily what reaction, if any, there was to today's newspaper stories.

At the door Monty welcomed him with "The *Daily News* certainly gave you a big plug this morning, Mr. Adler. Almost a whole page." He was even more effusive when he heard that Crystal Casalet, whose photograph had appeared with the story, would be joining Adam for dinner in a half hour.

"Let me know when she comes. As you could see from the photo, she's a good-looking blond. I'll be waiting at the bar."

Bob Kriendler greeted him with an even broader smile than usual. "Well, I was reading about you in the New York *Times* this morning."

"I didn't know you got as far as the ladies' page."

"You'd be surprised. We never miss them. They're full of helpful hints about friends who lunch and dine here."

Even the bartender said, "Congratulations," as he started mixing Adam's usual evening bracer, scotch on the rocks.

Adam was standing at the end of the bar, about ready for his second, when he saw Crystal come in.

He watched her laughing and talking to Pete and Bob Kriendler as they helped her take off her coat.

She was wearing a black dress that looked like taffeta. It had a big full skirt and a tight little waistline that showed her figure. On top of her head was a tiny black hat that looked about the size of a small cereal bowl. As he went to meet her, he thought: What a girl. Nothing throws her. Not even a day like today.

For the first time Adam was taken to a table in the restaurant's celebrity section just inside the door. Usually, in spite of lavish tips, he had been relegated to the impersonal section behind the first partition.

He and Crystal slid behind the table that the captain had pulled out and sat down together on the banquette.

"It's a celebration, Adam, so I want a champagne cocktail."

"I thought you might, so it's on the way."

He reached for her hand that was lying beside his on the banquette, and when he felt the warm pressure of her fingers against his, he thought: What a fool I've been. I should have suggested drinks at her place. He looked at Crystal's skin that the neckline of her black dress and the pearl necklace didn't hide. "God, baby, you don't know how much I want to kiss you. It's driving me crazy."

"I suppose people sometimes kiss in restaurants."

"Perhaps, but not the way I want to kiss you."

"Then let's talk about business. Today was so exciting. If I'm late tonight, it's because I was getting so many telephone calls. A Bob Bach called and asked if I would be a guest on 'What's My Line?' "

"That's great, but to hell with business tonight." He ordered more cocktails, a sirloin steak for two with french-fried potatoes and a green salad.

"May I have a baked potato instead? I've learned to love them in America."

"Of course."

When the waiter left, he turned to her. "Let's talk about you, Miss Crystal Clear. We've known each other for nine or ten months, but we've never got down to brass tacks, as they say. You could have knocked me over with a feather yesterday when you started talking about sex."

"Really, Adam?"

"Hell yes! I had you figured as a virgin."

"How does a man tell by looking at a girl?"

"There are lots of signs, and I'm not usually wrong. But you certainly fooled me."

"Adam, you shouldn't take me too literally, especially when I'm making a speech."

"Tell me, baby, have you ever been in love?"

"Yes, once."

"Serious?"

"Yes."

"What happened?"

"He was killed. It was a horrible accident."

"Sorry. Does it still hurt, baby?"

"Sometimes, but I made up my mind long ago to try not to think about it."

When their steaks arrived, Adam cut into his quickly and then beckoned to the waiter. "I ordered my steak well done, and so did this lady. This steak looks as if it had been barbecued. It's brown outside and quite raw inside. I don't want a barbecued steak. I want it cooked under a broiler."

"I'm sorry, sir. I was under the impression you said medium rare." When he returned with the plates after ten minutes, he assured Adam that they had been under a broiler and not on a barbecue grill. "We should know by now how you like your steaks, Mr. Adler."

Adam ordered more champagne and they drank it with the steak. "I guess I could easily turn into one of those health nuts," Adam said.

"Oh, I do hope not. It could spoil all the fun of eating."

"Well, one of my brothers had a heart attack last year and it scared me stiff. Since then I've been listening to doctors. I guess you've seen me taking my pulse sometimes at the office."

"No, I haven't, but if I ever do, I'll take your hand the way I did a while ago and tell you to stop worrying and enjoy life."

Adam couldn't remember that he had ever felt happier than when they got up from the table and left the restaurant. He had stopped at the bar and bought a bottle of champagne from the bartender. "Just in case we're still thirsty," he told Crystal as they walked the two blocks up Fifth Avenue with his free arm around her.

Crystal's apartment was much prettier than he expected, but when she wanted to take him down the steps into the living room and show him the blue-and-white china and the plants, he said, "Come on, baby, let's have a drink first, and then the guided tour."

They went into the kitchen but, through a half-open door across the entrance hall, Adam caught a glimpse of Crystal's big bed. "Could I borrow your men's room, please, ma'am?"

"Of course. Go right ahead while I get some ice."

Adam closed the bedroom door behind him. He took off all his clothes, folded them on a chair. When he saw Crystal's blue terrycloth robe hanging on the bathroom door, he put it on. He glanced over at the bed, one of the sexiest he had ever seen, and he had seen quite a few, he thought as he tossed all the little blue-and-white pillows on the floor and turned back the covers.

When he came out Crystal was standing at the sink with her back turned. He came up behind her and put his arms around her. Then he began to caress her breasts, moving his fingers gently.

She didn't turn, but the same quiver went through her body that had tipped him off weeks ago to what might be in store for him. He dropped his arms. "I feel you like it, baby, but tell me you do, because if you don't I'll quit."

"I like it, Adam."

This time he swung her gently around and, though she was still shivering, she burst out laughing. "Oh, Adam, you do look so funny in my robe with those long hairy legs of yours sticking out."

He pulled her close and kissed her. "God, baby, I'm mad about you. It was hell keeping my hands off you while we were sitting there in '21' tonight, dressed up like a couple of store-window dummies. I'll tell you what I'm going to do now."

"What?"

He pressed her even closer. "I'm going to put you down on that bed in there and take off everything you have on, piece by piece. I'm going to make love to every bit of your body as I go along." He half carried her to the bedroom, laid her on the bed, took off her shoes and threw them into the closet.

"Turn over, baby." He pulled down the zipper of her dress and Crystal helped him take it off. He took off her bra, tossed it after the rest of her clothes and, as he lay down beside her, started kissing her as he gently slipped off her stockings.

"Oh, Adam, it doesn't matter if you tear them."

Once free from the nylons, she turned to him eagerly.

After a while he said, "I'm glad you like it, baby, but how about making love to me for a while now?"

It seemed to Adam that it must be morning when he woke up and found the room lights still blazing. Crystal was still sleeping, curled up against his back. He got up and looked down at her, and she must have felt his eyes, for she sat up quickly.

"Oh, Adam, you must go. You can't stay all night. What would the doormen think? And besides, Eva would worry."

He sat down on the bed and began running his hand over her body. "You're more beautiful like this than when you're dressed, and one thing I can swear on the Bible is that you are not forty-four. Your skin is as firm and moist as a child's and you can't tell me there's any cream that can keep it that way."

"Forget what you've said, Adam. No matter what you think, for both our sakes it's better for you to believe I'm in my forties."

"All right, I know you aren't but I get your point. There's one thing I wish you'd tell me."

"I will if I can."

"How did you get that passport?"

"It was my mother's. We look exactly alike and had the same name."

"You're a bright girl, baby." He lay down beside her again.

"Oh, Adam, you've got to go."

"Not a chance, baby. I want you just as much as I did a few hours ago."

It was almost four o'clock when Adam reached home, and Eva was wide awake. "Where on earth have you been, Adam? I was getting terribly worried."

"I told you I was going out with some out-of-town customers, honey. People who are visiting here never get tired. We started at '21' and then went from place to place."

"Was Crystal in the party?"

"Yes, she was. What made you ask?"

"I guess it was because Roy and I thought Crystal did such a good job yesterday. She was fantastic. She deserves some kind of night on the town."

"Well, that she had."

"Did she seem to be having a good time?"

"Yes! Yes! She was having a good time, Eva. As a matter of fact, she was having a hell of a time."

23

"I'm beginning to hate the telephone, Mary Jane,"
Crystal said to the girl that Adam had brought in as a
temporary secretary. She was young and pretty and
full of enthusiasm.

"Oh, I know how you feel, Miss Casalet, but you've
had some pretty exciting calls. We all think you deserve them, too. Mr. Adler came in very early this
morning, and he was swamped with calls before he left
on his ten o'clock appointment. His secretary told me
he has decided to put in the switchboard right away.
Also that he was going to increase the staff, too. Maybe that means I'll have a permanent job."

The telephone rang again, and Crystal heard Mary
Jane confirming her date to be a guest on the Martha
Deane daytime talk show.

Crystal had just put a piece of paper into her typewriter and was jotting down notes for the interview
when the telephone interrupted her again. "It's Diana
Vreeland from *Harper's Bazaar*," said Mary Jane.

Crystal picked up the receiver and Diana Vreeland's
voice boomed over it. "Well, my girl, I hear you put on
quite a show the other day."

"I did my best, Mrs. Vreeland."

"Your best was good enough to send Kathleen
Corey back here with a rave report. My editor-in-
chief, Carmel Snow, wants to meet you. She's leaving
for Paris tomorrow and wonders if you could manage

to pop in here for just a few minutes later this afternoon."

Crystal quickly agreed. She had expected to stay at the office all day answering calls, but she had just enough time, she calculated, to have her hair freshly done and to rush back to her apartment and change into the suit she had worn on Easter Sunday with the short jacket and full pleated skirt. She had heard Shelley say Carmel Snow was the autocratic empress of the fashion world, and to meet her looking less than her best would be disastrous.

At *Harper's Bazaar* she was led past one little cubicle after another, with well-groomed young women in each of them. Diana Vreeland's office was painted the brightest possible lacquer red and Mrs. Vreeland, all in black, was sitting at a red desk and dialing a red telephone when Crystal was ushered in.

"Congratulations! Sit down for a minute while I call in Kathleen Corey. She feels you've brought something fresh to the cosmetics industry, and she wants to include at least a reference to you in our next beauty story."

While they waited for Kathleen to arrive, Mrs. Vreeland went on. "One of my editors will soon be calling you about being photographed in some of the new American sportswear. Nothing to do with cosmetics, but in fashion we're looking for women with that clean soap-and-water look that you have. It's unique, especially at your age. You're quite unbelievable, you know."

"Thank you."

"I can only attribute it to your birth. Oh, Hungarian women! They all seem to lead charmed lives."

"But I'm not Hungarian. My family was Viennese."

Kathleen Corey, a tall, broad-shouldered girl who exuded enthusiasm, led Crystal to Carmel Snow's office. It was larger than Mrs. Vreeland's and furnished with eighteenth-century French furniture covered in pale blue brocade.

Crystal was surprised to find that she was a small woman. Her snow-white short hair waved casually around a sharp little face with pointed chin and up-tilted nose, but a wide mouth that seemed to smile easily. It was an Irish look, Crystal thought instantly.

"I've looked forward to meeting you, my dear," said Mrs. Snow. She spoke in a voice that was unexpectedly deep and throaty and made every word sound significant.

"I'm so glad you were able to arrange it, Mrs. Snow. I know what a busy life you must lead."

"I do, indeed, and I'm off to Paris tomorrow. You know Paris, my dear?"

"Not really. I was there only once when I was a little girl."

"But you come from Europe, where I'm afraid all of our most beautiful, creative things come from. That's why I wanted especially to see you before I left."

"As I've looked through your magazine I've seen many beautiful fashions by American designers. I fell in love with the white Galanos dress in your April issue."

"Oh, yes. The one with the layers of ruffles."

"It was lovely, but then the New York stores seem to be full of good American clothes."

"Beautiful and good, yes, but creative, no. In fashion the great, new ideas still come from Paris and in cosmetics from Switzerland, Austria and at one time Hungary. Perhaps that's why I believe you may become a great force here, if you follow the right path."

"I should like to, but what must I do, Mrs. Snow?"

Mrs. Snow picked up a pair of tortoise-rimmed glasses, leaned over her desk and peered even more closely. "You look incredible for having passed forty, my dear, and that alone will win half the battle for you. You must make certain, though, that you are not a one-season sensation. Enlarge your cosmetics line as fast as you can. I understand that the young man who heads your business is a progressive type."

"We're planning to enlarge but haven't had time."

"You must find time. The cosmetics industry has a tremendous future. It has everything in its favor. European doctors have been doing serious research on the causes of aging, and you should go to Europe and interview some of them."

"I want to, but in the meantime I must go in some direction with my own line here. I haven't analyzed the situation well enough to know in which direction it should be, but it must be in something I believe in."

"How do you take care of your own face, Miss Casalet? Do you wash it?"

"Yes, I do."

"Do you use soap and water?"

"Yes, I've never felt clean enough any other way, but I put on my own cream afterwards to keep my skin from drying."

"There is a Dr. Erno Laszlo in Switzerland whose technique and products are used by all the famous beauties of the world. The Duchess of Windsor has never used anything else. He prescribes an oily cleanser, washed off with a special soap and followed by an application of his special cream."

"Where could I buy these products, Mrs. Snow?"

"So far they're not available in stores, but only on order for the doctor's clients who come to him for private consultations."

"What a pity."

"I feel quite sure that I can at least get a piece of the soap from one of my friends so that you can take it to your laboratory and find out what it's all about. I'll see that my secretary has it delivered to you while I'm away, and I shall look forward to seeing you when I return."

"Thank you, Mrs. Snow."

"And, my dear girl, you have a very unusual first name. Use it. Drop the Casalet. Be known only as Crystal. It's sure to be a winner."

It was almost six o'clock when Crystal left *Harper's Bazaar*, but still daylight. As she walked the few blocks to her apartment, she found herself smiling and humming an old German song that she had learned as a little girl but hadn't thought of for years. For the first time since she had come to New York she felt elated and even confident of her future.

She longed to see Adam and to tell him the new directive that Carmel Snow had given her. She could see the whole concept developing, see the packages and hear herself explaining them.

As she came into the foyer, the doorman handed her a note. "You just missed the gentleman who left this, Miss Casalet." When she reached her apartment, Crystal unfolded the note that was scrawled in pencil on a piece of paper torn from a notebook. "Sorry to miss you, but there'll be lots of tomorrows."

As she stood in front of her little stove, fixing dinner for herself, she could still feel Adam's arms around her and his fingers caressing her. I wish he were here, but I mustn't take this too seriously, she thought.

The next morning, though, she found herself trembling with excitement at the thought of seeing Adam again. He was in his office, but she went on to hers. Ten minutes later he followed her and closed the door.

"It's tough to see you like this, baby, all dressed up in your working clothes. I like you better the other way."

"That's nice."

"Well, I have good news for you. For nine years I've been trying to do business with Wanamaker's in Philadelphia, but no luck. Yesterday they called after they read all the stories. They want me to come down day after tomorrow."

"That's wonderful."

"There's more. They've agreed to buy the whole Adam and Eve line along with Young Forever, and while I'm there I'll see what space they plan to give me and . . ."

"It gets better and better."

"You'll have to come along with me. Wanamaker's wants to meet you. They've suggested a four o'clock appointment on Friday. We'll go down in the afternoon and have dinner with them. It may be that we'll have to stay over and work the next day. Can you stand the thought?"

"I'll try."

"And by the way, where the hell were you yesterday? I hung around here hoping you'd get back and then tried your apartment."

"Oh, Adam, I had the most wonderful afternoon. Carmel Snow sent for me. We had quite a long talk, and she gave me some constructive ideas."

"Shoot."

"You know you've talked about adding more products to my Young Forever line, but I've never figured out what wouldn't be repetitious to your Adam and Eve things. Now I've found something I want to do."

"If it's as smart an idea as the cream, I'm ready to say yes."

"It's just as personal, at least. It's based entirely on the way I treat my own skin, and it would call for only two new products, an oily cleanser and a special soap to wash it off with. The third step in the routine would be an application of my cream. We would still sell the cream separately, of course, but we could also package the three items together as a treatment. I've even thought of a name for it—Crystal Clean. What do you think?"

"I think you've got a brain above my favorite body. The only thing is, I've thought all these years that women were afraid of soap. Eva would no more touch it than she would a snake."

"I've used it all my life, and lots of other women feel the way I do. Have you heard of Dr. Erno Laszlo?"

"Sure, I have. He's the European dermatologist who looks at all the fancy ladies through his microscope. Now that I think of it, he's the guy who sells the soap-and-water treatment."

"Mrs. Snow promised to send me a cake of her soap, and here it is." Crystal tore open the small package on her desk and held out a fat cake of greenish nonperfumed soap.

"God, baby. You must have really charmed Carmel Snow to get all this attention. She's the big name in the fashion world, isn't she?"

"Yes, she is. It was very exciting, but do you think we can do something with the idea?"

"Sounds as if we're on to something good, but why don't you take the soap out to Roy this afternoon and let him have a look at it? Tell him I want to know what it would have to sell for in this country. I bet Laszlo charges plenty for his, but we have to appeal to what is known as the average American housewife."

When Crystal reached the factory and laboratory in Long Island City, she found Eva and Roy just coming back from luncheon in a nearby restaurant. She had never seen Eva looking so pretty and full of life.

"We had a glass of wine at luncheon. I don't know what possessed us, but it was fun," Eva said.

"You've no idea how exciting things have been here since the press conference," Roy said. "We've been jogging along for years, and now, even if we gallop, it looks as if we can't keep up with the orders. It's not just cream, but the publicity has boosted everything else we make, too."

Roy was even more enthusiastic than Adam had been about Crystal Clean. "I think the timing is right. Plenty of women are going to respond to a back-to-soap-and-water campaign."

"Do you really think so, Roy?" Eva asked.

"Yes, dear, I do, especially if it's moderately priced. It shouldn't be too hard, since we don't have to actually try to duplicate the Laszlo soap, but just to produce something that's rich and nourishing." He picked up the soap and said, "I'm going to try it on my own face this minute," and left Crystal and Eva sitting together in his office.

"Roy is very reliable, and he knows what he's talking about. He's been with us since the beginning, and he's such a nice man," Eva said.

When Roy came back he was more convinced than ever. "I think it's a great idea, and the name you've thought of couldn't be better. Even if you're running upstream against the general stream of cosmetic cleansers, I think you can put it over."

"That's so nice to hear, because I'm so sure of the idea myself."

"Tell Adam that I'll give him an estimate tomorrow morning, not on reproducing exactly this soap but on making something else along the same line," Roy said.

Early Friday afternoon Crystal and Adam left the office and took the train to Philadelphia. They were both carrying suitcases, "just in case," as Adam had said.

"I've never been to Philadelphia," Crystal said.

"This is just the start, baby. You'll soon be off on a tour of most of the United States. What kind of traveler are you?"

"Pretty good. I think. I don't get train sick, plane sick or any kind of sick as a rule. I think I'm going to enjoy it."

"Be sure to take along that suit you have on today, it's the same one you were wearing Easter Sunday when I saw you on TV."

"What a memory."

"But you ought to have some new clothes for the tour. Your own dividends won't start rolling in for a while yet and I'm thinking in terms of a much larger expense account. The impression you make is worth a lot to Adam and Eve."

"Oh, thank you, Adam. Shelley can help me find some really good things."

"I wish he could do something about Eva. She doesn't give a damn about clothes. She lives in a smock all day at the lab, so she doesn't buy anything any more, and she's perfectly happy living in our new house in Brooklyn Heights and looking like a Brooklyn housewife."

"Then why don't you move to Manhattan?"

"I'm planning to. I've been talking about it for years but Eva adores the lab and doesn't like to get far away from it."

"She'd soon get accustomed to the city, and love it."

"I don't know about that, but damn it, I want to get my two boys into the best schools I can."

"What are your boys like?"

"Well, Jeff, the older boy, always has his nose in

some book or other, and Alan is just an all-around good-time boy."

"He's your favorite, isn't he?"

"I don't know about that, but he gets along with people, and that's something I admire."

Adam opened the *Wall Street Journal* and began reading the front-page stories, while Crystal roamed through the *Herald Tribune*.

Adam finally put down his paper and said, "Baby, I've been rushed out of my mind for the past few days. Not that I'm complaining, just explaining. I didn't have a chance to tell you that Roy Archer called me with estimates on the soap and the cleanser, and I want to go ahead and produce them both but it's really just a question of where. Our factory isn't big enough to fill the orders that have come in already. I've started looking for an auxiliary place to manufacture, and I think I've found one. Luckily, my bank is willing to loan me the money. It's a big step forward."

"You'll make it."

"You'd better put on your lipstick, baby. We're pulling into Philadelphia and Wanamaker's can mean a lot to us."

"Yes, boss. I'll do my best."

They checked into the Bellevue-Stratford and left their suitcases in their individual rooms, then went directly to the store, where they asked for Mr. Burke.

"What a place! Is this really a store? It looks more like a cathedral!" cried Crystal as Mr. Burke took them on a tour. The center of the store was a huge rotunda that reached to the roof five or six stories above, and the different departments were actually arranged on the balconies that surrounded it. On one side of the main floor was an enormous bronze eagle that brooded over the crowd of shoppers. Crystal noticed many people standing in the shelter of its wings.

"It's a traditional meeting place. Everybody in Philadelphia says, 'Meet me at the Wanamaker eagle,'" Mr. Burke explained.

"Miss Casalet was brought up in Europe. She's just

getting acquainted with American stores," Adam said.

"So I understand. My wife is looking forward to meeting her tonight."

As they went through the cosmetics section, Crystal could see that the established aristocracy, like Arden and Rubinstein, had the best spots, closest to the front door, and that the cleverest climber in the business, Charles Revson, had spotted the advantage of having Revlon set up near the elevator. She also thought that she and Adam were lucky to be there at all.

When they left the store, Adam said, "They're taking us to Bookbinders for dinner. It's not '21', but it's as much fun as anything in Philadelphia. I'll pick you up in your room in a couple of hours."

Crystal took a warm bath and spent some time making up her eyes with a pencil that made them look even larger and bluer. She had learned the trick from one of Adam's demonstrators at Lord & Taylor, and was becoming quite adept at putting on too much and then taking almost all of it off so that it looked natural. She was ready when Adam arrived.

"You look pretty cute for a middle-aged girl. That's a great little hat, but don't forget you're letting your hair grow long."

"When I brushed it tonight, I could already feel that it was longer."

"You did a good job with your lipstick, too, but I think you ought to use something with more pink in it. You'd be better in Delilah than in Scarlett. Just remember next time."

"I have Delilah right here. I didn't think it was quite strong enough to wear with black."

"Try it and see."

She went back to her dressing table, rubbed off the red and applied the pink. She could see in a minute that Delilah was not only more flattering, but more interesting and elegant.

"You have an amazing eye for color," she said when she came back to him.

"It's something I was born with. It used to startle my mother when I was a kid."

The Burkes were waiting for them at Bookbinders. Mrs. Burke was a short little lady and had what Crystal always thought of as a pincushion figure, so soft and round all over that you feel you could stick pins into her and it wouldn't hurt. She was wearing a nondescript crepe dress, but Crystal could instantly see that her pearl necklace was a good one, and that she was wearing a big pear-shaped diamond ring.

"I've been so anxious to meet you, Miss Casalet," she said when they were settled at their table and had all ordered vodka and tonic. "I read the stories about you in all the papers and I said to my husband, 'Bob, we have got to get that girl down here with her cream.' "

"That's nice, Mrs. Burke. It's my first visit to Philadelphia."

"I was born and brought up here. I was born in Chestnut Hill, went to school at Miss Shipley's in Bryn Mawr and now we live near Ardmore. All on the Main Line. It must sound very provincial to you after your fascinating life."

"It sounds very nice." Crystal could hear the two men talking about comparative prices of cosmetic lines, so she decided to give her full attention to Mrs. Burke.

"Looking at you, it's hard to believe that you're forty-four," Mrs. Burke went on. "Is it really true?"

"I'm afraid my passport says so."

"Then we're almost the same age. If your cream has kept you looking the way you do, I must begin using it right away. Do you really think it will help?"

"I do, but you mustn't expect changes overnight. Any cosmetic has to be used regularly and over quite a period of time to be effective. I'm afraid most women tend to be inconstant."

"I know. Sometimes I buy a jar of something, start to use it and then forget. I guess I'm a happy woman. I have four children and a generous husband, but just recently I've begun to realize that I look older than he does though I'm actually three years younger."

Crystal longed to say to her, "Lose twenty pounds, start exercising, take up a sport and, for goodness' sake, travel around the world and forget the Main Line." Instead, she said, "When you use my cream, Mrs. Burke, remember the other important things in your life that must go with it."

"Oh, I do remember. I thought it was so modern of you to speak out the way you did about sex, and so did my friends."

Crystal could feel that the evening was going just as Adam had hoped. When she turned later to talk to Mr. Burke she could hear Adam saying, "I've been looking at you all evening, Mrs. Burke, and I have exactly the perfect shade of lipstick for almost anything you wear."

"How nice. I never seem to get the right color. They all look so different in the stick from the way they look on your face."

"You'll be happy with Cynthia. It's a tawny pink that will go perfectly with your lovely hair and eyes. It will be mailed to you the minute I get back to New York tomorrow."

When they left the Burkes, a definite date had been set for Crystal's personal appearance at the store along with the inauguration of her cream, and she had promised to be in Philadelphia a day earlier for Mrs. Burke's luncheon in her honor. "It's better to have a luncheon than a dinner, because the girls can ask more intimate questions," Mrs. Burke had said.

In the taxi on the way to the hotel, Adam said, "I can see this is the breakthrough. He's giving me a big order and a big ad for you and your cream. Philadelphia isn't known to be too hot on cosmetics, and if this can happen here, it will be even better everywhere else across the country." He bent over and kissed her, and they held hands going through the hotel.

Adam opened the door of her bedroom and followed her in. "You didn't think I was going to let you sleep all alone, did you, baby?"

He pulled her towards him and held her close. "Take off that dress, baby. I'm crazy for you, and thank God there's no doorman for us to worry about. Tonight I'm spending the whole night here."

The next morning they were back at Wanamaker's when the store opened. Adam pointed out the location he and Mr. Burke had decided on last night. It adjoined Helena Rubinstein.

"You'd be surprised, Crystal," Adam said. "It's good to be next to an established name. Women sometimes shop in such a hurry that they think they're buying one name and actually they're buying another. If they're Rubinstein customers, they can't miss seeing us, too."

When Mr. Burke arrived, Crystal decided to leave them and see some of the rest of the store. Mr. Burke was gone when she returned half an hour later and Adam was deep in conversation with a pretty red-haired girl she had already noticed who was selling DuBarry cosmetics in the location they planned to take. Even from a distance, she could see that Adam was giving her his biggest smile, and that the girl, who was leaning both elbows on the counter, looked flushed and happy.

As she watched, Adam put out a finger and touched the girl's cheek. He's telling her what beautiful skin, thought Crystal, and she felt a twinge of pain. It was enough to make her turn and walk away for a minute, but after a few seconds she made herself turn back. It isn't as if I hadn't heard the girls in the office talking about Adam and his buyers, but it suddenly makes me feel cheap, she thought.

As she came up to them Adam was putting away his little black book, in which she was sure he had just written the redhead's telephone number. "This pretty girl has promised to stay just where she is, but to work for a different boss. She's going to leave DuBarry and work as a demonstrator for Adam and Eve."

"That's wonderful," said Crystal, smiling at the girl.

On the train Adam sat back in his parlor-car seat and smiled at her. As he unfolded his *Wall Street Journal*, he said, "We've put over a great deal, baby, but the best part of it all was our night together. I wish we were still back there in the old Bellevue."

He leaned over and put his hand on her knee and she hated herself for feeling it quiver. While he buried himself in the news, she studied him carefully and made a mental list of his assets—the wavy hair just starting to turn gray at the temples, the slate-blue eyes under the heavy black eyebrows and the big mouth that could laugh easily but turn tight and fierce when things weren't going his way. They were all part of Adam's performance that made both men and women feel that he was irresistibly attracted to them.

I know what this man is like, and I'll never let him hurt me, she promised herself, but she wasn't sure it would be easy.

"You're very quiet today, baby. What's on your mind?" Adam asked as he closed his paper.

"I was thinking about business."

"What's bothering you about the business? Let me take care of that."

"What I was thinking is that I'd like to be known just as Crystal. In business I want to forget the Casalet. Did you notice how Mrs. Burke was fumbling over pronouncing it last night, and if she does, millions of others will, too."

"That seems sensible."

"I think the whole line of whatever products you make for me should be known as Crystal. Crystal soap, Crystal cleanser and Crystal cream."

"I get it, and when we make the next set of labels for your cream, they would read, 'Young Forever by Crystal' or 'Crystal's Young Forever.' "

"Exactly, and when I'm introduced to anyone from now on it ought to be 'This is Crystal' instead of 'This is Miss Casalet.' If I make a personal appearance like the one in Philadelphia, it should say in the ads, 'Crystal will be here on such and such a date.' "

"Agreed. I'll speak to Bob Taplinger about the press releases," Adam said.

"It will be much more dramatic to say Crystal the

way they do Garbo. You never think of Garbo having another name."

"Just like Garbo?" he repeated, and a big smile came on his face. "You believe in shooting high, don't you, baby?"

24

Crystal's trip to Philadelphia gave her an idea of what her trips across the country to promote her cream would be like, so she started immediately to plan her clothes. Shelley confided to her that he had signed a contract to design dresses as a side issue but hoped someday to make it his main career. Since summer was the firm's slack season, he volunteered to provide most of her clothes, saying that the resulting publicity would be his payment.

Crystal's closet soon held a long and a short evening dress, two cocktail dresses, a suit, some daytime wool dresses for fall and winter and an all-purpose black coat. Shelley also made her some hats, but all packable. "Hat boxes are a damn nuisance," he said.

The *Herald Tribune*'s summer pages carried a feature headed "Crystal's Cross-Country Clothes" with sketches by Joe Tula of some of the pieces. The text expanded on the collapsible hats, the coordination of the colors and how this could be worn with that, and that with another.

After the story appeared, she was deluged with offers of shoes by Delman, handbags by Judith Leiber and costume jewelry by Kenneth Jay Lane. All in return for a credit line along Crystal's route.

"I know it's difficult to think about in this warm weather but you will need a fur coat next winter. You'll have to manage that for yourself, but whatever you do, get a good one," Shelley advised. "American women are mad for furs. They don't pay much attention to fabrics, but they know their skins and their labels."

One night as Crystal walked home from the office, the front-page headlines of the *Journal-American* caught her eye as she passed a newsstand. She stopped and bought a paper, and when she reached home read the headline story:

EISENHOWER
UNDERGOES SURGERY
President's Operation Lasts One Hour
and Fifty-three Minutes
Thirteen Attend Him

When she turned the page a photograph of Lynda Lancaster was spread over four columns with a small insert of Montgomery Lance. The story was headed "Multimillionaire Real Estate Tycoon Weds Fashion Model." It went on to describe Lance as owning vast Manhattan properties and Lynda as one of New York's top fashion models. The two had been married the day before in a judge's chamber in City Hall, it continued. The bridegroom, who gave his age as sixty-seven, wore a dark business suit and the twenty-eight-year-old bride was in a Dior dress. The couple would be at home in Lance's Rye estate, said to be one of the most luxurious in the East.

I'm so glad for Lynda, thought Crystal. She picked up the telephone and dialed Rye information. The Montgomery Lance number was unlisted, but there was a gatehouse number available, so she tried it.

It was a secretarial-type voice that answered. "This is the gatehouse, but I will communicate with Mrs. Lance and ask her to return the call if you will leave your name and number."

Ten minutes later the telephone rang and Lynda's voice came over the wire.

"God, am I ever glad to hear from you, Crystal. You've got to see this place. You're not going to believe it."

"How wonderful, Lynda. Are you going to keep on modeling?"

"Not me. I've retired, like I told you. Retired at twenty-eight. Can you believe it? All I do is lounge around and eat. You know what an appetite I've got."

"I'm so happy that everything has worked out just right for you, Lynda."

"You can say that again. Listen, we want to see you, but we're leaving tomorrow for Hawaii. We'll be there about four weeks. Monty's right here and he's dying to meet you. Wait just a minute." She came back to the telephone. "Monty says, what about the weekend of August twenty-first? We get back just two days before. We'll send a car for you that morning, which is a Saturday. Be sure to bring a bathing suit."

Crystal liked to sleep late on Saturday mornings, and on August 21 Lynda's call awakened her. "Just wanted to know what kind of car you like best. You can choose between the Rolls and the Mercedes."

"What, no Bentley?"

"We'll try to get one by the next time you come. Monty has just given me a Porsche, but it's a two-seater. We'll toot around in it when you get here."

It was a Mercedes town car with a chauffeur in livery that arrived later in the morning to drive Crystal to Rye.

It was Crystal's first trip to one of the wealthy suburbs. I haven't been in the country for a year. I haven't even seen a real tree, except from a train window or those in Central Park, she thought as they rolled along the parkway and the landscape became greener and greener.

Just then they turned into one of the Rye exits and the chauffeur volunteered, "Mr. Lance's place is on the Sound, miss. We're headed in that direction now and we'll be there in about five minutes."

Soon he pointed out the tall black iron fence that apparently surrounded Montgomery Lance's country home. They turned into a driveway between two stone posts and arrived at the house, which was long and low and framed by enormous trees.

The door was opened by a butler, who took Crystal's suitcase and said, "Mrs. Lance is waiting for you on the terrace, Miss Casalet, or would you rather go to your room first?"

As she went through a long living room, she could see through the open glass doors at its end that the land sloped down to the Sound. The water was close enough for her to hear the waves as they lapped against a stone retaining wall.

Lynda was lying face down on a white wicker chaise lounge, but she jumped up when she heard Crystal's footsteps. "At last! I'm still trying to catch up on the change in time. Hawaii is a hell of a long way out in the Pacific."

After they had kissed each other on the cheek, Crystal said, "You told me you were going to be rich but I didn't know you meant this rich."

"I don't mind telling you I love it. I love the air, the sun and the trees up here, but I'd really like to live in a penthouse right in the middle of New York."

Lynda was wearing a brown two-piece bathing suit that had the smallest bottom piece Crystal had ever seen. It left her belly button as well as almost everything else in plain view. Since Lynda had the bosom of a five-year-old girl, she looked like a sliver of polished wood, Crystal thought.

"Your suntan matches your suit, Lynda."

"Sure it does. I know it makes me look naked but I like it that way. Monty had a fit when he first saw it."

"It makes mine look like Queen Victoria," said Crystal, who, up to then, had thought her one-piece suit, with the top cut like an evening dress, was fairly sensational.

"Borrow one of mine. I've got them in different colors and you can see which one you like."

Crystal went upstairs to her room, which had windows that looked out over the Sound. The maid had unpacked her suitcase, and was just bringing in a bikini like Lynda's. "Mrs. Lance thought you might like this blue one," she said.

When Crystal came downstairs, feeling rather bare

but comfortable, a table had been set on the terrace and Lynda told the butler to bring the luncheon.

"I must say, for a woman of your age, Crystal, you've certainly kept your figure. You look good in that suit."

"It's nice and cool."

"You see, I don't really like wearing clothes. I don't mean that quite the way it sounds, especially since I've made my living wearing them. But at home I like wearing nothing at all. I walk around our own suite naked all the time. The other day I ran downstairs that way to get a magazine and ran right into the butler. Monty was furious."

The luncheon, a big bowl of spaghetti Primavera with fresh green vegetables and another bowl of salad, was brought in, and Lynda explained, "Monty works on Saturdays, too. He has an office down in the gatehouse and he keeps secretaries around the clock. I try to get him to forget work sometimes, but I don't get very far."

After luncheon, still in their bathing suits, they walked to the orchard. Later they swam in the pool and lay on mattresses around the edge to dry.

"How's your love life, Crystal?"

"I don't know that I really have any."

"I read all the things you said about sex. Wow, kid! Then last week I saw the piece in *Business Week*. It had a picture of your new boss."

"Oh, yes, Adam."

"He's damn attractive, and a sexy-looking dish, if I ever saw one." She looked at her watch. "We have a masseur on the place. Monty has already had his massage and now it's time for mine. How about sending him to you later?"

As she lay waiting for the masseur, Crystal's mind roamed idly through the richness of Lynda's life, with the butlers, the greenhouses and no problem except to keep herself combed, manicured, massaged and companionable to a busy millionaire husband. Lynda's question about her love life had been a pinprick in a tender spot. Her calendar was full and almost every evening she came home from work, changed into nonworking clothes and went somewhere with somebody, but she had soon found that most men regarded her as a sort of curiosity. After they had said, "I don't believe you're as old as you say you are," and she had smiled and answered, "But I really am," there was always a slight feeling of distance between them, as if they were looking at each other from opposite ends of a long table. Even the men she had enjoyed most at a dinner party either left her at the door of her apartment or came in for a quick drink and then went away. Hostesses often told her the next day, "Your dinner companion had a marvelous time. He thinks you're simply terrific for your age."

It was a routine she had accepted, because she was locked into her own lie. It was only when she was tired that she had time for self-analysis and admitted to herself that she felt a desperate need to get out of her own trap.

When the masseur had finished giving Crystal a hard rub, and she was lying comfortably between two blankets, she asked him, "Do you have many customers, Serge?"

"Oh, yes. I seldom have a free hour. More and more women are turning to massage."

"What cream were you using on my body?"

"It's a lotion that I buy in large quantities from one of the mass manufacturers. It's only available wholesale, and not packaged for sale in stores."

"It was so delicious. Could you leave me just a bit to rub on my arms and legs before I go to sleep tonight?"

She sat up, reached for a robe and rummaged in her makeup bag, where she found a small bottle. After Serge had filled it and left, she made sure the bottle cap was secure, so that the lotion wouldn't leak out, tossed it into her bag and went downstairs.

At dinner Monty talked about his business. "One of my properties in New York is the block on Sixth Avenue between Fifty-third and Fifty-second streets," he said. "I am planning to build a great international hotel there, the equivalent of the Waldorf-Astoria on the West Side."

"Of course, I know the location. My boss is talking about taking office space at 666 Fifth Avenue. It's just up the street."

"That's a good building. Bob Tishman built it."

"What are you going to call your hotel, Monty?"

"I have a dandy name. I'm pretty proud of myself for thinking of it, and Lynda likes it, too. I'm going to call it the Lancelot."

"You're very clever. It's a perfect name."

"The plans have already been drawn and I hope to start building a year from now. Lynda will have her penthouse on the top."

"It will be a dream, and I can walk to any of the Fifth Avenue stores. The movies are just down the street and so are the theaters, and Monty has promised to put a terrific nightclub right down in the hotel basement, so I can stay out late without any problem," Lynda said.

The next morning Crystal's breakfast was brought to her while she was still in bed. The maid set down the tray and said, "Mrs. Lance wonders if you will come to her bedroom when you're finished. It's the door at the far end of the hall, Miss Casalet."

Lynda wasn't nude, as Crystal expected, but lightly covered by a thin silk robe. "Monty likes you very much. He thinks I should see more of you. I guess he hopes you'll be a good influence."

"He's an interesting man, Lynda."

"He's more like a father to me than anything else, but I love him."

When the Mercedes brought Crystal back to the city and she opened the door of her apartment, Crystal breathed a sigh of relief. Her clean blue-and-white living room and even the little kitchen had never looked so calm and so comfortable.

She could hardly wait to get to the office and hand

Adam the bottle of lotion the masseur had used on her body.

"We have to do this right away, Adam. Everywhere I go the women are always talking about massage, but I never thought of the product masseurs use until I had one this weekend."

"Good idea, baby. I don't see why we can't cut in on what Jergens has been making millions on with hand lotion and advertise ours for the body, too."

"I'd like to add this kind of product to my line. You see, we can promote it for a body rub after bathing, for millions of women who can't afford masseurs. It's a natural."

"I'll send it to the QL, and get it going right away."

The QL was Adam's new secret weapon, a small lab where new products that were just starting could be analyzed overnight and reproduced in a hurry if they seemed to be any good. It was a sure way to keep a beginner with a new idea from getting into the big game, because Adam felt he could always beat them to the store counters with the same thing better produced and widely promoted. He had kept the QL a secret from Roy and Eva. He wasn't sure they would approve, and he was in too much of a hurry to argue.

After the business of the body lotion was settled, Crystal went on to give Adam a play-by-play account of Lynda's new life in Rye. She told him about Monty's plan for the new Lancelot Hotel with their penthouse on top.

"It will be great for the West Side," he said, "but what was that you were telling me about Lynda reading the story in *Business Week?*"

"She thought your picture was attractive."

"Do you think we could get her for an ad next year?"

"I don't know, but I'll try if you still feel that strongly."

From then on Crystal kept track of the tearing down of the old buildings on the site of the new Lancelot-to-be. She imagined it rising tall and white, with forty stories, teeming with international celebrities arriving and departing, and Lynda lying serenely on the top, utterly relaxed on a chaise longue sunbathing in the nude.

25

On November 15 Adam and Eve Cosmetics was scheduled to move to 666 Fifth Avenue, where their neighbors would be Revlon and Estée Lauder.

"I've taken the whole floor," Adam said as he took Crystal up in the elevator for the first time. "We'll use just about half of it now, but if things continue to go along as they have been, we'll be using the whole space within another six months."

When the elevator doors opened, Crystal saw a man painting letters on the wall behind the reception desk.

"Don't say I never take your advice. You always said we should have an apple on the Adam and Eve logo, and it will be there by the end of the day. We'll use it on the stationery, too."

"It's like moving into Buckingham Palace from a gardener's cottage," Crystal said.

"I've done only the basics now. We'll get around to decorating the offices later. In the meantime we have a hell of a lot of work to turn out, and you have a big traveling schedule ahead of you."

It was early in December when Crystal made her first personal appearance in Boston. She spent several days there, arriving each morning at Boston's Bonwit Teller and staying all day, making an hour's speech over a microphone and then talking to the hundreds of women who milled around asking questions. Are you really that old? What can I do about dry skin? Do you dye your hair? What kind of diet do you recommend? Do you recommend wearing a makeup base? Do you really like long fingernails? And much more.

Though Crystal returned to her hotel totally exhausted every night, had dinner served in her room and went to bed early, the sales of her soap, cleanser and cream were far beyond what she and Adam had dared to expect.

Each morning she telephoned an account of the previous day to Adam at his office.

"The store is reordering and they want immediate delivery."

"I know. I've just talked with them."

"And yesterday some of the women started asking for my autograph. There was a regular stampede."

"I know that, too, baby, but I'm not surprised."

At the end of the last day in Boston, as she limped wearily into the hotel, she stopped at the newsstand as usual to get the evening papers. When she reached her room she kicked off her shoes and lay down on the bed. She closed her eyes and was half asleep when the telephone rang. She was tempted not to answer but finally picked up the receiver. It was Adam.

"What are you doing, baby?"

"Nothing. I was half asleep."

"Then wake up and put on that short evening dress that shows a lot of you. We're going out."

"Where are you, Adam?"

"Right here in this hotel, ma'am."

"But what are you doing here?"

"Could I have had a yen to see a middle-aged lady friend?"

"She feels middle-aged right at this minute, but I guess a quick shower will wake her up."

"Take your time. I've got tickets to a new musical playing here prior to Broadway. I'll be around in an hour, but remember to put on that dress."

Crystal jumped up, already feeling completely refreshed. She put on the dress that Adam had asked for. It was black chiffon, shorter than most of her clothes. The halter top left her back bare and the big, swirling black chiffon skirt had a narrow band of sable around it.

"It will be a divine dance dress," Shelley had said.

When Adam arrived, he was carrying a box under his arm. "I heard it was chilly up here, and I brought you a shawl."

She tore open the box, pulled aside the tissue-paper wrappings and pulled out a mink coat. "Oh, Adam, it's so beautiful." She lifted it in her arms. It was very dark and felt like silk in her fingers. "How could you possibly afford it right now?" She felt tears coming to her eyes.

"Luckily, my family's in the fur business, baby, but I picked those skins all by myself."

"I love it."

"I thought you would. It's an early Christmas gift."

"Thank you, Adam, I really love it."

"Say, I got that friend of yours, Shelley, to design it. That fellow's got a lot of talent."

"Yes, I know," Crystal said as she tried on the coat.

"It is cold tonight, but if you don't need it, just drape it on your shoulders, but you'll sure want it when you get to Chicago and Minneapolis."

As they walked out the door Adam said, "Tonight is just your surprise party. No business talk. It's all just for fun."

When Crystal woke the next morning, Adam had already showered and ordered breakfast. He sat down on the edge of her bed and smoothed her hair.

"I love your hair, baby, it's very special."

"Oh, Adam, it was such a perfect night. First the coat and then the play. I think I was singing the song in my sleep."

"Yes, you were. You woke me up once, and I could hear you humming."

"It's going to be a great hit, don't you think?"

"I'm betting it will go on for years on Broadway."

Adam liked a big breakfast. When she sat down at the

table that had been wheeled in and Adam lifted the silver cover from the platter of bacon and eggs, Crystal said, "The only time I'm hungry for breakfast is when I'm with you. When I'm at home, I just settle for a piece of fruit and coffee with toast."

"Don't let your public hear that, baby. They think of you eating this way every morning." Adam poured himself another cup of coffee. "Take your time, baby. I figure it may be a while before we're able to be together like this again."

"Yes, I'll be off across the country."

"I don't know how I'll make out without you, baby."

"Somehow I think you'll survive."

He laughed. "It won't be easy. I'm not kidding you, baby. You're one of a kind and there'll never be anyone like you in my life."

It was early in the afternoon before they finally reached the airport and boarded the plane to New York. Crystal had her new mink coat over her arm, folded with the lining side out. "Oh, do be careful," she said as Adam took it from her and put it in the compartment above them.

"You like it, don't you?"

" 'Like' is a silly word for what I feel."

After the plane took off, Adam turned to her and said, "It's a crazy business we're in, isn't it? It's not even Christmas yet, but I've been sitting here for the past few minutes thinking of next spring and next fall. Before I left, I saw the Easter packaging for your line. It's swell. That mauve of yours comes off great with violets and the Easter egg kind of thing."

"I've got some new ideas for fall, too."

"Save time for the office when I can get it all down on paper."

Adam unfolded his *Wall Street Journal*. Crystal started reading about Young Forever in the Boston *Globe*. Suddenly Adam interrupted her.

"Wasn't that friend of yours married to Montgomery Lance?"

"Yes. Why?"

"Well, he died of a heart attack yesterday."

"I can't believe it."

"It says his estate is estimated at a hundred million."

"Will that all go to Lynda?"

"Not likely. He's got a grown son apparently and grandchildren, but she'll certainly get a big hunk."

Crystal couldn't get through to Lynda by telephone, so she wrote her a letter. The next morning she left for Cleveland and Detroit, and it was almost Christmas when she came back to New York. This time she reached Lynda instantly.

"For God's sake, Crystal, can't you come out here? I haven't got a living soul to talk to except the butler and the chauffeur. The neighbors have always given me the icy shoulder. They like to say I married Monty for his money."

Actually Crystal had been dreading another lone Christmas with no family, no tree and certainly not the wine and cookies she remembered from her childhood in Berlin. Last year she had slept late, pretended to her solicitous landlady that she was joining friends and hidden her loneliness in a dark movie house where she sat through a double feature twice.

This time Lynda sent the Rolls-Royce to drive her to Rye. It was upholstered in red velvet brocade and had a cut-glass vase filled with red carnations attached to one of the window frames.

"Mrs. Lance thought you might be amused with the flowers," said the chauffeur. "She also asked me to tell you that if you press the button on the wood panel just behind me, a portable desk will drop down and you can work on the way out."

Crystal pressed the button. The desk unfolded and she actually took some notes, to the amusement of passing cars.

Lynda had lost her suntan and her hands were icy cold. "Why don't you put on some old pants and a sweater or something? I've got a tree and we're going to trim it. Anything to keep busy."

When Crystal came downstairs, Lynda was on a ladder fastening a star to the top of a ten-foot-tall live spruce in a green wooden box. "They brought it in from one of the terraces. I thought I'd keep it all silver, so hand some of that stuff up to me, will you?"

"I still love Christmas trees."

"So do I. Like I told you, I was underprivileged when I was a kid and I always wanted one like this. Now pass me some of those tin animals."

"At least you're not underprivileged now."

"No, and I never will be. Monty left me a million in cash and the interest on twenty-five million in trust. He always treated me like a kid, so, thank God, he fixed it so somebody will manage it for me and I can't make too much of a fool of myself.

"Now some of that tinsel, please. It's old-fashioned, but I kind of like it."

Lynda asked the butler to set up a table in the library and to serve their dinner there. "It's a lot more cheerful than the dining room. I would have asked Giorgio and some of the boys out, but Monty didn't like designers, and it didn't seem right."

"What are you going to do, Lynda?" asked Crystal later as they sat in front of the open fire, drinking their coffee.

"I don't quite know. It all happened so fast. He came home from golf with a pain in his chest, and I drove him to the hospital for a checkup. They told him he should stay to hear the result of the tests, so we sat there talking and holding hands. After a while he said I must go home for dinner, so I did, and when I got in the door the phone was ringing. He was gone just like that."

"You mustn't stay here, Lynda."

"Don't worry. I'm not. Monty left me the place, but I'm closing it next week but keeping the caretaker, the gardeners and a couple of the staff, so it won't run down."

"Where will you go?"

"Who knows? But I'll tell you one thing. It'll be some place warm and sunny. One of the models I used to know married a rich fellow with a ranch in Texas. That's going to be my first stop. Then I guess I'll be heading further south."

"I'll miss you."

"Don't worry. I'll turn up again," Lynda promised.

26

When Adam came out of his bathroom after showering and shaving, he was humming one of his favorite tunes of the moment, "Just in Time." The smell of freshly made coffee was permeating the apartment, and he knew that his breakfast was ready, but he went on choosing what he was going to wear with great care. Though he had always made it a point to look as dashing as possible, wearing the right clothes had become an important part of his new life. He realized that some of his efforts at being well turned out had, for lack of experience, been somewhat crude. He was now geared to a sober kind of elegance that he had observed on many successful men. As he put on a pale blue shirt and chose what he thought was a subdued navy tie, he was thinking of calling the tailor recommended by a friend he had lunched with the day before.

As he left the bedroom, he looked happily down the long expanse of hall that ended in a drawing room and library with windows on Park Avenue. In the kitchen Eva was standing in front of the stove with her back turned, and the little table in the alcove was set for his breakfast.

"Where's Anna?"

"She left with the boys on their way to school. She wanted to pick up something at Gristede's."

When Eva turned around, he saw there were tears in her eyes. "What the hell's the matter now?" he asked.

Eva brought the coffee pot and filled his cup. "I'm homesick," she said.

"Homesick! You've gotta be out of your head. Here you are in a new Park Avenue apartment that most women would be out of their mind over. You've got your own dressing room that you've talked about for years, and each of the boys has got his own quarters. And they aren't all over us the way they used to be. So just tell me, Eva, what the hell are you homesick for?"

"In Brooklyn Heights I could look out over the water and see the Statue of Liberty. She always made me feel so safe and serene." Eva set down a plate of freshly made muffins in front of him, and he saw that the tears were now rolling down her cheeks.

"Eva, I can't bring the Statue of Liberty uptown, but isn't there anything you can see from these windows that can help you feel safe and serene?"

"No, and I miss my neighbors, too. There was little Truman, and next door that other young writer, Norman Mailer, who used to have such interesting people coming in and going out."

"We might manage to have some interesting people ourselves, Eva, if you would listen to what I keep telling you. I am hiring a decorator, but you will have to take enough time off from the laboratory to oversee everything. I've told you, too, that we've got to hire a butler. Anna can't take care of this whole place alone."

"A butler? Whatever would he do? And these things cost so much money, Adam."

"Let me worry about that, honey. I'm telling you for the last time that things have changed. We're already in the chips, and I have every intention of becoming a whole lot richer. I want a place to live in that I can be proud of."

"You think I'm silly, don't you, Adam?"

"Just hard to understand, like most women. You wanted us to be a success, and now that things are going our way, you seem to hang back."

"I suppose so." Eva had stopped crying.

"Actually, what I really want, Eva, is for you to leave the goddamn lab. With Roy there and the new scientist I'm bringing here from Switzerland, they don't need you there any more."

"Oh, don't say that."

"I mean it. It makes me feel like a fool to have my wife keep working hours and wearing a lab apron all day. I think it's about time for you to start creating a new image. You ought to start making women friends, going out to luncheons and hearing what's going on and what people are talking about. Maybe you could take a course in something, like lots of women do."

"Oh, Adam, I love my work."

"You can damn well learn to love some other kind of work, if you try. Just like you can find something else to look at besides the Statue of Liberty."

"What would I take a course in?"

"How do I know? I just know that I want a hostess when I entertain and not a lab assistant as a wife."

Eva sat down at the table. She was staring at him with wide-open eyes, but Adam felt her mind was somewhere else. "Wake up, Eva. You're already a rich lady. I want you to say that a hundred times a day so you'll get used to the idea. Say it right now and let me hear you."

"I'm a rich lady, but who are we going to entertain?"

"You can help with that. You meet people. You ask them to dinner and when they ask you back you meet other people and you invite them. It's just like a chain letter."

He got up and patted her head. "Come on now, Eva. A life of leisure while I'm slugging it out can't be too bad. When we get our next apartment, I promise you a terrace and a view of all New York. I'll even toss in binoculars so that you can get a glimpse of your favorite statue on a clear day. Fair enough?"

"I'm thinking."

"Then think in terms of quitting your job within the next few months. I'm going to talk to Roy about it right away."

When he was ready to leave the apartment, he saw that she was still sitting at the table, drinking another cup of coffee. He stopped in the doorway just long enough to say, "Cheer up, honey. We're going places and from now on it's going to be a real sleigh ride."

A year ago it had been one of the happiest days Adam could remember when he closed the doors for the last time on the Brooklyn Heights house. It had been pleasant for a while but he soon found it soporific and boring, probably all right for the intellectuals, he thought, but not for him.

He prided himself on being right on target. When he had signed the lease for a whole floor at 666 Fifth Avenue, he had boasted that within six months he would be able to occupy the whole place, and it had been a triumphant day when he was able to keep his word.

Adam was genuinely in love with New York. He was constantly stimulated by the background noise of the city, made up of subways and millions of motors, pierced constantly by the screaming sirens. He wasn't bothered by all the tense, anxious faces he saw on the streets around him. They even provided him with a certain satisfaction, that he might have been one of them, if somehow he hadn't learned the trick of success.

He was pleased that Jeffrey and Alan took to New York just as he did. They had responded to Dalton School. Though Jeffrey held back a little, Alan quickly made friends. They had started tennis lessons, were enrolled in ice-skating lessons and, at Crystal's suggestion, were admitted to dancing classes that would lead later to the right debutante parties. All the things I never had myself, Adam thought.

He was thinking of Crystal when he went into his office, which he never entered without a surge of pride. One of his recent extravagances had been a huge, antique English table desk on which stood a silver-framed photograph of Eva with the two boys. Picking up his inter-office telephone, he said, "Please check to see if Miss Crystal is in, and ask her to see me as soon as possible." Crystal was something of a problem, he thought as he waited for her to arrive. She was one of the most exciting girls he had ever made love to, but, in a way, she was almost too stimulating. She expected more continuity and attention than he was able to give. Somehow casual contacts were easier, and he had had so many of those that the quality of the response was no longer all that important. What really mattered was the variety and his ingenuity at becoming the conqueror.

When she came in a few minutes later, he was intrigued all over again by the color of her skin and the shape he could see under the shapeless little dress, almost knee high, that she was wearing.

"What's that thing you've got on? It looks like a bag with your head and legs coming out of the top and bottom."

"You don't keep up with the news, Adam. Haven't you read about the sack dress? It's the latest look from Paris."

"On you I think it's pretty cute. I like having to feel for you under all this stuff." He ran his hand slowly and gently up and down her body.

"That's nice, but not if we're going to talk business. I can't concentrate."

"All right, sweetheart, but I need you. Come back when we've both finished our work tonight and we'll have dinner together."

She sat down in a chair across from him at the desk. "What's on your mind, Adam?"

"Besides you, advertising in general and ours in particular."

"Yes?"

"You're one of the few people I can think out loud with. We have a pretty large margin of profit for promotion, and I plan to put it right now into a better advertising campaign."

"I couldn't agree more."

"It's terribly important to know a long time ahead what the other fellow is going to do. Revlon has been such a whiz at it that they already have two lawsuits on their hands. Hazel Bishop is suing them for wiretapping their phones and Coty is suing them for stealing their advertising ideas."

"What are you going to do?"

"At the moment I'm not going to hire spies to steal copy ideas or tap wires. I just want to make a good informed guess at what shade of lipstick to bring out six months from now, and you must help me."

"Just how do you want me to help?"

"The whole clue is fashion. You're going to case the fashion industry to find out as much as possible what women are going to wear next year. I don't want the word to come from your expensive friend Shelley. I want to know what color and fabrics the cheap guys are going to use, too. They've got it all figured out by this time, and if you can come back to me with a report in three weeks, say, we can be way ahead of the game. Our whole campaign has to be ready at least four or five months ahead, for next fall."

"I'm sure I can get that for us easily. I'll enjoy doing it, and it shouldn't take three weeks."

There was a glint in Adam's eyes. "What's your rough guess now?"

"I think they'll stop calling it the sack, but we'll all be wearing short, unbelted dresses. The middle of a girl won't matter as much as her legs and her face. It should be a great time for eye makeup and lipsticks."

"I'm willing to bet my shirt on it, not only in magazines but on TV."

"You're going to try TV commercials?"

"Two agencies have come to me with ideas for national network programs. What tempts me is that everything broke for Revlon after that quiz program of theirs. I'm a good gambler, and if I'm going to lay my money for something, I'd rather do it on something big like a national program than a commercial like lots of others do."

"Adam, that's terrific, but what kind of program ideas have they brought you?"

"I've been stalling up to now because they all seem to be variations of the quiz idea. They're good but they haven't bowled me over. I want to get something that will make both men and women look and talk."

"You're so right. The quiz has had it. Why couldn't it be something involving beauty? After all, that's our subject."

"What do you mean?"

"This is right off the top of my head, but when you were talking, I began seeing the Miss America contest in my mind. I know it's terribly corny but people just love it. I even find myself getting involved every time I see it. I was wondering if we couldn't do it on a more personal scale."

"I think you've got something, baby."

"I think I have, too. I can see how we could infiltrate it with our makeup all through and have just enough sensible beauty talk to intrigue the women and not bore the men."

"I'll take the idea to an agency tomorrow."

"Do you have an agency you absolutely believe in? I'm just asking because I know such an interesting girl. When I was doing Ohio last year, we met in a Youngstown department store. She told me then that she was coming to New York, and she did. I've had lunch with her once, and I hear through the Madison Avenue grapevine that she's a sensation."

"On your recommendation, I'll call her."

"Her name is Mary Wells. She's with Doyle Dane Bernbach and she's very smart but soft-sell."

After Crystal left his office, Adam sat quietly visualizing Crystal's idea. From her first mention he had known it would be exactly right. The personal appeal of young, pretty girls would sell makeup like nothing he had ever paid for. Besides, he liked the idea of becoming a kind of patron of beauty, a kind of TV version of Florenz Ziegfeld.

"American Beauty" made its debut on CBS prime time the first Sunday night of the following October. The contestants had been picked by stores across the country, and the original group was scheduled to narrow down through four successive Sundays by means of beauty contests, quizzes and personal interviews until the final American beauty was selected. The grand prize was a year's contract to model exclusively for Adam and Eve Cosmetics. Adam had managed to round up mink coats, automobiles and trips to popular resorts to make the runners-up happy and keep the interest going.

"Eva, I want you to take off what you're putting on. I want you to wear your best, and your best is that short sequin thing from Norell that I just bought you."

"I thought it would look overdressed at just a TV show."

"It's not just a TV show. It's our own show and it's a social occasion. Besides, I want you to give those girls some competition. You've still got a good shape and that dress shows it."

He waited until he saw Eva take the sequin dress out of her closet and then went on to his sons' rooms. Jeffrey was lounging in a chair reading a book, already meticulously turned out in a navy blazer, the right shirt and tie and slacks. He was an elegant boy, Adam thought. His face was a fined-down version of his father's, but his hands, unlike Adam's, were long and slim. He had often wondered what ancestor was responsible for Jeffrey's instinct for the best of everything.

"You look all right, Jeff."

"You said it was going to be a big night, Dad."

"It will be. It's costing me a hell of a lot but you're going to see some of the most beautiful girls in the country."

He closed the door and went on to his younger son's

room. Alan, still in a dirty turtleneck sweater, was watching TV and hardly looked up until his father said, "Son, I want you to start getting dressed. Take a shower, wash your face and put on your best suit. This is a party."

"Oh, Dad, I gotta watch the end of this World Series game first."

"Not tonight. Do as I say or the TV set comes right out of your room." Adam strolled across the room and turned it off.

"If this show is any good, can I ask some of the kids from school to come with us next time?"

"Yes, I'll arrange it sometime. It's a good idea."

Before they left the apartment, Adam had sent Eva back to their bedroom twice, once to put on more eye shadow and the second time to spray her hair. He had objected to Alan's shirt, chosen another and retied his necktie, but on the whole he was well pleased with his family and the picture they presented as they entered the glass-walled sponsor's box in the CBS theater. Eva's glitter, he felt, was the perfect complement to his black suit and silver necktie.

"Where's Crystal? I certainly thought she'd be here, since she's been so keen on the idea," Eva asked, looking around and smiling at Wally Nelson and his wife and other executives who were huddled in the back of the box.

"Out on tour somewhere. I can't remember what city, but she'll have to be back for the final show, when they choose the winner."

The theater was filling rapidly, and in the crowd Adam was able to spot Sophie and Adam Gimble, Nena and Andrew Goodman, and some of the other important retail executives in town, as well as his buyer friends, many of whom had flown in from stores all over the country that had candidates in the contest.

Adam was feeling no real doubt that the show would be a success. Mary Wells and the agency had assured him that it would be. He had spent most of the past week since the girls arrived attending rehearsals, picking out his favorites and getting acquainted with a few of them. He looked forward to the succeeding weeks, when they would be fewer and he could give them more personal attention and even show them the town.

"They're all sweet kids, full of fun and are they ever built," Adam told Eva. "They seem to feel I'm kind of a rich uncle."

He turned around as a man came into the box and sat down directly behind them. "Are you part of the Adam and Eve organization or of CBS?" he asked, looking at the brown tweed jacket and the camel-color sweater.

"Yes, Mr. Adler. I'm the associate producer."

"If you have any respect for your work, why the hell do you turn up in that getup. Brown is the color of you know what. Why don't you get out of here and put on some decent clothes!"

Eva and Jeffrey were quiet, but Alan burst out laughing. "Well, Dad, you certainly told him."

The red light signaled that they were on the air. Though he watched it critically, Adam felt that it managed to combine the best aspects of beauty and quiz shows. They paraded in bathing suits and reappeared in sweaters and skirts to answer quiz questions. Most of them came through fresh, natural and bright, and Adam was glad that there were adequate prizes for all the losers.

The next morning the reviews were better than he had hoped for. The critics even praised the commercials for not having the pretentious hoopla typical of cosmetics presentations.

Crystal telephoned from Atlanta. "The show was great and everybody at Rich's is ecstatic that their girl is still in the running."

"She's a natural for the camera, and nothing throws her. It wouldn't surprise me if she made it to the end."

"How old is she?"

"Nineteen, and I'm thinking of hiring her, even if she doesn't turn out to be the winner."

"I'll tell everybody here. They'll be pleased," Crystal said. She had held back as long as she could from making a personal appearance in Atlanta, but by now she had visited almost every other major city and Rich's had become insistent about having her. The first day had been harmless, since, in a sense, the store was just like other stores, except for the southern voices. She had been sure that Mat's mother would never be part of the kind of crowd that milled around her, begging her to help them look young again.

The meeting of the Historical Society might be different. As her chauffeured car took her through the northwest section of the city, she looked at the big houses, set back from the roads and sheltered by big trees that hadn't turned yellow yet, and rolling green lawns that looked as if they had been designed and tended by the same person. If I had married Mat, I might have been driving my own car to this meeting as one of the members, she thought.

The car turned off West Paces Ferry Road into a long private driveway lined on both sides with trees. At the end she could catch a glimpse of the pink Italian-like house that she supposed belonged to her hostess, Mrs. James Robinson. Inside, the rooms were full of Venetian furniture and the soft chatter of ladies.

Crystal took a glass of sherry from the butler's silver tray and after she drank it began to feel a little better. She assured Mrs. Robinson and her neighbor Katherine Riley and dozens of other guests that, yes, she was really pushing fifty. For the first time since she had come to New York she hated the deception and didn't find it amusing as she usually did.

Fortunately, Emma Lou Perkins' success on the Adam and Eve "American Beauty" show on TV the night before was creating as much excitement as Crystal's age. Everybody in the room knew Emma Lou's mother or aunt, or had a daughter who had gone to school with her at Westminster.

It was almost at the end of the party, while chatting with Louise Allen, the mayor's wife, that she was introduced to a lady she would have recognized without an introduction. It was Mrs. Lanier.

"It's so nice to have you visiting us here. I'm sure very few women have had such a successful career as yours. I have no special reason for wanting to rejuvenate my face and no rainbow hopes of accomplishing it if I did, but I admire your ambition and spunk."

They talked a few minutes about Emma Lou and the contest, and then Mrs. Lanier said, "I know you must be exhausted, my dear, but I am having a few friends for tea this afternoon and, if you're not too tired, I would love to have you at my home."

As she took Mrs. Lanier's card, she almost said, "I know the address."

It was all just as Mat had described it to her, the gateposts, the dogs, the old-fashioned porte cochere and the big rooms with polished floors, the walls hung with family portraits and long mirrors in gold frames that reflected the English country house type of furniture.

"I'm afraid you'll find all this very old-fashioned compared with New York cocktail parties," Mrs. Lanier said. She led Crystal into the dining room, where a long table was spread with an embroidered, lace-edged cloth. A dozen or so pink-and-white porcelain plates held tiny sandwiches, different kinds of cookies and candies, and coffee and tea were being served from tall, polished silver urns at either end.

"This is my daughter Sue," said Mrs. Lanier, guiding her to the urn, where an outdoorsy jolly-looking girl was dispensing the tea.

"Mother has read that you're European and she thinks all Europeans prefer tea," Sue said. "How do you like Atlanta?"

"It's very beautiful, and it looks very rich."

"Oh, well, it's not poor but it's cozy and fun to live in, and I don't think I would trade it for New York or any place else."

They talked for a minute about Emma Lou, and Crystal told her that she had talked with New York that morning and heard that Emma Lou had a good chance of coming off with one of the prizes.

As soon as Sue found another customer for the tea urn, Crystal left the dining room and wandered back to the big living room to look out the windows. She wanted to see what Mat used to see when he woke up every morning. Suddenly she came face to face with his photograph, framed in silver and standing beside a lamp on a small mahogany table. He was wearing his uniform and his happiest, most confident smile. It was exactly the way he looked the last time she saw him.

She heard Mrs. Lanier's voice behind her. "That's a photograph of my son Mathew. He was killed in an accident after the war was over."

Crystal was trembling, but she pulled herself together and managed to say, "He looks like a wonderful person."

"He was, and he was just about to be married when the accident happened. In the interview with you in the Atlanta Constitution this morning, it said that you were born in Berlin. By any chance, did you ever know a girl named Chrissy Schultz?"

"Chrissy Schultz," Crystal repeated the name. It seemed like a century since she had heard it. "Chrissy Schultz. No, I don't believe so."

"Of course, Berlin is a large city, but I've always hoped to find her. She and Mathew were planning to be married here and she wrote me such a sweet letter, but there was no return address. We did everything to find her. My husband even flew to Berlin and tried to investigate, but there was never a trace. We wanted so much to have her come here and live with us."

Crystal managed somehow to find her way out to her car and then the tears came. On the way back to the hotel she had the driver stop at a florist shop, and she sent a big white azalea in a green tub to Mrs. Lanier with her card, saying, "Thank you so much for the tea party that was so much more charming than cocktails in New York." I couldn't bear to send her anything that would die, she thought.

When she reached her hotel room, Crystal called the cosmetics buyer at Rich's and said she had developed a bad cold and couldn't come to dinner. She undressed quickly, took an aspirin tablet and went to bed. It was still dark when she awakened the next morning, but she packed quickly, ordered breakfast and went to the airport to wait there for her plane to New York.

It was only after the plane was in the air and on its way that she could bring herself to look back at Atlanta and to think what her life would have been like if Mat's father had been able to find her in Berlin. Everything would have been easy and polite, she thought. It would have been almost like the early part of my grandmother's life. No lies, no undercover love affairs, no struggling to get somewhere, everything just handed to you by a butler on a silver platter. With Mat it would have been right, but without him it wouldn't have worked. . . . Maybe I'm too restless or maybe, like Grandmother, I'm at my best when everything seems bad. Perhaps, in the end, I might even have disappointed Mat. He was so easygoing and would have been happy forever living on his plantation. But maybe with everything I might have grown restless and wanted to do it myself. . . . After Mrs. Lanier's tea party, though, she knew she would never be eager again to see Adam.

During the next few days, Crystal was grateful that Adam seemed no more anxious to see her than she was to see him. There were no telephone calls and no notes at her desk. She spent several peaceful evenings at home and one night had dinner with Shelley.

One of the first things she did was to call Emma Lou Perkins, who was now one of the twenty-four girls rehearsing for the second go-round of "American Beauty." She asked her to luncheon at Sardi's to tell her about her hundreds of Atlanta fans.

Emma Lou was a real peaches-and-cream southern belle. She was small but shapely, a miniature Venus. Her hair fell to her shoulders in natural curls and her eyes were the color of aquamarines. "Oh, Miss Crystal, it's so sweet of you to ask me here with all these celebrities. I'm so sorry to be late, but I'm having such a terrific, wonderful time that half the time I just don't know what I'm doing," she bubbled.

"I heard from Mr. Adler that you did very well in the first contest. Mr. Adler, you know, is the president of the sponsoring company."

"Oh, yes, I do know Mr. Adler. He's been very nice to all of us, but especially to me. I don't know why. I guess he likes everything southern; biscuits and grits and especially girls, or at least that's what he says."

"I'm sure he does, and we all do, Emma Lou."

Over the luncheon, Emma Lou went on. "I've read all about you, Miss Crystal, and seeing I know your age—and it's unbelievable—I feel like I can confide in you. I think Mr. Adler is real attractive, but I hear he's a married man. Is that true or false?"

"Yes, it's true, and he has two sons."

"Well, thank you, Miss Crystal. Right at this point I don't want to get myself mixed up with a married man, if you know what I mean."

"Of course I do, and I think you're a very smart little girl."

The reaction to "American Beauty" across the country was overwhelming. Though the stores had been thoroughly informed of the program, most of them were totally unprepared for what was at least a 75 percent and sometimes a 100 percent increase in sales of all Adam and Eve and Young Forever Products, and a complete sellout of anything that appeared in the commercials. Marshall Field alone was holding three hundred orders for lipsticks that they couldn't fill.

Even with her office door closed, Crystal could hear Adam pounding his desk and shouting, "Get off your fat asses, you damn fools, and start producing, will you?" There was a long silence and she imagined that one of the factory managers was protesting at the other end.

Crystal saw the second "American Beauty" show from the sponsor's box with Adam and Eva and the two boys. Emma Lou was still holding her own.

"That little southern blond really has the stuff," Adam said.

"She's adorable," Eva agreed, and Alan chimed in with "Gee, Dad, she's my idea of pretty."

Emma Lou was again chosen by the judges as the group was narrowed down to twelve girls in the third show, which Crystal watched in the bedroom of her Kansas City hotel.

Crystal was glad she was going to be in New York for the final night. All of her friends seemed to have a favorite girl. Shelley was rooting for the girl from Nashville who sang her own folk songs and played her own guitar. "She's kind of tough and today," he said.

Diana Vreeland called to say, "That contest of yours has class, and I mean real class. You can't get anyone out to dinner on Sunday night, unless you can promise them a comfortable chair in front of a big TV set." Diana's favorite was long-haired, long-legged Allison MacKay from California. "But I doubt if anyone can put down that little southern charmer. The men are all spellbound by her."

Crystal felt that Emma Lou's strongest competitor might be Janet Brooks from Boston, a blue-eyed brunette with a Madonna-like face and a high rating in the IQ test the girls were given in the second show.

Though Crystal called Emma Lou, she didn't get through to her until the weekend. "Oh, Miss Crystal, I'm so nervous. We know we're going to be asked to tell our life stories, and I just don't have all that much to say. That Janet Brooks is writing hers on a typewriter, and I'll bet it will be fascinating, because she kind of is."

"Just be natural, Emma Lou, and don't be afraid to admit that you're happy. Tell what you like to do besides going to parties."

"I'm not much of a tennis player and I'd rather just float in somebody's pool than splash up and down the length of the pool ten times or more. I guess the only thing I do especially well is cooking, but I don't think the folks who are listening to this program would be much interested in that, do you, Miss Crystal?"

"I think they might be very interested if you tell how it all started and what you can do."

"Oh, I can do almost anything. I've read some of the French cookbooks, but I still like southern cooking better."

Since Adam was to appear on camera the fourth and final night of the first contest to fill the winner's arms with long-stemmed American Beauty roses, and Crystal was to present certificates to the five runners-up, they both appeared early for backstage makeup and, instead of going to the box, had been assigned front-row seats so they could reach the stage easily.

When the girls made their first appearance to be rated on their choice of evening dresses, Crystal held her breath. She was afraid that Emma Lou might decide to wear something too sophisticated, but she needn't have worried. Though several of the girls appeared in the long, white dresses Crystal thought they must have worn at their high school graduation, Emma Lou, smiling and completely at ease, came out looking like a blond Scarlett O'Hara. She was in the palest seafoam green. Her bare shoulders were framed in a ruffled top and the dress was nipped in at the waist and billowed out again in yards of lace and ruffles that were held in place by lace-edged crinoline petticoats that showed when she came down the few short steps.

Each girl was allowed three minutes to talk about her life. It was one of the most genuine programs she had ever listened to, Crystal thought. As Allison Mac-Kay discussed the discipline she forced herself into to succeed in athletics and Janet Brooks talked seriously about race prejudice, she found herself wishing that all the girls could win.

When Emma Lou reached the microphone she began: "I guess I figured out pretty early that I didn't have a talent like all my wonderful new friends that I'm competing with here have, so I just got myself out to Westminster and signed up for a special home economics class. I just took naturally to cooking, and after I saw my first soufflé puffing up, there was no stopping me. My family just couldn't keep me out of the kitchen and they didn't try too hard. Almost everything came out right, except a few messes at first. I don't like to brag, but they do say I make the best corn bread and the best corn muffins in Atlanta. I hope none of those people who make the prepared mixes are listening to this program, because I always start from scratch with fresh-ground cornmeal and everything else fresh. I can also make a honey-baked ham that's just as good as the professionals'."

"Good God, this kid is making me ravenously hungry," whispered Adam.

"You and me and millions across the country," Crystal whispered back.

Emma Lou was winding up with "So maybe if I don't have a great big serious talent, I can make some nice man happy."

"She'd better hire a secretary out of the prize money she's going to win. She'll get fan mail by the bushel," said Adam as the applause began to die down.

Ted Straeter's band had started to play while the judges, who were the editors of *Life*, *Look*, *Esquire*, *Glamour*, and *Mademoiselle*, went into a final huddle. It didn't take long.

The band stopped the song it was playing and struck up the program's theme song, "The Most Beautiful Girl in the World." The master of ceremonies started to sing: "The most beautiful girl in the world isn't Garbo, isn't Dietrich . . ." He paused dramatically and then went on: "She's Emma Lou Perkins of Atlanta, Georgia."

Pandemonium broke out on the stage. Adam and Crystal went forward, and Adam filled Emma Lou's arms with dozens of red roses and Crystal presented the runners-up with checks for ten thousand dollars. After that the contestants all kissed each other, and the first of Adam and Eve's "American Beauty" programs faded out on the screen.

Towards the end of the week, Emma Lou telephoned. "Oh, Miss Crystal, I've just got to see you."

"Of course. Come to my office anytime."

"I'd rather not come to the office. It's about something very private and personal."

"Then come to my apartment late this afternoon. If I'm held up, my maid, Grace Johnson, will let you in and give you a cup of tea."

Emma Lou was already sitting on the couch in her living room when Crystal arrived.

"I just had to talk to somebody, Miss Crystal. I have decided to give up the prize money and the year's contract and go back to Atlanta. I started packing up this afternoon, but I thought I should tell you, and not just disappear."

"What's this all about?"

"The truth is that I'm just madly in love with Mr. Adler. I've liked boys before, but nothing like this. I know it's not right, though, and I just can't go on."

"How far has it gone, Emma Lou?"

"He spent the night with me in my hotel room. You see, it happened this way. Monday night he called me and asked me to dinner. He said it would be sort of a celebration."

"At '21'?"

"How did you ever know? We celebrated with champagne cocktails and then he brought me home to my room. I guess he could see I was crazy about him and he kept staying and staying. It was like we couldn't get enough of each other, and the next thing I knew it was morning."

"Then why do you want to leave?"

"Because he came again yesterday afternoon and it was the same way all over again. I know it could never work out, and besides I might get pregnant. It looks as if the only thing I can do is to leave."

"Don't go, Emma Lou. All of us who watched you in the contest say that you have real talent that you can turn into a modeling career, or acting on the stage or the movies. It would be disastrous for you both if this story ever even reached the whisper stage, and Mr. Adler will be the first to understand it when I point it out to him."

"Then you will talk to him?"

"Of course I will. Unpack your suitcase tonight and plan to stay."

"And you are sure that Mr. Adler's feeling for me had nothing to do with my winning the prize? I wouldn't want to feel there was any kind of obligation."

"I promise you, dear, that Mr. Adler had no influence over the judges. Enjoy your year's contract and make the most of it. We'll see each other when you come for the photography session with Avedon. Then at the end of the year, if you and Mr. Adler still feel about each other the way you do this week, it will be nobody's business but your own."

The next morning Crystal went directly to Adam's office. He was sitting behind his desk, which was piled with clippings from papers across the country. Many of them carried photographs of Emma Lou looking up at him adoringly as he filled her arms with the red roses.

"Adam, you are a real bastard."

He smiled. "I know that, and I always thought you did, too."

"You're also a fool."

"That's different. Why?"

"Because you are willing to jeopardize your business success and your own private life for a silly flirt with a little nineteen-year-old girl."

"Somebody's been blabbing."

"Not necessarily. But what I know is easy for almost anyone else to find out. There are hotel clerks, chambermaids and best friends, you know."

"Where did you get this?"

"That's not important. Have affairs with anyone you feel like, Adam, except the girls on your own TV program. Don't you realize you can ruin your entire business and your own reputation forever, if you insist on going on this way?"

He didn't answer.

She went out and closed the door.

27

The "American Beauty" program raised Adam and Eve's sales, profits and consumer awareness so dramatically as to put it way ahead of most of its competitors.

Sales, which had been growing from 15 to 20 percent in the past two years since Crystal's Young Forever had been introduced, shot up 50 percent. Profits tripled.

Adam's own prestige sky rocketed. He was asked to be on the board of Mount Sinai Hospital, and investment bankers started to pursue him about going public.

One morning about six months later he called Crystal into his office. "I've got some news for you."

"Good, I hope."

"How would you like to become an officer, say a president, in a public corporation?"

She looked startled. "What is this?"

"I've been talking with Dillon, Morgan and Giles, who my friends on Wall Street tell me are the most prestigious banking firm in the country. They want to take us public, and I like the idea. You know Revlon did it five years ago, and the Ford Motor Company followed right afterwards."

"It's a big step, Adam."

"I'm aware of that, but I think we're ready."

"What happens next when you go public?"

"You'll be a very rich lady in a damn short time. I

intend to give you ten thousand shares in advance of the public offering. It should be a nest egg of at least a million in your old age. You'll become president of the company and I'll be the new chairman of the board."

"I can't quite believe it."

The Adam and Eve stock went public six months later, on November 9th at 10:30 a.m. with a million shares. Half of them were sold for the company. The other half Adam kept for himself. It started at 15 and there was a huge demand. Before the end of the same day the stock was trading for between 16 and 17. A week later it was trading at 17½ making it one of the most successful initial public offerings of the year.

One evening after a happy session of congratulations at the King Cole Bar, Adam arrived at their Park Avenue apartment looking even more flushed and triumphant than usual. He started calling Eva as he opened the front door, and she came quietly out of the dark library.

"Why the hell are you sitting in a dark room? Why don't you turn on the lights?"

"I was just resting."

"And what have you done to get yourself so tired?"

"I drove out to the factory. It was the annual pre-Christmas party for the employees. It was sweet. Crystal came."

"Eva, do me a favor. You've got to forget the factory and the lab. I've got news that will help you stop moping."

"Tell me."

"We're going to splurge and go to Florida, you and me and the two kids. I called the Eldorado in Miami Beach and asked for the Presidential Suite. When I told them I'd be staying through the holidays, they took it away from somebody else and gave it to me."

"I'd really enjoy some sunshine."

"Okay. Get yourself some new clothes and some cute bathing suits, and we'll start the day after tomorrow, the minute the boys are sprung from Dalton."

Like the hotel's foyer, the Presidential Suite at the Eldorado was a vast sea of white marble. The long living room had the master bedroom at one end and separate bedrooms for the boys at the other. There was a glassed-in garden room with a dining table and chairs painted white with a gold stripe. In the center of the dining table, oranges, grapefruit and bananas seemed to be piled so high that they looked ready to spill out of the basket with the management's card tied to the handle. The flower arrangement on the glass-top coffee table in the living room came from the manager of Burdine's department store.

I used to send flowers to that guy when I came to Florida, and now he's sending them to me, thought Adam. It was a delightful thought.

"Get ready. We're going to dress for dinner and go downstairs," Adam ordered. "It'll be breakfast in our rooms, luncheon around the pool, but always dinner in the dining room."

"Do we always dress up and eat with you?" Jeffrey asked.

"There may be exceptions, but tonight it's a must."

Adam was aware that they created quite a stir as they entered the main dining room. He suddenly realized he had become a real celebrity, first with "American Beauty" and more recently with the successful sale of his stock that had made him many times a millionaire. He relished every minute of his progress to the best table. If he had turned around, he was sure, they would all have their heads together talking about him.

The next day he engaged a cabana at the pool, and he was happy to see that Eva really seemed to be enjoying herself as she sat in a canvas chair and worked on a piece of needlepoint.

"That's right, Eva, stay out of the sun."

"Yes, I know. Women used to burn themselves into looking like pieces of leather, but Roy says it destroys the skin."

Later Eva went into the pool, paddled around with her deliberate breaststroke, came out and let her hair down to dry.

"That's pretty. You ought to do that more often," Adam said.

As Eva looked up she saw Alan balancing on the high diving board ready to jump off. She cried, "Stop him, Adam. It looks so dangerous."

"He can handle it," he said just as Alan leaped from the board, made a clean dive into the pool and came up laughing.

"Where's Jeff?" Adam asked.

Eva looked up from her needlepoint. "He likes the ocean better. He always loved the sound of it when he was a baby and we used to have the house at Far Rockaway."

The days passed quickly. Almost every morning after a late breakfast, Adam visited a different store at Bal Harbour or Miami, always checking the location of the Adam and Eve counter.

In the evening he usually invited a buyer or merchandise manager to dinner. He always ordered caviar upstairs for cocktails in the penthouse and the best possible champagne when they went down to dinner. It was the happiest holiday he had ever had, he thought as New Year's Eve began to come close. He was proud of his two handsome boys, and even Eva seemed less remote than she had been recently.

New Year's Eve passed in a montage of champagne bottles, paper hats, confetti and what he felt were friendly faces. When he finally reached the Presidential Suite around 3 a.m., he knew he had had much too much to drink.

Both he and Eva slept late the next morning, and when they finally woke, the suite was quiet and empty. Eva went out on the wide terrace that overlooked the grounds of the hotel and part of the pool. She thought she could recognize Alan's red head, but there was no sign of Jeffrey.

Over breakfast she said to Adam, "I can't believe it's 1962, can you? Just think, next July we will have been married twenty years."

"It sure has gone fast, especially this past year."

Adam folded his newspaper. "It's twenty-two degrees in Westchester. I spoke to Wally Nelson in New York a little while ago. He says it's still snowing. Why don't we go down and soak up some sun while we can?"

The pool area wasn't crowded yet, and they both stretched out on canvas chairs in their cabana.

Alan and his friends were jumping in and out of the water. "Where's your brother?" Eva asked.

Alan ran over to her. "I don't know, Mom. The last time I saw him he was with Roger Martindale. They got bored playing shuffleboard and they were talking about hiring a sailboat."

"But Jeffrey doesn't really know how to sail."

"Don't be a worrier, Eva. The kids are both water rats. He'll turn up in time for lunch."

Adam was sleepy. He dozed off and Eva had to wake him. "I'm getting hungry, Adam. It's after two and I'm worrying about Jeffrey, too."

"Oh, come on, Eva. The kid's around somewhere, but if you're all that bothered, I'll go down to the beach and talk to the life guard."

The life guard hadn't seen the two boys. "Our catamarans were all rented early this morning, and I know who has them. They may have walked down the beach to one of the other hotels to find one."

"Have you seen any sign of a small catamaran in trouble?"

"No, sir, and I've had my binoculars on the water all morning."

Adam walked back to Eva. "Honey, why don't you have lunch? I'm going to walk down to the next hotel. They probably decided to eat there."

"I can't eat, Adam. I'm too worried. Where did he get the money to hire a boat?"

"I suppose he used some of his Christmas money."

She began to cry. "I told you not to give him so much."

"Now, Eva, don't get excited. I'm going now to find out what I can."

There were no small-boat warnings posted, but as he strode down the beach he had a sinking feeling at the pit of his stomach. The surf seemed to be pounding in very loud and very high.

At the next hotel, the man in charge of the boats consulted his list. "Yes, sir, one of our boats was rented at ten o'clock this morning by Roger Martindale. I remember he had a young friend with him. They had a basket of food with them, I seem to recall."

"Don't you check up on boats that are hired by underage kids?"

"We do the best we can, sir, but the young fellow who rented the boat seemed to be a qualified sailor. I watched him handling it as they took off."

Adam wasted no time. "Do you have any fast motorboats for charter?"

"Yes, we have several."

"I want all of them for the next few hours and I want capable men to run them. We'll span out at different distances from the shore and run up and down the coastline to see what we can find."

He called the manager of his own hotel, explained the emergency and asked him to alert the Coast Guard. He hired three more motorboats and asked for Roger Martindale's father. "I don't know you, Mr. Martindale, but we haven't got any time to lose. Try not to excite your wife until you have to. Get into one of the boats I've ordered, and we'll see what we can do."

As he stood at the bow of the boat, turning his binoculars first out to sea and then towards the sand, he kept praying for the slightest sign—a sail, a piece of wreckage with a boy clinging on, or best of all, two wet boys running along the shore. A tiny island gave him hope for a minute, but after that there was nothing.

It was three hours later that he saw the farthest-out motorboat pause for a minute. As it came alongside the officer said, "There's a piece of sail still floating out there and a few bits of wood."

"Oh, God," said Adam. He ordered his boat to follow the other to the scene of the wreckage. When he saw the pitiful bits of white cloth and wood tossing on the waves, he began to cry. His face was caked with salt spray and the tears tasted salty in his mouth. He wasn't willing to give up, and somehow, through sheer force of will power, he was going to find Jeffrey alive and well. It was only when he saw the sun beginning to drop out of sight that he realized he had to give up. He ordered his boat to go alongside the Coast Guard cutter that some time ago had joined the search.

"We'll do everything we can, Mr. Adler," said the captain.

"Is there any chance at all that they could have reached shore?"

"We've covered as much of the shoreline as we thought possible, but there are always miracles."

"Thank you."

"We will go on searching. In case there has been a drowning, it may be some time before we are able to locate the bodies."

As he got out of his boat at the hotel, Adam was cold and shivering. "I'm afraid we're licked," he said to Roger Martindale's father, who was waiting for him.

"I can't accept it," Mr. Martindale said. "My son is a born sailor. He won all the cups. He was big and strong for a sixteen-year-old."

"My son was only fourteen," Adam said.

"I've been standing here for fifteen minutes wondering how I can possibly face my wife."

Adam was wondering the same thing as he strode through the foyer of the hotel. When he opened the door of the suite, Eva was sitting on one of the couches with her hands folded on her lap. She looked at his face and began to scream.

"Oh, God, my baby. He was my first."

"Now, honey," Adam walked towards her.

"It's the money. You gave him too much money."

"It was this older friend of his, Martindale, Eva, who hired the boat."

"If you had only worried about him like I did, you would have gone for him earlier," she screamed.

"My heart is breaking just like yours. I'm doing everything I can and screaming won't help."

He took Eva's hand and led her to the bedroom. "Lie down and try to rest for a while."

She lay down obediently but went on moaning and sobbing. Adam went to the house telephone and called the resident doctor. "One of my sons has had an accident. My wife is hysterical. Would it be possible for you to give her a sedative?"

The news of the boys' disappearance had spread quickly through the hotel. The doctor arrived in five minutes, and after a sedative Eva lay quietly, though her eyes were still open.

Adam closed the door and came back into the living room. He saw that Alan was huddled in a corner.

"Gee, Dad, it's awful." Alan burst into tears.

"Not now, son. We have to be brave for your mother. Thank God that you didn't go along with them." He told Alan to call room service and order anything he wanted sent to his room. He wanted to be alone.

Though he slept occasionally in his chair, he went time after time to the terrace. He watched the lights of the Coast Guard cutter scanning the shoreline for what he knew by now would only be his son's body.

After a two-day nightmare of waiting, Roger Martindale's body was washed up on the beach about two miles from the hotel and Jeffrey's followed with the next incoming tide. Adam answered the Coast Guard's call to come down to the beach and identify the body. The small crowd that had gathered around the blanket-covered form on the sand moved to a respectful distance. He bent down, turned back the blanket and gently smoothed Jeffrey's hair from his face.

"Yes, this is my son," he said.

As soon as Adam could make the necessary arrangements they left for New York.

The next two months were hell for Adam both at the office and at home. He plunged desperately into work and many nights found himself still at his desk as late as ten or eleven o'clock. Eva had gone into a shell and there was no communication with her at all. The one thing he dreaded most was going to the apartment, where she had moved into the guest room. The door was seldom open.

The first time he was able to smile was when he opened the *Wall Street Journal* one morning and read a front-page story about Adam and Eve. A&E, as it was known on Wall Street, was described as having been one of the most successful initial public offerings of the year. It was going to split two for one, in less than six months. For the first time in many weeks, he called Crystal's office and asked her to come in.

"You're looking better, Adam." She had gone to Mexico to visit Lynda for the holidays, and hadn't heard of the tragedy until she returned. She had written to both Eva and Adam and had called, but without any response. At the office, which was full of tales about Adam's bitterness and his unreasonable outbursts of temper, she had only managed to catch occasional glimpses of him, sitting pale and tense at his desk.

"Well, at last I've got something to smile about today," he said. "Have you read the *Wall Street Journal* this morning?"

"Yes, and I guess everybody else has, too. They are all talking out in the office, and I've had several calls."

"It means you've made a hunk of money in the last six months and so have I, and we're going to make a lot more."

"So I understand."

"Crystal, why don't you start living it up, with a bigger and better apartment, or are you hung up on the charm of your little blue-and-white place?"

"I *have* moved to another apartment, but it's in the same building and just like the other except for an extra bedroom that I'm turning into a library. I need more space at home for my papers and . . ."

"You're very cautious."

"Not necessarily. Someday when I feel like it, I'll go all out, but right now this is so easy for me. I love the location and can get anywhere without too much trouble."

"Live where you like. I'll have to drop by some time and take a look at the new place." When she smiled but didn't answer, he quickly changed the subject. "I have a new idea I've been wanting to talk about, and you're the best sounding board I have."

"Sometimes I'm brutally frank."

"Be frank this time. I'm thinking of launching a line for men."

"Fabulous. I think you're right on target again, Adam. It's funny you should bring it up today, because I've been researching men's fashions in the library recently."

"What on earth for?"

"Well, there's been a lot of talk going around about men being tired of looking drab. Some women designers turned out a group of fashions they'd like to see men wear. Everybody laughed at the evening shirt with the ruffles down the front, but some manufacturer reproduced it, and it's selling like crazy. The fashion industry is getting ready for a male peacock revolution and a men's cosmetics line would tie right in with it.

"In the seventh century there was an Abyssinian king who rouged his cheeks, and a hundred years ago the men in England were all dyeing their hair, beards and mustaches."

"I'm confident the timing is right."

"And of course you have the perfect built-in name for your men's products."

"I hadn't really thought. You mean Adam?"

"It couldn't be more appealing, both to a man and to the woman who's buying it for a gift."

"I'm glad you like the idea. I plan to go ahead with it fast."

"While we're on the subject of names, I've been wanting to suggest something for a long time. I'd like to add a perfume to my own Young Forever line."

"And call it Crystal, of course."

"Yes, and package it in a beautiful cut-crystal bottle."

"Or a less expensive imitation, if we can find it."

"No, I want it to be very elegant and to cost a great deal. I might even go to Grasse this summer to study French secrets."

"I like the idea, but the scent will have to be made in this country. It's much better from every angle to have production close by. I'll get Wally Nelson to talk to you. What kind of scent do you want? Any idea?"

"Yes, none of that fresh, green nonsense. I want it to be like old French perfumes. Sexy."

"Good for you, baby." Adam was surprised to hear himself laugh aloud.

She stood up to leave the office, but he stopped her. "There's one thing more I need help with. Eva and my twentieth anniversary is coming up in July. She's had a rough time of it lately, and I want to give her something really nice like a piece of jewelry. I had an idea for something I'd like to have specially made, but I don't know which jeweler would be best."

"I'd suggest a talented new fellow, David Webb, and, if you like, I'll telephone him to expect your call."

Adam went home feeling almost like himself again. Eva's door was open, and he breathed a sigh of relief when he saw that the dinner table was set for two. Eva was quiet through dinner except when they spoke about sending Alan to a summer camp the first of June, and seemed to be listening with some interest to his plans for the new Adam cosmetics line.

As they were drinking their coffee she said, "You know, Adam, Roy isn't happy working with the new chemist you brought in from Switzerland."

"What's the problem?"

"He thinks he's a complete phony."

"What the hell is all this grapevine chitchat you're always bringing me from the factory and the lab? Why the hell don't they have the guts to speak for themselves? You can damn well tell Roy Archer that he has another think coming. That Swiss chemist has one of the best names in Europe."

"I'll give him your message, but I think he'll leave if you don't change your mind."

"Not on your life, he won't. I know he's been with us since the beginning. It's auld lang syne and all that, but chemists are getting to be a dime a dozen these days."

Eva dropped the subject, but from then on her bedroom door remained closed. She came regularly to meals and Adam told himself she was well on her way to becoming her old self again.

It was late June when his secretary came into his office and said that Judge Lambert was on the phone. Adam picked up the receiver and spoke with his most winning voice. "Yes, Judge Lambert, what may I do for you?"

"It's about your wife that I'm calling."

"Christ, has something happened to Eva?"

"She has asked me to inform you, Mr. Adler, that she has left you. She has retained me as her lawyer and I'm calling to arrange an appointment with you or your legal counsel."

"I don't believe it. What kind of shit is this? It's not April Fools'."

"This is not a joke, Mr. Adler. Your wife is now installed in an apartment in the Essex House. She moved from your residence at noon today."

"Well, I'll be goddamned," Adam said as he hung up the receiver.

He sat stunned for almost a quarter of an hour and then picked up the phone and asked his secretary to get the Essex House. "What's all this shit, Eva?"

"I expected to hear from you, Adam."

"Well, what the goddamned hell is this all about?"

"I'm sorry, Adam, I've been instructed by Judge Lambert not to talk with you for the time being."

"What kind of crap is that?"

"I'm not happy, Adam. I haven't been for a long, long time. I want a divorce."

"A divorce? For God's sake, why? We've been married almost twenty years. I don't get it."

"My mind is made up, Adam. It's final."

He hung up the receiver, and his secretary could

hear him banging his desk and shouting every four-letter word in the alphabet. In a few minutes he pressed the buzzer and asked her to get his lawyer on the phone.

That night as his secretary, Miss Haley, was leaving the office she said to her best friend, who was secretary to Wally Nelson, "Don't say anything about it to anybody, but I think the boss is having trouble with his wife."

The rumor spread quickly around the office, especially since Adam was more than usually impatient and irritable. After two weeks the Cholly Knickerbocker column in the *Journal-American* broke the news. "Adam Adler, the cosmetics tycoon, is having a new kind of makeup problem. Two weeks ago his wife, Eva, the less heard and seen half of their business, packed up and said goodbye to their Park Avenue flat. She is suing for divorce."

It was almost Labor Day when Adam's secretary, quivering with excitement, announced, "Mrs. Adler is here to see you, Mr. Adler."

Adam stood up to greet her. "Well, fancy seeing you here, Eva." He motioned her to a chair by his desk.

"Don't be sarcastic, Adam. Now that the settlement has been signed, Judge Lambert says there's no reason we shouldn't talk together, especially since we're going to share Alan."

"I don't see much future for a long and beautiful friendship between us."

"I'm sorry to hear that, Adam, and I hope someday you'll change your mind. I came here to talk about Alan, but first I want to tell you that I'm very happy about the settlement. Judge Lambert says I should have taken you for twice as much, but I didn't want to do it that way."

"If you thought you could get more money out of me, why the hell didn't you try? I would have."

"I told you I was here to talk about Alan. It's soon time for him to come back from camp. He has a few weeks in New York before he leaves for school, and I think it would be easier for him to stay with you in his familiar room. That way it will be better for him to accept the new situation."

"I was hoping to have him."

"I expect to be settled permanently somewhere by winter. Then I'll be able to have him for the holiday vacation."

"You're leaving New York?"

"Oh, yes. I want to live in a warmer climate. I don't want to ever see Florida again. I've been thinking of California. I'd like to buy some land and raise grapefruit, maybe, or I might even try a vineyard."

"It sounds like quite a project for a lone woman."

"I'm not planning to be a lone woman. I'm planning to be married when our divorce becomes final."

"You're what?"

"Don't shout at me, Adam. It's one of the reasons I couldn't stand living with you any longer. I said I'm going to get married. I'm going to marry Roy Archer."

"Don't kid me."

"I'm not. I'm going to marry Roy."

"I get it. So that's why all this shit about your loving the lab. You and that Mickey Mouse have been shacking up all this time."

"We have not been shacking up. We have always been good friends and we both like the same things. I think we'll be very happy together."

"What the hell are you going to live on? Your money, I suppose. Because I can tell you one thing, he's fired."

"It won't be necessary to fire Roy. He has already handed in his resignation to take effect at the end of the year, but I'm sure he'll be glad to go sooner. He owns considerable stock in the company, you know, and he has never lived extravagantly, so I don't think we'll have to worry about where our next meal is coming from."

"Eva, I can't believe all this."

"I don't see why. You've always had your own interests and I've been aware of most of them. So why shouldn't I have a man of my own at last." She stood up to go and picked up her handbag from his desk.

"Wait a minute, Eva." He opened a drawer and removed a small box and slammed it so hard on his desk that it tumbled to the floor on the other side. "I had planned to have this delivered to you, but since you're here ..."

Eva stooped and picked up the package that was wrapped in gold paper and sealed with red wax. "What on earth is this?"

"It's something I had designed for that twentieth anniversary we were going to celebrate. Remember?"

"Do you mind if I open it?"

"Do as you like. That's what you've been doing anyway."

She broke open the seals, looked for a minute at the velvet case and then opened the lid. Inside was a small replica of the Statue of Liberty, the kind that tourists buy, but wrapped around it was a gold chain with some of the links separated with cabochon emeralds.

"It's a beautiful gift, Adam. You can be very sweet and generous when you're in the mood." She began rewrapping the package.

"Wear the necklace in good health, Eva."

She stood up again and dropped the jewel case into her handbag. "Even if I don't have much chance to wear it in California, I promise to keep it carefully for one of our grandchildren to wear someday." She hesitated for a moment. "Well, I guess it's goodbye, Adam."

"Maybe on a clear day, Eva, you'll be able to get a glimpse of Catalina from your new place."

"I'll still miss the Statue of Liberty." She turned back, smiled at him and went out the door.

That evening when he met Wally Nelson at the King Cole Bar for a drink, Wally had already heard from his secretary that Eva had visited Adam's office. He wondered if there was a reconciliation in the air. "Any new developments about Eva?" he asked casually after the bartender had put their scotch and sodas in front of them.

"Hell, no. That's past history. I've just been thinking. It cost me exactly two dollars for the marriage license to marry Eva, and it cost me exactly two million for a divorce settlement."

28

A few months later Crystal learned she was about to become an American citizen. The notice to appear before Judge Wells at the Federal Courthouse had arrived in the same mail with her first invitation to the White House.

She had applied for citizenship as soon as she felt her career secure in America, but since the list of German applications was long, she was kept waiting two years. Then after that it had taken the customary five years, although Adam exerted himself to try to expedite the legalities.

"Can you take time off next Wednesday to be a witness for my good character?" she had asked Adam when the notice arrived.

"Sure thing, but you need two, don't you? Want me to get Wally."

"I thought of asking Lynda. You and she are my two oldest friends here. I met Lynda on the plane coming to America and you a few days later."

"What's she up to these days?"

"She has been spending a lot of time in Mexico ever since her husband died. She just happens to be here now."

"Does she still have that million-dollar shape?"

"Yes, and a million dollars to go with it. Her husband left her quite a lot of money."

On Wednesday, Lynda picked up Crystal in her car

and they met Adam at the courthouse. While she was answering questions in one room after another, Crystal could see that the two of them were sitting on a bench, dividing a morning newspaper between them and drinking coffee in paper cups from a coffee machine.

It was almost noon when she was ready for the final ceremony. "I think I passed. I remembered that George Washington was the first President, that there were thirteen original states and that there are fifty now, along with lots of other fascinating facts," she told them. They went into the judge's chambers, where both Adam and Lynda raised their right hands, swore that they had known Crystal for more than seven years and that her character was thoroughly reputable.

"Welcome to our group, Fräulein," Adam said as they left the office.

Lynda hugged her. "Little did Pan Am know what they were doing when they seated us next to each other on that plane."

Adam put his hand on Crystal's shoulder. "I'm having dinner with Wally Nelson tonight. He's a bachelor this week. Why don't you girls join us and we can go out on the town."

At El Morocco, Angelo gave them the number-one table, right at the foot of the long staircase. The room was full, but Crystal saw that she and Lynda were wearing the shortest evening dresses in the room. The skirt of Lynda's was even cut in handkerchief points and showed her sheer black panty hose up to the thighs as she danced.

"You sure know how to wear clothes, Lynda doll," Crystal heard Adam say when they were back at the table. He leaned over and fingered the thin gold-and-diamond chain that was wound around her neck and looped a couple of times on the front of her dress. "And you know how to wear jewelry, too. Some women tend to play it down and others try to show it off. You handle it as if you just don't give a damn."

"I guess I feel that way."

While they were drinking their after-dinner coffee, Adam suggested they move on to the Peppermint Lounge, where suddenly everyone was flocking to learn to dance the twist.

"I really shouldn't go," Crystal said. "I'm taking a ten o'clock plane to Washington tomorrow, but I'm longing to see the Peppermint Lounge."

"Washington? Does that mean Garfinkel's again?" Adam asked.

"No, I'm going to the White House."

"The White House? Why didn't you tell us?" Lynda cried.

"I can't believe it myself. An American citizen today and the White House tomorrow. It's all very thrilling."

At the Peppermint Lounge, the crowd at the front door was overflowing the sidewalks and spilling into West Forty-fourth Street. Adam pressed a bill into the doorman's hand, and they all went around to the back door that led them through the kitchen.

The low-ceilinged main room was as crowded as the sidewalk had been, and the small dance floor was full of turning and twisting figures, all revolving to the rhythm of Chubby Checker.

"I'm mad for the twist. Come on, Adam," said Lynda.

"I bet you do a mean one, but you'll have to teach me what to do." Adam took her arm and led her out on the floor.

Crystal was longing to dance, but Wally, who was on the plump side, said, "Sorry, but I never got any farther than the two-step, Crystal." She was looking around the room and beginning to wave to magazine editors like Sally Kirkland and Nancy White when a small, limber man she had seen performing on the floor approached the table.

"I'm Killer Joe, Miss Crystal. Like to learn the twist? I give lessons, but this is a personal invitation."

She laughed and got up. "Yes, I'd like to."

It was midnight before she asked Wally to take her home. They left Lynda and Adam twisting. Next morning she was just ready to leave her apartment when

Lynda called. "Happy White House, Crystal. Last night was more fun than I've had in years, but I just wanted to ask you one question. Is there anything between you and that boss of yours?"

"Not a thing."

"It's funny. I always had a hunch there was, and I wanted to make sure. He asked me for another date, and one thing I've never done is to cut in on somebody else's guy."

"Feel free, darling, and call me soon."

In Washington she went directly to the Mayflower Hotel, where she changed to a beige tweed suit about the color of her hair. She had brought a small hat as a gesture of respect to the White House, but when she tried it on she decided she looked much better hatless.

Everything was exciting about the White House, the guards at the door, the paintings of former Presidents, even the ladies' room. She went up the marble staircase to the music of the Marine Band, and on into the Blue Room, where Jacqueline Kennedy was receiving. Crystal joined the line, and when she reached the First Lady, Mrs. Kennedy's eyes widened and she said, "Oh, I'm so glad you could come," as if she had particularly wanted her to be there.

When Crystal looked around the room she saw that the guests were all professional women from newspapers, magazines and businesses, like hers, slanted entirely towards women. There were no men.

Soon Letitia Baldridge, one of Mrs. Kennedy's staff, began circulating among the groups to say, "Outside in the gallery is a huge crystal bowl full of numbers. The number you draw will be your table. Mrs. Kennedy is going to draw just like the rest of you, so there will be no favoritism about where she is seated."

Crystal could hardly believe her good luck when she found that number eleven put her at the same table as Jacqueline Kennedy, who was already seated between a French magazine editor and a correspondent for a London newspaper. Across from her, Crystal found Jacqueline Kennedy even more attractive than the rave notices in the press had presented her. She was wearing a sweater and skirt and her hair fell naturally instead of being lacquered into place, a look Crystal thoroughly detested, even though the spray that produced it was one of Adam and Eve's best sellers at the moment.

Crystal stayed in Washington for several days. She felt herself becoming more and more caught up in the scene. Everyone talked about policies and appointments. When she made her promised public appearance at the store, she found it hard to concentrate on problems like dry skin for the first time and had to force the magnetism that always drew crowds of women around her.

I wish I could meet a man with an important post in the government, or even an ambassador, she thought. She could imagine herself running an embassy residence, managing the servants perfectly and planning menus that would make her a top Washington hostess. She felt she would enjoy plotting and scheming to help advance a politically minded husband.

When she came back to New York, nothing looked quite the same. Her apartment, which just a short while ago had seemed so cozy, so comfortable and so sensible, now seemed uninteresting, and unimportant.

The first thing I'm going to do is to move, she thought. She began checking the "For Rent" and "For Sale" pages of the Times and Tribune every night. As she sat in bed, propped up by pillows she found them fascinating reading. Rooms with wood-burning fireplaces, paneled walls, parquet floors, terraces or gardens were like bits of description from a novel, but all of them seemed to be right for someone else rather than for her. Everything seems to be directed at the beginner I was when I came here and not the successful woman I am now, she thought.

Crystal seldom stopped long enough for self-analysis and her own admission that she had become a successful woman startled her. She got out of bed and went to look at herself in the full-length mirror on the back of her closet door. The woman in the glass smiled back at her confidently. I'm better-looking than I was when I started working, she thought. My figure is better and there still isn't a gray hair on my head. As she slid back between the sheets of the bed, she felt a wonderful, warming sense of security, but as she closed her eyes, she warned herself: I mustn't stop. I must invest in myself and go on farther and farther.

The next day she called one of the top agencies, and the search began. Crystal shopped up and down Park Avenue for a new home, but even the most expensive apartments seemed to her to be one similar box after another.

"Had you thought of a town house, Miss Crystal?" the agent finally asked.

"I really hadn't. As much as I like the idea of a house, it would be rather ridiculous and much too expensive for a woman who lives alone. I would rattle around in it."

"You'd need to occupy only a small part of it. Most town houses have been remodeled and divided into apartments. You would choose one of them, and the rent from the others would probably pay your taxes and even the loan on any mortgage you might take."

"Then show me some that are available." The idea instantly appealed to her. To own property would be a step forward into security. She realized that she could soon, and without too much trouble, pay off a mortgage. Then she would own something tangible of brick or stone that she could reconvert into cash or even retreat to if worse came to worst.

It didn't take her long to find the house she wanted. It was in the East Sixties between Madison Avenue and Park, and it was quite old and very elegant. The second floor had a drawing room twice as big as her present one, a second large room she would convert into a combination dining room and library, a kitchen with a tiny maid's room adjoining and a big bedroom. It had an iron balcony and steps leading down to a tiny paved garden that she would share with whatever tenant occupied the ground floor.

At the moment it was rented to a stockbroker whose

lease would soon expire, and she could easily find another tenant if she didn't like him, she felt sure. The four tenants on the floors above had all been there for years.

"You've made a great investment," her agent assured her after the final closing papers had been signed. "In ten years this property will be worth more than triple what you're paying for it today."

Since the second-floor apartment was in relatively good shape, Crystal decided to move in immediately. On her first night there she went ecstatically from one room to another running her fingers over the marble fireplaces and the carved paneling. She realized that it was all hers and the reward of her own ingenuity. When she set her grandmother's jewel box on the dressing table in her new bedroom, she felt that, at last, it was in the kind of setting it ought to have.

She had just gone back to the living room, where her old furniture looked suddenly dollhouse size, when her doorbell rang. As she hesitated for a minute with her hand on the knob, a man's voice said, "It's your tenant downstairs. I'm calling to say welcome, but if you're tired I'll try it again sometime."

She flung open the door. He was tall with quite a lot of dark, curly hair and interesting green eyes, she thought. "Come in," she said.

"I'm Douglas Knolls," he explained as he followed her into the living room. "I'm sure you're my new landlady, though you're not at all the kind of landlady I expected."

"I'm sorry to disappoint you. Just how should your landlady look?" She saw that he was carrying a bottle of wine under his arm.

"Don't change. I like pleasant surprises. I've brought along a housewarming present to ingratiate myself." He held out the bottle of wine.

"Oh, do let's open it. I'm tired and thirsty," she said. In the kitchen she managed to find two wine glasses in a carton. There were a few crackers in a box on the pantry shelf and some cheese in the icebox. She put them all on a tray and carried them into the living room, where her tenant had already opened the wine and lighted the fire. "I want you to feel warm and happy on your first night in your new home."

Crystal curled up on the couch in front of the fire and he began to laugh. "Forgive me. I had heard that you're the successful cold-cream lady and that you're much older than you look. So I expected you to have big boobs, a kind of plastic hairdo and lots of jingling bracelets."

"Perhaps I can improve my image as time goes on."

"You're beautiful, and you know you are. My mother was blond, but her hair wasn't as gorgeous as yours." He poured himself a second glass of wine and began to talk about the state of the stock market.

Crystal felt the warmth of the fire on her face and, in spite of herself, her eyes were closing.

Douglas Knolls stood up. "Sorry. I know you're dead tired. Maybe as my landlady you'll have dinner with me in my place downstairs some night."

Later, as she took off her clothes and fell into bed, Crystal thought: At least he doesn't talk the cosmetics lingo, and he may make a good escort for some of the places I like to go.

The next morning a potted tree in a huge wicker basket arrived at Crystal's apartment with Douglas Knoll's card. It helped to soften the stark look of her new living room, and she dropped a note of thanks into his mailbox as she went out.

It was several weeks before she saw him again. Early one rainy evening they arrived home at the same time.

"I've been meaning to call you," Douglas said. "I was going to work up a little dinner party but I couldn't decide who to ask. Putting things off and not making any decisions is one of my worst faults."

"I'd like to have dinner with you anytime."

"How about tonight, then? It's a wretched night to go anywhere. I told my man to stay in and cook dinner. It won't be anything special, but we can sit around and talk."

Crystal went upstairs, peeled off her work clothes,

put on a long, comfortable knit sweater dress and went downstairs again.

Douglas' apartment was almost as large as hers, but he had taken the plaster off the walls and fireplace to show the old brick, and had hung some interesting modern art. The kitchen that was a combination stove, sink and refrigerator was installed in a passage between the living room and the rather small dining room.

"How comfortable this looks," she said as she sat down on a couch that faced the fire.

"Oh, well, it's got a little of everything in it." Douglas waved his hand at the books, the desk and the Chinese cook who was setting the plates on the round glass-top table. "What would you like to drink?"

"Some wine, maybe, just like the other night."

Douglas went to the kitchen and came back with a tall glass of white wine poured over ice cubes. "This is the way all the ladies seem to like it."

She took the glass. "I see at least one lady must have liked it this afternoon. You have some lipstick smeared on your cheek," she said, reaching for a piece of Kleenex in her handbag. "And it's not even Adam and Eve."

"It must have been my mother's when I dropped her off this afternoon, but how could you possibly tell it's not your product?"

"I always know. First by the color and also by the smoothness. Ours is much softer. I must send you some for your mother. I think I know exactly the shade she would like."

The Chinese dinner was delicious, and just as they were finishing it, she said, "You've been married, haven't you, Doug?"

"Yes, I have, but what makes you think so?"

"Because you have the kind of nice possessions like plates and glasses that look as if they came from an organized life. Most bachelor's apartments are full of assorted Christmas presents that women have given them through the years."

"I suppose you've seen more than your share of them!"

"No, just about my share, I imagine. After all, I've been a single girl in New York for a while, and I go out to dinner with someone almost every night. Some of my experiences would make a good book."

They moved back to the couch, and the cook brought a pot of tea and two cups. "You pour it," Douglas suggested. "I feel like having a woman wait on me while I give her material for another chapter. You're quite right, you know. I've just recently become a bachelor. My divorce has just gone through and I'm still terribly shaken up."

"What a pity. Most people seem to survive very easily."

"I waited a long time to get married. I guess I was overcautious and thought every girl I took out was after me for something. I was past thirty when I met Alice. After we were married everything was all right for the first five years."

"Then what happened?"

"Evidently I didn't give her what she wanted, and out of the blue she fell in love with a painter. I was too routine, she told me. Since then I've been going to a psychiatrist, but nothing seemed to be happening, so I've tried group therapy too."

While he was talking, Crystal's eyes had wandered to the water color of a beautiful nude girl that was hanging on the brick wall across from her. She had admired it before dinner, and now she asked, "Is that a portrait of your wife?"

"No, but it reminds me of her. That's the way the trouble all began. Her artist friend asked her to pose in the nude and they started having an affair."

The nude painting made Crystal think of Lynda, and Lynda reminded her of the body lotion that they had christened Head to Toe. Lynda had loved it, but the sales had been only mediocre in comparison with Crystal's other products. If I could only have promoted it with a beautiful nude girl, she thought. It crossed her mind that she might ask Douglas if she could reproduce his painting in an ad, but suddenly a more daring plan popped into her head. Why couldn't I hire a girl to pose in the nude? The magazines have been undressing models and suggesting nudity for the past year, and I believe right now is the psychological time for an ad to show a girl stark naked.

She was so quiet that Douglas leaned over and kissed her. "Am I boring you with my troubles, Crystal?"

"Of course not."

Since she smiled and didn't draw away, he pushed her back against the cushions and began kissing her face and as much of her bare throat as was visible.

"Crystal, you seem so strong and so sure of where you're going. I desperately need a woman like you."

Crystal closed her eyes for a minute. She found Douglas appealing. It might be pleasant to lie in bed with him and she felt she could easily drift into an affair, but not right now.

She sat up. "I like you, too, Doug, and our apartments are so locked together that inevitably we're going to see a lot of each other."

"Stay now, please."

"I really have to work. I had planned to stay all evening at my desk and your nice invitation was all unexpected, you know."

He released her reluctantly. They talked for a few minutes and planned to telephone the next day. Then she said good night and went upstairs.

Before she reached her own apartment, Crystal had forgotten Douglas' psychological difficulties. She was obsessed with the thought of a lovely naked girl posing for Head to Toe in some way that the top magazines would accept. It would be a dramatic first as well as a booster for all her products. She felt it would startle the whole cosmetics industry and make her one of its leading figures. She pulled a list of models out of her desk drawer and went through them, but she was not satisfied. It should be a nonprofessional woman, someone with a name if possible.

As the weeks passed, Crystal was surprised not to hear from Lynda, but the office grapevine had heard all about her. She and Adam had started to become a constant column item. They were on again and off again, and when Adam's divorce from Eva became final, Suzy predicted that their marriage would take place any day now.

One afternoon Adam called Crystal into his office.

"Congratulations, Adam. Is it true what I read about you in Suzy's column, along with the story about Henry Ford and Christina Austin?"

"Yes, that's what I wanted to talk to you about. You seem to be responsible for lots of good things in my life, baby. First you walk in here and bring me Young Forever. The next thing—you introduce me to Lynda."

"So far it's all to the good, isn't it?"

"You're damn right it is. I've had a hell of a lonely year and Lynda is the only bright thing that's come into it. I haven't asked her to marry me yet because I want to make sure Alan understands. He's coming home from school soon. I thought I'd take him somewhere this summer and then when he goes back to school we'll get married."

"I think Lynda and Alan will get along well."

"I do, too. I've already tried it out. He was crazy about her, but I just want him to be sure that he knows that he'll always come first."

"I hope Lynda won't mind taking second place."

"It's not that it's second place. It's just that Alan is part of me."

The next week Lynda telephoned to Crystal and said, "You know I once told you I'm a born collector."

"What are you collecting these days?"

"Well, it looks like I'm starting a collection of millionaires, doesn't it?"

"You mean Adam?"

"Yes. He said he'd more or less told you. We fight like hell, but I'm really crazy about him. Monty was a kind of father image, and I've never had a real lover before. Anyway, I've said yes."

"I'm truly glad, Lynda. When will it be?"

"I'll let you know the date in plenty of time, because you're going to be my bridesmaid. It won't be until fall because of the kid, but I don't mind. I'll just rest up in the country, because life with Adam is sure to be pretty strenuous."

If Lynda was resting all summer, Suzy and Cholly Knickerbocker were fabricating. They reported her here and there, especially with young Trevis Howard III of the old Newport family.

A few days after he came back from his pack trip in the Tetons with Alan, Adam called Crystal to his office again. "Lynda and I are going to be married next week just before Alan goes back to school. He's all for it and we'll get settled in some new place before he comes home again. Call Lynda, will you? She wants you to stand up for her."

Lynda was full of excitement. "We had a hell of a fight the night he got back. Some kind friend sent him all the clippings about me and Trevis, and for twenty-four hours I thought it was all off. He decided to forgive me, especially since it was his own fault leaving me alone so long. Trevis is a nice kid, but the rest of the family are stuffed shirts. I wouldn't want to be a leaf on that family tree."

"I happened to meet Trevis last week."

Adam and Lynda were married in a judge's chambers in City Hall the end of the following week. Crystal was bridesmaid and Wally Nelson was best man. Lynda wore a violet tweed suit by Mainbocher. Afterwards there was a luncheon at Henri Soulé's Pavilion. Since the event had been widely publicized beforehand by all the newspapers, there were almost as many photographers as guests.

Adam's plate was piled with uproarious telegrams from his friends in the industry. He read some of them aloud, but one he opened and tossed down the table to Crystal. "You might be interested in this."

It came from Carmel, California, and said, "Our best wishes. Eva and Roy Archer."

The honeymoon lasted until the following June,

when Adam decided to take Alan for a few weeks at a fishing camp in Newfoundland. Eva had asked to have the boy with her in California for the rest of the summer.

The day Adam returned to his office he fired one of his executives and rejected an advertising campaign that had been started in his absence. According to office gossip, he had sent back the proofs to his advertising director with SHIT written all over the copy in a red pencil.

Crystal wasn't surprised when Lynda called her at her apartment that night.

"Crystal, you've got to help me. Adam has cleared out of here and taken all his clothes."

"I can't believe it."

"I'm calling you at home because I didn't want to discuss it over the office wires, and I'm at the pay phone in a gas station because I think he's had my telephone tapped."

"What happened?"

"Well, when Adam went off with Alan, it was all right with me. Alan's a good kid and we get along fine. I said I'd stay in the country, but I never said I'd take the veil."

"Why should you?"

"I did come in town a few times and I went dancing at the Little Club with kids like Trevis Howard. When I think back on it, I believe Adam was having me watched all the time, though it's hard to believe. Anyway, he came back a day earlier than I expected him."

Crystal heard the operator's voice and the sound of more coins being dropped into the telephone.

"Trevis drove over to our place in the country that afternoon. We sat around the pool, and finally I asked him to stay for dinner. When Adam came, he saw the car and instead of coming in he went around the house and looked at us through the windows."

"Go on, Lynda."

"We weren't doing anything but drinking some champagne and laughing and talking. It was early and we hadn't even had dinner, but Adam came in and made the most terrible scene. He said we'd been swimming together in the nude, because as he passed the pool my suit was lying on a chair and it was bone dry. That's the kind of mind he has."

"Were you?"

"He knows that's the way I like to swim and I always do with him. This time I was wearing a bikini. I've got dozens of them and the one he saw was just an extra one, but Adam wouldn't let me explain anything. Obviously Trevis faded out in a hurry. Adam roared through the house and went upstairs and packed a suitcase. I haven't seen him since, but yesterday he sent his driver out for some more clothes."

"It's too bad, Lynda."

"I swear I've never gone to bed with this guy or any other guy since I met Adam, but if Adam goes away for a month, he ought to know by this time that I'm not the one to sit around and mope. Can't you tell him that, Crystal? You're one of the few people he listens to."

"I can try."

Crystal waited twenty-four hours and since no second call had come from Lynda she went to Adam's office. "Adam, I've been talking to Lynda."

"I expected she would cry on your shoulder."

"I believe everything she told me. You know as well as I do how much Lynda loves having a good time, and you can't expect her to sit alone for a month while you're away . . ."

"I got pretty well burned up by Eva's goings-on behind my back, and I'm not the trusting fellow I used to be."

"It's too bad for Lynda that you're carrying an old resentment into your life with her. I don't think she did anything wrong."

"Why does she have to pick that Newport pipsqueak to annoy me with?"

"Probably because she finds him so much less attractive than you are that she doesn't expect you to feel jealous."

Crystal knew Adam so well that she was sure this

idea would appeal to him, perhaps enough to send him home. She quickly changed the subject to her new perfume that was in the stage of being packaged and would be launched in the fall.

Two nights later Adam drove to the country. Luckily, there were no cars in the driveway and Lynda was upstairs in their little sitting room, stretched out on a chaise longue in a lacy robe and watching television. They fell into each other's arms.

Two hours later Adam telephoned downstairs for the butler to bring up a bottle of Dom Pérignon for a reunion celebration. After he had poured the two glasses, he said, "I've got a surprise for you, doll baby." He went to the jacket that he had thrown over the back of a chair and took a long envelope out of the inside pocket. "Start packing, because we're going to Europe and we're going to take our time about it. I've only been there once, when we opened our French office. You're going to show me around and we'll pick up some new clothes for you."

"Oh, what fun. The Paris collections will just be going on the end of this month."

"Then we'll go on to Rome and to Greece and to anywhere else we feel like."

It was mid-July when they finally took off for Paris, and September when they reached Greece. As they drove into town from the Athens airport, Adam commented that he hadn't expected to find such traffic problems in Greece. At the Grande Bretagne Hotel the general manager greeted them warmly. "Welcome to Athens, Mr. Adler. We are delighted to have you and your wife with us. We have a nice double room for you overlooking the square, but I'm sorry to say not the suite you requested. We have people flying in from all over the world for the royal wedding, you know."

Adam didn't know, but he said quickly, "Can you arrange for us to see it?"

"Some parts of it, certainly. Tomorrow I can make reservations for you on a chartered boat that will be going out towards the Corinth Canal to watch the royal Danish yacht arrive with the bride, Princess Anne

Marie, and her family. Many famous yachts will be coming, too."

From the moment he set foot on the chartered yacht the next morning, Adam fell in love with the sea. He liked the motion of the boat, and the slightly salty smell of the air was more invigorating than a drink.

It was a genuine September day with bright sunshine but enough cool breeze to flutter the Greek and Danish flags flown by the ships in the harbor. The route to the Corinth Canal was filled not only with the Greek flotilla that was steaming out to meet the Princess but with dozens of elegant private yachts. Adam heard friends calling to each other and watched stewards serving trays of drinks. At one point a speedboat dashed past them, towing a young man on water skis. Just after he passed them he took a bad spill and Adam heard an English passenger next to him say, "Oh, that was Prince Henry of Hesse."

As their boat approached, a gray warship emerged from the high rocky walls of the canal. It was followed by two minesweepers and then the royal Danish yacht, which was white but heavily encrusted in gold. At this moment a helicopter landed in the sparkling water near it, and again Adam heard from the English passenger that it carried Queen Frederika and her son, the bridegroom, who couldn't wait another minute to greet his bride.

The greatest sight of the day to Adam was the arrival of the two most famous yachts in the world, the *Creole* owned by Niarchos and Onassis' *Christina*. They came side by side cutting through the water at the same speed and both carrying large parties aboard.

That night they had dinner at an open-air restaurant at the foot of the Acropolis. He reserved a table, but before they ate, they climbed to the top and looked at the broken ruins turned white again by the moonlight.

Back at the restaurant there was Greek singing and dancing and customers were urged to express their approval by throwing the white plates. Adam, though, sat quietly while the crockery crashed around him.

"What's on your mind, darling?" Lynda asked.

"I was just thinking that I ought to get us a yacht."

Adam kept the overseas operators busy all winter, placing calls to ports, shipyards and even private yacht owners in Holland, Genoa, Monte Carlo and Athens. He read everything he could about boats, and his enthusiasm even spilled over to the history of the America's Cup races, past and present.

One drawer of his office desk was soon filled with photographs and statistics about yachts. It was April when he finally found one that he felt would be right for them. It was 135 feet, owned by a wealthy Athenian who was selling it in a hurry to buy a bigger one. It was only ten years old and said to be in good condition. Adam ordered it repainted both inside and out, with its new name, Lynda, painted on the stern in gold.

In July he and Lynda, along with Alan and a school friend, boarded the Lynda in the Athens harbor and spent most of the summer cruising among the Greek islands. Adam had a telephone installed, and since he carried a radio operator, he was able to talk to his office every day if he felt like it, and he usually did.

The Lynda was well designed and comfortable with a screened afterdeck that had a bar in one corner, a pocket size salon and what seemed to him three fairly adequate state-rooms. What he objected to constantly was that the galley was so close that he could smell the cooking. It dulled the pleasure of dinner, he felt.

On the whole he was pleased with the Lynda until they moored one afternoon late in August in the harbor at Monte Carlo. In most of the ports he had been a big fish, but here he shrank quickly to a moderate size. He was annoyed when he sat on his afterdeck and had to crane his neck to look up at the deck of the boat next to him.

Every day while they were in Monte Carlo, Adam

walked around the yacht basin studying the new arrivals and assessing all their good and bad points. He visited several that were for sale, but didn't see anything he liked.

On his first day back at the office Adam was in a happy daze, talking and thinking about nothing but boats. On the second day he started leafing through the papers neatly stacked on his desk for answering, okaying or delaying for another date.

When her buzzer began sounding as if someone's thumb was placed permanently against it and the crash of breaking china added to the noise, his secretary rushed into his office to find out what the hubbub was all about.

"What the hell is this?" roared Adam. "I knew nothing about this ad, let alone given a chance to say yes or no to the copy." The crash was the glass paperweight he had thrown across the room.

"We were all a little surprised but Miss Crystal took the responsibility." Pat Haley looked over Adam's shoulder at the final proof of the ad that had Crystal's okay on it. The photograph in the ad showed a tall girl who was unmistakably naked though her face was slightly blurred, one half of her was in shadow and a long lock of hair partially hid a breast. The copy read, "Contessa Cristina di Nicolini says, 'Face makeup is not enough. It must be Head to Toe.'"

"I want Miss Crystal here in my office in ten minutes and no fancy talk about some luncheon date she has."

When Crystal reached his office, the broken glass had been swept up and Adam was sitting quiet but unsmiling behind his desk.

"Oh, Adam," she cried, "I'm heartbroken that you don't like my new Head to Toe ad."

"I didn't say I don't like it. I just want to know why the hell I didn't know anything about it."

"I thought you deserved a happy holiday with Lynda and it would come as a gorgeous surprise."

"Surprise is not quite the word for what I'm feeling."

"The whole idea started with Lynda and her not wanting to wear clothes, you know."

"Yes, I do know, unfortunately."

"Oh, come now, Adam, you know this is all very exciting. You like to be first in everything and this is a real breakthrough. What with all the talk about Rudi Gernreich's topless bathing suit and the beaches on the French Riviera where people are lolling around with nothing on, somebody was sure to come out with an ad like this and we might as well be the first ones."

"Where did you find the girl?"

"It wasn't easy, and it took a lot of time. I know there are lots of people whose only assets are their titles, and I sent out an SOS to find one who was young and beautiful."

Picking up the ad, Adam said, "She's all of that. If I weren't a married man I'd go for her myself."

"Marriage hasn't ever stopped you yet, has it?"

"I suppose not, but tell me, how did you talk Vogue and Bazaar into accepting the ad?"

"I went to each of them separately. We talked about the whole new nudity trend and brought up all the pros and cons. In the end they were all ready to pioneer in something that seems inevitable. Besides, the photograph is so historic that it will sell out their magazines as well as our cosmetics."

"Does everybody know all about it?"

"Not really, but the story has leaked a little and they'll all try to follow us in their own ways."

"I have to admit that it's a good idea, and the timing is right."

"Then I'm forgiven?"

"For the time being, but just remember one thing, baby. Don't get too big for your britches."

29

It wasn't until the following April when Adam had received an urgent call from a Dutch shipyard that he flew to Amsterdam and found something he felt lived up to everything that a yacht should be.

It was 236 feet long, 101 feet grander than the *Lynda*, and he felt that when he brought it into a harbor its impact would be only slightly less than the *Christina's*. It carried a crew of twenty-nine, had two galleys, the latest in mechanical developments and six spectacular staterooms.

Adam bought it on the spot. He met with the captain of the former owner and engaged him along with the entire crew. He gave orders for the yacht to be painted and refurbished throughout, and the name on the stern to be *Lynda II*.

He telephoned to Lynda that he had found the perfect yacht and why didn't she fly over to see it, and they could go on to Paris and spend a couple of days there.

When Lynda saw the yacht her eyes widened and she said, "Well, kiddo, we are really getting into the big league, aren't we?"

Before leaving for Paris, Adam told the captain he wanted the yacht in Monte Carlo ready to sail on August 1.

In Paris they went to the Hotel George V, where Adam's tips had quickly made them favorites. They were given an enormous suite. Adam sat down at the telephone in the living room, and before he started calling New York, asked the concierge downstairs to reserve a table for him that night at Maxim's.

Lynda spent the afternoon at Givenchy, ordering the kind of clothes she wanted to wear on the yacht that summer. She had modeled a few times for Givenchy on her working trips to Paris ten years ago, and he had tried to persuade her to return. He had come out from his workroom wearing his white work jacket to consult with her. They decided on an all-white wardrobe, tailored pants suits in both wool and cotton, white bathing suits, robes, sweaters and evening dresses.

"It will be a pleasure because I know how well you'll look in them," he said. "Not many women who can afford to order custom clothes have a figure and ideas like you have."

Before she left, Lynda also commissioned Givenchy to design special terry-cloth robes for both the men and the women guests to wear while they were on board the yacht. She fancied the idea of a group all in related clothes lounging around the pool on the sun deck. She asked the tall, handsome designer where he was going to spend the summer and invited him for at least a weekend cruise with them, if he could.

Lynda felt totally happy. As they walked through the hotel lobby, she knew that she in a long hot pink brocade dress and Adam in his dinner clothes made an effective couple. She could see heads turning as they walked past.

At Maxim's, Roger, the maître d' who knew everybody, greeted Adam with "Ah, Monsieur Adler, welcome to Paris again." He bowed to Lynda and added, "And a special welcome to *la belle* Lynda."

It was Friday night, and the room was full of men and women in evening clothes. Lynda was able to recognize the Duke and Duchess of Windsor at one of the parties they passed on the way to their table.

"Did you hear what Roger just said?" Adam asked as they sat down side by side on the banquette that was built along the wall at one end of the room.

"You mean when he called me *la belle* Lynda?"

"He gave me a great idea. I'm going to change the name of the yacht. It's going to be called *La Belle Lynda.*"

"How fabulous. I love that."

"I'll call Amsterdam tomorrow. It happened just in time. I never really was satisfied with *Lynda II.* Everybody does that when they get a bigger boat."

As Adam gave the waiter his order and handed him a tissue-paper-wrapped bottle of corn oil for his salad dressing, Lynda sat back, listened to the music and looked over the clothes. It was a super-fashion spectacle, she decided, but she wondered why the orchestra didn't switch occasionally to something jazzier.

As they ate dinner they talked about the yacht and their first cruise. "Who should we have with us?" Adam asked.

"Crystal, of course," Lynda said.

"Yes, I'd rather have her with us so I can keep an eye on her instead of back in the office trying to take over."

"What do you mean?"

"When I got back the last time we were away, everyone was running to her instead of to me, and I think she liked it."

"I wonder who she will bring along. She never seems to get too tangled up with anyone."

"I guess her age gets in her way. The guys she likes to go out with shy away from getting too serious about a girl in her fifties."

"With that face and figure, why should age matter?"

"Seems to."

"We'll have Alan, of course."

"Unfortunately, not this time. Eva has already said she wants to take him to Hawaii in August. When I spoke to the office yesterday, I intimated to Wally that we want him and Peggy. That'll make a party of six, which is nice, and maybe we'll pick up some other people we know as we go along."

As soon as she reached home, Lynda called Crystal and told her about the new yacht and that she was invited on the maiden cruise. She was to pick her own partner for the six weeks they'd be away.

"Oh, thank you, darling, but I couldn't possibly spend six weeks so far away from the office." The past nine months had been a complete triumph for Crystal. The naked contessa advertisement for Head to Toe had created a real furor. She had been interviewed in newspapers, appeared on talk shows and been praised right and left for her courage and ingenuity. "You're getting more telephone calls than Mr. Adler," an operator had told her when they met on an elevator recently. She hoped no one had told Adam.

"You've just got to come, Crystal," Lynda urged. "It's just not healthy to go without a vacation."

"I know that, but I don't plan to go so far away or stay so long." Actually, she had promised to go with Douglas Knolls for two weeks at an Adirondack camp that a friend was loaning him.

"Wait a minute, Crystal. Adam wants to talk to you," Lynda said.

Adam's voice came booming over the wire. "Get ready to pack your sailing clothes, girl. You're coming on our boat. It's orders."

"But, Adam, I have so much to do. I'm going to use a beautiful Polynesian girl for my next naked ad, and I haven't found her yet. She's going to be lying clear across a double spread in a kind of Rousseau jungle. It will be an elegant version of *Playboy*'s double page, and it will sell our cosmetics like nothing has yet."

"Sounds promising, but just get a move on and do it fast. We sail the first of August and you can bring along any guy you like."

Damn it, she thought. I hate to be ordered to do anything. But I'm sure Adam's cruise will be an experience.

The day after Lynda's telephone call she looked out of the bedroom window and saw Doug was digging around the bushes in the small garden below. She threw on a sweater and skirt and ran down the outside stairs to tell him the news.

"Doug, how would you like to go with me on a six weeks' cruise on the Mediterranean and the Adriatic?"

"My God. What an invitation! Anything with you, Crystal, would be heaven, but I have to warn you now that I'm not the best sailor in the world."

"Oh, don't worry about being seasick. Adam's new yacht has all of the most modern stabilizers. You won't feel a ripple."

On the last day of July the two of them flew to Paris and changed to another plane. Late that afternoon they arrived in Nice.

"We're being met, Doug." As Crystal spoke she saw a tall, white-uniformed man, followed by two others, coming towards her, and as they came closer she could see that they had *La Belle Lynda* embroidered on their breast pockets.

"Miss Crystal?"

"Yes, and this is Mr. Douglas Knolls."

Their hand luggage was taken from them and they were led to a car and driver. "Your baggage will follow in another car, Miss Crystal. Just give us your luggage tags."

As they drove through Nice, Crystal asked to stop at the flower market, where they got out and bought a huge bouquet of tuberoses for Lynda. Their fragrance filled the car as it climbed the hill and started the long, serpentine drive to Monte Carlo.

"They're just a little bit too-too, don't you think?" asked Douglas.

"They're certainly definite in the scent department, but I guess I like things to be definite."

When the car reached Monte Carlo, it followed the road that dipped down towards the harbor. They started to circle the yacht basin. Just as she looked up and saw the palace of Monaco at the top of the hill, they stopped in front of the two largest yachts in the harbor. One, she saw, was Charles Revson's *Ultima II* and the other was *La Belle Lynda*. They were exactly in the center of the circular basin, like two choice diamonds with the smaller boats arranged like baguettes on each side.

They crossed a small gangplank and on the main deck the captain came forward to greet them. "Welcome to *La Belle Lynda*, Miss Crystal. I'm Captain König."

"*Sie sind Deutsch, ja, Herr Kapitän?*"

Crystal and the captain went into a cross fire of German words that left Douglas Knolls standing dumbfounded.

"Sorry, I forgot introductions. This is Mr. Knolls." She turned back to Doug. "The captain just explained that Adam and Lynda are resting. He will show us to our rooms, and we're expected on the upper deck for cocktails at eight-thirty. We are to wear whatever we like."

The wall of Crystal's stateroom was covered in pale yellow fabric, and Doug's, which was two down, was done in a masculine plaid. As she unpacked, Crystal felt she had never been so pampered. The hangers in her closet, which was part of a dressing-room alcove, were pale yellow to match her room. Her own Young Forever products were laid out on her dressing table along with the best of Adam and Eve. Some of the latest books and magazines were arranged on the table beside a comfortable chaise longue, and there was a telephone beside her bed. A small desk held the special stationery she remembered that Lynda had ordered from Cartier when they first bought the yacht. The notepaper, correspondence cards and envelopes were a pale blue paper, embossed with *La Belle Lynda* in a navy blue. They looked so tempting that she sat down and wrote a letter to Shelley.

Crystal decided to walk up the carpeted stairs to cocktails instead of taking the elevator to the upper deck. She was wearing a long white jersey dress with a sailor collar and a middy tie that Shelley had made for her. She was glad it had sleeves, since the room was cold as the inside of a refrigerator. The low end of the thermometer had become a status symbol ever since air conditioning came in, she thought.

Douglas was already at the bar talking with Peggy and Wally Nelson. When Lynda and Adam arrived Adam was sniffing one wrist and then the other, and as he came up to the bar he held out both hands to Wally. "We've got to make a final decision on our new perfume. I've narrowed it down to these two, and I'd like your opinion."

Wally bent over, sniffed each wrist. "The one on your right wrist is my favorite. It's really got a message. It's definitely on the whorey side, and I think women are in the mood for that kind of scent right now."

Adam went around and shook hands with Doug. "Welcome aboard, Knolls." Then he extended his wrists. "What's your opinion?"

Doug took a long time sniffing. "I'd say the left. It's more delicate and romantic."

"How about asking the girls?" Peggy Nelson interrupted. "After all, we do the buying."

"Not really," Adam said. "Most perfume is a gift from some man, and it's men's reaction—not just husbands and lovers, but what taxi drivers say when a woman gets into a cab—that makes or breaks a perfume."

Crystal burst out laughing. "The crew are fascinated by us. They must think we're crazy, going around sniffing wrists."

After another round of drinks, Adam announced, "We're going to the Sporting Club for dinner," so they all piled into the car. Afterwards Crystal had her first glimpse of the Casino, which was full of anxious faces bending over tables of black jack, chemin de fer and roulette. Adam bought ten one-hundred-dollar chips and promptly lost them on the roulette wheel. "That's my gift to Prince Rainier for the season. Let's go home," he said.

The next morning Crystal was sunning herself on deck beside the pool when she heard a commotion on the pier. She went to the railing and saw that Lyn and Charles Revson were arriving, and most of their Oriental crew was lined up at attention to help with the luggage.

"Maybe we ought to invite them over for drinks," Lynda said to Adam at luncheon. "We're so close together, it seems sort of rude not to. Besides, I'd like to know her. I like her looks."

"Why not?" said Adam, who was longing to see the interior of the *Ultima II* and to show off to Charles Revson his new radar equipment. He and Lynda went below, wrote a note and sent it over by one of the crew.

Several hours later a return note came from the *Ultima II* regretting that the yacht's owners had made previous engagements. At cocktail time, though, no guests appeared. The Revsons remained on their deck and made no effort to disguise the fact that they preferred to remain alone.

"Son of a bitch," said Adam. He had planned to stay in the harbor for several days, but he called the captain and told him that they would leave the next morning.

The noise of the engines awakened Crystal, but after a while everything was quiet again and, looking out of her stateroom window, she could see that Liz Taylor and Richard Burton's unglamorous yacht was still alongside, without the Burtons but full of children and dogs. She was equally sure that the *Ultima II* would still be on the other side.

Later on deck, Lynda was already splashing in the pool. She came up the ladder wearing a mini bikini that was open at the sides and held together by cords. "Adam's furious, so don't ask any questions. Our anchors have somehow got stuck together with the *Ultima*'s, and we have to send for help to get loose. The two large boats, it seems, have been together in the harbor for so long that they formed a permanent attachment for each other."

All day the crew was in and out of the water and the engines were starting and stopping, while the *Ul-*

tima II maintained a dignified silence. Adam sat grimly in a deck chair and the only time he smiled was when he and Doug had a drink together at the bar and Douglas said, "I've been following the success of your stock from the very beginning and I'm terribly impressed that it made the New York Stock Exchange in just over a year."

Later Adam told Crystal, "That friend of yours is a very pleasant and intelligent fellow. Glad you brought him on board." He had just telephoned to Nice and engaged a crew of deep-sea divers. They would come at dawn, disentangle the anchors, and *La Belle Lynda* would go on its way.

The noise of the divers woke Crystal in what seemed to her the middle of the night. Hours later, when she heard the engines turn on, she quickly put on a bathing suit and rushed to the deck.

For days the two big yachts had been a source of entertainment to all Monte Carlo. The pier was already crowded to watch the crew cast off the lines. As *La Belle Lynda* slid slowly away from the pier, hands waved, children yelled and every boat in the harbor blew its whistle. Even the *Ultima II* joined the din. It was the customary salute to a new boat sailing on its maiden voyage.

"Thank God, we're out of there," said Adam as they finally cleared the harbor. Peggy and Wally had their heads buried in books and Crystal and Adam started to play backgammon. Lynda and Doug were deep in discussing yoga and he gave her a first lesson on the deck that afternoon.

They moved slowly towards the Italian coast. The sea was silky smooth and they made brief stops at all the ports like San Remo, Portofino and Porto Ercole. The minute she saw land approaching Lynda always rushed to her stateroom and covered her bikini with a long skirt. Wearing dark glasses and carrying a big straw bag on her arm, she was ready to go on shore to shop the minute they either docked or anchored some distance off and sent in their tender.

Crystal usually went with her, but only as a polite

gesture. She had always been totally bored with shopping as a pastime and never went to stores except when she knew exactly what she wanted. Usually she and Doug strolled around the ports together.

Looking at her watch in the afternoon and calculating the difference in time, Crystal would think, "Pomeroy will have just finished the morning mail. I almost wish I were back there, no matter how beautiful this place is."

The day after they left Porto Santo Stefano, the water, which had been smooth as an ice-skating rink, began to break into white-crested waves and they felt the motion of the boat for the first time. "How glorious!" cried Crystal, who loved the wind and the slight spray she felt on her cheeks.

"This yacht has the best and latest thing in stabilizers. Guaranteed to keep anybody from getting seasick," Adam promised.

As the motion became more pronounced, Doug disappeared to his stateroom. By dinnertime the going was so rough that the plates and glasses slid off the table one of the crew was setting. Doug didn't appear and neither did Peggy and Wally. Adam, Lynda and Crystal spread a cloth on the floor and decided to eat picnic style.

The next morning they were anchored in the slight shelter of the rocky island of Capri, and the wind was beginning to die down. Everyone reported for breakfast except Doug, and when the steward reported that he had been quite sick, Adam went below to see him. He had gone back to sleep, so the five of them went ashore.

When she saw the narrow cobblestone streets, lined on both sides with shops and full of shoppers that looked as if they were in costume for an operetta, Lynda told Adam that she had to stay in Capri at least three or four days. She made a minor purchase of five pairs of espadrilles before they went back to the yacht for lunch.

On deck the chief steward handed Adam a letter addressed to Signor and Signorina Adam Adler. "I don't know a damn soul in this place," Adam said as he tore it open.

"Look at that crest! It's an invitation from some count and countess for dinner," said Lynda, who was reading over Adam's shoulder.

"It seems like the Conte and Contessa Enrico Bonini request the pleasure of our company, along with our guests, for dinner tomorrow night. Does anybody here have any idea who they are?"

"We can ask Doug, but I doubt if he has any more idea than we have," Crystal said.

Adam was all for tearing up the invitation and forgetting it, but Crystal suggested that she and Doug were going back for more shopping after lunch and that she would telephone the Contessa from the Quisisana Hotel and deliver their regrets.

At the Quisisana, Crystal asked the concierge to call the Villa Bonini and to stand by in case neither she nor Doug was fluent enough in Italian to cope with the Contessa. When the Villa Bonini answered she asked for the Contessa, and after a stream of *"Momento, momento,"* an unexpectedly American voice came on the wire.

"I'm calling for Mr. and Mrs. Adler. It won't be possible . . ."

"Oh, Miss Crystal, honey, is that really you? I recognized your beautiful voice instantly. You were so sweet to me when I was just Emma Lou Perkins. Remember?"

"Emma Lou! Of course I do."

"You see, I read in the papers about Mr. Adler buying this yacht and naming it for his new wife, so when I saw it come into the harbor this morning, I said to Enrico, 'You've just got to meet all these darling people who were wonderful to me in New York.'"

"We had no idea that the Contessa was you, Emma Lou."

"I do hope Mr. Adler isn't too mad that I left right after my year's contract and didn't want to continue modeling for Adam and Eve. I just wanted to see the world and it all worked out like a dream. The very first country I saw was Italy and one of the first people I met was Enrico. It was love at first sight, but I'll tell you all about that tomorrow night at dinner. You all will come, won't you?"

"Yes, of course. I can hardly wait to hear the story and I'm sure Mr. Adler will be interested, too. You probably remember Peggy and Wally Nelson. They are with us, too."

"Then how many of you will be coming?"

"We're six."

"That's wonderful. Then we'll expect you at nine."

After some brief shopping, Crystal and Doug rushed back to the boat, where Adam and Lynda were sitting on the deck with the Nelsons, sniffing each other's wrists. Adam was saying, "I still like the whorey one the best."

Crystal interrupted. "You'll never guess who the Contessa is, Adam."

"Somebody we know?"

"Somebody we know very well—Emma Lou Perkins. I accepted for all of us."

"Emma Lou Perkins a contessa? I'll be damned. It will be worth seeing," Adam said, laughing.

The Villa Bonini was not too far up the hill from the port. They entered through an iron gate connected to a high concrete wall and walked along a path that smelled of roses and jasmine. When they reached the villa itself, they could see that the path continued on down the hill and Adam guessed it led to a small private beach.

They walked up the stone steps into a marble foyer just as Emma Lou fluttered down the stairway in pale blue chiffon. "Oh, you darlings, am I ever glad to see you!" She went from one to the other embracing them, including Douglas. "Oh, Mr. Knolls. Perhaps I shouldn't have, seeing that I just met you, but I got carried away."

"My pleasure," said Douglas.

Emma Lou was soon followed by Enrico, a good-looking young Italian, and finally by his mother, the senior Contessa.

"Enrico doesn't speak English too well, but I'm teaching him, and the Contessa doesn't speak a word, but she doesn't mind us talking," Emma Lou said.

She took Adam's arm, and the others followed as she led them through the big, airy rooms.

"Quite a place you have here," Adam said as they reached an open patio where a long table with lighted candles was waiting for them.

"I just love it, Adam, if you don't mind my remembering I used to call you that." As she indicated where they were to sit at the table, she said, "I've got a surprise for you-all. We're going to have a south'n dinner, served Italian style. I've learned to love pasta, but I didn't have the slightest intention of leaving my favorites at home. Everybody here likes it, especially Mama Bonini, and I guess I have the distinction of bringing sweet-potato soufflé and corn bread to Capri."

The southern dinner was completely compatible with the soft Italian night, Crystal thought. She sat by Enrico, who not only was quite inarticulate when he tried to speak, but also seemed quite shy. From what she understood, he had become a confirmed bachelor until he met Emma Lou, who smiled up at him while drinking a glass of Coca-Cola all by herself in the Capri square. Until he brought her to the villa his mother had never approved of any of his choices.

Crystal heard Emma Lou ask Adam where the yacht was going after it left Capri. Adam answered it would stop in Naples for refueling and then probably go to Taormina and Palermo and then head up the Dalmatian coast to Venice.

"Oh, I'll bet you're going to the masked ball. I'm just dying to go, but Enrico doesn't like big parties."

"Yes, we are. Crystal got us invited," Lynda said. "We already have our costumes. You are supposed to wear red, white or gold."

"Oh, I know. I've been reading all about it."

"Come along with us, if you want to," said Adam. "There's lots of room."

The next night when Emma Lou and Enrico came aboard the yacht for dinner, Emma Lou announced that Enrico had decided to forget his hatred of big parties for the sake of the Venice Ball. "We'd just adore to come with you," she said, "and Riki—that's what he wants all of you to call him—says he'll be happy to telephone ahead and reserve a place for this big beautiful boat of yours, if you haven't already done it."

"I never thought of it."

"Well, Riki says there are going to be dozens of yachts in Venice and that you've simply got to be anchored in the Grand Canal, opposite San Marco, where Mr. Onassis always has his boat. It's just one of those things, like the main floor of Harry's Bar."

"Well, Miss Dixie, you certainly know your way around Italy. Tell Riki he would do me a great favor if he telephoned the harbor master." After Emma Lou and Riki had gone ashore and most of the group had said good night, Douglas pulled Crystal down beside him on the built-in couch at the stern of the yacht.

"It's too spectacular a night to turn in early," he said. "Did you ever see such a sky?"

Crystal lay back and listened to the sound of the water and the Italian music that came drifting over it from the pier. It couldn't be a more romantic setting, she admitted, but all she wanted was to go to her stateroom and fall asleep.

"You don't give a damn about me, do you, Crystal?" He put his arm around her and pulled her closer.

"Of course I do, Doug, or I wouldn't have asked you to come with me on this cruise."

"I hoped so when you asked me, but now I know it's not true." He leaned over and kissed her.

"That was nice, Doug."

"Nice is not enough, darling."

"Well, then, I like you better than any man I know. You're the most interesting, and fun to be with."

"That's not enough, either. At this point in my life I

want someone who is warm and loving and, perhaps, needs me a little. You don't seem to need anybody to reassure you. You're very self-contained, aren't you?"

"I've learned to be. But I do need you in my life, Doug."

"As an extra, yes. But what I really want to be is the only man."

"At the moment I don't care about anybody else, Doug."

"Don't worry. I'm going to hang on a while and see if I can make you change your mind, but not for the next ten days. I'm going to leave the yacht tomorrow."

"What a pity. I'll miss you very much."

"I'm no sailor. The least motion of this boat kills me, but I would have stuck it out if I thought you really care about me."

"But I do care."

"As things stand, darling, I'll go to Rome, kill some time and join you in Venice, unless Adam finds someone else he wants to occupy my stateroom."

Doug left the yacht the next day for Rome and Emma Lou and Riki came aboard. *La Belle Lynda* weighed anchor and headed for Sicily.

30

Thanks to Riki's intervention, *La Belle Lynda* lay at anchor in one of the most eye-catching spots in the Grand Canal, close to the domed church of Santa Maria della Salute, which was beginning to glow pale pink in the late-afternoon sun. Across the wide stretch of water they could see a colorful crowd moving along a promenade outlining the Canal, and in the distance they could distinguish the tall Campanile of San Marco.

The approach to Venice had been even more dramatic than they had expected, and they had all been on deck to look at the seeming myriad of small green islands with pastel houses rising out of the blue water. As they drew nearer, a pilot boat had come rushing out to show them to their place. Adam had been happy to find himself alongside the *Christina,* separating him from the *Ultima II.*

The next morning, they were all on deck and eager to go ashore. Their own launch, which had to be lowered, was waiting for them. Lynda, carrying a big empty tote bag over her arm, was the last to appear. "Adam isn't coming. He doesn't like the smell of the water and would rather stay on board in air-conditioned rooms. But Riki has invited us all for lunch at Harry's Bar and he'll meet us there at one."

"It's unbelievable! Far more beautiful than the picture postcards I've seen of it," Crystal said as they entered the Piazza San Marco. She was looking at the pigeons as they fluttered up in a cloud of white wings against the mellow golden color of the Byzantine cathedral. "It's like being inside a kaleidoscope the way the colors change around every minute." They stood and watched the little group of figures parade in front of the clock as it struck eleven and then separated, each going in a different direction.

Crystal chose the narrow street under the clock and walked along a path that turned and twisted, sometimes wide and sometimes narrow. Every minute there was a different scene—a miniature bridge, a gondolier with a big hat, a window full of antiques, a pastry shop, a curly-haired little Italian child with melting brown eyes begging for money.

This has to be the most fascinating place in the world, she thought as she began to retrace her steps slowly.

On the outside, Harry's Bar looked like anything but the international play place Crystal had heard so much about. It was on a small side street near the Canal and flanked by tourist-type shops. Once inside the doors, though, she found that the crowd around the bar was already three deep and the tables that filled the rest of the room were full of people from all over the world who all seemed to know each other and were exchanging hilarious greetings.

Luckily Riki had made reservations and most of their party was already seated at a table when Crystal arrived. They were drinking Bellinis, Harry's famous combination of fresh peach juice and champagne. Riki introduced Crystal to Consuela and Rudi Crespi, sitting with Countess Vendramin Marcello on one side of their table, and to Clara von Furstenberg and her daughter Ira on the other. He seemed to know everyone in the room.

It was the afternoon of the ball, but Crystal was still lying on the deck, feeling the last slanting rays of the sun on her body and watching the Canal that had a never-ending fascination. Motoscafos were darting back and forth like dragonflies across the water, and occasional gondolas slid quietly by filled with people, luggage, or flowers. She watched a gondola detach itself from the far shore and come towards them. When it arrived alongside, she saw that it held the hairdresser, the manicurist and the makeup man they had all been waiting for.

When she had asked Shelley to design her costume, she had said, "I don't really want a drop-dead kind of thing. It would be too hard to carry around for weeks ahead of time, but I want to look as good as possible." The result was a Grecian tunic of pleated white chiffon with a long white chiffon cape outlined with gold braid that tied at her throat. Shelley had made her a crown of pale gold leaves and fastened a sheer gold veil to it that she could take off when they unmasked. As she dressed, she began to wish she had let Shelley design the gold-sequin mermaid dress he had first suggested, but it was too late to do anything about it now.

The makeup man that Adam had ordered to fly in from the firm's Paris headquarters had at least given her interesting eyes. Their usually direct look was camouflaged by blue shadows.

She reached into her dressing-table drawer and took out a little jewel box. It held her grandmother's necklace, which she had decided to take out of the bank vault before she left New York and wear for the first time. It's old-fashioned, she thought as she looked at the little circle of mine-cut diamonds. The women who will be wearing the millions of dollars of jewelry that I've been reading about won't give it the time of day, but I still love it. She fastened it around her neck and it fitted perfectly at the base of her throat.

Thanks to Riki, their whole party was included in a dinner that Countess Volpi was giving before the ball. When they met on the deck for a drink before taking off in their tender, Crystal felt very plain indeed compared to Lynda, who looked like an Indian in bright red chiffon and a long red feather headdress. Peggy was in deep red brocade, and Emma Lou had managed to borrow Marguerite's gold-and-white jewel song costume from the wardrobe of Venice's Fenici

Opera Company. She had also cajoled the wardrobe mistress into loaning a red Satan suit for Riki to wear.

Adam and Wally Nelson had both flatly refused to put on a costume and were wearing their usual black tie. Crystal was happy that Doug, who had returned to the boat the night before, had brought with him from Rome a gold-embroidered white satin cape to cover his sober black dinner jacket.

Their launch joined the parade of private boats, all heading down the Canal to drop their costumed passengers at different palazzos. Crystal was glad that the Palazzo Volpi was at the far end of the Grand Canal, since it gave her more time to look at the elegant old buildings, one more romantic than the other, some of them with waves already breaking over the doorsills.

Their launch came alongside a pier at the Palazzo Volpi and they walked into the lower entrance hall across a small bridge. Upstairs in the big, high-ceilinged room where cocktails were being served, Crystal saw Princess Grace was in gold and white, wearing a Venetian gold collarpiece as a face mask. She recognized Douglas Fairbanks, Jr., and a lady wearing a satin tricorne hat was Clare Boothe Luce, yet she was as interested in the palazzo as she was in the guests.

It was three stories high, including the half floors, and built around an inner court with many balconies, from one of which she could see formal flower beds below. "I don't know how many rooms we have in the palace and I don't think my mother does either," Giovanni Volpi told her later. "I'd guess it might be around eighty, including the chapel, but with all of them we still don't have an electric dishwasher or washing machine."

Giovanni led her to the front of the palazzo and onto a balcony that looked down on the Canal. Launches were still drawing up and discharging guests, but she was aware that only a very small group out of the seven hundred who would be at the ball had been invited to the Volpi dinner.

It was eleven o'clock when they left the party to go

to the ball. As they walked to the launch, Crystal felt a few light drops of rain on her face. It couldn't be, she thought, since only a few hours ago she had sat in the stern of the launch looking up at a sky that seemed to be peppered with stars.

"It looks to me as if a lot of beautiful people are going to get their feet wet," Doug said.

They were only halfway to the Palazzo Rezzonico, where the ball was to be held, when the downpour started. Raindrops rattled against the windows of the launch. A strong wind whipped the Canal into waves and the launch began to rock.

Around the landing float that was anchored in front of Rezzonico, there was a traffic jam of launches, jockeying to get alongside, where attendants in costume were waiting with umbrellas. The launch from the Onassis yacht pushed itself noisily through the scene, and though some of the launches moved politely to let it pass, it collided with a more stubborn boat. The launch that was drawing along beside them was suddenly sideswiped by a passing boat, and the noise of breaking glass added to the confusion. The injured launch went on, and inside it they could see Clare Boothe Luce adjusting her tricorne hat.

The rain was already slacking when they finally reached the Palazzo Rezzonico and once inside they forgot it quickly. The huge ballroom, carved and gilded, with its lofty ceiling painted by Tiepolo, was lighted with Venetian chandeliers. It held, Crystal realized instantly, a unique collection of people in the most lavish costumes that she would ever see.

Even though Elizabeth Taylor was still masked (her hair was covered with a glittering white sunburst), Crystal quickly spotted her by her figure and the fabulous emerald necklace. The tall girl in a cloud of net embroidered with beads and sequins and an enormous headdress turned out to be Jacqueline de Ribes of Paris, whose photographs she had often seen in Vogue.

"There's Rose Kennedy, in the white dress, talking with Nicole Alphand. Her husband was the French

Ambassador to Washington when her son was President," Doug said.

Crystal had fallen in love with Italian palazzos, and she was longing to see more of this historic one. She wandered out on one of the balconies where Ira Furstenberg was standing with a tall man, whom she introduced as Eliot Tyler Young. They talked about the party for a few minutes, but when they left, Crystal remained on the balcony for a while.

When she came back to the ballroom the orchestra was playing a Viennese waltz. She was looking around for Lynda's red feathers when she felt a hand on her arm. It belonged to Eliot Tyler Young.

"Will you waltz with me, Vilia?"

"Why do you call me that?"

"I see I've shocked you, and I don't quite know why I did. It may have been those gold leaves in your hair. Vilia was the witch of the woods, wasn't she?"

"Vilia was also my grandmother's name."

They reached the dance space in the center of the ballroom and began to waltz. "I'm not surprised," he said. "There's something about you that doesn't seem to fit with the all-American group you're with."

"How do you know about my group?"

"I saw you all at Harry's Bar yesterday, and I saw you come in tonight. If Ira hadn't happened to introduce us, I was going to ask you to dance anyway."

"That's nice. I like dancing with you."

"Good. That's the first step and I can tell you right now that we're going to do plenty of dancing together."

The music stopped and he guided her through the crowd and onto the balcony again. They leaned over the railing to watch some of the crowd that was still arriving.

"I was admiring your necklace as we danced."

"That's rather ridiculous, isn't it, with Elizabeth Taylor's emeralds and the other millions of dollars' worth of famous stones here that you could be looking at."

"Yours is more charming. I can see that it's an old

one. I like mine-cut diamonds because they glitter instead of staring the way the marquise-cut stones do. The setting is European, I'll bet. I'd say it was made in Austria or Hungary. Did your grandmother give it to you?"

"Yes, she did."

"Don't look so shocked. Am I still stirring up bad memories?"

"No, just good ones. I'm surprised that you're so observant."

"I'm an interested observer of most people, but I'm deeply interested in you."

"Why on earth? You don't know me at all, and you may not even like me in half an hour."

"I intend to follow my instinct. It tells me I'm going to like you even better."

"I think you're a little crazy."

"It's possible. Other people have said so, including my mother, but the fact is, I always know what I want."

They returned to the dance floor for another waltz, then went out to the balcony and were back in the ballroom again when Crystal saw Lynda's red feathers approaching them through the crowd.

After she had been introduced to Eliot Tyler Young, Lynda said, "Sorry to interrupt, but we've been looking all around for you. Adam's bored and wants to go home now that he knows Charles Revson and Estée Lauder have seen him. Doug seems tired and the Nelsons are taking an early plane tomorrow for New York, but if you're not ready we can send the launch back for you."

"She's not ready, and I'll be responsible for returning her safely to the yacht," Eliot said.

"Yes, I'd like to stay. We may be going on to another party given by Marina Cicogna for the Burtons," Crystal said.

"Come whenever you want. One of the crew will be on duty all night." Then, turning to Eliot, Lynda said, "You know where our yacht is, don't you?"

"Who in Venice doesn't know where *La Belle Lyn-*

da is anchored?" Before Lynda left she had invited him to have dinner aboard the next night.

Crystal and Eliot left the ball soon after. Once they were settled in his launch, he told the sailor to take them to the Hotel Cipriani. "I thought we were going to Marina's party," Crystal said.

"That would have been pretty silly, wouldn't it, when I could hardly wait to get you away from that one, and you knew it, didn't you?"

She didn't answer for a minute. "Why are we going to the Cipriani?"

"Because I want to talk to you away from all the music and crowds of people, though I know quite a lot already. I know that you work with that gloomy guy who has the fashion model wife dressed like Minnehaha, and I know the fellow you came with but didn't seem too interested in is a somewhat neurotic New York stock broker. I also know Enrico and his southern baby doll."

"You're well informed."

"I like to know my facts."

There were still a few motor launches on the Canal with both Venetians and tourists curious to see celebrities and their costumes. The water was rougher than usual from the storm, but Crystal enjoyed the motion as their launch wove its way among the others. Soon they were passing Santa Maria della Salute and the lineup of the three giant yachts. Crystal didn't mind the slight spray from the waves, and as they turned off the Canal, passing pillared San Giorgio with its lighted dome, Eliot pointed to the new moon rising in the distance.

They came alongside the pier of the Cipriani. Eliot jumped out and took her hand to help her out. They went through the foyer to the bar, which was completely dark. "I've got some champagne up in my suite. Let's have a nightcap there."

When they entered his sitting room, which opened onto a large terrace overlooking the swimming pool, he said, "May I remove your crown?" His fingers searched for the clips and pins and he lifted off the wreath of golden leaves. "Your hair is extraordinary," he said.

He filled a glass with ice and poured champagne into it. "I noticed you drank almost nothing tonight, so I gather you don't go for the heavy stuff."

"No, I don't. I never drink anything but wine or champagne."

"That figures. You have a kind of undiluted, crystal-clear quality that goes with your name. It's a good name, but I find it cold. I like Vilia better, and now that I know that it belongs to your family, I'm going to call you that. Do you mind?"

"No, I'm getting used to it, and I rather like it."

"Tell me about the first Vilia."

"I don't feel like telling my life story tonight."

"Then I'll give you a capsule version of mine. I'm an only son who was spoiled rotten, and since I don't get up early in the morning and go to an office, I suppose I rate as one of the drones of the world."

"Don't you ever get bored?"

"Not so far. I've wandered all over the world and found plenty to amuse me."

"Where do you live?"

"Wherever I happen to feel like. I've lived in Rome for a little while, but I'm tired of it. Before that I had a farm in Kenya. I found it satisfactory, but I'm not sure you'd like it. Too primitive. Any more questions, or have I passed the exam?"

She laughed. "I can't think of anything else to ask."

"Come, Vilia, it's customary for a lady who's drinking champagne in a man's hotel apartment at two in the morning to ask him about his love life or, at least, whether or not he has a wife tucked away somewhere."

"Why should I care?"

"You don't take me seriously, do you?" he said, turning serious for the first time. "I'm not a flirt. I've always found it a waste of energy to flirt with a woman who doesn't violently attract me."

She looked at him intently. He was certainly the most extraordinary man she had ever met.

Everything about Eliot Tyler Young was on a generous scale—his height and powerful shoulders that his obviously well-tailored dinner suit only accentuated, his mane of salt-and-pepper hair, his gray eyes. Even though his nails were manicured, his hands gave her a sense of strength.

"I'm really beginning to be interested. Do you have a wife tucked away somewhere?"

He laughed, and his laugh was on the same generous scale. "No, I'm forty-six and still *totally* untamed. Not that I haven't had any woman in my life or deliberately shied away from being tied down. Maybe I never met the right girl at the right time."

"What do you do with your time? Some kind of sport, maybe? Even in your evening clothes you look as if you had just come from outdoors."

He laughed again. "I've shot big game occasionally, and I'm a big golf nut, but I guess my favorite sport is cards. I'm a chronic game player but I'm not a gambler. I find the casinos a big bore, and I think I'm beginning to bore you."

"No. I find you unique. I've never met a man like you before." She was looking at him and smiling as she thought: Finally, here's a man who doesn't seem to be bothered by my age.

He came over to her and took the glass out of her hands. "I'm violently attracted to you, Vilia. Let's not talk any more. We can do that tomorrow." He pulled her to her feet and kissed her, and then picked her up as easily as if she had been a baby.

Still holding her in his arms, he carried her into the bedroom and dropped her so hard on the bed that she bounced and sat upright with her dress falling off one shoulder.

"What's this all about?"

"You look a little angry, Vilia, and it's very becoming to you. I have the impression that you have been in a deep freeze, or at least slightly refrigerated, for the past few years."

As he pulled off her dress, she could hear the fabric

tearing. He took off his clothes and lay down beside her.

"Another hunch I have about you, Vilia, is that you like sex, just good simple sex." He kissed her gently. "If I'm not right, I'm going to take you back to *La Belle Lynda*. I'm sure I'm right, aren't I, Vilia?"

She put her arms around his waist. "Yes," she said.

Just before the sun came up, Crystal returned to *La Belle Lynda*. The sky was still pale gray, and there was no one in sight except a member of the crew as they came alongside. Eliot Tyler Young kissed her, helped her onto the landing platform and watched her climb the companionway and reach the deck safely. She was wrapped in one of his raincoats over her torn dress and was carrying the gold leaves.

Crystal went to her stateroom as quickly as she could, and breathed a sigh of relief, when she had closed her door, that no one had seen her come in. She took off the dress, folded it neatly and put it away on a closet shelf so that the cabin boys wouldn't see it and speculate on the damage. The covers of the bed had been turned back, so she lay down. I'll sleep just a couple of hours, she thought, but it was noon before she woke.

She jumped up in a hurry, took a quick shower and put on a fresh white shirt and pants. How did it all happen and what have I got myself into? she wondered as she brushed her hair and put on her lipstick.

This time she took the elevator to the upper deck, where she found Adam and Lynda, stretched out on deck chairs, sipping fresh peach juice from tall glasses.

"The Nelsons and Doug told us to say goodbye for them," Lynda said.

"Doug? Did he leave, too?"

"Yes. He was feeling in a lousy mood this morning and on the spur of the moment decided to go with Peggy and Wally."

"I feel so guilty," Crystal said. "I meant to be on deck earlier. I wish someone had called me."

"I knocked," Lynda said, "and when you didn't answer I even opened the door, but you were so completely out that I didn't have the heart to wake you."

"Well, it was a big night," Adam interrupted, "but I can take that kind of thing or leave it."

Lynda got up to sit on the arm of Adam's chair. "I've got a sourpuss for a husband. I just loved the whole evening. I saw all my fashion pals from Paris, like Pierre Cardin, Marc Bohan and Hubert Givenchy. By the way, I asked Hubert and Capucine to have dinner with us tonight, along with your new pal, Crystal. What's his name?"

"Eliot Tyler Young."

At that moment the chief steward appeared. "Mr. Young to see you, Miss Crystal."

They were all laughing as Eliot appeared on deck a moment later wearing crisp white slacks and a navy open shirt. He laughed, too. "Good afternoon, I've come to ask if I could borrow your beautiful guest and take her to lunch at the Lido?"

Crystal took his hand and introduced him to Adam, who said, "Sit down and have a drink with us first."

"Please do," Lynda said. "Adam and I are just going to have a lazy afternoon together, just the two of us. Three of our guests left for New York this morning and Emma Lou and Riki have gone off to visit some of his relatives in a nearby town and won't return until tomorrow night. Go ahead and have fun, Crystal."

Once they were in his launch, bouncing through the waves towards the Lido, Eliot leaned over and kissed Crystal. "Darling, Vilia, I didn't want to startle your friends by greeting you the way I wanted to. By this evening they'll be more accustomed to me and by tomorrow I'll become a friend. I enjoy people and I tend to make friends quite fast."

She laughed. "I think you've already proved that to me."

"I said friends, just pleasant, casual friends, not deep relationships. I've had very few of those." He took her hand and held it in his.

"Where are we going?"

"I'm taking you to the cabana of some old friends of mine, Count and Countess Brandolini. They'll have a lot of people, Romans and otherwise, and it's always fun. The luncheon will be very casual and, afterwards, we can walk on the beach or do whatever we like."

The talk at luncheon was all about the ball and the rude behavior of the Onassis launch, and Onassis himself, who never left Elizabeth Taylor's side.

"He's not camera shy, and neither is Mario. When they started photographing that Swedish film star, he was right in the picture, too," said Countess Brandolini's sister-in-law, whom everyone was calling Kiki.

"She was the worst dressed woman at the party. She didn't have to show her belly button to be attractive," Irene Galitzine commented. Crystal knew that she was a Russian princess who had become a successful fashion designer in Rome, and she liked her dark Gypsy looks and hearty laugh.

Not too long after they arrived, liveried servants appeared, loaded with large straw baskets. Under the canvas canopy of the cabana they set up a long table, covered it with colorful linen cloth, and set it with silver and wine glasses. The cold lobsters, the mousses, the bowls of green salad were delicious, Crystal thought.

"Thank God, Vilia, you enjoy food and eat like a human being. You don't even apologize for having an appetite and say that you're going to start dieting tomorrow," Eliot said.

I've never had to diet yet, she thought to herself. I can still remember never getting quite enough during the war, and maybe I haven't caught up yet.

As they were drinking their Italian espresso, Count Brandolini came over towards them. "How about a game?" he asked Eliot.

"Not today. I've got other plans, but tomorrow, maybe."

"I've got to have another crack at you. You were too lucky yesterday."

"Yes, you are right. Yesterday was my lucky day." He smiled at Crystal and then turned back to Brando Brandolini. "All right, we'll play tomorrow."

"I like your friends," Crystal told Eliot as they left the party and walked along the beach together.

"They liked you, too. They were all asking questions about you."

"What did you say?"

"I said that you're a beautiful girl whom I met at the ball last night. I didn't say that I made love to you, because I figure that's nobody's business but our own. I did say, though, that you're more European than American."

"It might interest you to know that I've just become an American citizen."

"It does interest me. Everything about you does, and there's so much I still don't know."

"What do you want to hear first?"

"Nothing now. We made a beautiful beginning and I look forward to finding out all the rest piece by piece and finally, or perhaps never, putting all the pieces together."

As she was dressing for dinner in her stateroom Crystal faced the fact that she was more than just attracted to Eliot Tyler Young. It was the first time since the brief period she had spent with Mat that she had felt any real emotion for a man, and she felt warm and happy as she relived everything that had happened last night.

Suddenly she was in a panic. She had almost forgotten that this enchanted kind of life wouldn't go on forever. In a day or two, whenever he made up his mind, Adam would order the captain to weigh anchor and leave Venice. She might never see Eliot again.

That night at dinner she heard Lynda say to Eliot, "If you haven't anything else to do, why don't you come along with us on the yacht? We've already lost three of our party, and Emma Lou and Riki have decided to stay on with his cousins for another week. So that means there are only three of us left to go back to Monte Carlo, where we will leave the boat."

While she pretended to be listening to Hubert Givenchy, Crystal was actually straining her ears to hear Eliot's reply. He didn't hesitate. He would come on board tomorrow night, he told Lynda, and he was in no hurry to reach any special destination.

31

Eliot Tyler Young took the motor launch to the Cipriani Hotel feeling a little guilty about being late for Crystal but otherwise happy. At the Brandolinis' cabana he had held miraculous hands all afternoon, and as he thought back over some of the bridge games, he didn't think he could have played them better.

Eliot enjoyed cards. In New York he could play twenty-four hours a day if he could find three other people to fill a table. He was popular at the Brook and Regency clubs because he was a consistent winner with an iron memory for every card, and because he was an equally relaxed loser. He never had to worry about paying his debts. His grandfather founded the Tyler Tool Company and left all the stock to his family.

When Eliot found that Crystal hadn't returned to the yacht yet, and had left a note telling him she had gone off to an island near Venice with Lynda and Adam to buy some linen, he was not displeased. It made him feel more independent about his own comings and goings.

From his childhood in Lake Forest, Eliot had always been a somewhat solemn-looking young man who concentrated on one thing at a time to the exclusion of everything else. But he did that thing well. As a small boy he had concentrated on collecting toy soldiers. Since his mother gave him everything he asked for, he wrote for all the collectors' catalogues and soon accumulated some intricately made miniature soldiers. He was an only child and often without playmates, so he used to set up opposing armies in the ballroom of the Lake Forest home. Occasionally, he set off firecrackers in the ballroom to create the sound and smell of war, but the practice was frowned upon by even his mother.

When he was sent off to Culver Military Academy because of his passion for war, the soldiers were packed away carefully in the boxes. He checked on them at the time of his last visit to Lake Forest and found them still safely stored away in closets.

When his lead soldier collecting days were over, Eliot had gone overboard for boxing. At Culver he won the Golden Gloves competition for teen-age boys. It took some tutoring to get him into Princeton, but he boxed for a year at Lawrenceville School. At Princeton he made a good eating club as well as the boxing team. In the ring he became famous for his special technique of appearing to be somewhat slow and inept just before he delivered a knockout punch.

He was not quite halfway through his senior year when Pearl Harbor came along. He decided to forget any further education and to enlist in the Navy. When his mother heard the news she became hysterical. Born Charlotte Tyler, she was sculptured in the same generous proportions as her son. Nobody ever thought of opening doors or carrying packages for her. She was never called anything but Charly by her husband and son and, behind her back, the servants and delivery boys.

Charly's tears, though, were wasted on Eliot. Off somewhere on a destroyer in the Pacific he was as safe as if he were spending the time at a summer camp for boys. He passed through the experience totally unscathed emotionally and physically but with lots of new friends who had similar tastes.

When he came home and the crowds and the shouting were over, he realized that his mother was campaigning to get him into the Tyler Tool Company as well as to marry the Chicago debutante of her choice. She wanted to make sure there would be another generation to carry on the family business.

Both ideas bored him to death. The girls telephoned him endlessly but he found them completely without guts or imagination. To please his mother, he promised to spend a month at the factory, but he dozed off every afternoon in the office they gave him.

"Come now, Charly. The war's over and I want to see what's left of Paris, London and Berlin. I may even get to Tokyo," he said one day.

He spent several years getting acquainted with all kinds of people in all kinds of places before he discovered the love of his life, Africa. The mood of Kenya suited him exactly—beautiful, mysterious and wild. The people were either completely primitive or completely sophisticated, but there were no dull people.

He began looking around for a home and finally found an old farmhouse surrounded by a hundred acres, some cultivated and some wild. His nearest neighbor, just far enough away to make him look forward to seeing her occasionally, was Baroness Blixen, who wrote under the name Isak Dinesen.

With the help of some of the natives he started renovating the farmhouse. It was the kind of work he enjoyed. He especially enjoyed the big kitchen and he decided to keep the old wood-burning stove and learn to cope with it. He enlarged the windows and liked to sit by them in the early evening. The thick woods just behind the house were full of wild animals and an occasional zebra often stepped out timidly and posed for just a minute against the tangle of brush.

Occasionally he took his rifle and came back with game, but he was not a compulsive killer. He was simply one of those who believe that a certain number of animals must be killed so that the rest have enough food to survive.

He had lived in Africa five years before he went to Nairobi one day and first saw Swana. A crowd of gypsies had come to town for a street fair and Swana was traveling with one of the tribes.

When Eliot looked back over his past, which he seldom did, he could still remember his disbelief at the sight of Swana. Standing there beside one of the bazaar tables, she was the most beautiful woman he had ever seen. She was at least six feet tall in her long, narrow bare feet that looked totally untouched by shoes. Everything about her was long and narrow, the straight body with small breasts, all such a delicious color under the sheer piece of cotton printed in a bizarre combination of hot pink, pumpkin and jade green.

Even her features were exciting, a delicate little nose between long, wide eyes and a big mouth. Swana's most beautiful feature, though, was her long neck that rose straight from between her shoulders, supporting a small head thickly covered with short black curls.

When she saw him staring at her, Swana smiled at him, showing her even white teeth.

He went over to her and asked, "Who are you?"

"I'm Swana."

"Would you like to have a cold drink with me?" They walked along the row of booths to a refreshment stand and sat down on two little chairs with a table between them.

Swana told him she didn't know who her parents were. She had been traveling with nomads who lived in tents, and as the weather changed they picked up their tents, packed their belongings on camels and moved to another place. After the drink they stopped at some of the booths, and whatever she fancied, whether it was a piece of cloth or a string of beads, he bought for her. Wouldn't I like to take her to Cartier in Paris, he thought. She would look magnificent in diamonds.

As he saw twilight coming, he felt desperate at the thought of leaving her and never seeing her again, but Swana solved the problem. "I go home with you," she said.

Neither of them spoke on the way to the farm. When they reached the house Eliot took her upstairs and opened a door. "This will be your room," he said.

"Where you sleep?" she wanted to know. When he showed her his bedroom full of rifles, binoculars, dirty shirts and old books, she said, "I sleep here, too," and put down the sarongs hē had just bought her on one of his chairs.

He showed her the bathroom, drew a warm bath for her and tossed in some of the bath salts he ordered from Paris every few months.

"I'll go downstairs and fix us something to eat," he said, and she smiled and nodded.

What have I got into after all these years? Eliot kept asking himself as he lighted the stove and put together some meat and rice. He was stirring it when he heard a faint rustle behind him and turned around.

Swana was standing there completely nude except for a pair of miniature gold-plated boxing gloves tied around her neck. He had given them to her that afternoon when she had admired them on his key chain. She held out her arms and this time she laughed out loud.

As they came together they were almost exactly the same height, and their lips and bodies were like pieces that suddenly find each other in a jigsaw puzzle. Swana's lovemaking was wild, free and uninhibited. The stove went out and the dinner was forgotten as they discovered each other upstairs.

Eliot's old casual African way of life was never the same again, but it became ever more fascinating. Swana was the perfect companion. She hardly ever talked, but often laughed. She made only sporadic attempts at keeping house, but she made herself excitingly available when he wanted her, whether it was in the kitchen, the bathtub, the woods or in the cabin of his boat.

He loved to lie beside her and touch her smooth, dark neck. One night he couldn't go to sleep for wondering how long it was. He got up and tried to find a tape measure, but couldn't.

To decorate her swan neck became such an obsession that he finally wrote to the president of Cartier

Paris, an old friend of his: "Would it be possible for you to make me a coil of 18-carat gold wire for a lady whose throat, I'm sure, is at least eight inches long? It should be Ubangi style, but slightly more delicate and studded occasionally with tiny eighth-of-a-carat diamonds to make it glitter. Price is no object in this case, but it must be delivered in time for Christmas." He wrote a second letter to Paris designer Jacques Fath: "The lady is six feet tall. I want a simple white dress that leaves her shoulders bare and is sheer enough to show the color of her body."

Eliot invited all the neighbors to a Christmas Day dinner. The two of them went into the edge of the woods, took up a small tree, planted it in a tub and brought it back to the house. Swana tied colored ribbons on the branches and draped it with strands of glass beads they had bought in Nairobi.

On Christmas morning Eliot gave her the packages as they were having their breakfast together in the kitchen. As always, she stood up and dropped what she was wearing on the floor so she could try on the new clothes. She was frantically excited over the necklace, but he had no idea whether she understood its value.

The living room was lighted with candles that evening and the guests were all there when Swana came out of their bedroom, down the steps and across the living room with the white dress just slipping off her shoulders and the diamonds like tiny sparks around her neck. Tied to her wrist were the gold-plated boxing gloves.

"My God, what a beauty you are!" said Peter Beard. He spent the evening urging Swana to leave Eliot, come to New York and make her fortune as a fashion model, but Swana only laughed.

It was after the episode of the necklace that, back in Chicago, Charly realized that her son was living with a native African girl. The bill from Cartier was sent by mistake to Eliot's Chicago address and Charly read it along with the accompanying note: "Dear Eliot, I do hope that coil of gold and diamonds suits your lady's lovely eight-inch neck. If you should bring her to Paris, I hope to see your African beauty."

Charly had to sit down and ring for a Bufferin when she saw the size of the bill and read the words "African beauty." She thought seriously of packing up and flying out to Africa to talk some sense into Eliot, but she remembered some of his other phases and began to hope that this one, too, would pass. She couldn't resist telling her troubles to several of her best friends, who promised not to tell a word of it. The story of Eliot and Swana was dinner-table talk from Chicago to Palm Springs that winter.

Swana, from the beginning, had always led an independent life. She spent hours walking alone and, as time went on, she became more and more capricious. Sometimes she disappeared for two or three days at a time, and Eliot never could discover whether she had found nomad friends somewhere or had thumbed her way to Nairobi and back.

Once, when she had been away three or four days, he got into his car and drove to Nairobi. The nomads were there again. This time he walked quietly and inconspicuously along the street. Suddenly he saw her in the distance. She and an African boy of about her own age were sitting at the same little table where they had had their first cold drink. They were leaning across the table with their heads close together, and they seemed to be talking seriously.

He turned and went home without her seeing him. A few days later she reappeared in high spirits and more loving than ever. There were no questions and no explanations and their life of eating, loving and sleeping went on again.

Three months later he came back from hunting one day to find her white evening dress folded on a chair with the diamond-and-gold spiral necklace laid on top of it. She had taken with her only the cotton sarongs and the cheap little gold-plated boxing gloves he had won at Culver.

The next morning he drove as fast as he could to Nairobi, but the nomads weren't there this time. When he asked for Swana and tried to describe her, he got nothing but nos and negative headshakes.

For a while he desperately missed her warmth and excitement. Whenever he started to cook something he found himself turning around and expecting to see her drop her clothes invitingly on the floor, but Swana never materialized.

Peter Beard brought him the rumor that she had indeed gone off with a young nomad and had died in childbirth. For a minute he wondered if it was his child or the African's. But in the end he doubted the whole story.

Eliot stayed on in the farmhouse for about a year. Finally he decided to fly to Rome for a while and look for fresh distractions. He arranged with his lawyer to pay the African caretaker to keep the place in order and to inform him by cable if Swana reappeared.

He left the white evening dress hanging in the closet but took the neck ring with him. He made a quick trip from Rome to Geneva to put it in the vault of his Swiss bank, and it was still there. He thought of Crystal, and briefly of giving it to her, but her neck wasn't eight inches long. Instead, he would have to buy her a long strand of big, milky white pearls, or maybe a bracelet to go with her small diamond necklace. Anyway, he must buy Crystal a special present right away.

32

Crystal had just come back from an extensive shopping tour of Venice with Lynda and Adam when Eliot Tyler Young arrived on board with his bags. Since the Adlers had gone to their stateroom to rest, Crystal rang for the chief steward, who quickly installed him in the second-biggest stateroom and dressing room. Lynda had wanted her to move into it, but she had become accustomed to the yellow room and loved the sunny color.

Before dinner she took Eliot to the bridge to meet Captain König. The German captain proudly pointed out the radar equipment and all the other new safety devices that Adam had had installed on the yacht. When *La Belle Lynda* weighed anchor at midnight, both Eliot and Crystal were on the bridge for a last look at the lights of Venice as they left the Grand Canal and headed for the Dalmatian coast.

The next morning Crystal was just finishing the little bowl of fruit that she liked with her toast and coffee when Eliot arrived on deck. He sat down at the table with her and ordered a three-minute egg with crisp bacon and coffee.

"This is our first breakfast together, Vilia, and it has just occurred to me that I don't know your full name. You were introduced to me as Miss Crystal, but that hardly seems adequate for a long-term acquaintance."

"My last name is Casalet. I more or less stopped using it because people had trouble pronouncing it, and that's no good for business."

"It's very pretty, though. I like the sound of Vilia Casalet."

When they reached Dubrovnik, the yacht dropped anchor and they went ashore with Lynda and Adam. Lynda discovered a fascinating shoe store, and while she and Adam investigated it, Crystal and Eliot crossed the drawbridge into the old town. As they walked along the old streets they could hear the sound of their own feet on the cobblestones. There were other shoppers in town, but more were looking at windows than actually buying, and Crystal thought that even the children's voices seemed subdued.

The yacht cruised along the coast between green islands on which picturesque old stone churches and bright-colored farm buildings seemed to have been arranged for their artistic effect rather than to have just happened naturally.

When they had come back from Dubrovnik, Adam and Eliot started a game of backgammon and Lynda asked Crystal to go to the top deck and sunbathe with her. It was a ritual Lynda insisted on because, as she often said, she hated to wear clothes. She shed them at home as often as she could, but Adam had refused to let her run nude on the yacht, even in their stateroom. When she went to the top deck, Adam had arranged to have crew members posted at all the companionways to keep any of the sailors from going up.

As soon as she and Crystal were stretched out on large monogrammed towels, Lynda said, "Eliot's a very attractive man, Crystal."

"Yes, he is."

"You're crazy about him, aren't you?"

"Yes, I guess I am."

"What I like about Eliot is that he's different, though I can't explain it. Adam likes him, too, partly because he doesn't think he's about to make a pass at me. He's crazy on the subject. He actually kicked one of those French guys off the yacht the other night because he kissed me goodnight. When I say kicked, I really mean kicked. I was standing just behind them and saw it happen."

It was late that night and Crystal was sitting up in her bed. She was holding a book in her hand, but she hadn't been reading it. She was thinking about Eliot. Since he had joined them on the yacht they hadn't spent more than a few minutes alone together. She had been intrigued about him in the beginning, but now she found herself thinking of him more and more. She was eager to see him again.

When she thought of their night together after the ball, she stirred restlessly in her bed and began willing him to come to her stateroom. Why hadn't he? she wondered.

Thinking of Eliot made her think of Mat, whom she had consciously blocked out of her mind. Now she could, for the first time, remember him with less pain. She had heard someone once say that a voice is the first thing that fades from a memory, but she could still hear the way his voice sounded when he smiled. Mat had been an innocent sweet love, but Eliot was different. Maybe it was his age that attracted her, or was it his complete security in every situation?

Suddenly there was a knock on the door and Eliot came in.

"Oh, I thought it was the steward."

"Shall I call him, or will I do?"

"Please stay."

"I feel deprived, Vilia darling. I had hoped to be with you constantly, but you are harder than hell to get to. Every time I've started to your stateroom, I've looked behind me and a friendly young cabin boy, all smiles and teeth, is peering around the corner. To save your reputation I've always retreated, but I think I got away with it this time."

"I'm glad."

"Then put down whatever you're reading. I can't make love to a girl with a book in her hand."

She closed the book, tossed it on the floor and threw back the covers for him to come in.

Hours later, Eliot woke her. "I'm going back to my stateroom before the crew turns out in full force."

Adam announced the next day that he had been talking to Wally in New York. "I'm getting antsy to be back at work. There are lots of things I can't settle from here, so we're not stopping anywhere but Naples, where we'll take on some fuel, and then on to Monte Carlo."

Crystal hated the thought of leaving the yacht, but the days were pleasant. They sunbathed, dipped in the pool, talked, read, played backgammon, and she and Eliot slept together every night.

The night after they left Naples he said as he kissed her good night, "Meet me at the pool tomorrow morning at nine o'clock, will you? It's important."

"Yes," she answered sleepily.

Crystal was in the pool, standing in the Jacusi, when Eliot arrived.

The water in the pool was always low when they were cruising, to keep it from spilling over onto the deck, so he walked across the pool and took her in his arms. "Good God, you're icy cold, quite different from the way you felt a few hours ago."

"Why are we standing here like this then?"

"Because I want to tell you that you and I are getting married. The only thing I want to discuss with you is when."

She looked at him for a minute and smiled. "I don't believe you."

"Well, you should. I love you. You love me and we get along, so why should we waste time? You do love me, by the way, don't you?"

"Yes, I do."

"Then, for God's sake, let's get out of this ice water. I'll get into action and see what I can do about it."

Adam and Lynda were just coming on deck when they came up the pool ladder. While he was drying himself with a towel Eliot announced, "Crystal and I are going to get married. Any suggestions about where? We want to do it as soon as we can."

"Oh, Crystal, I'm so happy for you." Lynda and she

hugged each other, and Adam exclaimed, "That's great." He ordered a bottle of champagne to be opened.

The bartender told the chief steward, who told his three cabin boys, and within minutes the news was spread all over the boat.

After the second glass of champagne, Eliot turned to Crystal. "Darling, what about Monte Carlo for our wedding?"

Adam interrupted. "I'm not sure it's all that simple to be married in a strange country. You might have to hang around a while for a license."

"In that case we'll fly right back to New York, but since we met over here, I thought it would be nice if we could spend a few days somewhere near, before we get back to the whole business of finding somewhere to live," Eliot said.

Adam got up and rang for the captain. "He's been cruising around these parts for a long time, and he may be able to tell us what the rules are."

After the captain had offered his formal congratulations, he turned to Crystal and spoke to her in German and she replied at length.

"I didn't realize I was about to acquire such a bilingual wife," Eliot said. "I speak bits and pieces of several, but nothing complete."

"Captain König was making the most amusing suggestion," Crystal said.

"I beg your pardon. So few people come on board who speak my language that I indulge myself when I talk to Miss Crystal. I was telling her that any licensed captain has the right to marry a couple at sea."

"What a romantic idea!" cried Lynda.

"It would only be necessary for me to spend a few hours in Monte Carlo, picking up a few required papers. Then we could leave the port and cruise out to sea six miles. That's the legal limit, and then I could perform the ceremony."

"Perfect," shouted Eliot. "A close friend I'd like to have for my best man has just bought a villa near Monte Carlo. I'll telephone and find out if he's there.

Maybe you know him, Harding Lawrence, head of Braniff?"

"Wasn't he recently married to Mary Wells?" Crystal asked.

"Yes."

"Then I know his wife very well," Crystal said.

"It just happens we all do. She's a whiz. She did a great job on a TV show I sponsored a few years ago."

Harding Lawrence was still at his villa. He and his wife were leaving almost immediately for New York but would postpone it a day to attend the wedding.

The sea was smooth, so Adam ordered the captain to travel as fast as possible, and Crystal felt a great surge of excitement and anticipation as she felt the yacht accelerate its leisurely pace and move swiftly through the water.

"Lynda, you'll be my maid of honor, of course, and Adam and Mary will be the witnesses," Crystal said as they made their way up to the top deck for their daily sunbath.

In her own stateroom Crystal faced the fact that her life was no longer completely her own business and that her decisions from tomorrow on would be shared with Eliot. It may not always be easy but I'm sure I can manage, because I love him, she thought.

That night as they were sitting on deck after dinner, she said to Eliot, "Darling, there's something I must tell you right now before we're married."

"I'm bracing myself, but I only have to look at your face to know that it's not fatal."

"I've been living a lie ever since I came to New York, and I've grown so accustomed to it that I hardly think of it any more."

"Go on."

She saw that he was smiling. "Well, I'm not in my fifties, as I let you and everyone else think. I'm just barely in my mid-thirties. No one knows the truth but Adam."

"The news comes as no surprise, but actually I've never given a damn about your age, Vilia."

"When I first came to New York, I hadn't the

vaguest idea what I wanted to do. It was sheer chance that I went to Adam's office and he would never have hired me if I hadn't showed him my mother's passport, and told him it was mine."

"It was quick thinking, it seems to me, and I admire you for it. Go on with the story."

When she finished he was still smiling. "So your slight hoax was the rocket that set off Adam's millions?"

"I don't suppose he thinks much about it any more and neither do I. We've done so much and have been so successful."

"I'll keep it a deep, dark secret, I promise."

"My cream is really good. The original Vilia always used it."

"As soon as we reach New York, I'll air-mail ten pounds to my mother, if you have such a thing."

"What is she like?"

"Oh, Charly's a good old girl. When we get to Monte Carlo, I'm going to call Chicago and tell her about you."

Early the next morning they arrived at Monte Carlo and went ashore as soon as they finished breakfast. Adam had decreed that the wedding was to take place at four o'clock, and he and Lynda would leave for New York the next morning.

"What are you going to wear, Crystal?" asked Lynda as they were riding up the hill to the shopping center in a taxi.

"I don't know. I have to find something. About the only thing I didn't bring along was a wedding dress."

"Then let's go shopping together. I'll get a dress for the wedding at the same time."

At one of the French boutiques Crystal was lucky enough to find a simple shirtwaist dress of pleated white chiffon. Lynda bought a similar chiffon in a beigy pink shade to wear as the bridesmaid.

"It's pretty traditional for me, but I kind of like it for a change." Recently Lynda had been buying nothing but the mad fashions from the rebellious young fashion designers.

While they waited for a few minor alterations to be made, Lynda and Crystal rushed to the florist along-side the Hotel de Paris and ordered their bouquets and the boutonnieres to be delivered to the yacht before three in the afternoon. They arrived at the yacht with their boxes just as the chief steward returned from a quick trip to Nice with a car loaded with flowers.

"Why don't you go below and rest or something?" Lynda said. "I'll help the steward with the flowers. It's something I like to do and I'm pretty good at it. Then I'll dress and come down to be with you. We've got to start out to sea around three, the captain says."

It was almost three when Eliot came on board, bringing Mary and Harding Lawrence. By that time the ship had been dressed in all the full glory of its signal flags, and the captain and the crew were in their dress uniforms. The news had spread through the port and a crowd had already collected around the gangplank.

"Sorry. It was a matter of finding the right ring in the right size," Eliot said. The sailors had cast off the lines and the boat was starting to move out of the harbor. Adam suggested he could give the Lawrences a tour of the boat while Eliot went below to change.

"You look great, Crystal," said Lynda as she came into Crystal's stateroom. "Just a little more eye make-up, maybe, and you're going to wear that darling little diamond necklace, aren't you?"

"Of course. I was just going to put it on."

"Did you know that the pier is already crowded and there are dozens of photographers taking pictures of the boat and even trying to bribe the crew to let them come on."

None of them were successful. When the boat reached its destination, the motors stopped. One of the youngest members of the crew sat at the piano and began to play the wedding march as Crystal and Lynda came into the salon where the others were waiting. The captain, in his white uniform with gold epaulets was standing at the far end of the room holding his book in his hand.

It was a simple ceremony. Crystal saw that her

bouquet was trembling, but she repeated the words clearly and firmly, and so did Eliot. Her eyes widened when she saw him slipping a circle of tiny diamonds on her finger, and she looked up at him in surprise. He squeezed her hand gently and then kissed her.

After congratulations and more kisses, the yacht's crew filed in to shake hands with the bride and groom. Almost immediately the motors were turned on and they began the return trip to Monte Carlo.

A four-story cake had been baked in the galley, complete with curlicues and a bride and groom on top. After Crystal and Eliot had cut the cake they sat talking with the Lawrences until they neared the port.

"Mary and I are leaving tomorrow morning, but wouldn't you and Crystal like to spend a few days, or as long as you want, at our place? All the people who work for us will be there, and I think you might enjoy it," Harding said.

"Oh, yes, I've heard it's the loveliest place on the Riviera," cried Crystal.

"I had thought of Paris," Eliot said, "but I'll cancel it right away. It would be great, exactly the kind of thing I was longing for."

"Its first owner christened it La Fiorentina. It means little flower. We liked the name and kept it. I'm sure you'll love the place as much as we do," Mary Lawrence said.

As they came into the yacht basin they could see that the crowd on the pier was three times as large as it had been. Men and women were cheering and waving, and children were throwing long ribbons of confetti into the water. Eager hands reached out to catch the lines the sailors tossed, and the yacht was soon firmly anchored once more.

"No photographers on board," said Adam.

The chief steward went below to deliver the ultimatum but returned in a few minutes. "They are asking as a special favor if the bride and groom won't come to the head of the gangplank so they can photograph them." He then added, "The crowd is calling out that they want to see them, too."

"Good God, I feel like a movie star," Eliot said, laughing.

"Let's go see them, darling. I don't know why they should want to see us, but they've been waiting for hours." Crystal picked up her bouquet and they followed the steward.

They posed for a few photographs, and the satisfied crowd began to drift away.

"It's getting chilly. I'm taking you inside," Eliot said, putting his arm around Crystal. After he had closed the door, he leaned over to kiss her. "I hope our photograph will help you sell a million more jars of your precious cream, my darling, but I don't ordinarily like to be photographed."

Early the next morning, after sentimental goodbyes to Lynda and Adam, Crystal left with Eliot for nearby St. Jean Cap Ferrat. La Fiorentina was even more enchanting than they expected. They drove between tall iron gates into the courtyard and up to the house that suggested a Greek temple. From a terrace on one side they looked down a series of stone steps bordered with cypress trees to the swimming pool and the Mediterranean beyond. On the other side they saw an herb garden laid out in geometrical beds and a hilly forest of gnarled old olive trees.

For their first dinner at La Fiorentina, Eliot ordered their table to be set out on the terrace so they could see the stars and the lights on the hills across the water. He chose the wine carefully and ordered what he knew she liked best to eat. Beside her plate, Crystal found a small, gold-wrapped package. She opened it to find a diamond bracelet. When she picked it up it was as flexible as a ribbon in her fingers.

"Oh, Eliot, this and my beautiful ring, too." She rushed to kiss him.

"Nothing gaudy, as you can see. I tried to find some stones cut as nearly as possible like Vilia's. I'm something of a jewelry fancier, and someday I'll come on something that exactly suits you. Until then this will do, Vee." He held her close. "I think I've just re-christened you. Vilia's too long for everyday use."

That night they made violent love, and after Eliot had gone to sleep, Crystal got up, slipped on a robe and went out on the little balcony beyond the glass doors. I can't believe it, she thought to herself. Two weeks ago I didn't even know this man and now he is as close to me as any human can be. Before I met him I was only part of a person, who was afraid to look back at the past, but somehow Eliot has put all the pieces together and I can think of all the people I've loved, my grandmother, my mother and Mat, without hurting. She could see her new life unrolling happily and securely with Eliot as her lover and her protector.

"What are you doing, darling? Looking for another Romeo?" he called from the bedroom.

"No, I only want you, Eliot," she said, coming back to him in bed.

33

Crystal found her office desk stacked with congratulatory letters and telegrams, all opened and neatly arranged on her desk, with the most important on top. She decided to spend her first day back at work dictating appreciative little answers to some of them and catching up on three pages of telephone calls that needed immediate answers.

The boxes for her new perfume had to be redesigned. Wally Nelson needed to talk with her immediately to make a final choice between several different versions of the scent. It had to be finished in a hurry to make the Christmas counters. Neiman Marcus was complaining about delivery. The Fashion Group in Philadelphia wanted her as one of its guests of honor at its annual awards and had to know immediately. Mr. Adler's name was underlined—"Urgent Please Call."

"Please tell Mr. Nelson that I'll be there. Sorry, but it's no to Philadelphia. Tell Tony I must see the box design. Try to finish a few of my notes while I run over to see Mr. Adler."

Adam's topcoat was draped over a chair beside his desk with his traveling bag beside it. "I'm flying up to Dartmouth for a couple of days to see Alan."

"Everything all right, I hope?"

"Great. The kid has made the varsity football team

and I'm going to stick around long enough to see him play."

"Did you want me to do something for you while you're away?"

"You've got enough on your hands right now. No, I just wanted to offer further congratulations, Miss Crystal Clear."

"You haven't called me that for a long time. What do you mean?"

"I guess I was just thinking about how you looked when you first came into the old Adam and Eve office."

"How did I look?"

"A little afraid, but you had a very determined look."

"How do I look now?"

"Not a damn bit afraid, and if you haven't got what you want, you're sure hard to suit."

"I am happy, very happy, Adam. I think I liked Eliot the minute I saw him and now I know I love him."

"He's a nice fellow, but why didn't you level with us about him?"

"I don't understand."

"You told me he wasn't a worker and I could see he wasn't a gambler, so I was curious." He paused, and then continued. "I had him looked up. As you probably know, he could buy and sell me and not bother to ask for change."

"How amazing! I really didn't know."

"Then let me be the first to tell you. He's a multi-multi-millionaire." He looked at Crystal's amazed expression, then continued. "Eliot's granddaddy founded the Tyler Tool Company that made all those plows and farm implements that civilized the Middle West, and your Eliot is the only son of granddaddy's only daughter."

"Oh!"

"You don't look happy."

"Eliot's money doesn't matter to me one way or another. I'm just terribly surprised."

Adam smiled. "You'll soon learn to live with it. I've

got to go." He picked up his coat and bag, and they left the office together.

Crystal and Eliot had returned from Europe only the night before. When they finally decided they must tear themselves away from La Fiorentina, Eliot had insisted that she come with him to Rome to help him pack up his belongings.

"I can't keep on living out of the two suitcases I took to Venice, and besides, there may be some other things we might like for our new apartment."

In Rome they had packed all day and had selected a few of Eliot's African wood carvings and pieces of sculpture to be shipped by freight. They were putting a few last things into a small trunk when Eliot had said, "I think we should keep the flat, Vee. We might want to come over for the weekend sometime, and it's much easier than going to a hotel."

On the plane they had talked things over and decided that they would spend the first night in Crystal's house and the next day Eliot would begin the search for the right apartment for them. To her surprise, he was up early and making an interested inventory of her things.

"It's all very blue and white and pretty, and just the thing for a single bird, but it makes me feel like the giant in a circus. We can use some of those porcelains of yours, though, in our new place."

"If we can't, I can always take them to my new office. General Motors is putting up an enormous building across from the Plaza. They're already starting to break ground, and Adam is thinking in terms of at least two floors. If he does, I'll have lots more space than I have now."

She could see that he was eager to get on with the business of finding their first home. "Any hang-ups about neighborhoods?" he called to her as he was shaving.

"None at all, but I do like a lot of light."

"And I'd like some ground to walk on, if I can find any. I'm not one for the dizzy heights," he said as he kissed her goodbye.

As Crystal walked back to her own office from Adam's, she was still thinking of what he had told her, and wondering what Eliot's great wealth would do to their marriage. He had given every sign of being a wealthy man, but, without ever discussing it, she had taken for granted they would pool their resources or that at least she would contribute something to their overall plan for living.

For a minute she felt rebuffed, and as if she had been holding out an unwanted gift to someone she loved and had even hoped to help. But how silly of me, she reasoned. I've always been so independent, but I'll soon get used to this new idea, just as Adam predicted.

A few of the notes were already finished and waiting for her signature. She smiled and said to her secretary, "What fun. I'm going to sign my married name for the first time." She wrote Crystal Young and stopped suddenly with her pen still poised over the paper.

Her secretary, Mary Jane, burst out laughing. "Oh, Miss Crystal, I know what you almost did. You almost added Forever."

"Yes, I did. I never thought of it, but now I really am Young forever."

"Several of the news headlines said so. You'll find all the clippings about your wedding in the top drawer."

When she came home she found it was already brightly lighted and Eliot was lounging in one of the chairs reading a news magazine. She was overcome with happiness at the sight. As she rushed to throw her arms around him, Crystal whispered, "Every woman needs a man in her life. I've needed a man and I've needed love, and now I have both."

"New York is fresh out of interesting places to live right now, Vee," said Eliot as he held her in his arms. "I don't like the boxes that they call apartments here. Most of them seem to have been built for dolls. I can walk across the drawing room in three steps."

"What are we going to do then? Don't forget, I own

this building. Maybe when some of the leases are up we can take more space here."

"In the meantime, I'd like to rent an apartment at the Pierre for six months. I saw one today that will do, but I want you to see if you like it before I sign the lease. Let's go over right now. If you do like it, we can come back here, pack enough of our clothes, move in and bring the rest later."

The hotel apartment was much larger than hers, with a big, open living room and an area that could be screened off for dining. The master bedroom had bathrooms at either end, and there was a second bedroom that Eliot could use as a study.

"It's perfect, and so easy," said Crystal.

"We won't spend much time here, anyway. Chris has asked us down to his South Carolina plantation for a week of shooting early in November. Charly wants us for Thanksgiving, and Jean and Tommy are expecting us the middle of December in Palm Beach to stay through the Coconuts Party on New Year's Eve."

"But, Eliot, I'm a working girl."

"An adorable one, I must say."

"No, quite a serious one, darling. I've just taken two months off to play, and I can't take all that time you're talking about so soon after my holiday. I have too many responsibilities. Don't forget, I'm the president of a public company."

"But you're also my one and only wife. I had hoped we would enjoy all these things together."

"We will enjoy most of them, darling, I promise you, but it's just that I can't always be free. At this moment, I have to see that my new perfume is what I want it to be, and more important, that it is launched just right. Before that I had promised to make a long list of personal appearances, and it would be ruinous to cancel."

"Ruinous to whom? I wonder."

"For something I have worked a long time to build up and that I care very much about. Before I met you I thought of almost nothing else."

"And now that we're married, what do you think of most?"

"Why you, of course, sweetheart, but I simply can't give up my work so suddenly. You wouldn't love me any longer if I got up in the morning with nothing to do. I'd be impossible."

"I'm willing to take a chance. I hoped that after we were married you'd be willing to give it up, maybe little by little. I'm well able to support you in any kind of style you want."

"It's not a matter of money."

"I know that and I know it was partly your independence and your obvious disinterest in money for itself that made me fall in love with you in the beginning, but I know, too, that I want a wife and not just a famous label on a cosmetic jar."

"That's brutal."

"I don't mean to be. Perhaps I don't understand what seems to me to be your blind dedication to work, because I've never worked myself. I've never had a serious job, but I'd like a chance to prove to you that the world is full of exciting things and incredible people. I've never had a boring day in my life."

"Are we having our first fight, Eliot?"

"Perhaps, Vee, but it seems to me we're just stating our positions. In the future we'll discuss our invitations, and you'll play hooky from your work whenever it seems feasible. Sometimes I'll go alone, because if I had to sit here or even played cards to kill time until you were through work, I might become impossible, too."

When the week for the shoot arrived, Eliot packed his guns and left by himself. Crystal took off to Houston to promote her perfume, but flew from there to the South Carolina plantation and came home with Eliot. "Naturally, I'll spend the whole week of Thanksgiving with your mother, and I can take ten days off starting with Christmas at Palm Beach. That's half of the time you plan to be there," she said.

When Crystal and Eliot reached Chicago, Charly's car and driver were waiting for them. It was a long drive, but amusing because Eliot kept pointing out some of the places that had figured in his young life, like the curve in the road where he had hit a tree because he was driving too fast, the kennels where he had once bought a fabulous Great Dane that he had named Hercules and the gates of the place where he had gone to his first dance.

"I like the Middle West. It's rich and comfortable, and I had a good time growing up!"

It was only when they turned off the road that she began to have any real comprehension of what Eliot's childhood must have been like. They were following a gravel road lined with evergreen shrubbery and enormous, bare trees that must be spectacular in summer, she thought.

Since the whole scene was as spotlessly neat as if it had just been swept and there wasn't a house in sight, she asked, "Is this a park? It's lovely."

"No, darling, this is where I was born. I guess I should have warned you that Charly is an avid horticulturist, and if you don't know the difference between a begonia and a gloxinia, you may be in for a bit of re-education."

"Luckily, I do love flowers, so I hope she'll accept me as an earnest beginner."

When the house came in sight, Crystal thought it looked as large as Buckingham Palace, which she remembered dimly from her year in England. Eliot told her the house had been built by his grandfather sometime before the First World War, and the architect had copied a French château turret for turret in American brick. Before he was born, Charly had camouflaged its severity with white paint and planted English ivy profusely to mellow some of its absurdities.

When the car stopped in front of the wide stone steps, the big double doors opened and Charly came dashing out, followed by four yapping schnauzers and a butler. She was wearing a tweed jacket over a turtleneck sweater and baggy pants tucked into boots, and her gray hair was tucked up under a boy's cap.

"You're early," she cried as she and Eliot hugged and kissed each other.

"Mother, this is Vee," he said.

"Down, down," said Charly to the schnauzers as she took Crystal's hand in both of hers. "My dear, I'm so happy to have a daughter at last."

They entered the hallway of the house, and after she had ordered their bags sent upstairs, Charly led them to a smallish, red-papered library where an open fireplace was blazing.

"I've just come from one of the greenhouses," she said, tossing her cap on a table. "That's where I spend most of my time, except when I'm in this room or my bedroom. I'm always threatening to sell this drafty old barn, but, of course, I don't do anything about it. Sit down near the fire and get warm, Crystal, while I pour you some tea."

"Secretly you love it, and you'd be bored silly in a place with fewer problems," Eliot said.

As Charly poured the tea, Crystal saw that she had the creased-leather kind of skin that she was spending her life trying to prevent women from having. On Charly, though, it was not unbecoming but a part of the whole scene with the dogs, the tweeds and the damp oak leaves that were still clinging to her boots.

While she was filling the cups and passing a tray with some watercress sandwiches, Charly was also taking stock of Crystal, whom she was pleased and surprised not to find the artificial kind of production she had expected.

When Eliot had called her from Monte Carlo to announce his imminent marriage, she had had a few minutes of panic at the thought of having to introduce an African daughter-in-law with an eight-inch neck decorated by a Ubangi necklace to her Chicago friends. When he said, "No, Mother, it's not Swana," she had breathed a sigh of relief that lasted until she heard that Crystal was in her mid-fifties. No grandchildren then, she had thought sadly.

Now, looking at Crystal's fresh, unlined and untired face, she said, "My dear, forgive me for saying so, but you are the youngest fifty-year-old woman I have ever seen in my life."

"Don't forget, it's her business, Charly," said Eliot.

"She's brought you a whole suitcase of this kind of stuff to play with."

Charly's bright eyes behind the old-fashioned gold-rimmed glasses were still trained on Crystal. "Why does my son call you Vee, dear, and would you like me to call you that, too?"

"Vee is short for Vilia. She looked like a Vilia the first night I saw her," Eliot answered for her again.

"He didn't know it, but Vilia was my grandmother's name," Crystal said.

"Vilia? That's not an American name, is it? By the way dear, please call me Charly, just as Eliot does."

"Thank you. My grandmother was Viennese." She hesitated for a second, then looked straight at Charly and smiled. "My grandfather was Count Curt Casalet. I never mention it here, but he was part of Kaiser Wilhelm's last cabinet."

"How interesting. Why didn't you tell me, son?"

"For a very good reason. I didn't know it myself. Vee is a very contemporary girl. She wants to do everything herself without leaning on a background."

When they went upstairs to the suite Charly had given them, they found another open fire burning. Crystal went from one window to another looking out at the greenhouses that were a quarter of a mile away and the artificial lake in which a few ducks were paddling.

"When I was a kid we always had a white swan and a black one," Eliot said, coming over to put his arm around her. "Charly took to you instantly. I know her so well, and I could tell."

"I like her very much, too."

"You two have a lot in common."

"Like you, you mean?"

"Other things, too. If I had brought home a pretty baby doll like Emma Lou, Charly wouldn't have bothered to cope. She would spend the rest of the week in one of the greenhouses."

His memory of the black and white swans on the lake had suddenly started Eliot thinking of Swana and Crystal, and as he showered before dinner he found

himself comparing the two. He could never forget
Swana's beautiful, mischievous face, her exotic body
or her uninhibited, impulsive lovemaking. She was
perfect for the time and place, but there was no way
she could have become a permanent companion. Crystal was equally warm and responsive and he had to
admit he was proud of her success and her independence even though they sometimes got in his way. He
wished that they didn't have to sit through dinner and
a long evening of looking through old photographs,
probably, before he could make love to her again.

The rest of the week passed very fast. Crystal
visited the orchid house, the indoor herb garden and
all the other greenhouses, and Charly confided that
her next year's project was to create gardens typical
of several different countries and to cover them with
glass.

Before they left, Charly gave what she called a reception for several hundred friends, many of whom
had wanted their daughters to marry Eliot when he
was still living at home. Now she wanted both the
mothers and the daughters to meet Crystal, whose
family title most of them had heard of from Charly by
this time.

Eliot begged off except for the last hour, but Crystal
went through the party easily with the same smiling
technique she had perfected for appearing in stores.

When the plane took off the next day Crystal felt
she had left a friend behind in Charly. "Thank God
we're on our way home," Eliot said.

It took Eliot several more months to discover an
apartment that he felt suited them both. He walked
through the Central Park fringe of the West Side, investigated upper and lower Fifth Avenue and Park
Avenue from Grand Central Station to the edge of
Harlem before he discovered Gracie Square.

The apartment that was available occupied two
floors and light streamed in freely through all the windows.

"It's more like a country house," Eliot said. "You
can watch the river and see trees. I can take a walk

along the edge of the water every morning if I feel like it."

Eliot volunteered to supervise the painting, papering and furnishing. It took another six months, and when they moved into it in September it was just in time to celebrate their first anniversary. That evening as they were eating their first dinner at a small table by the long windows of the dining room, the cook came in with a cake lighted by one candle, and Eliot took out a velvet box that he laid beside her plate. When she cried out at the sight of the canary diamond inside, he said, "I'm going to give you one each year until you have a real necklace, Vee. It'll be hard to find stones that match, but it will give me a project I'll enjoy."

Before she put it in the safe that Eliot had installed in her dressing room, she opened the lid of her grandmother's box and laid it on the faded satin lining. Besides a few blue-and-white porcelains, her grandmother's jewel box was the only thing she had brought from her old apartment to remind her of her past life.

PART THREE

34

New York, 1976

The morning after the Patino dinner party, Crystal was
still luxuriating in a warm, perfumed tub thinking of
last night. When she had reached her bedroom she had
sat down on the edge of the bed and while she undressed she was willing herself to go to sleep, just as
she always did when something went wrong in her
life. As usual, she succeeded. When she woke she felt
fresh and strong and even a little amused at herself for
considering Roderick Ramsey a real threat to her security.

The telephone rang, and as she raised her arm and
picked up the receiver of the extension, she felt her
annoyance and uneasiness coming back. It was Roderick Ramsey's voice at the other end of the wire, and
it was as sharp as his face.

"I hope I'm not calling too early, Mrs. Young."

"Not at all. But it seems as if we were talking only a
few hours ago."

"I wanted to thank you for a pleasant evening. I also
wanted to ask you a few questions, since I am flying
back to London. *World* is pressing me for the cover
story we discussed yesterday and my sources over
there seem to have more information than I can get
here."

"I'm sorry if we haven't been helpful."

"I'll try again. Do you remember a woman named Elsa Menz?"

"Elsa Menz? I'm afraid I don't."

"Oh, come now. She says she went to dramatic school with you, and that you shared a dressing room in some operetta that was playing in Berlin in the late thirties. She thought you had been killed."

"Yes. I remember Elsa now."

"No one here seems to know that you're a trained actress. The story should make good reading. You have a daughter, too, don't you?"

"I'm afraid I can't answer any more questions right now, Mr. Ramsey. I'm going to be late for my first appointment. If you write down everything you want to know and send the questions to my office, I'll try to answer everything as clearly and completely as I possibly can."

"I'm afraid that will be too late, since I'm leaving tonight. I'll just have to settle for what I can find out on my own. But don't forget Elsa Menz. That's an important link in my story."

As Crystal dressed hurriedly, she saw that her grandmother's little diamond necklace was lying on the night table beside her bed. She opened the safe that was hidden behind clothes in her dressing room to put it inside when Eliot walked in.

"Oh, Eliot, I'm frightened to death. Ramsey just called me and asked about Elsa Menz."

"For God's sake, who is she?"

"She was a friend of my mother's. They were in The Gypsy Princess together. I remember Grandmother took me to the opening night when I was a very little girl. The Storm Troopers were sitting in the row in front of us and were threatening to make a demonstration because Elsa was half Jewish. But nothing happened, and it was thrilling to see Mother on the stage for the first time. She had just decided to take the stage name of Marlene Duna, and she was wonderful in the part."

"What about Elsa? Did you meet her?"

"Oh, yes, afterwards we went backstage. Mother

and Elsa shared the same dressing room, and I remember Elsa made a big fuss over me. I was only about seven at the time."

"Did you ever see her again?"

"No, that was the only time, but I remember watching her take off her greasepaint, and her saying to me, 'My God, you and your mother and like two peas in a pod. In a few years you can do a sister act together.'"

"Well, even if Ramsey gets to see this Menz woman she can't prove that you're not your mother."

"Oh, Eliot, you make me feel much better."

"Try not to worry too much. I'm off to the Brook for an early lunch and to make some calls. If you need me, I'm there."

Before she left for the office, the telephone rang again, and this time it was Adam. "For God's sake, Crystal, what gives? This fellow Roderick Ramsey gets me out of bed this morning, acting as if it's a life-or-death matter. He talks more English than you do, and he wants me to tell him just what you said and what you looked like the day you first came in my office."

"What a bother. He called me, too. He's driving me wild."

"I told him you were damn good-looking and I can't remember what we said, but it doesn't shut him up. He questioned me if I know anything about your family, so I told him I never asked, and then I hung up the receiver."

"It's all about a cover story that World is supposed to be doing. I'm sorry I just didn't say no in the beginning, but I'm going to do my best to call it off now."

"Good idea. It might be better for you to try being low-key for a while. You've had your share of publicity, I'd say."

"You always said it was great for the business."

"It was, baby, but that was before we made the big league. Now I keep hearing from all sides that you're God almighty in our company."

"I don't believe anybody thinks that. What do you mean by, 'hearing from all sides'?"

"I mean it's just a general impression. I get it from my friends, other executives and even Alan."

"Alan?"

"Yes. He's a shrewd kid for his age, and he gets around."

"I'm surprised."

"Don't take this too seriously. Alan admires you and he's very fond of you, too. Just get this Ramsey and his early-morning phone calls off my back, will you?"

For almost the first time since she had started to work, Crystal faced the office with less enthusiasm than usual. Every day had seemed to fill her with a sense of discovery and achievement that had become the most important thing in her life. Suddenly she questioned all the smiling faces. Pomeroy was beaming as he laid the list of her telephone calls on her desk, but what was he thinking or what did he know about what other people were thinking? She wondered.

35

She met Lynda at La Caravelle for luncheon, and Lynda, who arrived first, had asked for a secluded table. "It's not that I've got any big news, but because I have to be careful of every word I say over the telephone. It's a big bore to have the telephone wires tapped."

"Isn't Adam ever going to get over that?"

"It was pretty silly of me to start the whole thing, because he'll never get over thinking women are cheats."

"I suppose he doesn't really like women very much, does he?"

"No, even though they're responsible for all of those millions he's made."

"Maybe they've all come to him too easily, both in business and in his own personal life."

"Could be, and it's the same with his son."

"Alan is a big charmer."

"And how. That's the kind of thing I've never been able to tell you over the phone. I don't think Adam has listened to one of those tapes for ten years but I'm damn sure he keeps them, just in case. He has already bailed Alan out of a couple of situations with girls. He's a nice kid but rotten spoiled and he wants to get places fast without taking any trouble."

"So I gathered."

"Adam's fond of me, that I'm sure of, and I can't

really imagine living with anybody else, but anything he feels for me is nothing compared to that kid. He can do no wrong as far as his daddy is concerned."

"It's because Alan is a real chip off him," Crystal said.

"You know, Crystal, it's because of Alan that Adam is bugging you about belonging to the Meadow Club in Southampton. He may tell you it's for me, but I don't give a damn for that kind of thing, and you know it. It's Alan who's ambitious as hell."

"Really?"

"Yes. I think he's even jealous of you."

"Me? Why on earth?"

"Don't kid yourself kid—he'd like to be President someday."

Back in their apartment that evening, she found Eliot rummaging in his closet. A small traveling bag was empty but open, along with some of his hunting guns, at the foot of the bed.

"What on earth are you doing?"

"I'm flying to London on the early plane tomorrow."

"What has happened?"

"I talked to Clive on the phone today. He says this Ramsey is an all-out, double-faced bastard, which is exactly what I expected to hear."

"So did I."

"He also says there are ways and means to get at Ramsey, and I get the impression he'll be happy to get in on the kill."

"Why are you taking those guns?"

"I'm not going to shoot unless I have to, Vee darling." He smiled. " 'In on the kill' was just my way of expressing the fiendish delight both Clive and I will feel if we manage to put this fellow in his place."

Crystal felt her spirits rising. "How wonderful."

"If we're victorious, Clive and I thought we might treat ourselves to two or three days of shooting in Scotland before we get back, but, naturally, I'll keep you posted."

In London, Eliot went directly to the Berkeley. He telephoned his friend Sir Clive Campbell, and they agreed to meet for lunch the following day at White's.

"Glad you decided to come over. You haven't turned up at a shoot for I'd hate to say how long," Clive said.

"I know. I'm out of the routine. I guess I'd had enough of it in Africa to last me for a while. Amazingly, I haven't missed it at all."

"Any sport gets to be a bit of a bore if you go at it too regularly. Besides, Myrna cries when I bring home any game. She's definitely anti-gun."

"Most women are. Crystal has never said so, but she never wants to touch mine. Every once in a while I take out my elephant rifle. I just point it across the room. It's unloaded and I'm just testing to make sure my eyes are good as ever, but she won't come close enough to sight down the barrel."

"Too bad you didn't bring her over. Myrna's going to fly over to Paris for a couple of days while we're away, and the two of them could have gone together."

"It's on account of Crystal that I came over, and I've got to clean up the Ramsey mess before we take off."

"Well, he's not a major criminal, but a slimy one that takes a bit here and there to eke out his salary, if you know what I mean."

"A blackmailer?" Eliot asked.

"Not quite that grand. I always think of a blackmailer as being something like a drug addict who starts something and can't stop until he's done for. So far as I know, Ramsey has sometimes been restrained from publishing unpleasant facts when a sufficiently generous gift has been offered but he doesn't go on pumping until the well is dry."

"Why hasn't someone gone to his publisher?"

"Because the publisher of the *Daily Globe* might fire him but still insist on his paper publishing the true story."

"Do you actually have friends who have paid Ramsey off?"

"That's what I'm telling you. Of course I have. One of them was involved in the Profumo case, but a tidy little sum kept him out of Ramsey's column, at least."

"Oh, yes. I remember reading about that case while I was in Africa. It made international headlines."

"Indeed it did. I used to spend a lot of weekends at Cliveden and was somewhat near the scene. But it's all but forgotten now. Years have a way of doing that to our memory."

"But you definitely recall Ramsey being paid to keep someone out of the press at the time."

"Absolutely. I have heard of another man who has paid him what I consider quite lavishly to insert his name and his wife's into any kind of socially important gathering that he talks about. This makes him a bad boy, since the press is supposed to be true blue."

"Then that's the strategy I will use."

"If he's threatening to say something detrimental to your wife, it will be quicker and easier to pay him off."

"My wife has nothing to hide. I simply don't want her to be exploited in Roderick Ramsey's kind of writing, and I didn't fly over here with any gentle idea like tipping him to get rid of him."

"What do you mean?"

"I propose to liquidate the bastard if I have to, though I'm sure I won't."

"He'll cave in fast when he sees that you mean business."

"When I go to see him I may take along my rifle with the telescopic sight. It might give him a jolt."

When Eliot arrived at the Fleet Street offices of the *Daily Globe*, he found the columnist sitting behind his typewriter in one of the many small offices that surrounded the city room. "It's a surprise to see you here so soon, Mr. Young. I had no idea you were thinking of a visit to London."

"I'm just passing through on my way to Scotland for a few days of shooting."

"I see you have your guns with you."

"Just a few of my favorites. Are you interested in guns, Mr. Ramsey?"

"Not really. I've never shot and I've strained my eyes to the point that I doubt if my focus is sharp enough."

"You'd like this one. It has a telescopic sight that brings anything at a distance right up in front of your nose so that you can't miss."

"You've shot big game, I assume."

"Not for the last few years, but I don't think I've lost my knack. If I had a grudge against a fellow I could still pick him off from quite a distance without his ever knowing where the shot came from."

"If there's something you want to discuss with me, Mr. Young, please put the gun away. Guns have always made me nervous."

"So sorry. I thought you might be a fellow sportsman." Eliot put the rifle away in its case.

"I suppose you are here, Mr. Young, to discuss the story for *World* that I'm involved in, but I must confess it's out of my hands now."

"I'm glad to hear that. My wife doesn't need the publicity and I don't like the idea."

"Strange. A cover story like that is the answer to most people's prayers these days."

"Not ours. My family originally believed their names should appear in the newspapers only three times— when they were born, when they married and when they died. Naturally we're not that strict today."

"I am sure your wife doesn't feel that way, unless she has something in her past that she wants to hide."

"She has nothing to hide. What publicity she has had relates to her business. Her private life is her own, and I plan to help her keep it that way."

"I see your point, Mr. Young, but you're wasting your time and mine. It's been killed."

"Killed? I don't know what you mean."

"I mean the story is in the wastepaper basket."

"Why?" For a minute Eliot felt as if Crystal had been slapped in the face. "Wasn't she good enough for a *World* cover story?"

"It was a great story. I worked like hell on it, both here and in America, doing all kinds of research, really digging into obscure places for bits and pieces about your wife. By the way, she's a remarkable woman."

"That I know, but what happened?"

"I really don't know, Mr. Young. All I know is that a month ago your wife's name meant very little to me. Yes, I had read about her and seen her photographs occasionally in magazines. I even wrote a small paragraph about her in my 'I Spy' column, but that was the extent of my knowledge about her until the *World* bureau chief in London called me out of the blue one day and gave me the assignment. He said he had read my small piece on Crystal and thought she would make a good cover story. When I agreed he gave me a big advance and said go out and find everything you can about her."

"And what did you find out?"

"That she had a remarkable past that nobody apparently knows."

"I don't think my wife has tried to keep any of her past a secret."

"Perhaps not deliberately, but I've never read anything in her clips about her stage career. Just by chance I dug up a former chum who shared her theater dressing room in Berlin before the war. Her name was Elsa Menz. She told me that her chum Crystal had a love affair with an Englishman and a child by him."

"When was this supposed to have happened?"

"In Berlin in the early thirties."

"And who is this woman, and where is she?"

"That's the funny thing. When I came back from New York the other day I tried to get in touch with her. The landlady of her boardinghouse said she's gone off to Australia with a theatrical company. She'd left no forwarding address."

"Was she such an important part of your story?"

"Not necessarily, but at least a link to your wife's life in Berlin before she went to America. After all, not much has been written about that. But that was a minor part of my real story."

"What was your real story?"

"That a has-been actress from Berlin could go to America after the war and become the president of a multimillion-dollar corporation by selling millions of jars of cosmetics to women who want to look as young as she does in her sixties."

"Why do you suppose the story was killed?"

"Frankly, I don't know." Ramsey shook his head in disbelief. "It was a damn good story. One of the best I've ever done, and I was paid well for it. The day after I turned it in I telephoned the bureau chief to ask when it might run. He hesitated and then said, never, he had torn it up."

"Wasn't that a strange thing to do?" Eliot asked.

"Yes, it was. Especially if you know the man. He's a scholar, easy to work with, and in the beginning he was very hot on the idea. Wanted me to find out everything I could. Called me twice while I was in New York to prod me along."

"Publishing is something I know very little about. However, I like World. I've read it regularly since I was in college."

Eliot picked up his gun and started for the door, and then turned. "By the way, what is the name of World's London bureau chief?"

"No one you would ever have heard of. His name is Dunston. Keith Dunston."

Eliot telephoned Crystal that evening. "Don't worry, darling, your World story has been scrapped."

"What do you mean?"

"I wish I could take credit for it, but some fuddy-duddy old editor killed it. He gave Ramsey no reason, but paid him for the article."

"How weird."

"Count your blessings, darling, and forget the whole thing. I'm off with Clive for three days in Scotland. Are you okay?"

"Oh, yes. I'm so relieved to have this Ramsey story off my mind because I have the most wonderful idea. It will be the best thing I've done yet. I'll tell you all about it when you return."

36

Crystal should have felt totally elated and carefree after Eliot's call from London, but, instead, she was restless and depressed. Since she had married Eliot, she had never faced a weekend alone in their New York apartment. The silence of the telephone was terrifying and even the sight of the water flowing past outside the windows failed to be soothing.

She traced her depression back to an encounter she had had with Adam the day before. He had called her to come to his office, and just as she approached it, the door opened and Alan came out.

He was a good-looking boy with his auburn hair and he was grinning from ear to ear just as Adam always did when he felt he had accomplished something especially smart. "Why, hello, Crystal," he said. "Fancy running into you around here."

"Alan, you look as happy as if somebody had handed you a million dollars."

"Well, I just told Dad that somehow or other I got on somebody's list of best-dressed guys along with George Hamilton and Prince Charles. He was pleased."

"Congratulations. I don't blame him."

"I guess it helped him make up his mind about making me president of all the men's divisions. He just told me the good news."

She hid her reaction under her pleasantest smile. "I'm sure you'll do a wonderful job."

When she opened the door and went into Adam's office, he, too, looked flushed and smiling. "I guess you met Alan, and he gave you the news."

"Yes, he did."

"You don't look too pleased."

"He's just a kid, with no experience, and you have lots of executives with years behind them who have been dying for the job. I wish you could have given me a chance to talk to you before you made up your mind."

"I don't need your help or anyone else's when it comes to picking my division presidents. Besides, Alan is the likely one to inherit the business when I feel like quitting. He needs more responsibility than I've been giving him. He keeps telling me that."

Before she had left the office that afternoon Lynda had called her. "Crystal, I just wondered if you had been able to do anything about getting us into the Meadow Club at Southampton."

"Things like that take time, Lynda."

"That's what I keep telling Adam, but every day he asks me if I've called you. It's all because Alan is needling him."

"Alan, Alan, Alan. Everything seems to center around him these days."

"You feel that because, as I told you before, Alan is jealous of you. If you weren't around, I guess he feels he'd be the big cheese."

"I'd like to see him produce as many ideas for Adam as I have."

"That's not the point. Adam would give me up in a minute if he had to choose between Alan and me. I realized that a long time ago. It drives me wild, but I don't try to buck it," Lynda had said.

As Crystal stood staring at a tugboat making its way down the river, she decided to adopt Lynda's philosophy. Yet to play the part of a disinterested observer, she had to find a new project that would keep her totally involved.

Her book on plastic surgery and surgeons had sold out its first edition within a week, and a second printing was due soon. To write another informative book on the heels of the first would be counterproductive. The beauty cruise she had suggested to Adam had just been announced and its registration was almost complete. She had promised Adam she would direct it and supervise hiring a staff of exercise, massage, makeup and hair experts.

There must be something fresh and new that she could bring to the beauty world, she thought while pacing up and down the hallways as she often did when she wanted to solve a problem. Eliot's door was open and she wandered into his room and sat down on a couch.

Eliot's room was always extraordinarily neat. It reflected his usually uncomplicated state of mind and his ability to move steadily in one direction instead of being torn between different directions, as she often felt she was. Everything in his room was in its place, except for an open gun case on the desk.

As she started to close it, she noticed the corner of a color snapshot taped to the inside of the lid.

The photograph showed the most beautiful black girl she had ever seen. She wore a white evening dress, and a coil of gold and diamonds encircled her elegant long neck. What fascinated Crystal most was the girl's makeup, the perfection of the eye shadow and the exactly right shade of lipstick. Probably someone Eliot knew in Africa. But where did she find cosmetics?

She returned the snapshot to its place in the gun case, and as she closed the door of his room she thought: That's it. Why didn't I think of it before? A high-style cosmetics collection for all the beautiful black girls in the world. Today, our most spectacular models are black, and now that I think of it, I've heard complaints that no good makeup is designed for the various hues of their skin. We've done a few products here and there for dark skins, she remembered, but we emphasized price instead of fashion. Crystal envisioned a line that would emphasize elegance.

A week later she took the idea to Adam, demographics and spending potentials carefully worked out.

As she entered his office he didn't give her his usual smile. Instead, he asked, "How are you feeling, Crystal?"

"I feel great, but why do you ask me that? I usually do."

"I suppose it's because when I look at you I never can understand how you manage to make people believe you are in your sixties now."

"It's lucky for us that they do."

"I've always known women were gullible and believe what they want to believe, especially when it comes to cosmetics."

Adam listened attentively to the plan and to the statistics, but somehow lacking his usual enthusiasm. "Yes, I think it's a timely suggestion. I've heard rumbles about black cosmetics from other directions but none of them seem actually to have got off the ground."

"I've even got a good name: Black Beauty. Naturally I'd like to head it."

"I don't know about that. Don't you think you have enough responsibility?"

"All my things are pretty well organized and are running almost on their own steam."

"Well, let's wait, at least until we have an executive meeting. It *is* a good name, though."

Crystal didn't let Adam's unenthusiastic response worry her. She had never felt happier. Now that the worrisome threat of Roderick Ramsey had been removed, she felt free to think and plan again.

Suddenly, she found herself thinking of fat old Frieda, the German cook who had looked after her when she was a little girl. She remembered that Frieda would sometimes say, "The sun will always shine on you, little Crystal." Now the sun, some special sun, was shining on her, and she could feel its warmth.

She was in the library, looking through some art books and taking notes on unusual new shades to set off dark skin, when the door opened and Eliot swept in, followed by the elevator man with the luggage.

"Darling, I had no idea you were coming. I would

have come out to the airport or at least sent the car."

"No problem. I suddenly had enough. I was lucky to get a seat on the plane."

She followed him into his bedroom. He had left with a minimum of clothes and there wasn't much to do. "You can't imagine how carefree I feel since you called me," she said.

"It seems it was all much ado about nothing."

"If you hadn't gone, we might have been watching and waiting every month for the ax to fall."

"Funny, but at the end I found myself less annoyed with Ramsey than with that damned editor for not thinking the story was good enough for his magazine."

Eliot sat down on the couch beside her. "I've missed you, Vee." He took her in his arms. "You know, I was ready to kill for you."

"I love you, and I've missed you, too, darling."

"Crystal, why don't we have our dinner on trays tonight and get to bed early?"

"Let's go to bed first," Crystal said.

Eliot was pouring his second cup of breakfast coffee when Crystal, wrapped in a little terry-cloth robe, appeared in their sitting room, where they often ate at a small table in the bay window.

"Good morning, darling." He poured her a cup of coffee. "I see you are about to take a cruise."

"A cruise? What do you mean?"

He smiled and unfolded the paper. "The *Times* seems to think you're off somewhere."

Spread across five columns of the family page was the headline "Crystal's Cruise Launches Mobile Beauty Spas." "Oh, that," she cried. "It's not till next fall and I'm not going the whole way. I thought I'd perhaps leave with them, spend a couple of days and then fly back. I might have to meet them again at Rio for the end. Of course, if you wanted to come with me, they'd be more than delighted to have us both for the whole trip."

"Thank you, Vee. But I can't think of anything worse than getting myself planted in the heart of a female self-improvement group. You know I think all women who talk about reducing, diets and spas are deadly bores."

Before she left for the office she brought up the subject of the Meadow Club, and Eliot seemed to feel quite sure of getting a junior membership for Alan. "It will just have to wait until the next membership committee meeting, but in the meantime I'm sure I can get the kid guest privileges. I haven't been near the place for years, but I pay my dues, so I guess I'm still a member in good standing."

Several weeks passed with no call from Adam to discuss further plans for Black Beauty. Finally, Crystal used the Meadow Club membership as an excuse to go to his office.

Adam seemed to be somewhat mollified that a guest card also allowed Alan to play tennis. "He's the stuff champions are made of," he said.

Yet he refused to make any commitments about Black Beauty. "We've got a lot of things going in a lot of different directions right now, and I haven't made up my mind."

"You mean you're not going to do it at all?"

"I didn't say that. I plan to produce the line, but I simply don't know how I'm going to handle it."

"But I'd like so much to start working on the right shades of eye shadow and lipstick. My research has produced some revolutionary suggestions."

"Just file them, Crystal, until I make up my mind. Besides, you should be concentrating on what the Times calls Crystal's Cruise. You and Estée Lauder get more publicity than any two dames I've ever known."

"I'm sure that headline was just the work of some writer who was looking for alliteration. They didn't intend to single me out."

"Okay, but it was a nice plug for you, I thought. The cruise was your idea anyway."

"And so is Black Beauty."

"Believe me, I realize that, too."

Crystal continued her research and soon found herself totally immersed in the study of black cosmetics.

She interviewed the major black models. She even persuaded Eliot to take her to a performance at the Harlem Dance Theatre.

"How did this all start, Vee?" he asked her on their way home.

"Didn't I tell you? I was trying to think of a new promotion and I happened to see the snapshot that was taped to one of your gun cases. You left it open in your bedroom when you went to London and I was putting it away."

"So she inspired you?"

"Yes, that unbelievably beautiful girl started me thinking. I was fascinated by her eye makeup. Would you have any idea what she used?"

"We never discussed it, or much of anything else. She spoke English but not too well and I knew only a few words of Swahili."

Before she could see Adam again, she discovered that he and Lynda had left for a month's cruise on the yacht. Eliot suggested taking Crystal to Africa. "You really should see the girls in Nairobi," he said. Crystal was in a mood for something nearer and easier. They compromised on the Bahamas, where Eliot could play golf and swim and she could study.

She saw quickly that the Bahamians were spectacular. She liked their posture, their style and their flair for color. Wherever they went she used her camera, and she filled a notebook with her comments. "I think this will be the best thing I have ever done," she said on their flight home.

She talked to Adam several times when he returned from the cruise on *La Belle Lynda*. Once again he failed to okay a go-ahead on Black Beauty. Lynda seemed as friendly as ever, so Crystal convinced herself that Adam was just in one of his moods. Eventually he would grant her request. Every morning she opened the newspapers nervously. She couldn't believe that someone else wasn't thinking along the same lines. She remembered, a little nostalgically, the excitement she and Adam used to share when they started a new project. For the first time since she had become a part of Adam and Eve, she began to listen to the office grapevine for any clues to what Adam was thinking, but there were no rumors. She was sure that none of the executives had any knowledge of Black Beauty.

It was just before the beauty cruise that a telephone call came from Mary Lasker. "You'll get a letter soon, Crystal, but I thought you ought to know right away that you've been elected the Creative Woman of the Year."

"How wonderful, but do you really think I've done anything special enough to deserve it?"

"You know you have. We all admire you and you would have won the award years ago if the contribution you've made to all our lives hadn't been part of such a fantastically successful business."

She laughed. "You mean that money should be enough of a reward?"

"Something like that, perhaps, though we've never analyzed or discussed it. You should be even more flattered that you're the first businesswoman who has won the award since I've been on the committee. The others have all been painters, sculptors, writers or involved in science or medicine."

"I'm very happy, and I accept with pleasure."

"I don't know whether it was the little book on plastic surgery or the beauty cruise that influenced the decision, but you might like to know that the vote was unanimous."

"Thank you. I still can't believe it." When Crystal hung up the receiver she was flushed and smiling. She had had several awards, but they had been quite frankly commercial pats on the back. This one put her in a category of real creators and contributors, like Louise Nevelson, Fleur Cowles and Diana Vreeland.

Crystal was reluctant to leave her office for the beauty cruise, but when the big ship slid out of its berth and began sailing down the river, she felt a wonderful release from the tension that had been building up for the past year.

As she stood leaning against the railing of the promenade deck, watching the Statue of Liberty fade into the distance behind her, she thought: Adam and I ought to get together and resolve whatever the trouble is. She was sure that everything could be straightened out.

She stayed aboard the ship for four days instead of the two she had promised Adam. It was a good group that sat together at special tables and ate the nutritious but low-calorie meals that she and an expert had planned. Her real coup had been getting Gayelord Hauser to come on board as a celebrity guest. His two lectures on health had each filled the ballroom to capacity, and Crystal found herself listening avidly. Nearly every hour was occupied with exercise, massage and lectures on everything from art to sex. There was scarcely time for late-afternoon walks around the deck.

Crystal knew that the women were loving every minute of the program. Already many of them had begun to look rested and younger and she felt she could see lines disappearing from their faces. They would look five to ten years younger by the time the cruise was over.

She departed feeling like a benefactor. When she reached her office, she was happy to find a memo asking her to call Adam, but when she made the call she found he had gone off skiing with Alan and Lynda. "He left a message for you, though, Miss Crystal. He wants you to organize a couple more beauty cruises, one for March if possible and another for next fall. He's very enthusiastic about the idea, and he knows that at least a hundred women had to be turned down for the present cruise."

"Actually it was a hundred and fifty-five."

"He'll be happy to hear it," his secretary said.

"Please tell him I'll arrange the cruises, but are you positive that was the only message?"

"I'm sure that was all."

It took Crystal several weeks to organize the cruises, and the two were completely booked within seven days after the announcement, and another waiting list was begun. As good as, if not better than, striking oil, she thought.

On the morning of the Creative Woman Award luncheon, Crystal stood at one of her office windows looking across at the Plaza, where the luncheon was to be. She had asked for a guest list and found that Adam had taken a table for ten. Several times she had made up her mind to call him and ask if he was coming, but some instinct had made her cradle the receiver without completing the call.

At times recently she had had an uncanny sense that something she didn't know about was going on around her.

When Crystal arrived at the Plaza, she took the elevator at the rear of the hotel to the ballroom floor. When the elevator door clanged open, she was projected into the ballroom's big foyer, which was already full. The many voices merged into a single sound, a kind of rich, contented hum that she had become familiar with from the many lectures and benefit luncheons she had attended across the country. It could only be heard in America, where women get together as a single force instead of wasting their strength by competing with each other, she thought.

"This is my big scene," she said to herself as she edged through the crowd. "Twenty years ago I would have sold my soul to be an extra at this party and today I'm playing the lead." She knew at least half the women by name and she had a smiling acquaintance with the rest.

Many of them managed to stop her for a moment to say, "Congratulations," or "How well you look, Crystal." If they had finished the sentence they would have added "for your age." She knew that. She had heard the words so often that they inhabited her dreams. A few nights ago, she had heard them sung, over and over again, by a choir: "How well you look for your age, Crystal, how well you look."

When she reached the dais Crystal saw that the centerpiece was an enormous red papier-mâché apple filled with white flowers and trailing sprays of ivy. She looked down at the ballroom, where the television cameras were already set up. The tables were so close together that the waiters could hardly navigate among them with their trays. On each table was a similar apple, a facsimile of the one she had suggested to Adam long ago as a logo for their firm.

Adam should be happy when he looks around and sees the room full of Adam and Eve apples, she thought. She scanned the ballroom to locate his table and finally spotted Alan's red hair and Wally Nelson's round face in one of the boxes that surrounded the room at a slightly higher level. Sitting beside Alan was a black girl, and even at a distance Crystal could tell that she was a ravishing beauty with an elegant little head and a long, slim neck. Just what I need for Black Beauty, she thought. One seat at the table was still vacant, and she guessed that Adam was waiting until the last minute to arrive.

When the luncheon was served, she sipped her white wine, played with her food but found she couldn't swallow a bite. It wasn't that she was nervous. For weeks she had looked forward to speaking to a crowded ballroom of distinguished New Yorkers. It was only that, for the first time since she had cajoled Adam into hiring her, she felt weighted down by an oppressive sense of guilt. What she had done in the beginning out of dire necessity to survive, and later excused herself for on the grounds that her products were good and seemed to make women happy, now appeared to her as a giant and unforgivable hoax. She wondered how she could possibly smile through Mary Lasker's presentation speech and, for a moment, she thought of pleading sudden illness and leaving the room. She even wondered what would happen if she went to the microphone and went through her whole story. She could imagine the dead silence and then the flurry in the ballroom and she almost laughed at the thought of Adam's face.

"You're not eating, Crystal," said the man on her right. "I would have thought you would be accustomed to this kind of thing by now."

She quickly glanced at his place card and saw that his name was Clay Cromwell. She remembered he was the head of a large publishing house.

"This luncheon is far from routine. It's a very special occasion for me."

She clenched her hands tightly under her napkin when Mary Lasker rose and went to the microphone, and they were still clenched when Mrs. Lasker finished with "Naturally, this year's award could hardly be made of anything but crystal."

Crystal felt herself trembling as she took the crystal bowl and read the date and the message that had been engraved inside. She ignored the rather impressive speech she had prepared, expressed her thanks very simply and briefly and went back to her seat.

"Crystal dear, our committee is very happy that you seem to have such real feeling for this award," said Mary Lasker, reaching over to pat her hand. "Don't worry about the bowl. It will be sent to your home."

Clay Cromwell turned to her. "May I offer my congratulations, too? Have you ever thought about writing a book?"

"A beauty book?"

"No. A book about you and your remarkable life. I think it would make a best seller."

She smiled and thanked him. Then she looked across the ballroom again at the Adam and Eve table, where she saw that they were still drinking their coffee. Adam's place was still vacant, and she wondered if he had left or had simply never bothered to come at all.

There was only one way to find out. As soon as she finished her thank-you's, she made her way to the box. Alan and the spectacular black girl had already left, but Wally Nelson was still there, finishing a cigarette.

"You were great, Crystal. Adam would have come but he was expecting a long-distance call from Bali by way of Tokyo."

"How exotic! And speaking of exotic, who was the lovely black girl with Alan?"

"Don't ask me her name. It begins with a t and ends with a, and it's something like Taharanda. She's nineteen and just arrived from Nairobi. Adam has hired her for our new Black Beauty line."

"Black Beauty? What do you mean?" She felt as if she had been slapped across the face, and she could feel the sting on her cheeks.

"Oh, you know. It's that new division of Alan's."

"No, I don't. Tell me more about it, Wally."

"It's a whole line designed for black skins, and it means a complete new color range of foundations, eye shadows and lipstick. Adam is all worked up about it, and I took it for granted that you were in on the details."

"We did talk about it a while back. I remember now. In fact, I believe I brought up the subject after I happened to find a color snapshot of a good-looking black girl."

"Well, this one is a knockout, anyway. You'll be crazy about her when you see her close up." He stood. "Let's go back to the office, shall we?"

As they walked through the hotel and across the street, Crystal was thankful that Wally kept on talking about inconsequential things. She felt as if her smile had been carved permanently onto her face, and though she interjected appropriate yeses, nos and how-wonderfuls at the right times, her mind was actually a tornado of dark emotions.

The bastard. How dare he do such a thing to me? Black Beauty is all mine and I could kill him for doing this to me, and I won't take it.

When they reached the GM Building, Crystal went directly to Adam's office. "I must see Mr. Adler right away," she said to Pat Haley, whose desk guarded the door of Adam's most private retreat. "It's very important."

"Mr. Adler especially asked not to be disturbed. Did you have an appointment?"

"No, I haven't had time to call him, but it's urgent that I see him. I'm sure he'll understand."

"Oh, yes, I know you've been taken up with the awards luncheon all day, but I don't feel I can interrupt Mr. Adler at this minute. The last time I buzzed him, he was quite irritated. Perhaps if you came back in half an hour."

"I'm sorry, Pat, but I must speak to him. I'll gladly take the blame if he is irritated." She swept past the desk, opened Adam's door and went in.

Adam was sitting at his desk, deep in reading the Gallagher Report. "Oh, hello there, Crystal. Sorry I couldn't make the big luncheon, but I made sure the rest of them were there."

"Yes, I saw them, but I rather missed you."

She pulled a chair forward, and as she sat down she saw that he had a large silver-framed photograph on top of his desk of the beautiful black girl she had seen at the luncheon.

"Who is this girl, Adam? I saw her at the luncheon with our group."

"Taharanda is quite a girl. She's just one generation out of the bush, but she's pretty sophisticated and I'm planning to use her for the new black cosmetics line. In fact, I've already signed her to pose for the first ads, if Avedon's test shots turn out to be good."

"So you're going to do the black line."

"You're damn right I am. I thought you took that for granted. I'm not fool enough to pass up an idea like that."

"Maybe you don't remember, but in the beginning it was my idea, Adam."

"Sure, I remember. I've got a good memory for all kinds of things."

"Then you will let me have it, won't you, Adam? I don't think I've ever wanted anything as much as I want Black Beauty. I've spent hours on research and have turned up what I think are some great angles."

"I've usually let you have your own way. In fact, you've always had it since the day we met, but this time, baby, I've made other plans."

Their eyes met across the table, and as they stared at each other, Crystal saw suddenly that his were cool and remote. It was as though he had never seen her before.

"What are the plans?"

"I've set up a new division and put Alan at its head."

"But Alan is still a kid, and this is a kind of delicate experiment. It's nothing cut and dried. It's a first and it will take someone older and more experienced to swing it."

"That's where you're wrong. We've got to give the young ones a chance. I think so, and so do all the board members I've talked to. Alan has a great personality and I'm sure he can handle it."

"Of course he has a great personality. He's so much like you. Basically I agree with you about all the young people, but surely I'm not so senior that you won't let me work out an idea that I suggested in the beginning."

"You can be sure that I've already set aside an adequate block of stock to repay you for the idea."

"I'd rather have the work than the stock."

Adam didn't speak for a minute. "Baby, you force me to bring up a subject that I hoped we wouldn't have to discuss for a while," he said.

"What do you mean?"

"I mean the matter of your age. How could I possibly turn over a new cosmetics division to you when you are pushing sixty-five?"

"Why should that make any difference, especially since you know that I'm not?"

"All that I really know is the age that is registered in our file. The one on your original application. I know, too, that the retirement age of this company is sixty-five and that you will be eligible for it within a few months."

"You must be joking, Adam. You used to tease me about claiming to be forty-three when you knew I was only twenty-three."

"When we were in bed together I guessed you couldn't be as old as you claimed. You were a great girl in bed, baby, but that was long ago, as you reminded me so righteously recently. Besides, what I find out in my private life has nothing to do with my company's policy."

"I can't believe that you don't want me and need me in this phenomenal business that I've worked so hard to help build up."

"Baby, I've always appreciated your brains, your guts and your sexy good looks, but rules are rules and there's nothing I can do about it."

As she finally took in the full impact of what Adam was saying, Crystal felt a terrible chill through her body. She opened her mouth but no words came.

"You'll thank me for this someday, baby. You'll have a great time once you're free."

"I don't want to be free. My life is my work," she managed to gasp. "You bastard, you really want to get rid of me, don't you? You've been plotting this for a long time."

"Don't be foolish. You'll have a more than generous pension for the rest of your days. Besides, you'll feel differently about it by the time we announce your retirement next fall. You're a rich woman with all your stock and I'm willing to bet you've been stashing away most of your salary since you've been married to that multimillionaire husband."

This time when she looked in Adam's eyes she saw a gleam of malicious triumph. She felt her heart swelling with such hatred that she thought it would surely burst. If I were only a man and could smash my fist right into his face, she thought. "You bastard," she screamed, and picking up the silver-framed photograph of the black girl, she threw it at Adam's head.

He tried to push back his chair, but it grazed the side of his face and broke into fragments on the carpet. She saw a small trickle of blood running down his cheek before she picked up her handbag and went out the door.

"If you have any Band-Aids in your desk drawer, he may need it in there," she said as she passed Miss Haley, and left the office.

Instead of going back to her own desk, as she had told Pomeroy she would, Crystal headed straight for the elevators and pressed the button for the main floor. She felt as if she were walking in a dream. A thin mist before her eyes seemed to be separating her from the real world.

Luckily, a taxi was dropping a passenger at the Madison Avenue entrance and she signaled to him. As she almost fell into the seat, she said, "Please go into the park at the Sixtieth Street entrance. I want you to drive clear around the park as slowly as you can, and when we come to the Seventh Avenue exit, I'll tell you where I want to go next."

It was still only four o'clock and the same beautiful day she had felt so secure in earlier that morning. Though the sun was dropping behind the Plaza as they turned into the park, the whole scene was bathed in the pale, watered gold light of an early-spring afternoon in the city. Children in bright sweaters were playing on the sidewalks and she could hear the noise of the animals in the zoo.

"Still pretty chilly, isn't it?" said the driver.

"Yes, but please don't talk to me. I have a problem I have to solve."

Now she was beginning to feel the actual pain of being violently and unexpectedly uprooted from everything that made her feel most secure. The office with all her own possessions around her, her desk, her own staff that knew and understood her and just the simple, daily routine of coffee and telephone calls and the constant excitement of seeing new faces and making new plans. They were the basic nourishment that she had worked hard for, and all the rest that had come so easily she had accepted and enjoyed but in her heart regarded as a rich, fluffy dessert. As she looked out the cab windows at the back of the Museum, the lakes and the trees that were just starting to bud, she seemed to herself to no longer be a part of it all. Once more she was deep in the frightening aloneness of her first days in New York, but this was worse. Then she had had high hopes and a sense of adventure, but now she was facing defeat.

As they slid past the Tavern-on-the-Green, the driver asked, "Where now, miss?"

I can't go home yet, she thought, and she gave the address of her town house, which, for the past few years, she had thought of only when Pomeroy showed her the rent checks before he deposited them in the bank. But suddenly she felt it would be a haven.

The next hour would give her enough time to pull herself together, she felt.

She paid the driver and stood on the sidewalk for a minute looking at the façade of the building. Though she admitted to herself that it was childish, just to know that she had bought it with her own money and that it was all hers gave her a feeling of security.

As far as she knew, Douglas Knolls was still occupying the ground floor, but if he wasn't, she decided, she would just go in and talk to the janitor in his little room.

She pressed Douglas' bell and in a few minutes she heard his footsteps. "Who's there?" he asked.

"A lady in distress."

He opened the door. "For God's sake, Crystal, what are you doing here?"

"Just checking on my property, I guess. Would you like to give me a drink?"

"Of course I would. It's the first time I ever heard you ask for a drink. Is anything wrong? You look pale, and not at all like your usual self."

She sat down on the couch and leaned back against the pillows. "This is nice and familiar," she said as she watched him pour vodka into a small glass and fill a larger glass with ice cubes.

"If you're feeling rocky, you'd better drink the vodka neat and follow it up with a chaser of ice water."

"Thank you, Doug." She was already beginning to feel better.

"Tell me, what's happened in your life?" she asked.

"I've just been working along. I was dying to rent

your old apartment upstairs, but you know what Wall Street has been like."

"It hasn't damaged us very much." She had forgotten for a moment that she was no longer a part of the enchanted cosmetics world, and felt a sharp twinge as she remembered.

"How is our garden? Did you do anything else with it this year?"

"I put in a lot of bulbs and the last time I looked they were just pushing up the first green shoots."

"Let's go see it." She slipped her coat over her shoulders and Douglas pushed open the glass doors. Most of the bulbs were well out of the ground and would be in bloom in about two weeks. "I'll try to come back and look at them," she said. The sun was going down and she felt chilly again. She glanced up at the windows of her old bedroom and said, "We'd better go in."

Douglas offered her another drink, but she refused. He had a fire going and she found it very comfortable for the next half hour listening to him talk about his latest enthusiasm—ESP and Uri Geller. When she saw that it was getting dark she picked up her coat and said, "I'm afraid I'll have to go."

"Surprise me again someday," he said.

At the door she put her arms around him and kissed him more tenderly than she ever had before. "I don't quite get you, Crystal. Why didn't you kiss me this way when we were next-door neighbors?"

"Sometimes I don't quite understand myself," she said.

She found a taxi, and as she rode uptown, she wondered how the day that had started as what she had believed was the happiest in her life could possibly have ended as the most disastrous.

When she reached their apartment, she found Eliot already in the library with the newspapers. She went over to him, kissed him on the forehead and took the newspaper out of his hands.

"Listen, darling. I have some really hot news for you. Adam has just fired me."

37

It took Crystal a few minutes the next day to realize that she wasn't the same person she had been the day before. The life she enjoyed so much had been sharply cut in two and it was as if she were waking up in a hospital after an accident and wondering how it all happened.

As she drank her morning coffee, she wondered what on earth she was going to do with all the long hours that stretched ahead of her today and what looked like an eternity of tomorrows.

She had decided she would never go back to her office, but it would be a while before she could contact Pomeroy and tell him to come to Gracie Square.

Though Adam had provided the setting for their wedding, she had quickly realized that there wasn't the remotest possibility of Eliot and Adam ever becoming friends. Eliot had never bothered to dislike Adam, but whenever they met he always seemed to be looking at him from a distance as if he were some kind of strange specimen. Adam had become definitely hostile to Eliot, and Crystal was sure if he referred to him he described him as a snob and embellished it with all the possible four-letter words.

When Crystal had given Eliot a play-by-play account of what had gone on in Adam's office, Eliot had said, just as she thought he would, "What the hell else did you expect of that s.o.b., darling?"

After that, Eliot had taken her in his arms, kissed her and stroked her hair. He tried to comfort her as if she were a child whose favorite toy had just been smashed instead of a woman who had suddenly been robbed of what she had put every ounce of herself into creating. Eliot had always gone along with her because he loved her, but he saw her work only as a charming caprice to endure. "Let the little girl have fun" had always been his attitude, she realized. He would never understand the pleasure of work, the thrill of success or the insistent need to push on, though to what end she was pushing, she herself hardly knew when she stopped to think.

She had never seen the hands of her bedroom clock move so slowly. It was still an hour before Pomeroy would arrive at the Adam and Eve offices and at least hear that there had been a scene in Adam's office yesterday. She was sure that Pat Haley would spare no details of the blood and the broken picture frame.

Crystal felt a sudden need for action. She put on pants and a sweater and opened her closet door. I've been trying to find some time to sort out my clothes, and that's what I'll do right now, she decided. She left the warm-weather clothes hanging in her closet, took out the heavy-duty winter things to be stored in a cedar closet and started making a third pile to be sent to the Sloan Kettering thrift shop. As she threw dresses she had never liked, coats that she felt looked out-of-date and even a mink that was worn at the edges on the thrift-shop heap, she forgot her problems temporarily in the pleasure of adding up in her head the tax deduction she would surely have.

When Eliot came into the room, it was full of not only the piles of clothes but stacks of shoe boxes, scarfs, feather boas and even hats that she had dragged from the back of her closet.

"What on earth are you doing, Vee?"

"Just killing time and trying not to think, I guess."

"Come here, darling." He put his arms around her again. "What a funny girl you are. Though you can't see it now, this may be the very best thing that has ever happened to you. In a little while, you may learn to enjoy doing nothing."

"I don't know how good I'll be at it."

"You can be good at anything you try."

He kissed her, and she almost expected him to call her "little Crystal" and to add, "The sun will shine on you."

When Eliot had left, Crystal dashed to the telephone and called Pomeroy. Just as she expected, the news that there had been a rumpus had spread like wildfire through the office. "Surely, there's no serious trouble between you and Mr. Adler? He always seemed to depend on you so much. But Miss Haley told the girls that you were white as a sheet when you left the office."

"Take a taxi and come up here, Pomeroy. We can discuss the situation better here than in the office."

While she waited for him, she finished with the closet and called the maid to put the thrift-shop clothes in a big plastic bag and said that she would call one of the committee members to pick it up. Now her mind was racing. She and Pomeroy would work temporarily in the library, but she had an unused servant's room that could be converted into an office. It was large enough for the desk that she had actually bought for herself, and the files that she intended to move before anyone knew exactly what she was doing.

If Pat Haley says I looked pale, I'd better put on some color before Pomeroy gets here, she thought. She put a little rouge on her cheeks, outlined her upper eyelids in dark blue and opened her handbag to reach for her favorite lipstick. A card dropped out and she looked at it casually before she tossed it in the wastebasket, but the name rang a bell. Clay Cromwell was the man who had sat beside her at the award luncheon yesterday, though it seemed months ago.

He's an important publisher and he was urging me to write a book, she thought. Suddenly the possibility of unveiling the backstage operation of Adam and Eve struck her in a blinding flash of joy.

She had never looked happier, Pomeroy decided

when he arrived with a shopping bag that held her engagement calendar, some stenographer notebooks, yellow pads and all kinds of pens from thin to felt.

As they went into the library, Pomeroy was convinced that the rumors that were spreading through the office must be fictitious or even wishful thinking on the part of some of the girls.

When they sat down in the library, though, Crystal said, "I'm leaving the cosmetics industry, at least Adam and Eve, and I'm not even coming back to my office. We're going to move it up here."

"Oh, Mrs. Young, I can't believe it. What will Mr. Adler do without you? Surely you'll change your mind."

"No chance, Pomeroy. It's all over, but I'm hoping you will stay with me."

"Of course I will, Mrs. Young. I'm sure you'll be swamped with offers of jobs."

"Perhaps not, since I've made such a point of being over sixty." She handed him the card. "Here's one offer I have already, though. Please get him on the phone for me right away."

When Clay Cromwell came on the wire, Crystal said, "I enjoyed so much meeting you, and I won't waste your time. As I remember, you told me to think about a book."

"I did, and I hope you have."

"Yes, I usually make up my mind very fast. I believe I would enjoy writing a book. Since we talked yesterday I have decided it's time for me to leave the cosmetics industry, and this will make it possible for me to write a better and much more honest book."

She made an appointment for the following day and had hardly hung up the receiver when *Women's Wear Daily* was on the wire, asking for a statement. "It's true that I'm leaving the company, but it's too soon to say anything definite. When I know what I'm going to do, I'll be happy to give you the first interview," she told Michael Cody.

When Eliot arrived home early, expecting to pet and console Crystal, he found the telephone ringing nonstop, Pomeroy trying to take the calls and Crystal looking her usual happy and enthusiastic self. "Good girl. She's already got over the worst of it," he told himself.

That night Crystal slept soundly. The next morning Pomeroy made his appearance promptly at ten o'clock to take care of the telephone calls. Crystal was already dressed and ready to keep her appointment at the publishing offices of Cromwell and Richardson.

As she sat across the desk from him and they exchanged platitudes about the weather, Clay Cromwell found himself looking with pleasure into Crystal's eyes. They were the clearest, most limpid blue eyes he had ever seen. He tried to find the right word to describe their color but couldn't.

"I've had no real experience in writing, except for my speeches and the special books on beauty, but I've always been told they were quite articulate," Crystal was saying.

"We want you to do the book, but give me just a hint of your story line."

"I would like to start with my childhood in Berlin just before the Second World War. The horrible bomb that wiped out my home and entire family, then my struggle to get to America and how I have succeeded as a working girl here."

"And what are you going to tell us about your part, at least, in the cosmetics industry?"

"The truth, even though it involves a hoax about my age that I have perpetrated on the world."

"Well, that is startling news." Clay Cromwell looked at the beautiful blue eyes again, but a sixth sense told him that, in spite of their softness, she had briefed herself thoroughly on the fantastic prices that were being paid for revealing autobiographies. He decided not to start too low and agreed to give her an advance of two hundred thousand dollars.

"I had planned on offering you an advance of seventy-five thousand, but a story like this sounds like a blockbuster, if you live up to your promise."

"I can assure you I will." Before she left she had

agreed to finish the book within a year and to sign the contract that would be sent to her apartment the next day.

Crystal arrived back at the apartment just as an enormous box of flowers was being delivered. It was as big as a coffin, she thought, and when she opened it, it was full of flowers of all colors and sizes, along with Adam's card. The message on the back of it read, "We miss you, baby. Come back and let's talk things over peaceably." She noted that the message was not in Adam's handwriting, but had either been telephoned to the florist or written by Pat Haley.

"He's a damn fool! Even if he gave me a whole flower shop I wouldn't go back to that office." She felt like throwing out the whole box but decided not to take out her anger on the flowers.

She went into the library, where Pomeroy was working. "Please call a moving company, Pomeroy. We must get my files out of the office and sent up here while they're not sure whether this is just a temper tantrum and may blow over. You must go down there and oversee the moving tomorrow, and make sure that I get all the papers and information I've accumulated. Also, see that my paintings and porcelains are packed carefully, and the desk, too. I bought it myself. And, for heaven's sake, don't forget the Roladex of telephone numbers."

"Oh, Mrs. Young, this sounds so terribly final."

"The moment all my private papers and possessions are out of the place I want you to call Miss Haley and make an appointment for me to see Mr. Adler later in the week."

Pomeroy's face relaxed. "That's good, Mrs. Young. So many of your friends down there are hoping that you will change your mind."

"Don't count on it, Pomeroy," she said.

Crystal was still arranging some of the flowers and putting them in different strategic spots when Eliot came home. "Good God, I can't believe it. What's going on? Are we having a funeral or a wedding?" As he took her in his arms, he said, "It's nice to see you at home once in a while, darling."

"Adam sent these. Probably after reading the front-page story in *Women's Wear* this morning."

"Why do you keep the bastard's flowers?"

"He doesn't bother me any more, so we might as well enjoy them. Besides, I've got a nice surprise up my sleeve for him."

"I hope it's a bomb," Eliot remarked as he left the room.

Crystal's contract for the book came the next day. After her lawyer had finally approved it and returned it to the publishers, she had accepted Clay Cromwell's invitation to lunch with some of the staff she would work with.

Pomeroy had managed to set up an office in the apartment and she found herself suddenly beginning to enjoy her new freedom. Her enthusiasm was already so concentrated on revealing herself as the person she really was that she no longer saw herself in other people's eyes as the sixty-five-year-old purveyor of a miracle cream to keep women young.

"I should have left of my own free will and never given him a chance to make the first move," she thought as she went into the GM Building for the meeting with Adam that Pomeroy had arranged.

There had been no trouble about making the date. "Anytime at all. In fact, Mr. Adler himself just asked me to try to contact Miss Crystal," Pat Haley had said when Pomeroy telephoned, and she was still all smiles and softness when Crystal came into the office.

"We've all missed you so much, Miss Crystal, especially Mr. Adler."

Adam was behind his desk, and she noticed that there were no framed photographs on top. His eyes were grim, but his face, at least, was smiling.

"Hello, baby. You're looking well. Sit down, will you?"

"I've never felt better." She sat down and waited for him to make the first move.

"I guess we both got a little hot and hasty at our last meeting here. I hadn't expected to talk about the whole situation right at that time, but you forced me into it when you started talking about seeing Taharanda at your award luncheon."

"Oh, really. I suppose you had planned a glorious surprise, like giving me an engraved silver bowl at a big dinner for executives and guests."

"Oh, no, I was going to discuss it with you before that, though, as a matter of fact, we were planning a dinner in your honor."

"Forget it. Nobody enjoys testimonial dinners and I can't think of anything worse than sitting through a dinner for myself."

"I only mention the dinner because you blew up so quickly when we were talking that I didn't have a chance to go into the entire plan."

"I have a very good memory, Adam. I understood every word you said. I even understood many of the reasons. I can't think of anything that could possibly be added."

"I don't need to tell you, I guess, that Lynda has been giving me hell ever since the board made its first decision. Finally we called an emergency meeting and decided that we want to keep you on for the next ten years as an active consultant."

He got hold of the board in a hurry. He must be worried, Crystal thought, but she said, "I don't really think I'd care for that, Adam. Consulting has always sounded a little passive to me. It's something I think I'll save for some of those later years that, as you know, I haven't reached yet."

"We would pay you a larger salary than you've been making or, if you prefer, the same salary with larger stock options."

"Even if you had told me this the first time we talked, I don't believe I would have accepted the offer. However, now I have a real reason for thanking the board nicely, but still saying no. I'm going to be too busy."

Adam said nothing for a minute, then looked up at

her and said, "You've always seemed to be crazy about your work, Crystal. It must be something fascinating you've found that makes you willing to forget Young Forever so fast."

"It will be fascinating, I think. I've just signed a contract with Cromwell and Richardson to write a book."

"Oh, a beauty book, of course. That will be right down your alley. But you ought to be able to manage that and still stay with us."

"It's not a beauty book, Adam, though the cosmetics industry will certainly play a big part in it. Clay Cromwell thinks my own story is interesting, and since it seems to be the fashion now to confess everything about yourself, why shouldn't I?"

"When you say everything, what do you mean by everything, baby?"

"Everything is everything, isn't it? I plan to start with my childhood, my first love affair, meeting Lynda on the plane, running my finger down the yellow pages of the telephone book and finding you just by chance on a Saturday morning."

"That all sounds very sweet, but of course you can't tell the truth about why I got involved with you and that cream of yours."

"Of course I can and I will. I'm going to tell the truth and nothing but the truth, Adam, about you, me and everything and everyone else."

"I thought you were smarter than that."

He's scared, she thought, but she gave him her best smile and asked, "Why on earth do you say that? The fact that I was using my mother's passport and that you went along with the hoax will make fascinating reading. The book can't miss being a best seller. Clay Cromwell said so."

"To hell with Clay Cromwell and your goddamned book. You little fool, don't you know it will ruin Adam and Eve? Your stock will take a nose dive along with the rest of ours. It will be the end of everything. You can't do it, baby."

"I can do it, and I'm going to," she said. "I'm not as greedy as you are, Adam. I've already sold some of my stock. I can live comfortably on my income without what you referred to as my pension. Besides, I have a rich husband." She paused for a moment and then added, "I'd almost forgotten, you have nothing to worry about, you have a rich wife."

"You bitch!"

"Besides, I'm sure I'll be able to make more money once the smoke clears and I'm able to establish my real age."

She could see the angry red coming into Adam's cheeks, and hear his voice rising. "Those fine friends you've made are going to drop you like a hot potato when they find out what kind of crap you've been handing them all the time."

"Perhaps they will. I've given it some thought, but I don't think so after they've read the story. But it's a chance I'll have to take."

Adam's hands were clenching and unclenching violently. It was an involuntary gesture, but she knew he would like to get them around her neck. She stood up. "I ought to thank you for hiring me when I needed a job so much, though I think I've paid my way ever since. I suppose I ought to thank you, too, for setting me free at just the right time in my life."

"What a bitch you are. I should have known you were too good to be true. You never needed me or anybody else to help you get along. Just get the hell out of here."

"Goodbye, Adam," she said, and as she left the room, she thought: Funny, I can still see why he's attractive to so many women.

When she reached the outer office, Pat Haley's eyes were glued to her with anticipation. "I hope everything's all right, Miss Crystal. We're all hoping that you're not going to desert us."

"I'm afraid I am, Pat, and there's something I forgot to say to Mr. Adler. Please tell him to cancel the silver bowl he told me he had ordered for my retirement dinner. If it comes to my apartment I will throw it into the East River."

38

Crystal said nothing to Eliot about her final scene with Adam, but at dinner that night she told him that she was going to write a book.

"Isn't it rather sudden?" he asked, but she could see that he was pleased.

"I suppose it is. I happened to sit by Clay Cromwell at my award luncheon. He suggested it then, but I didn't want to say anything, even to you, until the contract was signed."

"Will it be about people, or lipsticks and creams?"

"About fifty-fifty, I imagine, but it will be the story of my life, and if there is a hero, of course it will be you. I plan to keep regular working hours with Pomeroy every day, and though the publishers have given me a year, the format is already starting to take shape in my head, and I'm sure I may turn it out in less."

Later that evening as they were talking in bed, Eliot said, "I've been thinking about your book, Vee, and I think I've got a good idea."

"Go ahead, darling."

"I know I often talk about Africa, but it's an oddball kind of place that once you've lived there you keep thinking of and wanting to get back to. Why don't we go there for the next year? There are no telephones and not too many other distractions. You would have complete quiet and seclusion for your writing."

"Africa. Oh, Eliot, whenever you've mentioned it, it has always seemed so far and so frightening."

"Oh, come, Vee. You've never been afraid of anything unless it's not having enough to do. You've seen the photographs of my farmhouse. It's quite big and has more rooms than I've ever lived in. You could decorate it in your spare time. Nairobi is quite near and you'd go out of your mind over the native fabrics. I can imagine just how you'd look when you get your first glimpse."

"Let me think about it for a minute, Eliot. You know I don't care much about wild country. I always feel I ought to do something about it. It's like seeing children with dirty faces and wanting to scrub them clean."

"You and Africa will take to each other. You both have tremendous vitality. Yours shows in your face and every move. Africa's isn't so apparent but you feel it under the surface. It's like a native drum that you're just barely aware of, beating in the distance."

"I've never heard you so poetic, darling."

"It's truly beautiful and from our bedroom window you'll be able to look out over enormous wheat fields. In the far distance you can see the tip of Kilimanjaro covered in snow."

"It really must be something special and you have just managed to convince me that I want to go."

The more Crystal thought about it the next few days, the more a year on Eliot's farm in Africa seemed to be the right thing to do from every point of view. It would be a total change of scene, and there would be no possibility of meeting Adam or any other Adam and Eve executives either on the street or in a restaurant. There would be no tension, no telephone calls and no repetitious explanations to friends about why she had so suddenly given up her cosmetics career.

Her only concern now was how to convince Pomeroy that he could be happy in Africa for a year. They had already started the book, working together just as they did with her speeches and personal press releases. Each morning Crystal turned off her telephone, and since she seemed to think better on her feet, walked up and down her bedroom talking into her tape recorder. Later the two of them played back the tapes. She made changes and additions, and Pomeroy put the whole thing together with the proper periods, commas and quotation marks.

It wasn't long before she had to break the news. As soon as Eliot had started checking into plane schedules and had cabled the tenant farmer who managed his place, he had begun getting out his guns and checking through storage closets for old hunting clothes that Crystal had ordered put away in boxes.

Pomeroy, whose sharp little eyes behind the glasses never missed anything, complained to Crystal, "It makes me very nervous to see Mr. Young fingering those dreadful weapons of his. Is he planning to go off somewhere to shoot something?"

"He has a fabulous home in Africa, you know, Pomeroy. He's going there for a visit and you and I are going there with him."

"Africa! Oh, no." Pomeroy almost screamed. He turned pale and his glasses fell off his nose. He bent to pick them up and Crystal saw with relief that they weren't broken, since she wanted to get on with the work.

"Oh, come now, Pomeroy. You're going to find Africa fascinating. This is the good safe part of Africa. It's no more country than Long Island. There are no government problems and the natives are absolutely dears, Mr. Young says."

"But those dreadful animals, Mrs. Young. Even when I was a small boy I couldn't stand the smell of a circus and even closed my eyes when those tigers came into the ring."

"The wild animals are all in special areas now, and I'm sure the wildest thing you will ever see on our place is a rabbit." She must remind Eliot, she thought, not to tell Pomeroy that one of the charms of his farmhouse was the occasional glimpse of a zebra or once even a panther in the thick woods that began about a hundred yards behind his back door.

"How long must we be there, Mrs. Young?"

"Possibly a year, but you and I will fly back several

times with our manuscript, so it won't seem so very long. But I promise you it's not all that primitive. Mr. Young tells me he even has a projection room where he runs old movies and an occasional television show." Later she thought: Thank goodness Pomeroy's resigned to his fate and is coming with me. I don't care what I have to say to keep convincing him, and in the end both of us may learn to love it.

That week both *Time* and *Newsweek* came out with detailed accounts of what they called the eruption at Adam and Eve. Though they gave Adam's life story, his start in Brooklyn, his marriages and his tough treatment of his executives, both articles were critical of Adam's promotion of his son and seemed slanted favorably towards her. She was described as providing the inspiration of the firm's first step upwards but continuing to supply most of their fresh, forward-looking ideas and products.

The fact that she was still described as the sixty-five-year-old miracle woman no longer bothered her. The truth would soon be told. She realized now that for years she had lived in the shadow of her public image, conformed to it, sometimes even believing it. She had felt happier and more gloriously free each day since leaving Adam and Eve.

As a result of the two stories, she noticed in the stock-market listings that Adam and Eve had taken a sharp dip, and she smiled. "I'd like to see Adam's face, but it's nothing to the way he's going to look when my book comes out." She thought of calling Lynda, but before she found time, Lynda called her.

"Guess what! I'm on my own again and off to Hawaii," she said.

"What do you mean by 'on your own'?"

"I'm leaving Adam. It's just Alan, Alan, Alan day and night with him. Alan is the only human being he cares about, and he doesn't just care. He dotes. He's just like all hard-boiled people. Once they manage to feel something, they overdo it."

"In a way, I couldn't be more surprised."

"I'm not doing anything legally yet, and the way

things have been lately, I doubt that he'll know that
I'm gone."

"I'm sure he will. He'll be sending someone like
Wally Nelson to bring you back."

"I don't think so, but he'll have me watched. He'll
want to have evidence ready in case I sue. That's the
way he's stupid, because I'd never bother. I thought
you just might be in the same mood I am and feel like
coming along."

"Darling, I can't. I'm writing a book, and I'm going
to Africa with Eliot for a year while I do it." As she
spoke she felt a sharp twinge of regret at the thought
of leaving the new life that was unfolding before her
with some new excitement each day. However she had
promised Eliot and cared for him too much to disappoint him.

Clay Cromwell soon provided a reason for delaying
the trip for two weeks. After she had turned in the first
two chapters for criticism and direction, he asked her
to have luncheon with him to discuss what she had
written.

This time there were no executives along. "When it
comes to a piece of writing, each of us has his or her
very definite, individual opinion, so I thought it would
be better for just the two of us to talk it over."

As she sat beside him on the restaurant banquette,
Crystal found Clay Cromwell even more attractive
than on the three other occasions they had been together. I must have been terribly overwrought at the
awards luncheon not to realize that this man is almost
any woman's dream, she thought, and as he talked, she
checked his assets impersonally: the dark wavy hair
with a wide white streak running through it; the long,
oval face with bright eyes and a wide, humorous
mouth; the tall, slim figure; and even the soft, gentle
voice. He was saying, "You look particularly lovely
today, but you seem to have a faraway look."

"Maybe it's because I'm thinking of Africa, where
I'm going in a few days with my husband and my
secretary to write the book."

"Oh, I'm sorry to hear that. I was looking forward

to working with you closely. I feel that your book is going to be a tremendous success and I even intend for it to be my own special project." He turned towards her and she saw there was genuine disappointment in his face.

For the past few weeks he had been unable to put her blue eyes out of his mind and had kept inventing what he knew were ridiculous reasons to call her. Now that he looked at them at close range they seemed softer and deeper than he remembered. He suddenly thought they were asking him to provide some sensible reason for her not to make the trip to Africa. "I wonder if you couldn't possibly put off the trip at least two weeks, at least until you can give me a complete outline of what you intend to do."

He saw the blue eyes brighten and the color come into her cheeks, and knew that she was pleased.

"That sounds sensible. I'm sure Eliot will understand," she said.

"I believe your story may be more effective if you start with the first meeting with Adam Adler and just how the hoax about your age began. Then you can flash back to the years in Germany. But suppose you go on just as you are now, and we can go over it again when we meet for luncheon next week." He wondered if it was his imagination that she seemed as eager as he was for their next luncheon.

As soon as she reached home Crystal called Eliot at his club. It was something that she seldom did. He was probably in the midst of a good game, she thought, since his voice sounded gruff.

"Darling, I'm sorry to disturb you, but my publisher says I must stay here for at least two more weeks to get this book really started. It wouldn't be necessary, except that I'm going so far away. I thought you ought to know right away, so you can do something about the reservations."

"God damn it, darling. I've got everything packed and I'm in a mood to go."

"I'm sorry about it, but I know you're as anxious

for the book to be successful as I am. If the delay really bothers you, I won't be angry. You can go ahead and I'll follow you with Pomeroy."

"I'll wait this time, Vee, but I'm beginning to feel that you don't want to come with me at all."

"Of course I want to come, and it just means I'll stay at least two weeks longer." As she hung up the receiver, she felt terribly guilty, and though she tried hard all afternoon, she was unable to add even another paragraph to her manuscript. As she paced up and down her room with her tape recorder, she told herself that she should simply have told Clay Cromwell that the decision to go to Africa was irrevocable and that he would have accepted it. She realized that they had a mutual desire to see each other and to work together. It was strong enough to disturb her, and she made up her mind to cancel next week's luncheon date with him. She wouldn't have Pomeroy do it today or tomorrow, but at the last minute so that she couldn't change her mind.

By next week she had completely forgotten her feeling of guilt, and within five minutes after they met at their favorite restaurant both she and Clay Cromwell were happy together on the banquette. She had already submitted an outline and the first draft of several more chapters. He liked them, suggested a few changes and they soon found out that they were laughing over the same things, that they liked the same kind of food and had even reached the same state of mind on the subject of money. Too much of it seldom made people happier or more attractive.

"I don't know what time it is, but we seem to be closing this restaurant," Crystal said finally.

He put his hand over hers on the banquette. "We're not just writing a book. We're discovering each other," he said. "Don't go to Africa just now."

"I have to go, Clay. I've promised Eliot, but I'll come back as soon as I can."

She seemed so vague and absentminded when she returned from the luncheon that Pomeroy had to remind her twice to return Mr. Robert Friedkin's call. "He's a big shot in the TV world, Mrs. Young. He has already left three urgent messages and you have totally ignored them."

When Pomeroy spoke to her severely, Crystal always knew she had done something that he considered disadvantageous.

"I guess this idea of such a drastic change in my life is upsetting me a little. Please call him right away, Pomeroy."

As he dialed the number, Pomeroy spoke to her severely again. "Please remember, Mrs. Young, that your state of mind about Africa is nothing compared to mine." He held the receiver closer. "Mr. Robert Friedkin please." A moment later he turned to Crystal. "Mr. Friedkin has left for the day. His secretary says it's imperative that you see him as soon as possible. It's something about your award luncheon that was on TV. Anyway, I made an appointment for you at his office tomorrow at half past ten."

"I suppose I might as well see what it's all about," she said later to Eliot.

"Hell, I guess it's TV that wants you now," said Eliot, who hadn't been his usual jovial self since she had put off the trip. For a while after she had walked out of Adam and Eve he had been the strong man in control of the situation, but for the past few weeks he had felt her gradually slipping away from him again.

The next day as Crystal was ushered into Bob Friedkin's office, she was in a mood to feel totally unimpressed. She knew little about the world of commercial TV, its gods and goddesses, and she had had no time in her life so far to become familiar with the programs.

Bob Friedkin rose, circled his desk and held out his hand. "How are you, Crystal. Glad to meet you. I'm Bob Friedkin and I've had one hell of a time getting you over here."

He reminded her a little of Adam, but not in an unpleasant way. "I'm sorry. My life is somewhat topsy-turvy at the moment. I'm writing a book and getting ready to go to Africa with my husband."

"To Africa? Now wait a minute. I'm about to offer you something that millions of girls in this country would give everything for."

"Tell me."

"I'll give you the shocker first. We want to offer you your own talk show for a trial period of thirteen weeks. Sit down and think about it."

She sat down. "I must say it comes as a shock. I've hardly ever been on TV, except for interviews on the early-morning shows, so why me?"

"I like you." He looked her up and down. "You're a cool one, aren't you? Most girls would be yelling for a contract by this time, whether they thought they could perform or not. As far as salaries go, Crystal, this one is fairly astronomical."

She smiled. "Thank you, Bob, but I'm not on welfare."

"Just go on talking. It's that beautifully modulated voice of yours that got to me first. To level with you, we happened to send a crew over to the Plaza to shoot the Mary Lasker award luncheon. Since there was nothing big happening that day, some of it made the evening news and I happened to catch it. I said to myself, with that voice and that face, this woman could be a godsend to any TV program."

"I'm flattered, Bob, but the timing is wrong. I'm packed and we leave within the next few days."

"Come now, Crystal. Don't give me the love-and-duty ploy. This is today's world. You're writing a book and you'll be lucky if twenty thousand people outside the cosmetics world buy it. Once you are a TV personality, I can promise you millions of readers. That is, if you are good. And I think you will be or I wouldn't waste your time and mine."

"What makes you confident that I can be successful?"

"After I saw you on the evening news, I asked for everything they had shot at the luncheon and I watched you all through it. In fact, I ran it over and over and I got more and more excited. Now what do you have to say?"

"Of course I'd like to try it, but what about some other time?"

"It wouldn't work. *Time* and *Newsweek* have given you a tremendous buildup as a great businesswoman and I'm not entirely displeased to find that you're a real female under the slight glaze. Also, I'm sure, being a climber-upper, you must have acquired an understanding husband."

"He will not understand this time. I'll have to think about it."

"Then let me know as soon as possible. We want to start right away. The program will be based on interviews, but not just personality chitchat. The people you interview would be chosen for their association with special subjects, everything from abortion to seduction, with a dash of politics, racial problems and lighter things like your own health and beauty subjects in between. For such a wide spectrum, we need a mature, sophisticated woman instead of one of the pretty kids that are so easy to find."

Crystal left Friedkin's office in a daze. Instead of taking her car, she dismissed the chauffeur, and started walking up Fifth Avenue as she used to when she had only the simple problems of money and loneliness to solve. Now she was faced with more momentous ones. She knew that if she put off the African trip again she might lose Eliot forever, but if she gave up the chance for her own TV program she might hate herself for the rest of her life. Bob Friedkin had described her as one of the climber-uppers and she accepted the description. But aren't most of the people I know? she thought. And if I'm a climber-upper, how can I settle for just being part of the way up and not trying to go farther? She decided before she went to sleep that night she would plan how to make Eliot sympathetic to the idea.

As soon as she reached the apartment, she rushed

to her office to look up Robert Friedkin in her copy of *Celebrity Register*. The book carried his picture along with a full column that described him as a talented young producer with great sensitivity and a flair for finding the right people for his programs.

When she came into Eliot's room the next morning, he was almost ready to go out. "I just have to tie up a few loose ends before we take off," he said.

"Eliot, darling, something has turned up that makes it absolutely impossible for me to go right now," she said. "When I explain it all to you, I'm sure that you will understand."

He was taking his wallet and a handkerchief out of a drawer, but he turned around and faced her. "I'm afraid I've been expecting that this would happen, Vee. After the first shock of leaving that office of yours that you loved so much, I could see that you hadn't the slightest desire to go to Africa. I was proposing it to you as a romantic journey, but you thought of it only as a means of escape. When you found you were being sought after, you no longer wanted to escape."

"Eliot, you must listen to me. I've been offered a television program of my own, but it's only for a thirteen-week trial period. After that, I promise you that I'll come straight to Africa and do everything to make up for not leaving now."

"I do understand you, Crystal. I understand that you will come to Africa only if your program is not successful and you will need to be healed before you begin again."

"That's not quite fair, Eliot."

"I think it's quite fair, Crystal. Just after we were married and we had our first little argument, I told you that what I wanted was a wife, but you've always preferred to be somebody else of importance. When you and Adam disagreed, I hoped it was over, but now you still don't want to be my wife. You want to be the woman millions of people turn on their TV sets at a certain hour to idolize or to criticize or whatever. You want to belong to them and not to me."

"What a strange thing to say."

"It's a quite human reaction, I'm sure, and I've been feeling it for some time."

"Will you wait for me, Eliot?"

"Not here, Vee. I still love you and I admire your instinct for success, but at the moment I'm tired and bored. I'll try to change my reservations and get off this afternoon if I can. How long I'll wait for you in Africa depends on when or if you decide to arrive."

"Oh, Eliot, don't talk to me this way. I can't imagine living without you." She threw her arms around him, and he bent down and kissed her.

"I love you, Vee, just as I've told you, but I'm sure you'll get along very well without me. I like looking at you and making love to you and we've had a lot of good times together when your work didn't get in the way. I'm not sure that you need anybody to make you happy or that you ever needed me, but don't come to Africa because just for the moment you think you should. If you wire me that you're coming, it has to be because you are willing to lead my kind of life and on my own terms."

39

After Eliot left, their apartment was frighteningly quiet, yet when Crystal analyzed it, she decided it must be her imagination. Eliot was always quiet. She went into his bedroom and looked at the empty top of the chest of drawers, where he always tossed his belongings. It was usually a tangle of keys, glasses and memos, but now it was polished and neat.

She opened the door of his closet and saw with a rush of relief that he had left most of his heavier clothes. She took the sleeve of a tweed jacket and brushed it against her face, sniffing and enjoying the masculine tweed and tobacco scent. When he thinks it over, she thought, Eliot will understand that to have my own TV show is a challenge that I simply couldn't afford to turn down. It seemed to her to be a culmination of everything she had wanted to achieve, and since it had come to her at a time of crisis, it was like a gift from heaven.

If Eliot hadn't been so hasty, I could have explained all this better, she thought. Nevertheless, she felt confident that he loved her and everything would eventually be cleared up.

When she told Pomeroy the news, she burst out laughing at the sight of his face.

"Oh, Mrs. Young, you don't know what this means to me. Last night I was watching a nature program photographed in Africa, and there are hyenas all over the place."

"You're not safe yet, Pomeroy. This is just a breather. Mr. Young has gone on ahead, but we'll be joining him at the end of my thirteen weeks, unless he decides to come back before then."

"I admire you very much, Mrs. Young, and if you want to become a big TV personality, I know you will."

She telephoned Bob Friedkin and told him that her answer was yes. "I only hope my decision hasn't cost me my husband. He was impatient to get to his home in Africa, and has gone on without me. I plan to join him later."

"We'll do everything we can to help. After the first few programs, which I want to be live, we can do some taping ahead and give you a long weekend away."

Crystal realized that with the book contract signed and a debut into a totally new medium ahead of her, she would be working harder than she ever had before. Oddly, she was glad. It would keep her from brooding about Eliot and worrying what the reaction to the first broadcast would be.

Clay Cromwell was ecstatic when she called to tell him she was postponing her African trip. "Eliot has left without me, but I've promised to join him as soon as possible."

"That's wonderful news. If you are free, can we have dinner this evening?"

"That would be nice. I have some exciting news to discuss with you."

As he hung up the receiver, Clay Cromwell wondered whether Crystal's decision to delay the trip was the result of his urging her not to go.

He was thinking of her as he sat in La Côte Basque waiting for her to arrive. He lived alone in Greenwich and commuted every day from a monster of a house in which he had been rattling around alone since his wife died a year ago. He could picture Crystal playing tennis on his court, swimming in his pool and sitting at the foot of his dinner table when he gave a party.

While they were having their cocktails, she told him about the TV program. "You know, Clay, the only way Mr. Friedkin talked me into it was to convince me that we would sell millions more books this way. I was sure you'd be pleased."

Clay's first reaction was to feel deflated. He wanted all her attention and enthusiasm to be concentrated on the book and on him. He took an instant and violent dislike to Friedkin. Crystal finally convinced him that her primary interest was the book and that her best efforts would go into it. Only then did he relax.

When he took her back to Gracie Square he said, "May I come up for a drink, Crystal?"

She hesitated. Then she said, "Of course, Clay, but it has to be brief. I have to get up early to go to the studio."

They went into the library, where he mixed a scotch and soda. Crystal refused a drink, saying, "Since you're here, I want you to see our new glass-walled living room."

They stood for a moment looking at the water that looked almost near enough to touch. Then Clay turned to her. "What a fool your husband was to leave you alone. If you were mine, I'd never let you out of my sight. I can't think of anything but wanting to make love to you." He pulled her close and kissed her.

It was a long kiss and Crystal felt her heart beginning to pound, but she pulled away. "You're very attractive to me, Clay; for now that is enough."

When he had left, Crystal went directly to bed. She tried to sleep but tossed restlessly. When Clay kissed her, she had found herself wanting to return his kiss and let him take her to bed. It was hard to pull away, but to add Clay to her life was a complication she could not manage. She began to worry about what was happening to her marriage. How would she write about the lie about her age sympathetically? Could a novice in TV make good with so little experience?

She got up and took a couple of Bufferin tablets. I have to keep a very clear head, she thought. Then sleep came at last.

She and Pomeroy were like generals planning a campaign. They budgeted her time. Mornings, as far as possible, were devoted to TV. Afternoons she dictated sections of the book.

Liz Smith broke the story in her column. She wrote that Crystal had given up the cosmetics world for the TV screen. Her new program would be called "Today's Living." After the column appeared, excitement over the new program became intense. Every celebrity and would-be celebrity wanted to be on the show. Moreover, there was a waiting list of advertisers. Bob Friedkin was sparing nothing to make it a success.

Crystal made several test programs and she and Bob Friedkin watched them together in the projection room. "You know how to handle it, Crystal, I knew you would. Sure, there are some rough spots. You could come on a little stronger occasionally. But I have a feeling the less I say to you about yourself right now, the better. I'll tell you one thing that's just right. You're not a show-off and you come over as if you were sitting at home on a sofa with a handful of fascinating guests. It's a kind of throw-away quality that I like."

Bob decided the first program would be on beauty. She had been sorry at first because she considered it primarily a woman's subject, but it was also a challenge to handle it in a way that would interest men as well. "Why don't we try a more specific aspect of beauty?" Crystal proposed.

"What do you suggest?"

"Well, for example, what age do you think women are the most beautiful?"

"Aha, you've got ideas, too."

He arranged for the guests for the first show to be Diane von Furstenberg, who had just started her own company; Estée Lauder, who had succeeded Elizabeth Arden as cosmetics queen; Shirley Lord, representing Helena Rubinstein; and Taharanda, the new black beauty of Adam and Eve. She had cringed when she heard that Adam and Eve would be a part of the show but was relieved somewhat by the fact that it was being represented by someone in the company she didn't know.

As the premiere of "Today's Living" came closer, Crystal was outwardly calm. Only Pomeroy knew the truth, as he told his mother one morning: "She's living on nerves."

She had written to Eliot soon after he left, telling him everything that had happened and how much she missed him. Recently she had followed that letter with another. She was not surprised that she had not received an answer to either, as Eliot was notoriously a bad writer. His mother, Charly, had once told her that he occasionally sent a telegram but had never in her memory, replied in writing. She told Pomeroy to see to it that Friedkin made her a tape of the first show to send to Eliot. Perhaps that might persuade him to come home.

On the morning of the show, Crystal was up before daylight. She drank a cup of coffee, tied back her hair with ribbon and put on the bright blue dress that the cameraman had thought was the best color for her complexion. The studio was a hubbub. Cameramen and technicians were placing the cameras and adjusting the set. In her dressing room she ordered another coffee and began looking through her notes.

"Hope you're not nervous. We're all rooting for you, Miss Crystal," an assistant said, handing her a cup of coffee.

"Thank you, dear. But I'm not really nervous."

She was completely calm as she sat facing her mirror. She had worked at her top capacity during the past few weeks. She had studied her subject and thought of almost nothing else. She had rehearsed, corrected her faults, worried and even prayed.

As she listened to the countdown, Crystal watched the man standing by the camera directly in front of her. He raised his hand, then dropped it suddenly. She saw the red light flash on, and the show began.

Diane von Furstenberg was the first guest and she was easy. They were friends and laughed together as Diane talked about how she started her career, toting a suitcase full of clothes around town to show buyers at a time when she was very pregnant. She described how she made a fortune on Seventh Avenue before she started her cosmetics line. When Crystal asked her at what age did she think women were the most beautiful, she answered, "In their late twenties when they've just discovered that getting a man isn't everything."

Estée Lauder recounted the story of her family's origin in Vienna, where they were skin doctors. Then she went on to describe her social life on the Riviera and Palm Beach. When Crystal asked Estée the key question, she answered, "Beauty is ageless. My very best friend, the Duchess of Windsor, is a beauty at eighty."

The next guest was Shirley Lord, who told how her beauty education started in a school just outside London, and then proceeded to describe how she took the underground to apply for her first job on a London newspaper. She left a few years later in a Bentley. "As for the most beautiful age of a woman, I really think life begins at forty and certainly women are most beautiful at that time."

The show was going well, but Crystal was watching the clock and knew she had only four minutes left. Until then Taharanda hadn't said a word as she sat at the far end of the sofa playing with a little gold bracelet.

When Crystal said, "You are a newcomer to New York, Taharanda, and I understand you were born in Nairobi," she said, "Yes," smiled, and went on playing with her bracelet.

She's beautiful, Crystal thought, and so exactly what she had originally dreamed of as representing Black Beauty that it was hard to believe.

She decided to ask a more provocative question to stimulate an exchange. "Have you ever found that being black is a hindrance to your career?"

"No. It helps," said Taharanda. She smiled again, showing her beautiful, even, white teeth but seemed to be totally disinclined to talk and went on jingling the bracelet.

She must be nervous, Crystal thought, and for the first time she began to feel nervous, too. She was suddenly conscious of the lights, the heat and the clock that relentlessly ticked on. She felt perspiration starting to roll down her face as she sought desperately to think of some interesting question to end the show.

Finally she asked, "Tell us about that little bracelet that you've been playing with, Taharanda. It must be something that you love very much."

The girl held out her arm, then said, "They are little gold boxing gloves that say Culver. They belonged to my mother, who died in Nairobi when I was born. They're all that I have to remember her by."

"Then tell me about Nairobi," and for a while they discussed the girl's early life, the kind of clothes and jewelry that women wore there. Then it was time for Crystal to ask her the leading question, "At what age do you think women are the most beautiful, Taharanda?"

"My own." She smiled broadly. "I'm nineteen." Then suddenly the red light went out and the show was over.

Crystal said goodbye to her guests as briefly as she could, and went to her dressing room. As soon as she had closed the door, she burst into tears.

"I was a total disaster. I've failed," she said to herself as she started to take off her makeup. "Where was Frieda's sunshine today?"

Pomeroy had been a nervous wreck for days. The morning of the broadcast he moved from room to room in the little apartment, near the United Nations, that he shared with his widowed mother. He turned on their television set a full hour before the program and sat down in front of it biting his nails, a childhood habit that came back to him whenever he found himself faced with a crisis. He had worked with Crystal for nearly eight years and could imagine what she was going through at the television studio. As soon as the program started his mother came in from the kitchen and stood behind him. When it was over, he jumped up, hugged her and said, "Thank God, I'll never have to go to Africa. She's sensational."

Charly Young hadn't seen much of her only son and his wife during the past few years. She still lamented the fact that because Eliot had married an older woman there would be no grandchildren, but she read every word about Crystal that appeared in newspapers or magazines and bragged about her frequently to her friends. She even occasionally tried one of the creams or sprayed on some of the perfume Crystal sent her. When she read about the broadcast she invited her own little group to watch it over a late breakfast. They had just finished their hot biscuits and bacon and were still drinking their tea when the broadcast started. "Just look at her," Charly said. "To think she's only eleven years younger than I am."

Eva and Roy Archer were sitting on the patio of their rambling redwood house in northern California that overlooked their vineyards in the valley below. Roy, who looked tanned and happy, but was losing his hair, was stretched out on a brown wicker chaise, and Eva, plumper but still pretty, was just coming out of the kitchen with a coffeepot in one hand and a plate of hot muffins in the other. As she started to pour the coffee, Roy said, "Look, it's Crystal." After a few minutes of the show, Eva put her cup down and said, "I always wondered if she and Adam had an affair. God, I wish that cream of hers had done as much for me."

Lynda Adler had rented a house in Hawaii overlooking Diamond Head. She was lying nude at the edge of her swimming pool, screened by lush tropical foliage and orchid plants in full bloom. Propped up against pillows, she was watching TV and talking over the telephone. "No, you can't come over now, Bobby," she was saying. "You know I've told you that my house is watched. If you were caught here, nobody would believe we were just playing backgammon." She hung up the receiver just as a tape of Crystal's original broadcast began. "Christ, what a damn fool Adam was to let her go," she thought.

Keith Dunston saw the program on a replay in London three months later. He sat watching in his office at *World*, remembering Crystal as a bright-eyed little girl. He first became curious that she might be his daughter when he read a squib about her in Roderick Ramsey's column. When the program was over he flipped off the TV and said to himself, "Thank God I killed the story."

Shelley had two TV sets going in his New York town house with the three-story living room. He hadn't seen Crystal since the blowup at Adam and Eve that had kept his group speculating ever since. Every day there had been a new rumor. When the program was over he called down to Joe Tula, "The blue dress was too obvious. They ought to let me design her clothes."

Douglas Knolls was having coffee at Doubles with a stockbroker friend while they watched the program on the giant TV screen in the private dining room. "You see that beautiful blonde," he said to his friend. "That's my landlady, and I almost got her in bed once."

Alan Adler, who was living with his father since Lynda left, was having breakfast in the peach-colored sitting room that adjoined his bedroom. As the recently appointed president of the company, he was wearing a dark pinstriped suit and cultivating a mustache that needed touching up frequently with one of Adam and Eve's hair colors. He had just finished telephoning Bulgari to send a necklace of old Roman coins to his girl of the moment when Crystal's broadcast came on. As it ended, he said, "Christ, she's a beauty."

Adam Adler, sitting next to Alan, was still in his pajamas and dressing gown. He had not moved or uttered a sound since the program began. Suddenly he turned to Alan with a start. "Are you speaking of Taharanda, or the bitch?"

Clay Cromwell planned to watch the broadcast from his Connecticut home. He hated missing his usual 8:21 commuting train with his friends and the card game he sometimes joined, but to see Crystal on the screen was something he couldn't take a chance on missing. "Don't give me any calls," he told his housekeeper as he turned on the set in his bedroom. As he turned it off, he thought: It's probably goodbye to our affair, but she'll sell a million books.

Robert Friedkin watched the show from the monitor's booth. He was almost stuttering with excitement when he called the president of the network. "This girl is dynamite. We'd better get her signed to another thirteen weeks fast."

Eliot Young had just cooked dinner at his African farmhouse. It was something he often did to pass the time. He always managed to find plenty to do in the daytime but after dark there was little or nothing. Earlier in the afternoon he had toyed with the idea of inviting Peter Beard and other neighbors over to watch the TV tape that Pomeroy had mailed to him, but had finally decided he would rather watch it alone. As the program ended he almost shouted, "My God, my wife interviewing my daughter, or is it my daughter? I may have to go home to find out."

ABOUT THE AUTHORS

Eugenia Sheppard has written for *Women's Wear Daily* and the *Herald Tribune*. Her column on fashion and society, which appears locally in the *New York Post,* is syndicated by the Field Newspaper Syndicate and appears daily in more than eighty newspapers throughout the United States, England, Thailand and Canada. *Time* describes Sheppard as the "most outspoken U.S. fashion writer by far."

Earl Blackwell is the founder of Celebrity Service, Inc., and the editor of Celebrity Register. He knows more celebrities than perhaps anyone in the world and is world renowned as a host. (He has organized giant parties for Presidents Kennedy and Johnson.) His duplex penthouse is a replica of an Italian palazzo and boasts one of the few remaining ballrooms in New York City.

RELAX!
SIT DOWN
and Catch Up On Your Reading!

☐	11877	**HOLOCAUST** by Gerald Green	$2.25
☐	11260	**THE CHANCELLOR MANUSCRIPT** by Robert Ludlum	$2.25
☐	10077	**TRINITY** by Leon Uris	$2.75
☐	2300	**THE MONEYCHANGERS** by Arthur Hailey	$1.95
☐	12550	**THE MEDITERRANEAN CAPER** by Clive Cussler	$2.25
☐	11469	**AN EXCHANGE OF EAGLES** by Owen Sela	$2.25
☐	2600	**RAGTIME** by E. L. Doctorow	$2.25
☐	11428	**FAIRYTALES** by Cynthia Freeman	$2.25
☐	11966	**THE ODESSA FILE** by Frederick Forsyth	$2.25
☐	11557	**BLOOD RED ROSES** by Elizabeth B. Coker	$2.25
☐	11708	**JAWS 2** by Hank Searls	$2.25
☐	12490	**TINKER, TAILOR, SOLDIER, SPY** by John Le Carre	$2.50
☐	11929	**THE DOGS OF WAR** by Frederick Forsyth	$2.25
☐	10526	**INDIA ALLEN** by Elizabeth B. Coker	$1.95
☐	12489	**THE HARRAD EXPERIMENT** by Robert Rimmer	$2.25
☐	11767	**IMPERIAL 109** by Richard Doyle	$2.50
☐	10500	**DOLORES** by Jacqueline Susann	$1.95
☐	11601	**THE LOVE MACHINE** by Jacqueline Susann	$2.25
☐	11886	**PROFESSOR OF DESIRE** by Philip Roth	$2.50
☐	10857	**THE DAY OF THE JACKAL** by Frederick Forsyth	$1.95
☐	11952	**DRAGONARD** by Rupert Gilchrist	$1.95
☐	11331	**THE HAIGERLOCH PROJECT** by Ib Melchior	$2.25
☐	11330	**THE BEGGARS ARE COMING** by Mary Loos	$1.95

Buy them at your local bookstore or use this handy coupon for ordering:

Bantam Books, Inc., Dept. FBB, 414 East Golf Road, Des Plaines, Ill. 60016

Please send me the books I have checked above. I am enclosing $_____
(please add 75¢ to cover postage and handling). Send check or money order
—no cash or C.O.D.'s please.

Mr/Mrs/Miss_____

Address_____

City_____State/Zip_____

FBB—11/78

Please allow four weeks for delivery. This offer expires 5/79.

DON'T MISS
THESE CURRENT
Bantam Bestsellers

☐	11708	**JAWS 2** Hank Searls	$2.25
☐	11150	**THE BOOK OF LISTS** Wallechinsky & Wallace	$2.50
☐	11001	**DR. ATKINS DIET REVOLUTION**	$2.25
☐	11161	**CHANGING** Liv Ullmann	$2.25
☐	10116	**EVEN COWGIRLS GET THE BLUES** Tom Robbins	$2.25
☐	10077	**TRINITY** Leon Uris	$2.75
☐	12250	**ALL CREATURES GREAT AND SMALL** James Herriot	$2.50
☐	12256	**ALL THINGS BRIGHT AND BEAUTIFUL** James Herriot	$2.50
☐	11770	**ONCE IS NOT ENOUGH** Jacqueline Susann	$2.25
☐	11470	**DELTA OF VENUS** Anais Nin	$2.50
☐	10150	**FUTURE SHOCK** Alvin Toffler	$2.25
☐	12196	**PASSAGES** Gail Sheehy	$2.75
☐	11255	**THE GUINNESS BOOK OF WORLD RECORDS 16th Ed.** The McWhirters	$2.25
☐	12220	**LIFE AFTER LIFE** Raymond Moody, Jr.	$2.25
☐	11917	**LINDA GOODMAN'S SUN SIGNS**	$2.50
☐	10310	**ZEN AND THE ART OF MOTORCYCLE MAINTENANCE** Pirsig	$2.50
☐	10888	**RAISE THE TITANIC!** Clive Cussler	$2.25
☐	11267	**AQUARIUS MISSION** Martin Caidin	$2.25
☐	11897	**FLESH AND BLOOD** Pete Hamill	$2.50

Buy them at your local bookstore or use this handy coupon for ordering:

Bantam Book Catalog

Here's your up-to-the-minute listing of over 1,400 titles by your favorite authors.

This illustrated, large format catalog gives a description of each title. For your convenience, it is divided into categories in fiction and non-fiction—gothics, science fiction, westerns, mysteries, cookbooks, mysticism and occult, biographies, history, family living, health, psychology, art.

So don't delay—take advantage of this special opportunity to increase your reading pleasure.

Just send us your name and address and 50¢ (to help defray postage and handling costs).

BANTAM BOOKS, INC.
Dept. FC, 414 East Golf Road, Des Plaines, Ill. 60016

Mr./Mrs./Miss_____
(please print)

Address_____

City_____State_____Zip_____

Do you know someone who enjoys books? Just give us their names and addresses and we'll send them a catalog too!

Mr./Mrs./Miss_____

Address_____

City_____State_____Zip_____

Mr./Mrs./Miss_____

Address_____

City_____State_____Zip_____

FC—9/78